MERETE MORKEN ANDERSEN

Oceans of Time

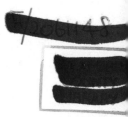

MERETE MORKEN ANDERSEN

Oceans of Time

Translated from the Norwegian by
Barbara J. Haveland

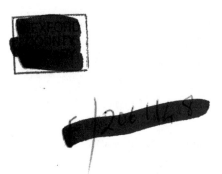

Published in 2004 by
The Maia Press Limited
82 Forest Road
London E8 3BH
www.maiapress.com

First published in Norwegian as *Hav av tid* by Gyldendal in 2002
Copyright © 2002 Gyldendal Norsk Forlag AS
English-language translation © 2004 Barbara J. Haveland

Merete Morken Andersen asserts her moral right to be identified
as the author of this work
Barbara J.Haveland asserts her moral right to be identified as the
translator of this work

ISBN 1 904559 11 5

A CIP catalogue record for this book is available from the
British Library

Printed and bound in Great Britain by Thanet Press

The Maia Press is indebted to the Arts Council England and
NORLA (Norwegian Literature Abroad) for their financial
support of this edition

*As death (when closely considered) is the true
goal of our life, I have made myself so thoroughly
acquainted with this good and faithful friend of
man, that not only has its image no longer anything
alarming to me, but rather something most
peaceful and consolatory; and I thank my heavenly
Father that He has vouchsafed to grant me the
happiness, and has given me the opportunity (you
understand me), to learn that it is the key to our
true felicity. I never lie down at night without
thinking that (young as I am) I may be no more
before the next morning dawns. And yet not one
of all those who know me can say that I ever was
morose or melancholy in my intercourse with
them. I daily thank my Creator for such a happy
frame of mind, and wish from my heart that every
one of my fellow-creatures may enjoy the same.*

Mozart to his father, 4 April 1787

from *The Letters of Wolfgang Amadeus Mozart,
translated, from the collection of Ludwig Nohl,
by Lady Wallace*, Boston, 1864

EBBA AND ERLEND

There are people moving about inside the houses. The summer evening is bright and dry, full of people raising arms, sitting down, then getting up again, people turning their heads to windows. They are living, they don't know anything else; they bend their knees, they yawn and walk into other rooms and close doors behind them. Or they open cupboards, making little clicks and bangs as they change their minds, turn away and go off to do something else instead.

In the cars driving along the roads, too, there are people who are living; they zoom off, they reach forwards and rummage in glove compartments for their sunglasses, sit back and settle heads against headrests. And maybe they run their hands slowly over steering-wheels covered in imitation leather, or tune in to a different channel on the car radio; all it takes is a light touch on the tuner button.

The town is bathed in light even though it is evening; light that streams from a strong, young sun. It hasn't rained for weeks. Sunlight on the cars driving by and the houses lining the roads, sunlight slicing across the glass pane as someone opens a window. Soon they'll go to bed; it's hard to get to sleep when the nights are so light. No one here has any idea what's going to happen in one of these houses early tomorrow morning.

There is no wind. But time is moving, gliding on, it never stops; comes the bright night and eventually they fall asleep, the children too; then a bright new morning dawns. No one knows how this comes about; the one just glides into the other.

She is a young woman in a nightdress. She is sixteen, but looks older. This summer there's been a stiffness about her when she walks along the street.

She wakes up in the house at the top of the drive around half-past four. The room is almost unnaturally bright, with not a single shadow; instinctively her left hand clasps her right wrist, around which she has wound the red rubber band from a preserving jar. She woke up several times during the night and fingered it, as if willing it to remind her of something.

She sits on the edge of the bed with her feet on the floor and combs through her hair with her fingers. Then she pulls off her nightgown and tosses it down to the foot of the bed, draws her hair back into a pony-tail and secures it with the rubber band from her wrist, picks her panties, trousers and a thin, pale-blue blouse off the floor and creeps softly into the bathroom. She pees, washes her face and hands the way she always does, gets dressed and tiptoes down the stairs. In the neat, tidy kitchen everything is just as it always is; she stands at the kitchen window, drinking a glass of orange juice while she gazes at the croquet mallets lying in a heap under one of the birch trees in the garden. Then she puts the glass in the dishwasher. This one glass was all that was needed; now the machine is full. She pours in the dishwasher powder, turns the little dial and presses the button to start the wash cycle and send the water gushing into the machine with a steady whoosh. By the time her mother comes down to the kitchen, a few hours from now, the dishes will be clean. Then she steps out into a morning that is already hot, gently closing the outside door behind her.

There are two pairs of wellingtons on the step, her own and her mother's. They are the same type, dark blue with a white trim, her mother's two sizes bigger than her own. Her mother has written their names on the insides of the boot tops: Ebba. Ebba. Judith. Judith.

She hesitates for a moment before sticking her bare feet into her mother's boots, then walks down the steps and across the gravel to the garage.

The car boot is not locked. She opens it and takes out the blue nylon rope; the noise of the boot lid banging shut sounds all too clearly in the still morning air. The coiled rope bounces against her shin as she walks across the lawn towards the fence separating their ground from the little grove of trees beyond. The dry grass forms a firm carpet that scrunches under the soles of her boots. Her breath whistles in her nostrils as she swings her legs over the fence; she presses her lips firmly together.

It is quiet in the wood, as if someone had turned down the volume, both inside her and outside. No movement anywhere, no wind in the trees, not a breath of air.

When she reaches the tumbledown shed known simply as the hut, she bends down and wraps her arms round one of the big tree stumps they used for stools at the secret club meetings they held here as kids. She half tips it, half rolls it towards the big fir tree against which the hut is built. She makes a loop in the rope with a knot learned from her father when out sailing with him. She cannot remember a time when she could not make this knot, one which allows the loop to tighten. She throws one end of the rope over the branch that juts out directly above the stump. Then she climbs up on to the stump and ties the other end of the rope around the branch, using the same sort of knot. She is deft and precise when it comes to practical tasks like this; she rarely has to do anything over again. She has given some thought in advance to which knot she should use, she knows quite a few. She pulls the noose over her head and tightens it.

Her eyes are open when she jumps.

And things move on, four and a half days have gone by already. The house is custom-designed, its wooden walls are stained black and the front door is of oak. A Virginia creeper covers one side, the leaves already starting to turn gold. Behind the house is the little grove of trees, and behind that again the car park attached to the graveyard that has been established here over the last year or so. There is no church next to the graveyard.

Someone is moving about inside this house too now, her name is Judith. She is not herself this evening; here she is, coming down the stairs from the first floor, her arms full of clothes from her daughter's wardrobe. She stumbles into the sitting-room and tosses the clothes on to the floor, then runs back up the stairs. A minute later she is on her way down again, carrying various items of clothing, together with a Discman, a set of padded ear-phones as big as protective ear muffs, several pairs of shoes, a hairbrush, books and magazines. These too she throws on to the heap on the sitting-room floor.

She used to love a man called Johan. He is still around; it's very rare for someone to disappear completely. He is not that far away, only a few blocks from the house he is driving slowly around in his old banger of a car. He is on his way to her. He knows the road, he has driven it hundreds of times, but he cannot bring himself to turn in her direction. Instead he pulls in at a nearby snack bar. And there he sits, smoking a cigarette.

It is midsummer.

The boy who found her is called Erlend. He cannot remember what he felt when he saw her hanging there in the wood. Maybe he screamed, a short, sharp scream like that of an animal.

He was her boyfriend, three years older than her; he would be starting at the university in town come the autumn. It had never bothered him before that she was so young, not until this summer; they had been good together, he had been very much in love. Ebba was pretty, and she had a certain way of looking at him, she seemed to sparkle – it made him think of the light just after a shower of rain. She was bright too, he knew that, and she had her own special way of putting things. It was hard to explain what it was that she did, but he liked it when she talked like that; it could put him into the sort of mood where it was easy to laugh with her, easy to see the funny side of things. But in other ways she could be quite childish, he thought, maybe a little too touchy, and not nearly as forward as the other girls he knew.

He had met another girl, a few weeks ago; she was the same age as himself and she too would be starting at the university in the autumn. She had a snake tattooed around her navel and made no secret of the fact that she liked him. She was a good dancer. So over the past couple of weeks he had been thinking that it was time to do a reality check, that everything would be different once he became a student. Ebba would be in her first year at junior high, while he would be staying in the halls of residence, really getting to grips with a subject. There would be parties, he would make new friends; to them she would be just a kid. It was never going to work.

He had been dreading broaching the subject with her. He hadn't known how to tell her – he had noticed that she often knew what he was thinking without him having to say a word. It's hard to explain something to someone who already knows. He had also noticed that she had become stiffer in her movements recently, as if her body knew something that it wanted to keep to itself. He was not an insensitive boy, not the sort to miss something like that. He was fond of her, wished her all the best.

The interview at the police station did not take long. It was purely routine. After all, it was he who had found her, he had to tell them what had happened. He answered all of their questions in monosyllables; he sat in that chair, bare to the waist, and stared out of the window. His knife hung from his belt in its sheath, no one seemed to have noticed it – or if they did they didn't let on.

When they were done asking him questions about Ebba, they asked if there was anything they could do for him. He shook his head.

They asked if he wanted anything to drink, but he said no. Later they arranged for a policewoman to drive him home. She had not been present at the interview; she asked no questions as to what he had been doing at the police station, but it was obvious that someone had told her what had happened, she was kind and considerate. She simply said that she was just finishing her shift and had to go in that direction anyway. She assured him that it was not taking her out of her way.

He sat stiffly in the passenger seat with his head turned towards the window as they drove along; he looked at the houses they passed. The bare skin of his back stuck to the imitation leather of the seat and made little smacking sounds when he moved, like two people kissing. He asked her to set him down in the car park behind the grove next to Ebba's and Judith's house. The policewoman glanced curiously at him as she stopped the car, and asked if everything was all right. Then she dropped him off, turned out of the car park next to the churchyard and disappeared down the road.

He stood where he was until the car was gone. A path ran from the car park into the wood. He walked slowly, his body heavy and sluggish. The ground was so dry, the thought of forest fires crossed his mind. You have to think of something; the mind doesn't stop thinking, it never stops. He thought: it had better rain soon, otherwise all of this could go up in flames.

He caught sight of his shirt straight away. It was lying where he had put it, rolled up on the ground next to the stump off which she had jumped. All was quiet.

Her grandmother had called him on his mobile, when it became clear that Ebba was missing. There had been a note of authority in her voice; she was very businesslike, as if it were some object that was lost. He had been going into town to meet someone when she called; as soon as he heard Judith's voice, hysterical in the background, he knew what had happened. He had thought: too late.

At that moment someone had begun to hollow out a cave behind his face. He had taken the train back out of town and started looking for Ebba straight away. He had felt it quite clearly, whoever was digging in there behind his face they were hard at it, working away like insects.

He had walked briskly out of the station and straight to the grove of trees behind Ebba's house. It was the first place he looked. Ebba had shown it to him once, and he had understood that this place was in some way special to her. This was just after they met, one cold, birdless day late in the winter, in the afternoon after school. She told him she liked the way he carried a knife at his belt. He felt ten feet tall, and asked if she also liked it that he wasn't wearing anything except a T-shirt under his jacket, but she didn't answer, merely smiled. He took his jacket off and laid it over one of the stumps outside the hut, then he pulled her down on to his knee. His pale upper arms were cold, the skin came up in goosebumps, he saw that she saw.

They listened to his music. They stretched the earphones of his Discman wide apart, so that they could put their heads together and listen with one ear each. An open channel seemed to run from his ear, through his head and hers, to the ear with which she was listening; a channel through which the music could pass, as if it were flowing water. She held the CD cover in her hands, inspecting it; the band was called Tool. She'd never heard of them before, but she didn't say so, and he understood everything without saying a word about it. He was in love.

But that was almost six months ago. If he hadn't found her here in the wood, he wouldn't have known where to look. He hadn't known her well enough to be familiar with her other haunts.

JOHAN SAYS

Ebba. Listen to me. Don't go.

There's something I need to explain.

It was Erlend who found you. I've spoken to him. I think he was in shock.

His mother answered the phone when I called. I heard my voice speaking to her. She sounded as if she had been crying. I hadn't been crying. It took a while for Erlend to come to the phone; maybe he was asleep.

He knew what I was going to ask, there was no need for too many questions. He had to use his knife to cut you down. He had to climb up on to the same tree stump that you had been standing on before you jumped; it was the only way. You were stiff, there were little red spots in the whites of your wide-open eyes. Your tongue had swollen, it was sticking out of your mouth. All of this he told me. I asked him how he had managed it. He said that he had wrapped one arm round you and cut through the rope with the other. You were so heavy, he said, once the rope was severed you slipped out of his grasp and fell to the ground with a thud. How clearly I could hear that thud. I asked him what he had done next; he said that he had jumped down off the stump just as you must have done, pulled off his shirt, rolled it up and put it under your head to support it, straightened you out until you were lying with your legs parallel and your arms by your sides. At least I think that's what he said. He ran his hand over your face and shut your eyes, like they do in the movies. You were cold, he said.

I asked if he would be one of the coffin bearers tomorrow. Apparently your grandmother had already called to ask the same thing.

I asked what made you do it; he said he didn't know. I asked again and again, until all he could do was cry, and his mother, or it might have been his sister, came to the phone and hung up for him. I felt bad about that, but when I called the number again to apologise, they had obviously unplugged the phone.

It was an odd conversation. We knew one another so well, and yet we were like strangers.

Don't go. There's more.

When your mother called me to tell me what had happened I had been out all night alone in the sailboat. I set out around ten; there wasn't much of a breeze, but I reckoned it would probably freshen up later on in the night, as the weather forecast had said. But instead the wind died away to a dead calm, the boat hung motionless on the smooth, oily surface of the fjord. By then I was lying just out from the cottage that your mother and I used to share. If I had felt like it, I could have dropped anchor and swum ashore to spend the night there; I know where the key is hidden. But I didn't. The cottage is in Judith's name, your grandmother wanted it that way. I made no claims upon anything when I left.

There was no wind, and I too was motionless, sitting there, gazing at the shore and the wooden cottage. I could see that her jetty was in need of repair.

It was so warm. I had taken a couple of beers with me, and a thermos of coffee, but no food. Everything was dry and still, even though I was out in the middle of the fjord. It occurred to me that once the beer and the coffee were finished, I had nothing left to drink, even though I was surrounded by water. I was struck by a sudden sense of the depths below me. I could picture the rock face that fell away below the shelf on which the beach lay, plunging downwards into darkness. No one knows how deep the water is just here, I thought. No one has ever reached the bottom at the spot over which I am sitting right now. Real perception comes, I thought, only from things we've experienced in real life.

Around midnight I had to call Minna on my mobile to tell her that it looked as if I would have to spend the night on the boat. I tried to describe to her what it felt like sitting there, but I couldn't;

I didn't want to scare her, you know how she worries, although she never says anything. She's not as easy-going as you. I switched off the mobile once I had said goodnight and blown her a silent kiss.

I saw a strange-looking cloud while I was sitting out there in the boat. I followed it for hours with my eyes. That cloud seemed to speak to me, I felt it was important to follow its progress; I thought to myself that I would have to tell you about it, that you like me to tell you about things like that. Ever since you were a little girl, no matter what I might have to tell, you've always had to know every detail. I kicked myself for not having taken the camera with me.

The cloud changed shape very slowly – as I say, there was no wind to speak of – and yet it underwent a quite radical transformation. To begin with it was shaped like a boomerang. It was moving eastwards. The upper wing of the boomerang was pale and transparent, the lower one was dark. It lay in shadow. Behind this boomerang cloud, which I thought of as mine, were a number of small fleecy clouds – delicate, but dark – some of which could be glimpsed through the upper wing of the boomerang. Then it changed, turning into a sort of globe, feather-light and wispy at the edges. It was bright pink in colour. Behind it the small, fleecy clouds hovered like a dark string of pearls over the horizon.

I saw a glorious sunset and an even more glorious sunrise. It was four in the morning before I had to pull on a sweater.

Just after sunrise four young men came along in a motor boat – you might know them, they may be lads that Erlend knows, I didn't get around to asking. I think they were a bit hungover; it looked like it. They must have felt sorry for me; at any rate they gave me a tow back to the dock. I felt strangely let down when I finally got the boat tied up and strolled up to the car park, carrying the empty beer bottles and the thermos. Already the traffic on the roads into town was pretty heavy. It grated on me, having to dive back into all that noise and commotion. I comforted myself with the thought that I could drive home and have a shower and a good breakfast before going in to work. I switched on my mobile, called Minna and woke her up. I asked her if she couldn't let Jennifer take it a bit slower that morning, then the three of us could have breakfast together before we dropped her off at nursery. Minna has a late start on Thursdays, she doesn't have to be at work until eleven, and I could take some of the time that was owing to me. She told me she had slept well and that she had not been worried about me. Not true, of course, but we tend to say that sort of thing out of consideration for one another.

I had just finished talking to Minna, still had the mobile in my hand, when it rang. I guessed it must be Minna again: something she'd forgotten to say, maybe something she wanted me to pick up for breakfast; I remembered that I had used the last of the coffee when making up my thermos the night before.

But it was Judith. She sounded upset. The moment I heard her voice I knew what had happened.

Come here. Don't go.

I've never been good about this business of the moment, Ebba. I'm better over the long stretch. It's a fault, I know, your mother was given to pointing it out, it made me feel stodgy and stupid. In her world you had to be spontaneous and playful and daring. Once, when we were at a party, she said, supposedly in jest, that she could never live with a man who didn't know how to play. I was left wondering whether she did actually think I was a playful man, or whether she was trying to tell me that she was growing tired of me.

Whenever I find myself in a situation where something crucial is about to happen I often feel a kind of . . . pressure. It's an almost physical sensation; as if the pressure of whatever it is that is lying out there somewhere on the horizon like a dark shadow, a storm that you know is on the way, settles over your nose, lies heavy in the stomach. It has the same effect as fear: a sort of sick feeling.

Sometimes the fear is so strong that I seem to be pushing this thing that's approaching away from me. As though I and the events waiting on the horizon are two like poles, repelling one another. I don't know if this protects me, or whether instead it holds the future at bay, so that it can never reach me. But it can make me feel terribly lonely.

Minna could tell, the moment I walked through the door, that something had happened, but I couldn't bring myself to say anything. I think Jennifer also realised that everything was not quite as it should be; she was clingy, hanging around us, wanting to hear what it had been like to spend the night in the boat out on the fjord. You know how she is, with all her questions, just like you at that age. Had there been pirates? Was I scared? Wasn't it right that Mama and I were both going to take her to nursery?

Minna and I went round and round one another in small circles, I could see that I was tormenting her by not telling her anything. Eventually, she followed me into the bathroom and locked the door behind us, she gripped my arm hard. So I told her. I had to tell her, you do see that, don't you.

She slid to the floor and I had nothing to give her; suddenly I felt as if I had to punish her. I was totally cold, I left her sitting there, went through to the kitchen and made up a packed lunch for your sister. Then I looked out her little slippers and drove her to nursery alone.

After I dropped off Jennifer I spent ages driving aimlessly around town. I couldn't remember where I lived. It was unreal. At last I turned on to the main road and drove here; I suppose I thought that I ought to be near your mother. Near your house. The petrol tank was almost empty by the time I got to the building site just before what used, of course, to be my neighbourhood too. I stopped at an Esso station and filled the tank. When I went to pay, I told the man at the till about you; I said that my older daughter had hung herself. I couldn't remember having been at that petrol station before. I had to ask him to tell me how to get back on to the main road. Then I drove home to Minna, I felt as if I had been out driving all day, I was stiff all over.

That was four and a half days ago, wasn't it? I can see the Esso station from here.

I came here from the hotel – this stiff body of mine feels as if it has driven here all by itself. It turned off the main road just before the petrol station, and into this car park. Then it put the car into neutral and pulled on the handbrake. My hands know what to do.

It struck me that I wouldn't have minded having another chat with that man behind the counter, check whether he remembered me, place myself in front of him with some coins in my hand and buy a pack of cigarettes, or a new lighter. I could do with a new lighter. See whether he showed any glimpse of recognition. A look in his eyes – something or other. I could have said: I'm the man who was here a few days ago.

But that's not how it went. My hands turned in and parked in front of the snack bar instead. Eddy's Snack Stop it says on the sign, but it's a woman who's selling the hot dogs. The poky little stall is lit by fluorescent tubes, it looks weird on such a bright summer evening; look, the light makes her shimmer.

People are crossing the car park towards my car, they drop their hot-dog wrappings on the ground. There's no wind, just the paper falling, it doesn't blow away. I'm shaking. Hold my hands.

Your mother is waiting for me in the house a few blocks from here.

I'll never learn to know any house as well as I know that house. It's a good, solid house, I built it well. My toolbox is still down there in the basement, isn't it? Well, it's not as if I had any use for tools after I moved in with Minna, there's a limit to what you need when you live in a block of flats with its own caretaker.

This could have been a very different evening. I could, for that matter, have been on my way down to the harbour again, or to a late meeting to do with work. I could have stopped here at the snack bar to buy a hot dog before driving on; I could have thrown the wrapping into the bin, checked my mobile – there might have been a text message from you, then I might have smiled to myself – you send such sweet, funny messages, you're so good with words, they remind me that you're thinking of me. I might have got into the car, released the hand brake, put the car into reverse and backed out of the car park. My hands might have been resting on the steering wheel, firmly, instinctively, while I munched on the last chunk of hot dog, I might have left the car to carry on down the road towards some place I knew well. I might have hummed along to some tune I heard on the radio.

Minna and Jennifer were tucked up in the big double bed at the hotel when I left them just now. They were lying there like two sisters in their matching nighties, watching cartoons. I said to them, from where I was standing over by the door: one little and one big sister, I said, one light and one dark. It was said with love, but I don't think they heard. Jennifer had just learned to use the remote control, she was experimenting with the volume button in her own cautious, concentrated fashion. Movements she has from her mother. They're so precise those two. Exactly like you.

It was only a little over half-past seven in the evening, and Jennifer had slept in the car on the way to the hotel. When I left she was wide awake and high as a kite; I saw how she had to force herself to lie still in bed beside her mother. She had both her hands on top of the quilt, like a doll, one of them clasped firmly around the remote control. She had about her an air of gravity and elation combined that almost prompted me to turn away. Minna was very pale, as pale as she can sometimes be when she is in pain; she avoided my eye. That hurt me.

She said she might just as well go to bed. After all, she could hardly leave Jennifer alone in the hotel when I went over to Judith's, and she hadn't brought anything to read. I offered to pop down to the news-stand in reception and get her some newspapers and magazines, but this she dismissed with a listless wave of the hand.

She and Jennifer unpacked our good, dark-coloured clothes for tomorrow, and hung them on clothes-hangers on the outside of the cupboard doors as soon as we got to the hotel room. After that they ran themselves a bath in the plush hotel bathroom. I would have liked to have sat there for a while, on the edge of the bath, and watched them, but they didn't seem to want me there. They chattered away and dug channels and caves in the bubble-bath foam, but behind all the chatter I could see Minna's tense, tired expression. I had no reason to believe that this was any easier on her than it was on me. I eyed her white body.

I thought to myself that I would have liked to scrub their backs too, lift them out of the bath and dry them off with big towels, as if they were two little girls. As if I were the father of both. But they did all that themselves, they dried themselves and combed out their hair, pulled their nighties over their heads and brushed their teeth. Then they climbed into bed and switched on the television.

Minna and I had discussed it on the way to the hotel, while Jennifer was asleep, and we had agreed that I should go to see your mother alone. There was no long discussion, we both knew there was no point in dragging our feelings into this. We're trying to be grown-up about it, Ebba.

It was there in the car with Minna and Jennifer that I really began to feel that the situation was pushing me away. Something lay ahead, in the future, that wanted nothing to do with me, dark weather. I didn't want to worry Minna with it.

She glanced across at me from the passenger seat with the same mute look in her eyes as Jennifer had had in hers when I collected her from nursery in the early afternoon. I think Minna felt flat too. Dark and flat and emitting the wrong magnetic charge.

I stepped out into the hotel corridor and shut the door behind me.

Further along the corridor there was an ice dispenser. I lifted the little flap and buried my hands in the ice cubes, kept them there for a long while. When I drew them out again they were white and chilled and pinched. My whole body was shivering with cold, even though I still felt hot and sick to my stomach. The lights on the panel showing which floor the lift was on kept changing, flashing on and off as though someone were constantly stepping in and out of the lift doors, sending it up and down the narrow lift shaft willy-nilly.

It's still unusually hot, the newspapers have been full of ominous pictures of parched fields and meteorologists posing alongside empty rain gauges; I remember we talked about it, you and I.

'It's a sign,' you said, looking up from the paper. You looked straight at me. 'It's so dry, it's like a sign.'

Oh, God. Tell me that's not what you meant.

It feels as if something horrible is working its way up my throat and out of my mouth. As if I might find myself saying something . . . disgusting, or spit out something, something way too big. Forewarnings of its terrible stench seep through my pores and mingle with the rank, rubbery smell of the seat covers – do you know the smell I mean? When I was a little boy, I was sure that other people could smell it too, that stench, I thought that was why they were always after me. It was the odour of age-old fear, older than my own short life, older than anything else that I knew of; I thought it must be something I had inherited. One of the first things that crossed my mind when I saw you in the hospital just after you were born was that you hadn't inherited that fear. I was so relieved. I knew right away that you were brave, you were the smallest and the bravest person I had ever met. I felt that everyone must be able to see that. You shone.

There was no snack bar on this spot when I lived here with you and Mama. But during the past few years new housing estates have sprung up all over the place. You know I've no time for these new standard houses, all pastel colours and small window panes; they annoy me, I can't help it, I can't look at them without thinking of the awful crassness that's creeping into everything these days. You're the only person to whom I could admit having such thoughts, did you know that? You know my likes and dislikes.

I might have started the car again, turned around and driven back to the hotel. Minna and Jennifer will probably have an early night. Minna has her own special way of settling Jennifer for sleep, I don't know how she does it. I could have sat there and watched them, sipping a whisky from the mini-bar while the hours drew on towards tomorrow morning when we would have to put on the good clothes that hung ready and waiting on the cupboard door.

I'm sorry. I don't know what I'm sorry for.

Everything. I'm sorry for everything, Ebba. Everything is beyond repair.

I told Jennifer about you when I picked her up from nursery that afternoon, that was on – Thursday. Yes: Thursday.

She responded with – I don't know what to call it. A kind of coolness. A mute, wide-eyed gaze at me. No questions, no comment. She just looked at me, then she turned and walked over to her cubby-hole to fetch her jacket and the little rucksack in which she carries her lunchbox. She took my hand as if I were an old man who needed to be helped out to the waiting car. She was right; I am an old man.

After I had buckled her into her car seat she asked me to put on one of the children's tapes that she always has scattered about on the back seat. I think she did this to prevent me from starting to tell her about you, as I had planned. She knows me so well, many's the time she's known what I was going to say even before I did.

I've never liked that tape, with its phoney, jazzed-up versions of traditional children's songs, by a charmless has-been who has latched on to the growing market in music for children. Dreadful synthetic arrangements. Things were different when you were that age, kids' records were simpler in those days, more innocent. Happy-go-lucky music-box tunes with clarinet and bass. I know you remember that music. *This old man, he played one –*

When I went to turn on to the main road the rush-hour was at its height and traffic was at a standstill in both directions. The sky over the new DIY centre was pale, almost watery, and a fine veil of herringbone clouds had formed far in the east. They looked clean and light. In the back seat, Jennifer was singing, I could hear how already her voice had taken on some of that affected, child-star twang.

Between the buildings I caught a glimpse of the fjord. Only hours earlier I had been sitting almost motionless out there in the sailboat. It was hard to imagine that I would ever sail across that fjord again.

Ebba. All the beauty has been taken from me, it's running through my fingers. Soon Minna and Jennifer will be lost to me too, I don't deserve them. I never deserved you, and I don't deserve them.

Don't let them leave me! Don't go!

I don't know the meaning of loss. No. I don't know the first thing about it, and I don't want to know. Don't tell me about it. My head's splitting, Ebba!

I have to concentrate. The car is in neutral. The hand-brake is on. There's a pool of light round Eddy's Snack Stop.

You were beautiful. You were the best of me. You were the best of Judith too. I don't know why you didn't want to live any more. Why you simply made an end of it.

I can light a cigarette. It doesn't matter if I smoke now.

You knew everything about us, didn't you? You never blamed us for anything. You trusted us. You were a song that someone sung inside me. Someone will have to go on singing that song, I can't sing it myself. Sing it for me.

Oh, it comes out all wrong! D'you hear me! I can't do it.

I don't know what it means for something to come to an end. I don't want to know. It mustn't go all quiet here. It's far too quiet.

Stars shining bright above you
Night breezes seem to whisper I love you . . .

Remember? It mustn't go all quiet here. It's far too quiet.

My lighter's almost empty, I ought to buy a new one. I could drive over to the petrol station, it's right over there.

I know there is something so beautiful that it hurts. You don't need to remind me.

You were . . .

It hurt to be your father, it hurt right from the start; you were too much for me, a gift that was too great, so great that I staggered backwards when you were put into my arms, I had to put you down.

You looked like your mother. And when Judith and I started seeing one another she was so beautiful that it hurt. I couldn't imagine who could have granted me such a gift, what lay behind it. I felt as though I was being tested.

I remember the day I collected the two of you from the maternity home. Judith was waiting downstairs in reception with you in her arms when I arrived; I was a bit out of breath after hunting for a parking space and fumbling about with the parking ticket machine, you know how I am sometimes, I had run all the way from the car to the entrance.

Judith was wearing her air-force blue blouse, and a hairband that made her forehead seem high and bright. You were asleep, all wrapped up in a white crocheted blanket, you were wearing a little bonnet knitted by your grandmother. I had on my brown leather jacket, my shoulders loose and easy. I looked at Judith and felt the corners of my mouth twitch at the same moment as hers twitched. She held you out to me, carefully, as if to show me something I had never seen before. We take pleasure in the same things, I thought, when she did that. All impressions are like a wave that reaches us together, because we are standing side by side on an endless beach, and all impressions roll in on a warm wave that hits us together; our child is one of them, she hits us together, we have never seen her before. That's how I was thinking. I suppose that back then I must have pictured life as being rather like a beach.

But of course I can see now that that image won't do. It would probably be more true to say, don't you think, that life was the wave that came rolling into the shore, and that Judith and me and you were already part of that wave. That we were hurled out into it together a few moments before the currents swept us away from one another again. There wasn't anyone standing on the shore, was there?

We were three wet heads in the waves, moving in the same direction for a moment or two, before the tide turned and we drifted away from one another.

Something like that. I don't know. But I keep thinking: you were lost in the water between us. I should have saved you, I should have swum to where you were, you were just a baby, babies can't swim. Listen to me, Ebba. Babies can't swim, can they, they can't get themselves to the shore on their own.

My hand seems to have forgotten how to release the hand-brake, how to put the car into reverse. My head and my left arm can remember, but the right arm has no memory. I'll have to sit here for a while, it's bound to think of it soon. Judith will just have to wait, I don't think she's going anywhere, do you? I don't think she's been over the door since she heard the news about you.

Look, there's no one at the snack bar now, the woman inside has sat herself down behind the counter with her face in profile, she's still shimmering, I think she's reading a newspaper. If it is a newspaper then she has folded it in four, but it might be a magazine. Do you think it's a magazine?

My head goes on thinking. Why do I think like this? It goes on running at night, too; it can't sleep, it's splitting, it can't do anything but think, it doesn't know what else to do, there's no rest for it. I wish I could sleep for a little while here in the car. Tip the seat back and let sleep . . . rise up like water.

Did I ever tell you how Mama and I met? I guess I haven't been all that good at telling you about us, it's been so difficult, what with . . . well, you know.

In a way, the town hall gardens are our place, Mama's and mine. I think you should know that she saved my life that day eighteen years ago. I can't take that away from her, it must be possible to keep that in mind, no matter how things turned out for us; I owe both her and you that much. If she hadn't found me in the town hall gardens that spring, I would have faded away, my contours would have dissolved. And if she hadn't put her hands over my ears, you would never have been born. I think I might almost say that that was how you were conceived.

I believe that on that day I was saved from becoming invisible. If I hadn't been visible, I couldn't have become your father. My contours were already starting to blur, I could feel it. I was a 35-year-old computer engineer, I had a steady, responsible job with a good salary, but I had no drive until I met your mother. I rested a lot in those days, you've never seen me the way I was then.

And then she came along and was beautiful for me, she was a flaming torch. You know how she can be when she shines like that! That torch made me visible to myself. Yes, it did. It made me visible.

Until that day I had only been visible in short flashes during my childhood and youth, flashes that reminded me of something, although at that point I didn't know what. Later on those flashes would make me feel vaguely ashamed, I would never have told anyone about them, they seemed to come under the same heading as masturbation or speculations about religion. How could I possibly have told anyone? I didn't have the words, they hadn't yet been invented.

But when Judith came walking through the gardens towards me, I became visible. and when I became visible the shadows disappeared, all the weight that had been hanging over me. And I realised that with her it didn't matter that I had no warmth of my own, in fact it was almost an advantage. She transmitted her warmth to me, that was what she did when she put her hands over my ears on that morning in March in the town hall gardens; I felt the warmth flowing into me from her white hands, and I became someone who could be a father.

I don't know why Minna and I feel that we have to punish one another, Ebba. It wasn't always that way. And it was never like that between your mother and me, or at least not to begin with. Judith and I didn't start punishing each other until everything was over between us, and the storm broke. By then you were around, you had been there between us for some years. We both had a hold of you, each by one hand.

It doesn't look as if there are going to be any more customers, look, the woman has put down her paper. Maybe she's going to shut up shop soon. It's not eight o'clock yet, but if no more customers show up she might as well close, don't you think. It's too warm for hot dogs anyway.

Of course I could get out and . . .

No. I'll switch on the radio. Maybe there'll be some music. I'll find something you like. Don't go.

You know Mama was playing the violin with the orchestra at the Opera House when I met her? I thought that was great, for me that was a big thing. I was a member of the Friends of the Opera. They were in the middle of rehearsals for *The Magic Flute* when we started seeing one another. Those first weeks were so intense that my work began to suffer, I would call in sick and go to rehearsals with her instead. It wasn't like me, but I didn't feel at all guilty about it.

Maybe that's why I felt it was so important to tell you about *The Magic Flute*, back there in the spring. Maybe I wanted to show you the music that Mama and I had once shared, the music that was part of all the beauty before you were born. I've always felt that that music was the start of what was to become you. That and her hands over my ears.

Never before could I remember having felt as I did with Mama back then. I suppose I must have been happy, but somehow the feeling seemed so unfamiliar to me. I sat up in the gods, at the very back, slumped down in my seat with my legs crossed and my jacket on, studying her and the other musicians. Mostly her, of course.

The music hit me with such force. It washed over me, and I suppose I must have been happy, the way you can be when you listen to music; I wasn't afraid, I didn't flinch, I sat back in my seat and opened myself up to it all. Something happened to my vision too, I developed a particular way of half-closing my eyes so that Judith slid out of focus. That way I could take in the whole of the orchestra at once and not allow my doting eyes to dwell on her alone. Suddenly I had masses of energy; the music made my thoughts crystal clear. I decided to use my eyes and ears objectively, democratically, I would impose this discipline upon myself, rather than follow my own eager impulse and let my gaze lap up, linger on and caress your mother. I would give the music as much room as her. I was keen as a razor-blade, Ebba. We're not so different, you and I.

The overture to *The Magic Flute* is only six and a half minutes long, I think I forgot to tell you that, the evening when I was trying to explain everything to you. But within that short space of time a brief metaphysical drama is enacted, I know I remembered to mention that, powerful forces are at work, all of these voices at one time . . . I remember I used to think to myself, sitting up there in the gods during rehearsals: this is what thinking is like. This music shows what goes on in my brain. What a relief to know that there's a language for it.

The piece opens with one strong chord, played by the entire orchestra at once. It is a statement – Mozart has presented a response, in advance, to a question that has not yet been posed. It's arrogant; necessarily arrogant.

But then that same chord is repeated, this time split in two and already more tentative, then it sounds for a third time, transformed by now from an assertion to an ambivalent question, one to which the musicians are not really sure they want to know the answer. Then comes the febrile, delicate rendering of this question by the strings; insect-like, vibrant, as if they have already released the question, sent it soaring into the air. And the rest of the orchestra follow their lead, each section in turn catching and letting go of the question, flipping it on, from one to another, and almost imperceptibly they start to offer their own suggestions for a response: the flutes notably to the fore here, followed by the other wind instruments; they egg each other on, the tension builds up –

I slid farther and farther down in my seat and waited for the moment when the whole thing would reach such a pitch that there would no longer be any way back, and it felt as though the musicians, led by the wind section, were having to formulate for themselves exactly what it was they were getting into, what this question with which they had been playing actually involved.

It was a magical moment. I no longer needed to screw up my eyes, I had lost sight of Judith, she had become one with her fellow musicians. And then, uncompromisingly, came the three dramatic blasts from the wind section, both an echo and an extension of the opening chord:

Ta-tam ta. Ta-tam ta. Ta-tam ta –

I could tell that the orchestra now realised that something was on the way. For one fleeting moment time had stood still, then everything moved on. Now there was no going back; the orchestra had surrendered to the music, they weren't musicians now, they weren't even the orchestra any more, they could no longer be considered individually.

Yes, I thought, that's just how it is. What a relief.

No; you're right, I ought to be getting on. Mama's expecting me. Help me now. My right arm will remember what to do if I just tell it, won't it? Lift the hand-brake up a little, press the button with my thumb, lower the lever. Push the gearstick all the way to the right and into the little notch; there.

When you reverse, you have to keep checking your mirrors. Check the blind spot as you turn out on to the road.

It was almost bewildering to watch Judith playing with her fellow musicians. I could see that she was somewhere else, she had been taken out of herself, become part of something greater. This was a side of her that was closed to me. I looked forward to the moment when the rehearsal was over and I could go backstage and be with her, put my arm around her shoulders, whisper something in her ear, feel her detaching herself from the others, putting her violin back in its case, sticking her arm into the coat that I held for her and becoming the Judith that I could take home with me.

Look, I'm just passing the Esso station. I can't turn my head to see if there's anyone inside, I have to keep my eyes on the road. There's hardly any traffic, but I have to look where I'm going, keep my eyes on the line down the middle.

Those first weeks when Mama and I were together, there was such an . . . intensity between us. I often felt that with her I found myself in situations that I couldn't even have made up on my own; laughter sat loose, high in my chest, ready to bubble up through me like warm little surprises. I was more dynamic when we were together, my fingers were somehow nimbler than I had ever known them to be; everything about me was lighter and easier, my chest was wide open and light as snow, and I developed a new way of walking, several people remarked on it. I suppose I had a name for being a rather close, standoffish character. A bit dull maybe, not very physical.

In those days, when Judith smiled, her torch lit up my face, making me beautiful and forceful too. I had been suffering, for a long time, from a terrible lethargy; engineering college and my job with the company I was working for when you were born seemed in some way unreal to me, a daze in which everything moved in a steady, rhythmic cycle of dreamlike repetition, the sort you sometimes fall into just before going to sleep.

The problem was not that I wasn't good at what I did. You know it doesn't cost me much to do something well, you're like me; doing things well is just a natural consequence of the fact that someone has placed a brain of slightly above average intelligence in my head, just as someone has done with yours, quite unmerited, and most likely inherited from an intelligent but socially inept father who never dared to excel at anything. Your grandfather was a cowardly man, Ebba.

The difficulty lay on another plane; it had to do with the fact that the work I did was always set by other, often less intelligent people than myself. There is something so disheartening about that. It didn't help that I was good at what I did, I couldn't rid myself of the feeling that what I did, didn't really matter.

But then Judith found me, and I realised that she was my work. I felt her hands burning into my ears, and all my restless energy which, until then, had had no focus, concentrated into one point and began to glow. I glowed at the music in her.

Ta-tam ta. Ta-tam ta. Ta-tam ta –

It was around this time that I started reading Nietzsche. When you get right down to it, he may have had as much to do with the change in me as your mother. He became my high priest. A high priest is someone who can change another person's life by altering the way that person thinks. Someone like Nietzsche. Someone who doesn't call himself Sarastro, the high priest in *The Magic Flute*, but Zarathustra. Someone who shines a light into the head of the reader, causing him to see things he has never seen before. Things that have always been there, but which have been invisible to all but the initiated. Someone who shows you a door that has previously been hidden, and opens it wide for you.

Reading *Thus Spake Zarathustra* was like being presented, at long last, with work set by someone far more intelligent than me. I had had no idea that anyone could think like this mad philosopher, it was unheard of. And yet these might have been my own thoughts, from when I was very young; I simply hadn't had the language to cover them, the words did not as yet exist for me, I had been living in the wrong world. I felt at one and the same time lucid and confused, my brain was working in top gear.

Your mother was, of course, a bit of a catch, I was well aware of that. All those of us who had spent some time watching her from afar knew that when it came to wooing Judith you had to go by a different set of rules than that which applied to other women. She had her game, and we played along, with greater or lesser skill.

I'm not saying that I set out to snare her or anything like that. But I had had her in my sights for a long time, you couldn't help noticing her. We live in a small country, there isn't room for too many divas. There is, however, plenty of scope for the few we do have. And there's room for many more nondescript computer engineers.

There was a group of us from the computer business who went regularly to the opera and were members of the Friends of the Opera. Sometimes we were invited to parties organised by the opera's sponsors. These gatherings had a determinedly ebullient, rather superficial air about them. I always had the feeling that everyone there was in a terrible hurry, as if they all had a particular goal that had to be achieved in the course of that evening and night, and a combination of alcohol and excitable conversation laced with lots of high-pitched laughter was the quickest way of getting there. In the long run it was exhausting, both for the musicians and for the rest of us. It occurred to me that we might end up burning one another out; eventually there would be a PUFF, and everything would go quiet, everyone would collapse.

The Magic Flute is an opera with a lot of *thunder* in it, don't you think? I found that very funny, back in the days when I was attending rehearsals, those claps of thunder every time something dramatic was about to happen on stage, as if Mozart hadn't trusted his audience to get the point.

Sometimes during rehearsals there was trouble with the thunderclaps – the sound man got it wrong and brought them in either a little too early or a little too late for the action and the music. You would have loved that, wouldn't you, it's just the sort of situation you find funny. He had the musicians and the singers in an uproar, anyone would have thought he was sitting back there in his booth rehearsing all by himself, paying no heed whatsoever to what was happening on stage; like a headstrong god, a weather god with little authority, but some powerful tools at his disposal. I couldn't help laughing, I put my hand over my mouth feeling very childish, but your mother, who was so big on playfulness, didn't find it at all funny. When I mentioned it on the way home after rehearsal, she seemed merely frustrated. She hated amateurs, she said. Not until years later did I realise that I too must count as an amateur.

When we had you, the light from Judith's torch seemed to grow even brighter. You were this sacred object, you shone too, lying there asleep with your face nestling into the hollow of her throat and your little mouth resolutely pursed. And in the dual light cast by her and by you my contours suddenly became too sharp; where before I had been vague, I was now far too clear-cut, both to myself and to you two. Before, I had been transparent; now my elbows were indecently bony, my chin intrusive, my shoulders all angles. Surrounded by so much beauty, I didn't know what do with my great clumsy hands; I was afraid I might break something, I had to take my hands into another room. It was around this time I discovered that hands can forget what it is they're supposed to do, that sometimes they have to be told. It was around this time, too, I discovered that beauty can hurt, Ebba.

It took me a long time to get used to it. It was some weeks before I felt able to hold you without worrying that something of me would rub off on you. I always washed my hands before I changed you, did you know that?

But you and Mama didn't become too clear-cut, in some strange way the two of you remained bathed in a shimering haze until long after you were born. Your own joint light rendered your contours beautifully indistinct, you blended into one body of gentle little breaths, in and out.

All through her pregnancy, I was convinced that the baby Judith was carrying was a girl, a little clone of herself, and it didn't seem quite right when you came out of her and I realised that you actually looked like me too, not just her. But while you were still only a tiny baby I used to talk to you in secret, as if you and I were bosom friends who had known each other for ages. You see, I felt that the tone of our conversations had already been set by the talks I had had with Little Judith. Little Judith is the little girl inside Mama. I don't think I ever told you about her either. I suppose I must have thought it was Little Judith who was going to be born back then.

My hands didn't know what to do with you, but my voice knew.

And in my infinite naïvety I took it for granted that in due course you would have a little brother who would speak with Little Johan's voice. It was only a matter of time.

I don't need to tell you who Little Johan is, I'm sure. Mama and I used to talk like that in those days. It seems a bit silly now, after all this time.

Here it is.

Your house is just up there at the top of the drive. See? Oh God, look at all those flowers. Don't tell me she's still at it, you'd think she'd have given that up by now.

I think I'll leave the car down here on the street; can't drive over all those flowers, I mean there's a whole carpet of them. I can't drive over that, can I?

She's drawn the venetian blinds. Why has she drawn the blinds?

The sweat's running off me, the back of my shirt is damp. Feel.

I know this area – well, I did used to live here. I'll just light one more cigarette and let you listen to the rest of the concert on the radio, then I'll walk up the drive and ring her doorbell. I will do it, I promise I will.

It's still almost like being in the country out here, isn't it. It's certainly very different from the high-rise estate where you live when you come to stay with Minna and me and Jennifer. Most of the houses here were built long after yours and Mama's, it stands out a mile once you know what to look for, they're different in style, all built to the same standard design. Some of our old neighbours must have sold off plots of their ground; there are new little side roads, and postboxes that weren't there before. Our house is the only one here that was custom-designed, did you know that?

It has a fair bit of ground attached to it. Mama and I used to be rather proud of that. On the other side of the wood behind the house is a car park, it's new too. On the other side of the car park lies the graveyard.

Oh, Ebba.

It was on an afternoon after a rehearsal for the opera that Judith and I drove out here to look at this bit of ground. I had skived off work again, I was feeling very daring. We fell for the spot straight away, there were hardly any houses here at that point.

We paced about the cleared plot, planning how our house should sit. We wanted a big bathroom with a window overlooking the wood, and an open-plan living area with sliding doors between the rooms. I said I wanted to leave the ground wild and untouched. Your mother agreed, so we didn't make a lawn or any flower beds.

I built the house myself, almost single-handedly. That was seventeen years ago. I only hired people to lay the foundations and to put in the wiring and the plumbing. I really put my heart into it in a way I'd never done with anything before. I felt so close to it all, to the materials, the ground, the wind gusting around the trees as autumn came and went and winter drew on. Once the roof was on I held a topping-out ceremony all by myself with a beer and a cigarette. We moved in in May; I finished off the last bits and pieces in the bathroom, put up the mirror and hung the venetian blinds after we moved in.

But once the house was finally finished, Judith seemed to forget that we had agreed to leave the ground untouched. She started planting nasturtiums in big pots and setting them down either side of the gravel driveway, giving no hint of what she was up to. She also dug flower beds round the sides of the house and planted begonias.

Those begonias got to be so huge, I didn't see how they could grow so fast; I thought it took plants of that sort years to reach any size. The nasturtiums grew like mad too, that first summer. The dense tangles of flower stalks, leaves and orange and yellow flowers spilled over the edges of the pots, which were widely spaced out towards the bottom of the drive, but set closer and closer together the nearer one got to the house, just as they are now. In this way she made it look as though the flowers were winding across the heath and working their way up to the house, as if they preferred to be close to people. Judith has an eye for that sort of thing, you know how she is; she has a knack for creating dreamlike codes of this sort in such a way that they seem quite credible. Sometimes I had the feeling that she did it in order to confuse things. As if she had access to something profound and secret from which I would always be excluded. It felt like some new sort of test, for what I couldn't say, but it was hard to be tested in such a way, it made me feel stupid.

But I lived through her, I breathed with her lungs, I could no longer remember how I had drawn breath before I met her. Those years when I was at the college of engineering – maybe I didn't breathe at all back then.

It must be getting late. Maybe I'd better see if I can find the jazz channel. You like jazz too, don't you?

I have to get her to listen. We have to come to some sort of agreement about the arrangements for tomorrow; a lot of people will be coming back to the house after the funeral. We have to sort out the seating in the church. It's very important to me that Minna and Jennifer should sit at the front in the church along with Judith and me. In the same pew. I know that's what you would want. I hope it won't take too long for us to agree on that.

It has been quite clear from my telephone conversations with

Judith and with the Moon Queen that I can't expect any help from that quarter. I need to be strong now, don't I. I have to understand. When you don't understand, you become weak and small and pathetic.

But there's something I have to explain to you before I go in to see her. It takes such a long time to understand, Ebba. Before you can explain, you have to understand, but it takes such a long time. You understand that, don't you.

I'm not sure it will do, that image of the sea and the current that changed direction and swept Judith and you and me away from one another. It's too passive, it was more like there was something about the very substance of the bonds between us that changed, some sort of chemical reaction; maybe it was the glue holding us together that almost imperceptibly began to come unstuck. I had been so sure that it was a strong glue, but as it turned out it wasn't good glue at all. Yes: glue. That's a better image.

I don't know what it was that triggered the process. It may be that it commenced quite soon after we started seeing one another, although it wasn't until much later that I began to notice the first signs: a slight physical irritation in certain situations where Judith was being herself in a particularly distinct fashion, playing up to me, letting me be her audience. Suddenly I felt that she was using me. It was as if she knew she was irresistible, and could not resist the temptation to have me confirm it. My love for her must have chimed with something inside her, given rise to an echo within her, perhaps it confirmed what she already knew: that she was worthy of love. This echo had caused her to lay herself open, with absolute trust, to me and to the world. And in this trust, which is a torch, and another word for beauty, there was also an assurance that she was safe, that nothing would ever be used against her. And so she could play up to me, revel in herself as I revelled in her.

Don't get me wrong, there was nothing calculated about this as far as she was concerned. I would be more inclined to call it a love so fundamental that it could allow itself to extend not just to me, the loved one, but in other directions too. In fact it was as if she shared in my love for her, as if my eyes on her made her reach out to herself with a particular kind of yearning.

And she was right, of course, she was irresistible, in the way that children and kittens are irresistible, and her authority in this was the supreme authority of children and kittens. There was no way you could guard yourself against it.

When you are head over heels in love as I was with your mother back then, the thought that it might pass, that in just a few years you could find yourself having the same strong feelings for someone else entirely, is totally inconceivable, not to say absurd. If anyone had ever suggested such a thing to me, I would probably have smiled indulgently and changed the subject, possibly fought down the urge to pat the hand of this person who had never experienced such a well of emotions as that granted to me.

We talk about falling in love. Nobody ever talks about the falling out again.

To begin with, Judith and I knew nothing about the fall. From the very first night we spent together we were one, and we couldn't fall anywhere. That first night came right after the afternoon when she found me on the bench outside the town hall.

I've always accepted her version of what happened: that it was she who found me, suddenly and unexpectedly, even though a more pragmatic version of events would have to allow for the fact that I had already loved her from afar for months, and had gone to all sorts of lengths to be near her – at those parties at the opera, for example – while she, for her part, had never given any sign that she was interested in me until that afternoon.

I know that at the time I had the naïve idea that that moment marked the start of something new, that I had been sitting there on that bench waiting for her at long last to come along, and that once she had found me we stood up, as if on command, and walked off side by side, almost like brother and sister, out of the town hall gardens. Not exactly hand in hand, but along the street, full of wonder and an almost hallowed sense that something utterly new was beginning. I had switched into another mode, or so I imagined, as if I had stepped into a story of some sort, a sacred tale from a hitherto unknown manuscript, possibly only recently discovered on a parchment scroll covered in symbols and primitive characters that someone had stumbled upon in a dark, dry cave somewhere out in the desert. The way that now and again we hear of a new discovery of pictures and writings from religions so old that one is left awestruck at the thought that there could actually have been people with religious aspirations in those days. That they didn't have enough to do just staying alive, finding food, procreating. The way you and I have often read about in the *National Geographic*.

It was because I was a part of this sacred tale that my strides were exactly the same length as Judith's as I walked beside her along the street. That was how it seemed to me. I didn't have to make any effort, even though my legs were, of course, longer than hers. That was why the sky above us was pale and hazy, that was why there weren't any clouds up there, just a sort of expectant mist. And that was why someone had turned down the volume on all the sounds round about us, in such a way that we could, in effect, hear each other breathing, amid all the noise from the traffic and other people on the street. It was as if someone were watching over us; we had stepped into the inviolable setting of the sacred tale.

We walked over to her flat. I carried her violin case, she said she didn't need to go to work the next day. It was a lie, of course, and it made me so happy. I remember she had to pop into the post office on the way, to post a letter; I went in with her, all the way up to the postbox at the counter. As if I had every right to do so I scanned the name and address on the envelope, it was a woman's name, your grandmother as it turned out. I didn't think twice about the fact that she was writing a letter to a mother who lived in the same town as herself. Further on we called in at a little shop selling foreign spices and exotic fruits and the like, things I'd barely heard of. Judith was on first-name terms with the dark-skinned proprietor, who evidently knew what she was in the habit of buying. He gave me a warm smile, as if it were already a well-known fact in this part of town that I was her new man. We left the shop with a carrier bag containing olives, freshly ground coffee and a special sort of round bread with a crispy crust that smelled of what might have been caraway seeds, I'm not quite sure.

I had a rough idea of where her flat was. And once we got there, once the water from the pasta was coming to the boil, once your mother had chopped the parsley with a an outrageously sharp kitchen knife and I went to open the wine bottle on the kitchen worktop, I found that the corkscrew was in the first drawer I opened, as if this were a kitchen I already knew well. I didn't make a mess of opening the bottle the way I usually do, the cork didn't fall apart, the action with which I pulled the cork out of the neck of the bottle was not too sharp; the hollow, resonant *plop* of a cork being pulled out of the neck of a bottle was a sign that I could safely surrender myself, that it was simply a matter of allowing oneself to be led. It felt so good to think of it in that way.

I don't remember what we talked about over dinner. Maybe we didn't talk about anything much. I don't remember it getting dark, or us drawing the curtains. But I remember standing, without knowing how it came about, with my hands cupped around her bare shoulders, and my lips at her throat. I remember the little moans she made as our movements became more and more intense.

I want to be completely open with you about this, Ebba. I know you know about such things.

I had to make a quick trip to the bathroom during the night. She had a large, full-length mirror in there and it was as if, in that mirror, for the first time I saw myself as I really was. It was a shockingly honest mirror, it presented the true story about me. Someone was in the process of deciphering the characters on the parchment scroll. Everything that happens to us has a meaning, I thought, it's just so old that it's almost been forgotten.

For the rest of that night we stayed in bed, telling one another things. To begin with I suppose it was mostly the usual sort of pillow talk that all lovers indulge in after a torrid session between the sheets, little stories intended to illustrate some aspect of ourselves or someone we care about. But after a while the conversation took a more serious turn. It was Judith who put me on the spot; she wriggled in under my arm with her face turned up to mine.

'What's the name of the boy who lives in there?' she asked, tapping gently with her fingers here, on my chest. It never occurred to me not to answer, everything in me was laid open to her.

'Little Johan,' I answered, without a second thought.

'Tell me about him,' she said.

And I trusted her, Ebba. I didn't hesitate, I started to tell her, it was like a piece of improvisation, as if someone had unexpectedly handed me an instrument and I had taken it without hesitation and begun to play, never thinking that I couldn't. Just like all the times later on, when you were small, when I used to tell you stories. You know I'm good at improvising, but I didn't know it myself, not back then. It was your mother who showed me the way.

'Once upon a time,' I said. 'There was a land far away in which a different time held sway. And in that time lived Little Johan, he was invisible, just a voice, he sat on a bench in the town hall gardens with his clenched fists stuck in the pockets of his jacket. He was alone. He was actually on his way to work, but all of a sudden he didn't know whether he could make it. He needed to rest, he was always so tired. He was waiting for something.

'Then one day he spied a woman walking towards him through the gardens. She was strong and beautiful, like you,' I went on. 'Even from a distance he could tell that she must be the Moon Queen's daughter, he could tell by the way she walked: swiftly and purposefully. In her hand she carried her violin case. She was wearing a fur hat, she had come straight from the hot coffee she had drunk standing by the kitchen window, it wasn't very hard to see, her step was so light, her calves were slim and strong. She recognised him, she could see him even though he was invisible, so she must have met him before; she was bright and breezy with a spring in her step, she looked like you, she walked up to him and sat down next to him with her knees pointing outwards, without saying a word. Her fur hat was like a helmet, gently she set down her violin case on the bench beside her. In her pocket she had a letter.

'It might be that they had met one another at a dinner party or something of the sort, they were able to exchange remarks about mutual acquaintances, the tone between them was light from the moment the first words were spoken.

'She understood that he was invisible, just a voice, he didn't need to tell her, and she saw that his ears were cold and that he needed to rest somewhere warm. And after a while, although neither of them could have explained it, she placed her hands over his ears to warm them. She blew on him. By the time she took her hands away he had surrendered himself to her, he had come out into the open and his contours had become clear. She took off her hat and put it on his head, tied the strings under his chin.'

Your mother lay perfectly still with her hand on my chest and gazed at me, bright-eyed. I looked down at her and felt the story growing out of me, the words linking up. I was amazed at myself.

'That was the moment when their story began,' I said. 'Judith tied the strings under Little Johan's chin and with that it was sealed. They got to their feet and walked out of the gardens and down the street towards the post office, they popped into a shop and bought food, then they lay in bed in her flat, they slid in and out of one another, all they had to do was reach out a hand and the other was right there at their side. They are lying there still,' I said. 'They are in a land far away, somewhere between "Once upon a time" and "They lived happily ever after." Time stands still.'

I put out my hand and drew breath, there was silence. There was no applause, as there usually is at jazz concerts after a great piece of improvisation, but I knew I had been good.

'Was that a good story?' I asked, after drinking in the silence for a while. I curled my fingers around her upper arm. She laughed at me.

'It was lovely,' she said.

I felt so open, in a wild, almost scary way, Ebba. Wild and free, as if something had burst open inside me. I bent down and bit her nipple. She moaned.

Afterwards, the sunlight lay in a band across the bed; I reached out my hand, it cut through the band of light, for a second the whole room seemed to swim and I knew with appalling certainty that we had nothing to hide from one another – how could we, we were one another. Her shy smile might have been my own. My words could have come from her lips.

'That letter I posted was to the Moon Queen,' she said. 'But I didn't know that was her name.'

That must have been when she realised that I had already dreamed up a secret name for her mother. I don't think I ever mentioned that name to you before. I don't know where I got it from, I mean I hadn't even met the woman at that point.

We laughed a lot in those days. We developed a language all our own. I continued to tell stories about Little Johan; gradually he seemed to become clearer and found his own voice, rather as if I were a ventriloquist. I felt a bit like an entertainer. It was a whole new side of me. You've seen me like that, I know, easy and free, but I wasn't like that until I met her. And as time went on and she came to trust me, Judith too would sometimes put on a small, piping voice, letting me know that this was Little Judith talking. Little Judith was actually a rather shy little girl, like you when you were small, or Jennifer is now. Quite different from the grown-up Judith. She got on well with Little Johan, the two children started talking to one another there in the bed. Occasionally they would say things neither your mother or I understood. But we assumed that they knew what they were saying; sometimes their talk became babyish and faltering, with clumsy formulations and long pauses. Now and again, when we adults allowed the conversation to lapse and lost ourselves in one another yet again, it seemed as if they sat a little further down the bed, watching us in awe. They weren't worried, they simply observed us.

And when we fell asleep for a few hours, worn out and running with sweat, those two children seemed to continue their conversation, each from their own dream. Our dreams always lay very close to one another. Sometimes they ran together.

It's those nights I remember best, I think. Although we did have our day-to-day routine too. The nights ran into days and then the night came again. We always looked forward to being able to climb into the same bed together at night. We never tired of it.

I can't remember whether people around us were particularly surprised when Judith and I got together. I don't think so. Nor can

I remember whether it took a while for people to start treating us as a couple. But there must have been something absolute about the way in which we fitted together that was hard to ignore. Lots of people remarked on us, even some of her former lovers, and she had had quite a few, she never made any secret of it. Your mother has always had plenty of admirers. But for some reason, to begin with it didn't worry me that she had a history of complicated relationships and romantic intrigue. I didn't see how it could have been any other way, and yet I felt certain that none of that had anything to do with us, it was as if we two were part of another story. If there were sides of ourselves which we had not yet revealed to one another, I told myself, then it was because we were not aware of them ourselves, we didn't know there was anything to reveal. If you don't know that something exists, then you can't draw attention to it, far less talk about it. It goes without saying.

I actually knew one of the men she had once lived with, one of the musicians in the orchestra, slightly. His name was Jørgen; you know him, we got on well together, there was never any ill will between us. If I harboured any special feeling for him it must have been a sense of gratitude for the fact that he was one of those who had helped to make Judith the person she was. It didn't bother me all that much that he had of course also been one of those who had helped to provide her the experience that made her a tiger in bed, although naturally I was sometimes visited by irksome images that could be ousted only by dint of a bit of concentration.

For my own part, I was much less experienced than Judith when it came to love affairs; I see no need to make a secret of it. I had lived with two women for short spells before meeting her, but neither of these relationships had been particularly passionate, they were really more in the nature of practical arrangements which meant I had someone to share expenses with and someone to sleep with when I had the urge. I have a strangely hazy recollection of both these women; it never occurred to me to have children with either of them, and their faces seem to have been wiped from my memory. They're both married and settled down now, you don't have to worry. Looking back on it, I can see that I must have been appallingly indifferent to them. I feel guilty just thinking about it.

No. I'm not explaining this properly, Ebba. I can't sit here. I'll have to get out of the car.

Look at those flowers. Clearly your mother couldn't care less about the watering restrictions; she never did pay any heed to other people's laws, she simply goes by her own laws. Hers and the Moon Queen's. Her mother has too much of a hold over her, I saw that right at the start.

There's something about this story of your mother and me that doesn't quite add up. I can't describe the strong distaste I feel when I think back to those early days with her. It arouses the same distaste as thoughts of the first two women I lived with. But that time with Judith was a happy time! I felt truly happy! Open! And yet when I think about it now, it seems as though something between us was falling apart right from the start. It's like a sum that won't come out right.

I can't stand it when things don't come out right, you know that, I think you're like me in that respect, halfway through the working out I'm overcome by a kind of lethargy, as if even my memory refuses to cooperate, as if my brain's asleep. My eyes insist on focussing on something a little to one side of the matter in hand.

She won't come out on to the steps to look for me, she never stands on the steps and looks for anyone. I doubt if anyone stood on the steps and looked for her when she was a little girl either, I guess there must be some connection there.

Did Mama stand on the steps and look for you, Ebba? Was she there for you? Was she there?

I'll have to go up there myself. The first time it was her who came to me, on that morning in the town hall gardens. After that it was always me who had to go to her.

She played up to me from the first. And because I was so hooked on her, somehow she also forced me to be my own audience. She forced me to look.

My eyes could not get enough of her, and because she was me and I her, she also forced me to look at myself. It may be that the seeds of my irritation lay in the hard look at myself that she forced me to take through my own eyes. I don't know. It was not pleasant, I wasn't used to it.

Most likely it all comes down to longing. Judith played upon the longing between us, longing was a kind of a game with her, and because she played with it, you could say that she took my own longing for her away from me, turned it against me, as if in a mirror. That's how it must have been. It's much more difficult to long for yourself than to long for a warm and beautiful woman.

No. There's no point. You could wear yourself out searching for words to cover such things. Maybe it has the exact opposite effect, maybe it simply draws one away, leads to a state of contourlessness instead of bringing one closer to the truth. You want to understand, but you are drawn further and further away, until in the end everything has dissolved into mist.

It has always seemed to me that you were a person who trusts in words. That you believe words can say all that needs to be said. You've been that way ever since you were a little girl.

But if I were ever to succeed in explaining to you what went wrong between Judith and me back then, rather than expressing myself in words I would have to show you with a gesture; a hand run over the face, for example, or perhaps a certain tilt of the head revealing how suddenly, through seeing oneself in another, one was made aware of oneself. The horror of that.

So.

Since I heard the news on Thursday I haven't been able to sleep at night, I just lie there wide awake next to Minna. I've talked and talked to you, Ebba. I've tried to be as quiet as I could. Sometimes whispering, other times just forming the words inside my head. Say that you've heard me.

And when I haven't been talking, I've been thinking. Can you hear my thoughts too? Sometimes it's hard to know whether I'm talking or thinking, it seems like it all comes down to the same thing; it feels exactly as if I'm being dragged back to things I thought I was done with, words keep churning round and round, stuck in a groove. It's so hard to get any further, get things clear, but I feel I have to force myself, for your sake.

I've been thinking so much about Judith and me. I feel I owe it to you to go over everything that happened between us, follow every little twist and turn that can take two people from the burning ecstasy of love to an icy cold front within just a few years, a few short, pitiful years.

I suppose my irritation with her was a physical thing long before it became a thought that could be conceived. An urge to shake something off, the way large animals shake themselves to rid themselves of flies and other insects. The picture I have of myself at that time is of a big, docile horse, standing in the shade giving itself a shake. A cloud of insects rising up.

The glue that held us together may have begun to dissolve before you were born; it may even have started while I was still building the house. I would often work on long into the night, I so much enjoyed working alone, and I always listened to the radio, as I'm doing now; I felt as if all the subjects in the world were presented to me through those radio programmes, subjects I barely knew existed suddenly became of enormous importance to me. It was spring, the nights were gradually growing longer and lighter, Judith was on tour much of the time. I didn't really seem to miss her, even though I knew that as soon as she was with me again everything would be different and I would fall back into the longing. But I didn't feel any longing when I was working on the house.

I liked the fact that the plot of ground we had bought was pretty secluded. The owners of the other plots had scarcely begun to mark off their preserves with wire strung between wooden stakes before I had the foundation wall built and the driveway laid, shingle and all.

I had already started thinking that once the house was finished it would be nice to build a cottage up in the mountains. Not in one of the usual holiday-cottage tracts, but up on the mountain top, that was what I had in mind. Sometimes it felt as if the house I was building was actually this imaginary cottage out on the high moors, in an area that I could roam for years without ever coming close to knowing it properly, because the terrain would be forever changing. I pictured myself striding along in a pair of well-used hiking boots, with a hunting rifle over my shoulder. Maybe I would have a dog that would run ahead of me, sniffing the ground, and looking back eagerly when it spotted something, to get me to follow. I would be able to live alone at that cottage for weeks on end.

The turning of the seasons, the different times of day – this motion would be there within me and I would be in motion, I would be as regular and as unpredictable as the light, sitting in the lee of the cottage and smoking a cigarette before going inside after my hunting trip; two dead grouse lying in the grass at my feet, the dog trained not to touch them. The wall of the cottage would be warm from the sun and reek of creosote. I wouldn't have a thought in my head.

These are probably the sort of thoughts that were running through my mind while I was building your house up there at the top of the drive. A custom-designed house on a new housing development outside one of the largest cities in Norway. Or maybe there wasn't anything running through my mind at all. Maybe this idea about the cottage in the mountains has only come to me now. Back then – maybe I really only listened to the radio, smoked and hammered in nail after nail without a thought in my head. In which case the things I've been talking about didn't exist. Didn't exist until now, when I find the words with which to give them to you.

Before I started reading philosophy, music was the closest I came to freedom. My moments of freedom were almost always musical moments. As a small boy I would sit perfectly still beside the radio during concert broadcasts, just the way you used to sit right next to the loudspeakers in the sitting-room. I would listen to any sort of music, from the simple, soppy ballads that my mother loved, to opera and brass band music. At those times my body seemed to lift itself out of my rather diffident skin and I became another, or perhaps not another, but something other, in the same way that, years later, Judith became part of the orchestra as I sat there in the theatre, watching her through half-shut eyes during rehearsals. I derived a sensual delight from the music which nourished me; it was at these moments that I became visible. A certain feeling would well up inside me: as if I was becoming my own person, as if I had a warmth within me, a warmth in which I could move around, in which I could jut out my hips, wave my arms about, open my mouth wide, be shining and solid and free.

As far as I know, no one in my family has ever taken music lessons, in fact I don't recall ever seeing a musical instrument in my parents' house. I don't think your grandfather would have liked it.

Minna is not particularly musical, as you may have noticed. And I didn't take my record collection with me when I left you and Mama, she seemed to think it belonged there with you two, although I don't think we ever actually discussed it. It was a long time before I could afford to buy a new hi-fi system and I didn't browse around the record shops the way I once had done. It just worked out that way.

Are you free now? Say that you're free. Say it. Shining and free. Say it.

One evening, while I was working on the house, Judith came out to the site to surprise me. She had been on tour for a couple of weeks, but the final concert in Germany had been cancelled, and instead of spending the last day doing the rounds of the museums with some of her colleagues from the orchestra she had managed to change her plane ticket and fly home a day early. I was in the middle of laying the floor in the bedroom when she arrived. There were no doors or windows in the house yet.

She had taken a taxi straight from the airport. Although from where I was working I could hear the sound of the car engine, and could easily have seen the taxi driving up the newly constructed driveway from the gaping hole in front of me where the bedroom window would be, something inside me made me pretend that my hammering drowned out the sound of the engine, and I kept my eyes on the floor. The stairs hadn't been fitted yet, so Judith climbed up the ladder to the first floor where I was working. I let her sneak up on me from behind and lay her cool, slender hands over my eyes without turning a hair. I could smell the heavy scent of her perfume; she must have drenched herself in the stuff in the taxi, she smelled the way women do when they have been at pains to make themselves irresistible. I rose to the bait, of course.

But while all this was going on, a fierce sense of irritation was welling up inside me. No, it was more than mere irritation, it was aggression, it was almost impossible to keep it in check. I stood quite still for a moment with the hammer dangling limply from my hand, before I let it drop to the floor with a bang and turned to face her. I grabbed her and pulled her to me so roughly that, when I finally let go of her, she staggered backwards.

That must have been the evening when you were conceived, if, that is, we are to go by the physical facts and not merely the poetic truth, which says that this event occurred in the town hall gardens at the moment when your mother laid her hands over my ears. Judith had been away for a while, so it wasn't hard to work out exactly when it must have happened. I remember that we were both slightly disturbed by the fact that you were conceived on the as yet unfinished, unlacquered wooden floor of what would one day be our, and is now her, bedroom. I think she had pictured a rather more . . . momentous setting for your conception. Maybe that's why I came up with the story about the town hall gardens and my ears. To be honest I don't really remember what I was thinking.

But I was happy that you were on the way. You mustn't ever think otherwise, Ebba. You made me happy even before you were born.

On the morning when we found out that she was pregnant, Judith came out of the bathroom in her little flat in town – you've never seen it, this was before we moved into the house; she climbed into the double bed beside me, clutching the pregnancy test instructions and gave me a look that was both candid and challenging: an odd look, one which I had never seen in her eyes before, but which made my stomach lurch. It was the same look that you have sometimes turned on me, although of course I didn't know that then. She settled herself in bed a little apart from me, with her back to me, and tucked the duvet in around herself, looking vaguely annoyed. I was cold and tense with excitement. I read the directions several times, they were printed in a number of different languages; I read them aloud to her in English and in Swedish to make sure she had understood them correctly. There was no doubt: the test was positive. We curled up together and made love solemnly, almost wistfully, twice in succession to celebrate, or as we said, to put the finishing touches to our work.

It wasn't planned, that pregnancy, I don't suppose it makes any difference to tell you that now. It didn't fit in at all well with Judith's career plans; she had her eye on a place with the symphony orchestra, and knew that she had to perfect her technique. The opera was no longer enough for her. And yet we were happy, we could hardly wait for you to arrive. At any rate I know that she wore a maternity dress for her very first appointment with the doctor. And as it transpired, during the following nine months she disclosed a new side of her character when it came to you, the baby she was expecting. This woman, formerly so single-minded and ambitious, became withdrawn and unsure of herself. Everything she said or did was in some way related to you. And her relationship with your grandmother grew, if possible, even closer than before; she had her own room in the Moon Queen's house in town, she would still stay the odd night there after a concert.

After we moved out here, to the new house, she would often invite the Moon Queen over. I would find them huddled close together on the sofa of an evening, leafing through books about pregnancy and writing lists of boys' and girls' names. Your grandmother began to look for a place near us, and not long after you were born she sold the house in town and moved into a terraced house out here. Judith had her own room there too; although to be sure that soon became your room at Granny's house, furnished exactly like your room at home with us, first with a cradle, then a cot and eventually with the bed that both your grandmother and Judith had slept in as children.

Judith was a different person when she was with your grandmother. I had the feeling that they talked a lot about me, about who I was and what I might possibly make of myself, my good and my not so good sides; everything was weighed up and assessed. I could see it in her eyes when she came back from a visit to her mother's, they had an appraising look in them that unsettled me. It always took a little while after she'd been at her mother's before I could be sure that she was looking at me with her own eyes.

There wasn't much to do about it, except bide my time. Fortunately I am a patient man, I don't need to tell you that. I can only assume that Judith and her mother often considered me dull, or spineless; I had the impression that they preferred bold, dynamic men. Your grandfather on your mother's side was, by all accounts, a very dynamic man: pillar of the community, businessman, a true king. Did you know he was a freemason? He died of a heart attack while in the middle of some important negotiations, one was led to believe that he had been in the middle of important negotiations all his life. I'm not sure if Judith has told you about him; to me she always spoke of him with a kind of dispassionate respect, and it didn't seem natural to bring his name up in conversation, except when Little Judith and Little Johan were talking to one another.

It took its toll on me, being assessed in this way. No doubt that was also one reason why I became so deeply attached to you; there has never been anything appraising about you, you were totally open to me, you took me in, and always all of me. Even when you were a tiny baby I could see the look of wholehearted delight that leapt into your eyes at sight of me. It moved me more than words can say.

The contractions started early in the evening while Judith and I were eating dinner. We were having fishcakes; I'd bought them earlier in the day at a fishmonger's next to the office, you've never seen it, it closed down a while back. They were particularly good fishcakes and Judith was tucking into them with a will, stopping every now and then to chew and turn her attention inwards, trying to decide whether this really was it. She was pretty tense.

I was sure I could feel those same contractions in the small of my own back, she said they were like really strong period pains and I thought I knew exactly what she meant; I'd often massaged the small of her back for her during the first days of her period, I could sense that same warm grumbling. When the contractions grew stronger and the intervals between them shorter, Judith pushed her plate aside, got up and went to fetch the bag she had standing packed and ready with the things she would need at the hospital. She asked me to call your grandmother. She said it so matter-of-factly; she wanted the Moon Queen to come with us to the hospital. I was surprised and a bit upset, I must admit; this seemed to me to be such an intimate moment, something that had nothing to do with anyone but us. At the same time though, I was all of a dither, I wasn't feeling too great, and Judith insisted. Besides which, the contractions were rapidly getting stronger, it would have been silly to start arguing with her just then. So I called your grandmother's number and asked her to come with us to the hospital. I got the impression that she too had been sitting there with her bag all packed and ready.

We got the taxi to pick her up on the way, the taxi driver flashed me a big smile in his rear-view mirror, he probably felt sorry for me. But in the end I was genuinely happy to have her there. She did, after all, know more about these things than I did. The whole thing suddenly became so intense, I felt as if it were a matter of life and death, even though a no-nonsense midwife would probably have described your birth as being a perfectly normal one, if a bit quick for a first-timer. Snow was falling heavily, the roads were like glass and by the time we got to the hospital the cervix was dilated enough for us to be taken straight to the delivery room. Only a couple of hours later Judith was able to start pushing.

I stood behind her head, pushing with her and trying to control both her breathing and my own, as we had learned at childbirth classes. Your grandmother stayed out in the corridor, waiting for it all to be over, she was the one who had to speak to the midwife and the doctor on duty when we got to the hospital. She's a clear-headed, forceful woman, your grandmother, you've probably got a bit of her in you too.

I'll never forget the look on her face when I came trundling out with you in a little cot on wheels. You'd been weighed and measured, washed and put into a nappy and a tiny matinee jacket, wrapped in a white crocheted blanket and tucked up under a microscopic duvet. Granny, who's normally so fussy about her appearance, always perfectly made up with not a hair out of place, looked pale and distraught, with black rings of mascara under her eyes and her skirt crumpled up around her heavy thighs. Imagine! And yet for a second there all the bad feeling between us seemed to melt away, I believe I can say that I felt truly fond of her at that moment. Suddenly I saw her as a real person. For a long time she had simply been an annoying, but necessary figure in the story of Judith and me, a Moon Queen with rather too definite opinions on what it befitted her precious daughter's spouse to do or not do. We hugged; she had had the foresight to pop a quarter bottle of brandy into her handbag; we used white plastic cups from a dispenser in the patients' toilet and drank a toast over your sleeping head, you who were to become so firmly rooted in me. In us. Who for fleeting moments would succeed in getting closer to me than I felt I could get to myself.

Don't go. I'll find you some other music if you like. There! There you are. The jazz channel. I like this presenter's voice. He tends mainly to play the old standards, you can hear that, maybe. I've told you about the standards, haven't I. A lot of good versions of the standards have been produced over the years. It all depends on the musician, you know? The standards are like an alphabet. Used as a basis for improvisation.

I think, in fact, that I'm quite a good singer. But in Judith's version of our family history, she was the one who did the singing and she was always talking about how important it was to sing to children. Singing was synonymous with vitality and spontaneity: qualities which she, of course, possessed, although to be honest her voice wasn't all that great, even if she was a musician. And I believed her, I felt merely embarrassed by the music that I could produce. My music was facile and I had never learnt to play an instrument; I knew nothing about the technicalities of music.

I think Judith would have been very surprised to hear that I actually had a better voice than she did, just as she was truly astonished to discover that you did not have a particularly good singing voice, and didn't display more than an average aptitude for playing a musical instrument. And you had a go at a few over the years: the violin, the piano, and wasn't there a flute for a while, too? I think it really bothered Judith that she had had a child who seemed, to her mind, to be not at all musical.

'She doesn't sing, Johan. When I was her age I sang all the time,' she said.

It was a year after you were born that I bought The Mammas & The Papas' record which was to be our secret. I'd heard Ella Fitzgerald singing this song when I was just a boy, back in the fifties, and it had been there at the back of my head ever since. It put me in mind of bright summer afternoons in the sitting-room at home, the little crocheted mats we always had on the occasional table, and my mum, your grandma, walking by, leaning over me and kissing me on the cheek as I sat there next to the radio; her fingers smelled of horseradish.

Suddenly I just had to get hold of that music and play it for you; it was more than a longing, it was a necessity, I had to find the right recording, the one with the right – *thrill* to it. The right smell. But how to go about finding it? I only knew a couple of lines, I wasn't even sure about the title. It would never have occurred to me to ask any of Judith's musician friends about such a thing, I felt they would think it an odd question to ask, and one that only showed what poor taste I had. But I knew I had to have help.

Eventually I decided to go to a record shop in a part of town that Judith and I never frequented together. It was a gloomy autumn afternoon; my shoes were soaked from splashing through puddles. I felt strangely excited, standing there in that poky little shop, waiting for other customers to be served, be handed their plastic bag and step out into the street.

Once the last customer had gone, I leaned across the counter to the girl who was serving and cleared my throat several times – it had gone all hoarse. She smiled at me encouragingly. At last I found my voice and sang the first lines softly, with what I thought were the right words. I asked if she knew of a good recording of that song. She didn't seem at all surprised or put out, she acted as if it were quite normal for a grown man to lean across the counter at her and sing a song he had heard on the radio as a child. For a moment I felt almost as if she was about to kiss my cheek.

She didn't kiss me. But her smile grew even broader, the title of the song was 'Dream a Little Dream of Me', she said, and Ella Fitzgerald had of course made a recording of it, that was probably the one I had heard, but she also knew of a more recent version, from the sixties, by The Mammas & The Papas, that was the one she liked best. She turned away from me and proceeded to sift through a pile of records behind the counter. She found it almost immediately, she asked if I would like to hear it.

I felt that was almost too much to accept, what service, but she had already placed the record on the turntable and was handing me a set of headphones that was attached to the counter; I took them from her and gave her a shamefaced smile in return. She brought the needle down on to the right track first go.

Then I was alone with the music. My ears were covered each with its own padded cup. It only took a few seconds. She studied me with interest while I listened. I shut my eyes. The music washed over me, it hit me so suddenly: I felt exposed, caught with my trousers down, there was something shameful about it; I felt suddenly flustered, I didn't hear the song all the way through, but whipped the headphones off after only a moment or two and nodded to let her know I would take it. She put it into a plastic bag for me.

I was so relieved, I would have liked to ask her to keep the change, but that might have seemed a bit odd.

As she handed me the bag she said: 'You have a nice voice.'

I stumbled out of the shop.

I walked along the quayside. The weather had cleared up; it had suddenly turned quite warm, it could easily have been spring rather than autumn. The houses on the other side of the fjord were bathed in yellow twilight, and above the houses dense clouds piled up one on top of the other, like towers; they looked as though they were lit from within. I stared and stared, I could not get enough of all that brightness – there was something insistent about it, something veiled and yet seductively simple, as if I were on the trail of something important, as if the solution lay in the record-shop carrier bag that I held in my hand, and in the luminous clouds over those houses. Suddenly it struck me that I was invincible, and that the woman in the record shop had deliberately presented me with the key to something that changed everything. I felt as though she was one of the initiated and I was a novice, and that this was what she had wanted to show me. And I, in turn, wanted to show it to you, Ebba. There was nothing else, there was just this, but it was enough, it would move you to tears.

When I got home I walked straight into the sitting-room, still wearing my wet shoes, and tucked my purchase right at the back of all my other records. You and Mama weren't home yet. I went back out into the hall, took off my shoes and sat them to dry, hung up my coat. Then I hurried through to the kitchen and put the plastic bag into the rubbish bin, got out the pots and vegetables and started preparing dinner. When I heard your voices in the hall, I tipped the potato peelings into the bin so that the bag from the record shop was completely covered.

It was some weeks before I dared play it. Well, there was no chance really; when we were at home, Judith and I were almost always in the same room. I had to wait until one afternoon when I was sure that she wouldn't be back for ages.

It was a Sunday. I stood at the window with the music playing full blast, I sang for you.

Perhaps it's the case that you can only feel really secure with someone you would dare to sing to. And when you were bigger, on those evenings when Judith had a concert we used to dance around the sitting-room together. She got the job with the symphony orchestra, it was a big step up the ladder for her. And it gave the two of us more time on our own.

I think you also looked forward to our evenings alone, didn't you? You had become a person in your own right by then, you understood a lot of things. It mattered a lot to me that you should understand what it was about this music that was so special to me. I drew you close and did as I had always done when there was something delicate and important that I wanted to say to you; I told you a story. I improvised, a skill I had learned with your mother, I made up a nice little story – do you remember it – about an invisible boy who sat on the rug in front of the radio at home with his parents and listened to the music pouring out at him. I told you about his mother, who came through from the kitchen and kissed him on the cheek, about how the little boy was so happy and thought that his mother smelled funny and nice. I described the smell of horseradish, didn't I, and his father who was out in the garden raking up leaves, his brisk, unapproachable movements. Remember? I think you understood. You certainly nodded, the way you sometimes do, you kind of shone, and gave me a big open smile. You liked it when I told stories.

I moved the needle back to the start yet again, lifted you up and whirled you round. 'Dream a little dream of me,' they sang on the record, and you tipped your head back, shut your eyes, making yourself dizzy, you squealed and giggled, your voice shrill and happy, a little siren, and you sang along in your babyish and charmingly mangled English. We had learned the song by heart, it was our secret.

'Seem to wispa ay buv yoo,' you trilled.

I was a father dancing with his daughter.

I kissed your cheek, and you kissed me back, I would never have dared to do that to my mother when I was a boy. We were shining and visible.

I don't know whether Judith can see me from the house. Maybe she's gone to bed. Maybe she's been in bed ever since she heard about you, maybe she was just fooling me, leading me to believe that she was up and about when I talked to her on the telephone.

One of the first things Minna said when I eventually got round to telling her what had happened was that Judith wouldn't be able to bear this. She won't be able to bear it, Johan.

I have to understand. I have to explain to you why everything turned out the way it did. I have to trust in words, the way you trust in them. Tell me I can trust in them.

True perception comes only from those things we have experienced in real life.

I had to put you down. I staggered backwards under the weight of this great gift I had been given, so I put you on the floor at my feet. That's how it was. But you didn't hold it against me, you just smiled your thin little smile and turned your face up to mine, you whispered: 'Seem to wispa ay buv yoo.'

Or it could have been another day entirely, in the middle of the day perhaps, when trustingly you took my hand and walked on by my side while you told me about something that had happened at nursery. Somebody had shown you something, somebody had stood on your foot when you were getting on to the climbing frame. You told me about the view from up there, you could see all the way over to the old folks' home on the other side of the street, there were people over there who were so old that they had to push a little trolley in front of them when they walked, you knew about such things.

You led me by the hand. That's how it was. You led me by the hand as if I were a little child, the way your little sister took me by the hand on Thursday, as if I were an old man, to stop me from telling her again and again that you were dead. She's so like you. I have been blessed with two daughters, and all I have done is to follow their lead. There's something pathetic about that Ebba.

I did the best I could. I thought I could protect you by loving you away from all the ugliness.

'Sleep facing me, Papa!' you used to whisper when you were small and you climbed into the big bed with Mama and me in the middle of the night. You slipped silently through the door and across the room in your little sleep suit with your teddy under your arm and crawled over Mama who lay on the outside; you always insisted on sleeping between us. Mama didn't wake up. She slept with her face turned to me, facing the middle of the bed, while I tended to turn in my sleep to face the wall, although I was always careful to be facing her when I fell asleep.

I didn't wake up either until I felt that warm little hand against my cheek:

'Sleep facing me, Papa!' And I would turn my face towards you and your mother and stroke your back, tuck you in under the duvet. We had a big double duvet in those days, but you probably don't remember that, you were so young then. Or do you? For all I know Judith may still have that duvet.

Judith and I were beautiful. To begin with, the story about us was a beautiful story, it was full of things like your warm hand on my cheek in bed at night, it was so beautiful it hurt. Mama and I were not aware of what we were doing, but our story progressed of its own accord. Beauty is a powerful motor that drives everything onward in one smooth, steady glide. It keeps on going long after we ourselves have stopped. It wasn't until much later that the story turned ugly. By which time you had also become a part of it, you were innocent, you just loved us, but there was nothing we could do to change it. We just let it continue.

I'm sorry.

When I finally became aware of the irritation which Judith aroused in me, it was as if it had always been there. She may well have detected it before I did, she certainly maintained that she was more sensitive to such things.

I don't like to think that she might have known what was happening before it dawned on me. I think, after all, that I prefer the image of the current that swept us all off in different directions, to that of the glue that began to dissolve. At any rate it did sometimes feel as if everything was being controlled from the outside, as if somewhere out there, there was someone who had a purpose with the story of which we were part. Something had to change, and it felt as if the three of us, Judith, you and me, were in fact utterly powerless to prevent what happened.

Someone must have decided that Minna should be there behind the desk in the library, a good three years after you were born, smiling at me. I had met her only once before, and yet I felt I knew her, a sense of recognition that went much further back in time than the last dinner party we had both attended with our respective partners.

I can see now that I must have been ripe for a new and overwhelming infatuation of this sort for quite some time. Like a bud that has long been on the brink of opening, and needed only a few concentrated minutes in the sunlight in order to burst into full bloom.

That was a clumsy metaphor. That's not really how I think of it at all, I'm not as good with words as you are, you're so precise. It's not words I'm trying to get at, it's a feeling. A fierce itch.

I scratched and everything changed. It feels stupid to put it like that, I feel I've already used up that expression on the time your mother found me outside the town hall and took me home. But 'everything changed' is the only phrase that fits, which must mean that everything can change several times in the course of a life. Everything changes and you think this time it's forever, but then all of a sudden it happens again, and once things have changed twice you start to feel pretty sure that they could do so yet again. And that scares me.

I want the beautiful story about Judith and me to live on. You had your beginning in it. If that story is to live, then someone has to tell it. And who is there to tell it, if not me? Judith won't do it. Judith let it die out a long time ago, no doubt she has her reasons, you'd know more about that than me.

'Snip, snap, snout,' that's what we always say when we reach the end of a fairy-tale we've been telling. Whatever that means. But long before we get to that point, we may have begun to think: soon it's going to come to an end. The end looms up ahead, like a shadow on the horizon. You keep staving it off, you know it's over, but you can't bear to believe it. Snip snap snout! you cry in fear. But it just goes on and on, because you keep staving off the end.

The clouds above your house are light and fluffy, they hang down from the sky. They are moving fast; it almost looks as though they are moving in different directions, do you see? But that can't be right.

This is just a little story. It bears telling, it's not dangerous, say it's not dangerous, it has its beginning and its end, it has a first-person narrator – no: it's told in the third person. Let's see now . . . it's a story about Johan, your old dad, who has driven out here from the hotel, that's me, you see. He's been sitting in the car, smoking, for quite a while, he has listened to the radio and talked to you, he's stiff all over. But look, now he's getting out of the car, he locks the door, look, he's starting to walk slowly up the driveway. That's the way. Now let's see what happens.

He's weak with nausea, I think he'll have to sit down on the step for a moment before he rings the bell – here – he'll sit down here. Just for a little second, Ebba.

There's a pair of boots on the step here. They've got your name in them. Written by her.

Oh, God.

The steps could do with staining.

She has lowered the venetian blinds, hasn't she? She probably can't bear to look out. She doesn't want the light to get in.

The hate inside her was so ingrained, Ebba. I can still sense it. I could see it in her back then, and I couldn't feel anything but loathing.

After I met Minna it was as if I had to come up with a new version of the story about Judith and me. I had to rewrite it in such a way that there was room for Minna as well, also in the time before I knew her. You have to make room, in the past too, for those you love. Suddenly I found myself remembering all the minor sources of irritation between Judith and myself, which had been there right from the start, all the things unspoken, all the little ways she had of manipulating me.

And instead of recalling the heady, exhilarating feeling of togetherness that we had shared, I now remembered my own rather sulky protests when her plans for our life together became too high-flown. I remembered all those friends of mine who were dropped, all the professional interests of mine that were dismissed because they did not fit into her world of extravagant gestures and what, in her vague fashion, she referred to as Art, as if everyone would instinctively know to what she was referring. Her way of using this word had clearly been borrowed from your grandmother, and she gave the impression that by this word 'Art' she meant everything that was beautifying, enriching and exalted, all those things which only a person of some refinement could truly appreciate. She employed it in the same airy way that she employed the word 'Imagination'. I would never have dreamed of entering into a discussion about this with her, although even in those days, had I taken a little trouble to consider the matter, I would have realised that my own conception of art was of a very different order from hers. Nevertheless, I could not deny that one of the reasons why I loved her as ardently as I did was that back then she actually was a great artist, that what she could do with music far exceeded her own childish ideas about the nature of art; and that she was also a person with a lively imagination, whatever that last word might in fact cover.

I suppose you could say that falling in love with Minna was, in a way, the saving of me, at least in the short term. It got me out of my marriage to Judith before all this unpleasantness rose to the surface and started souring our existence. We never got to the stage of wearing each other down with resentment, petty games of tit-for-tat and painful taboo subjects that are allowed to lie and smoulder, as I have seen so many other couples do before they finally get a grip on themselves and split up. To some extent your mother and I could be said to have made a clean break.

And you could say it was Minna who got me to start reading books again. I met her at the library. Looking at it objectively, books may have been as much the saving of me as Minna.

It was around that time that I started taking you for runs in the car in the afternoons after nursery. We went for little trips out of town; I needed to have you to myself, to give us a little peace and quiet. I liked having you in the car with me, a car's a good place to be alone in, don't you think, a little haven on wheels that keeps the world out, while at the same time making you feel that you can move on, that it is actually possible to leave something behind.

We drove out to the aquarium, do you remember, and to the swimming pool and the library in the next town. At the aquarium we always made a beeline for the seals. You loved the seals! At the library we headed straight for the children's section. As time went on we found that we preferred the library to the aquarium or the swimming pool, it was free and it was open for longer. You soon got to know your way around the picture-books, found your own favourites; after a while all I had to do was start you off by reading the first couple of pages of a book to you, and then you would carry on 'reading' out loud to yourself, pointing at the pictures as you went along and making your own little remarks about them. You looked so comical and so adorable sitting there, I don't see how the other people in the library could have helped but notice you too. It wasn't long before I could leave you to yourself and find myself a seat next to one of the magazine racks in the adult department.

Minna was at the issues desk. We recognised one another from the dinner party.

She had such a soft, welcoming smile for everyone, you know what she's like; I saw how much they meant to the library regulars, the old age pensioners and mothers with young children, their little chats with this friendly librarian. Talking about books they'd been recommended to read, asking to be put on the waiting list for them.

She was well aware of my presence. I think we had both known that there was something going on between us, ever since that evening. She had been there with the man she was living with at that time, you've never met him, I don't know if she has ever mentioned him to you; their relationship was obviously on its last legs, they hardly looked at one another during the whole of that dinner. I was with your mother, of course. As usual you were sleeping at your grandmother's that night. The Moon Queen always insisted that you sleep at her house when we were going out somewhere, so that Judith and I could sleep late the next morning and 'have some time to ourselves' as she so archly put it.

Your mother was blooming, as always when she had an audience, but both Minna and I felt out of place in that company, which consisted for the most part of professional musicians; and the talk around the table was of little else but internal strife within the orchestra. We were seated directly across from one another at the table and the conversation being carried on by the others was so loud that we had no real chance to talk. But we've discussed this a few times since and we have both admitted that something was going on between us that evening. We were partners-in-crime, non-musicians in a world of conductor gossip. That in itself was a strong bond. We were about to break loose.

That was our prehistory; not much to work from maybe. But one afternoon when business was slow at the library she came across to where I was sitting, smiling that big smile of hers. She drew up a chair and asked what I was reading. So I had no choice but to show her the magazine I was flicking through; fortunately I had taken time to select one that would make a good impression: a journal whose rather more scholarly appearance set it apart from the other magazines on the rack: glossy, lavishly illustrated publications devoted to gardening, parenthood and the like. This one looked as if it belonged in a university library rather than an ordinary Norwegian public library. It was called *Classical Philology* and it was published, so I had noted, by the University of Chicago Press.

When I showed her what I was looking at her round face broke into that lovely smile once again, she gave a little laugh and said what a funny coincidence, because she was the one who had actually arranged for the library to take out a subscription to this particular journal, for purely selfish reasons she had to admit; it was a journal that she herself had wanted the chance to read in her spare time. She had always been interested in Greek studies, at one point it had been a toss-up between the College of Librarianship or reading classics at the university.

Already I could tell just how much classical philology mattered to me. Although somehow I hadn't realised it until that moment. It had a weird effect on me, to sit there leafing through this journal under Minna's gaze, I felt that it lent me a special air; in the course of one short afternoon I almost began to feel like a scholar of classical philology, attached, so I fancied, to the University of Chicago; in my mind's eye I saw my office there, with a view of the whole university campus and bookshelves laden with volumes written in Greek and illustrated with ancient vase paintings of women in flowing Hellenic drapery, rendered in profile. I caught the delicate scent of Minna's perfume.

And then of course I had to read that journal. I was allowed to borrow an entire volume. Minna was only too glad to be of service and I took as long as possible over the formalities, until you came and tugged at my jacket, wanting to go home to Mama and children's television.

Once you were in bed I spent the rest of the evening sitting in my reading chair, flicking frantically through those journals; it was hard to know which article to read first. Judith was upstairs in the music room practising, the orchestra was about to go on tour and she was a bit nervous. I sat there long into the night. Judith went to bed without coming down to say goodnight. She had never done that before, it wasn't like her. From the moment we met hardly a night had passed without us wishing each other goodnight, not even when she was tour, when we used the phone.

Summer came and Judith went on tour with the orchestra. The day after she left I called Minna.

She was on holiday. We met. I skived off work as often as I could. It was crazy. We were totally besotted with one another, spent as much time together as possible; we took ridiculous chances, I invented fictitious meetings and logged out of the office. Minna waited for me in cafés or in the tiny, over-furnished bedsit with separate bathroom that she had moved into after breaking up with her boyfriend. I bumped into her landlady late one morning when I was sneaking along the narrow corridor from the bathroom to the bedsit with just a towel round my waist. The landlady gaped at me in astonishment. It couldn't have been too hard to figure out what we were up to in there in the middle of the day.

I felt dreadful picking you up from nursery after one of those days with Minna. I didn't doubt for one second that you knew how things stood with me. I really had to force myself not to act too jolly, not to sing songs to you while I walked you home from nursery, bring you little presents as some sort of compensation for the fact that I was doing you a great injustice. I emptied my pockets of chewing-gum and throat pastilles for you, I asked about every little detail of your day. Who had you played with? Had you played with the building bricks? Had you been digging in the sandpit? What story had you read at Circle Time? Your hand rested quietly in mine as you walked by my side, patiently answering all my questions.

I knew only too well that what was happening to me was a betrayal of you, of your childhood. It was not your mother I had been moaning ecstatically with between sweat-soaked sheets only an hour before turning up at nursery with my hair still wet. My whole body was jangling; I had to hold you tight for a long time after I found you among all the other children in the nursery playground. I stepped into the sand-pit to get to you or bent double to get inside the Wendy House and give you a big hug. The staff at the nursery probably found these scenes very touching, and took me for an unusually doting and soft-hearted father. One of them was, of course, Bodil, who's married to Jørgen from Mama's orchestra, we saw them socially now and again; you might remember their son, Harald, he was at nursery too, a sweet little boy the same age as you. I always got an especially warm smile from Bodil, I think she liked me, maybe she felt sorry for me. And maybe I played on that a bit. That made me even more pathetic in my own eyes. We chatted about this and that, what we'd heard about the tour our spouses were on, the telephone calls from them, reports of good reviews in the British press. We were going to take you and Harald out to the airport in a couple of days' time to pick them up.

Only once did I allow you to spend the night at your grandmother's while Minna slept at our place with me. Minna and I had never had a whole night together, we'd been talking about it for a long while and time was running out. In a couple of days Judith would be home, the hour was approaching for what would either have to be the end of a brief and passionate affair or the start of something else, something far more serious. Naturally we knew that the latter alternative was the only option, even though we did not want to admit it to one another. It was absolutely vital for us to spend those hours of the night together. We each had to find out what the other was like in sleep, the bridge that linked together our days. I was feeling so confused.

Obviously it was awkward for Minna, coming to my place and having to spend the night in what could hardly be described as anything but our marriage bed, Judith's and mine. But her bedsit wasn't a good option either, I absolutely had to be at home to answer the phone. Judith usually called once she got back to the hotel after the evening's concert, to say goodnight and ask how our day had been, and I had no excuse not to be home at night. Both Minna and I knew that this night together outweighed any awkwardness, outweighed any thoughts of betrayal or immorality.

There was nothing remarkable about you spending the night at Granny's, she was always offering to take you and give me a break when Judith was away. The Moon Queen is the sort of woman who believes that men need to be helped, that they become totally helpless the minute their women aren't there to see to them – I'm sure you've noticed it, she probably talks about men to you in exactly the same way.

I'm not sure if you'll remember that evening, you were only three and a half after all. You and I had packed your little rucksack with your nappy for night time, your teddy, pyjamas and toothbrush. You were looking forward to sleeping at Granny's I think, you would be allowed to stay up as late as you liked; you were all keyed up and a bit clingy. I drove you over to Granny's house and sat for a while on the sofa, making small talk over a cup of coffee, before blowing kisses to you both and driving home. I remember regretting that cup of coffee, my stomach was churning, I'd had to use your grandmother's toilet several times before I got out of there.

We had arranged that Minna would come around nine, and that she would arrive on foot – there was no need to let the neighbours see a strange car parked outside the house all night. We had discussed these details most matter-of-factly the previous forenoon while taking a walk in the park like an old married couple. We were deeply serious, we didn't take this lightly, Ebba.

As soon as I got home I started to change the bedclothes on the double bed, but had to stop several times to run to the toilet. My stomach was in turmoil. When the doorbell rang I was sitting there again, I had to stand up with my trousers round my knees and call to her out of the bathroom window, telling her to come on in, I would be down in a moment. The front door is, as you know, on the other side of the house, so it was a while before she heard me calling. It was a ludicrous situation, I know, but neither of us laughed about it.

When I finally emerged from the bathroom I found Minna in the bedroom. She was finishing making up the bed with the clean linen. She had put the pillows at the foot of the bed. It was the only right thing to do.

We were woken at the crack of dawn the next morning by the loud, almost unearthly sound of birds singing outside the window. During the night we had moved quite far apart from one another in the big bed, I could barely recollect having my arms around her at all. I didn't remember much of what had taken place before we fell asleep, but I was glad that my stomach had settled down. It was strange to wake up lying with my head at the foot of the bed.

The window was open and the air was heavy with the scent of the wood behind the house. It seemed to have a life of its own that morning.

Minna asked me what was in the wood. I replied that it was just a little grove of trees, there was a hut there that you and the other kids from the neighbourhood were building, but not much else. And yet the sounds and smells drifting through the window could have come straight out of some nature programme about the Amazon. Minna eyed me solemnly and said she thought it was a primeval forest. For a split-second I froze: it was exactly the sort of thing you might have said.

Neither of us had slept much; from that point of view all the trouble we had gone to in order to have the chance of experiencing each other sleeping would have to be said to have been in vain. Minna didn't want any breakfast, she just took a shower, got dressed and left. She didn't kiss me, and I could see that she was close to tears.

When I went into the bathroom after she left I found that it was icy cold in there: I had left the window standing wide open all night. Minna had used your mother's towel, she had hung it to dry in exactly the same way as your mother always did. Not that she could have known that, of course, but still it made me feel uneasy.

I had to step over the pile of bedclothes that we had taken off when we changed the bed. I decided to wash the linen that Minna and I had used, and put the old set back on the bed. Judith had changed the bed before she left, and it might seem odd for me to have changed it again while she was away, it was always her who saw to that side of things.

When I came to pick you up an hour later it was still early. Your grandmother was sitting at the kitchen table drinking the same explosive brew as we had had the previous evening, she was truly surprised to see me so early. You were nowhere to be seen, Granny said you weren't awake yet, but that I could go up and wake you myself.

I climbed the stairs to the bedroom. The door was closed. I opened it to find you lying naked on the bed on top of the duvet with your spindly arms stretched straight out on either side. You had taken off your pyjamas and your night time nappy and laid them neatly on the chair. The nappy was dry. When you saw me you jumped up as if I had caught you doing something wrong. You ran to me and huddled up close to me. You were freezing cold. Alarmed, I asked if something had frightened you, and why hadn't you gone down to Granny, couldn't you open the door, were you afraid to go down the stairs on your own? But you didn't answer, just huddled close to me.

After a while you whispered that you had to pee. My heart went out to you, you must have been holding it in for far too long; I remembered it so well from when I was a child, that feeling of almost losing control over your body. I carried you through to your grandmother's bathroom and gently set you down on the toilet. Sitting there, you looked so appallingly like your mother as she was early on in our relationship, when she used to watch me showering in the morning while she sat there peeing. It was as if you and she were the same woman. But in those days Judith used to tell me about her dreams and you didn't tell me anything. I shuddered.

Afterwards, I got you dressed, took you by the hand and led you down to the kitchen and Granny. She simply could not understand why you seemed so fretful and pensive all of a sudden, you'd had such a nice evening together the two of you, and you had slept like a log all night, as far as she had heard, anyway.

You appeared to pull yourself together when you saw your grandmother. You dutifully ate the breakfast that was put out for you and told me all about what the two of you had done the previous evening, in just the way you knew she liked. You smiled hesitantly and soon you were running around, serving us tea from the little doll's tea set you kept in the toy basket at Granny's – you know, the one with the tiny hand-painted flowers on it that she bought for you in Japan – looking like your old self.

But back at home you grew solemn again. You wanted me to come out to the wood with you, it was as if there was something that wouldn't wait. You led me by the hand through the garden, over the fence and into that little grove of trees, you acted as if it were your grove. The powerful sounds and scents that had come to me through the window a few hours earlier, as I lay in bed with Minna, were there no longer. I told myself I must have imagined them. Now it was quiet and cool among the trees, we saw no signs of life anywhere, neither of animals, nor birds or people.

You led me in among the trees. We sat for a long time in the hut that you kids were building, whispering to one another, the little stories and secrets that we were so good at making up together. Then we went home.

I didn't speak to Minna on the phone until late that evening, after you were in bed. I wanted to wait until after Judith's good-night call.

I don't remember what stories I told you out there in the wood. But I think you enjoyed them, you helped me with the details, with the improvisation. We sat with our backs against the board wall of the hut, looking straight head. But I don't remember what the stories were about. The invisible boy maybe? I ought to remember that. They're back there in my mind somewhere, they must be. Everything is stored away in there, right? I won't rest until I remember.

I wish they would tear down that wood.

I lied to you. I may not have told any lies, but I lied to you none the less. Only in truth is there beauty. I should have given you beauty, Ebba. No one should ever give their child anything but beauty, I know that. I've known it all along.

When your mother got back from her tour, Minna went abroad with a girlfriend. We had decided to have no contact with one another for a month, it seemed an age. I don't know whether either of us really understood what was happening, I mean truly understood. We were both unhappy, but I don't think one is possessed of any greater understanding when one is unhappy than when one is happy. One is simply unhappy, confused. It all becomes too much.

We drove out to the airport to meet Judith, you and I, do you remember? She had never been away from us for so long before. It had been hard for her, leaving you in my care, it was kind of silly really that she hadn't ever gone off on her own before, she had had to turn down a number of big jobs because of her excessive worrying.

We met Bodil and Harald at the airport; I'll never forget how thrilled you were to see Mama. Judith, on the other hand, seemed almost disppointed that everything had gone so well while she was away. The first thing she said after after we'd all finished hugging one another was: What are you doing, letting her run around without any tights on! Are you crazy!

I felt such a clod.

She had brought us far too many presents. Chocolate and toys for you, and for me enough booze to completely restock the drinks cabinet. It wasn't like her to buy more than the permitted amount. There was something different about her, out there in the arrivals hall, a frenetic air that was new to me.

By the time we reached home she seemed her old self again, but then she went upstairs to put you to bed and didn't come back down again. I was relieved. I sat for a long time by the window with a glass of the whisky she had brought from London. I swivelled the whisky glass round and round in my hands and gazed out at the wood. It looked dark in there now. The sounds in there, and the scents, they . . . It was a stupid little wood, of course, just a tiny clump of trees, but for a three-year-old like you it was more than big enough. And if it was big enough for you, it was big enough for me. It also brought us into contact with the people round about us, with that easygoing neighbourliness to which Judith appears to be so infinitely superior. She's never been one for popping in next door for coffee, getting involved in the local Christmas tree raising or neighborhood work days; there was always something more important that required her full attention. Something that had to do with her, naturally. Her own artistic development and so on. Either she needed to practise, or she had to rest. You know what I mean.

For a moment I managed to fool myself into thinking that I had warmed up the whisky glass with the heat of my hands, rendering it so soft and pliable that it moulded itself round my fingers like gelatin. I sat like that for a long time.

I listened to the radio. There was a programme about the golden age of variety. The presenters sounded so enthusiastic, as if they were discussing some new phenomenon. They played snatches from old archive recordings of famous performers. Some of them were really wonderful; I sat there chuckling to myself.

I would have liked to stay down there in the sitting-room, with the view of the garden, the whisky and the chirpy voices on the radio. I thought: well, there'll be another programme after this. And then another. Something about farming, maybe.

But in the end, you do always have to go to bed. You have to get out of the chair, switch off the lights, turn off the radio, get undressed and climb into bed beside your wife, even if you cannot get to sleep. That is how you preserve your reason, Ebba. You mustn't lose your grip.

Your mother's averted back in the bed next to me seemed somehow shrivelled and pinched under her nightdress. You and she were wrapped in each other's arms.

Several times during those first few days after she got back, Judith told you that she wasn't happy about the hut that you and the other kids were building, and that you were far too young to be running around in the wood with no adult to keep an eye on you. And you took her words to heart. I could see you dutifully starting to think of the wood as a dangerous place where terrible things could happen, and you let her know in all manner of small ways that she didn't have to worry. You took to shaking your head yourself when the other kids came to the door to ask if you were coming with them, sometimes you didn't even come to the door, but simply shouted down the stairs from your room that you were playing and didn't want to be disturbed. I don't know what the other kids thought. You didn't seem to care either way, it was probably much more important to you that your mother should not worry.

Gainsaying Judith has never been easy. It may be that I was actually staging a little protest of my own against her obdurate worrying in joining some of the other fathers one afternoon to cut up the trunk of a huge pine tree that had been felled in one of the gardens. I used a chainsaw to slice the tree trunk into stumps just the right size for sitting on; the idea was for you kids to use them as stools when you were playing in the hut. We carted them to the wood in the wheelbarrow, three or four fathers and a crowd of kids, but not you. There was a lot of laughter and carrying on, that's what I mean when I say that I'm actually a sociable person.

We cut across our garden with the wheelbarrow. Through the window of your bedroom upstairs I could see Judith putting you to bed. It was far too early to go to bed, I felt; it was a beautiful, bright summer evening after all. I think children should be allowed to stay up as long as they like in the summer, they shouldn't be coaxed into bed with bedtime songs and stories.

We walked across the grass. When we reached the fence one of the other fathers lent a hand to lift the wheelbarrow full of stumps over, then I lifted the kids over, one by one. My arms were heavy; suddenly I felt so weak, too weak to face what was to come.

I can see the wood from here. It's not big. The remains of the hut are still in there.

I had to make a choice that summer. I had to choose myself; that was the summer when I discovered that a person cannot choose anything but himself. All else is a lie. When you stop choosing yourself, you start to die slowly.

I remember my fictitious evening strolls, the secret, despairing phone calls to Minna from the phone box over at the petrol station. She didn't want to put any pressure on me, she said, although in our situation any talk of pressure was clearly pointless.

Over the latter part of the summer Judith's worrying got even worse. She began to develop physical symptoms, she started having premonitions of some sort which caused her fingers to stiffen up and hence, according to her, made it impossible for her to play. At any rate they led her to act like some misplaced and rather exasperating soothsayer from a tragedy by Aeschylus. It was a good thing that it was the summer holidays, with the tour behind her; I don't know how she would have got on at work if this had happened before she left.

She also started to have terrible nightmares. More than once she woke up around four in the morning with a horrified look in her eyes. I had to stroke her back for ages before she calmed down, nestled in to me and fell asleep. As for me, I spent the greater part of those nights lying awake anyway, I had my own worries. During the day, her face fell into tense, introspective folds. I had seen her like this a couple of times before, but I had never known how to deal with it, I couldn't tell whether she was putting on an act or whether it was for real. I had the schizophrenic sensation of being under surveillance and yet, at the same time, forsaken.

She seemed to have crossed into an unseen, irrational world that was hidden from me. It was evidently a world fraught with omens and forewarnings, but when she told me about them I just felt stupid, I didn't know what to say. We found ourselves in a difficult situation; one of us had to keep a clear head and I couldn't help but notice how the omens she believed she was picking up made her do things that were almost touchingly clumsy and out of place in the real world.

She was wrong, and yet she was right, that was what was made it all so distressing. Now, of course, I can see that she misread the forewarnings she thought she had received, so that to her they seemed to speak of a disaster that would strike you, not our marriage. She was sure that there was someone out there who meant to do you harm. She behaved as if she were fighting for your life, she wanted to push the wood away. I think she scared away the neighbours' kids who came to the door to ask you to come and help with the hut; she stood on the front steps like a witch and shooed them away. She looked strained and unkempt. Maybe she scared you too. Did she scare you, Ebba? Did she tell you scary stories about the wood?

I'm sure she could read me like an open book. But I didn't want to be a book, I didn't like the way she read, it was somehow unassailable, closed to all logic. There are no arguments against being read in such a way. You just have to sit there, caught up in the shame of something all unknown to you, which is clearly written all over you, and which speaks of some dreadful secret. You are bound hand and foot.

And alongside this, in the middle of this, there is the other story. Our story, yours and mine and Minna's; I have to keep it alive, it is my job to make sure that it doesn't fade away. That is why I have to say this yet again: Minna came over to me that time in the library, and *she was happy in that surprised way that makes people look fresh and clean.*

There is no arguing with that either. In that lies freedom. And in freedom lies joy. That joy – it is so intense. Minna smiled at

103

me, and I saw that she was a lifeline, she was quiet and happy and warm.

My decision to leave your mother was born of a necessity that went far beyond my own person. It was as if some sort of formless garment had been pulled over my head, one which could not possibly be taken off again. I could find no holes in that garment through which to stick my arms. I kept tripping over.

For fleeting moments I would dream of carrying on as before, after Judith got back from the tour, carry on seeing Minna in secret at the bedsit, carry on with my ostensibly idyllic family life with Judith and you. But that was, of course, out of the question.

And all the time your mother lived within me, somewhere on the inner side of my arms, like a kind of lining. Minna was the blood coursing through my veins and making my thoughts unclear, but Judith was the fine silken lining on the underside of my skin.

It was all very confusing and I couldn't very well talk to Minna about it. After our night together in my and Judith's bed and my disastrous stomach problems the bonds between us had simply become that much stronger.

I really did try to behave decently towards your mother once I realised that things had gone too far, that a break-up was inevitable. I tried to talk to her, and I wrote little notes to her and left them lying around the house in places where she couldn't fail to see them. I wrote them at night after she had gone to sleep. Often I had to get up again, having lain awake beside her for hours, staring at the ceiling.

I tried out various metaphors in those notes: 'glue that's starting to dissolve', 'bonds that are wearing out', 'ocean currents sweeping us off in different directions'. She never gave any sign that she had read them, but she certainly found them and removed them from wherever I had left them, that much I could see. It was a strange, unreal time. I started wishing that I would soon wake up, although I hadn't slept in a long time.

But I couldn't bring myself to say that I had met someone else.

It was difficult to see the reality of our situation for all the irritation, the shame, the longing for Minna, the fear of what was bound to come. I felt like a blind man. Things were not made any easier by the fact that Judith seemed to play on the tension in the air in a cheap and histrionic fashion; those so-called premonitions of hers were presented in a way which made it plain that, all unknown to me, she had developed a particular knack for setting herself into strange and seemingly significant situations, as if she were part of another story than that which I had imagined we were in together. I can't explain how she did it, except to say that she went around with this vaguely agonised, slightly ironic look in her eyes, while at the same time giving the impression that her story was far more soulful and exalted than mine, that she was in fact playing the lead in some piece that I would never be able to comprehend, a tragedy of inconceivable depth, while I was but an extra, an amateur player in a tacky soap opera.

But I know that I believed her. I was extremely vulnerable, my bad conscience would not allow me to be otherwise.

Only recently did it occur to me that this premonitory gift of hers reminded me in some obscure fashion of my own knack for staving off whatever was looming on the horizon, the thing I told you about earlier. Your mother and I seemed, at that point, almost like a brother and sister who had inherited the same essential nature from some distant ancestor, one which manifested itself in a slightly different way in each of us: she had some inkling of what was about to happen, feared it and yet drew it to herself; while I, for my part, longed for what was going to happen, but involuntarily held it at bay.

Minna is so much simpler to live with – blessedly so. She views what lies ahead with her eyes wide open, and one of the great things about her is that she generally tells me how she is feeling, which means I don't have to guess. When she doesn't tell me, it's because there's no point in saying, either because I already know, or because there's nothing I can do about it. There's nothing underhand or secretive between us. I know you love her too.

I remember that I was leaning up against the fridge when I told Judith about Minna. She was standing by the kitchen bench, laying slices of cheese on some halved bread rolls. I could feel the warm thrum of the fridge motor against my back.

Our story took a new turn at the moment when I told her. I looked at her eyes, they changed. Behind them little Judith curled up in a ball and turned away. At that same moment the thermostat in the fridge cut out and behind me everything went quiet.

Her white hate came as a shock. She was capable of hating in a cold and calculating manner that stunned me. She seemed experienced, almost an expert in her hate; compared to her I was a complete amateur. On those few occasions when we tried to talk about it and she pressed the start button on her hateful talking machine, which seemed to be hooked up to a dynamo that never ran down, I realised that any summing up of how things actually stood between us was out of the question. We didn't have the words in which to tell the true story. Not only that, but such a confrontation would also have forced me to recognise just how deeply I had deluded myself in my blind infatuation with her back then; to what a great extent I had been manipulated. I don't know whether I could have borne it, it would have been too much for me. Seems like I can't cope with just anything either.

So I let her go on living out her own version of how she and I had been one, even if it didn't really fit with the way the story ended. For the most part I said nothing, merely listened to her venomous outbursts and descriptions of all the ways in which I had let her down. It seemed the least I could do for her.

The beautiful version of the story about us was, of course, also true in its fashion. But it could not stand being contradicted.

One of the first weeks after I left home she was standing on the front steps with you on her hip when I came to pick you up. She told me that she had put all of my books out in the garden a couple of days earlier and unfortunately, as I was no doubt aware, it had rained pretty heavily since then, so I probably shouldn't count on them being worth much now. She added that she would appreciate it if I would remove them as soon as possible, as she would be holding a garden party at the weekend. And I would have to bring you home earlier on the Sunday than previously agreed; she wanted you to meet the people who were coming, they were all so fond of you.

I saw that she was already starting to create divisions among our mutual friends, she wanted to be sure of getting them all on her side as soon as she could. It wasn't hard to imagine what they would be saying about me at that party.

She stood there on the steps with you on her hip and watched me lug the disintegrating cardboard boxes full of sodden books out to the car; I had to make several trips. You wailed and kicked, wanting to come to me, but Judith jutted out her hip and held you in a vice-like grip. This particular action was to become her hallmark. Years later, long after you had grown too big to be carried, I would still imagine I could see your mother jutting out her hip in that same fashion, whenever she came up with some new means of punishing me. I could picture it quite clearly, the way she clamped you to her side, even when you weren't anywhere near her and the argument of the moment concerned a birthday that I had been unfortunate enough to forget, or some other misdemeanour which she had taken it into her head that I had committed.

I'm so sorry, Ebba, that I sometimes forgot your birthday. I feel so bad about that. You know I've never had a head for dates.

It wasn't the fact that she deliberately ruined my books that really got to me, that upset me most that day. The worst of it was that she should bring me down like that in front of you.

Women seem to me to be so ruthless when it comes to taking revenge. In exacting punishment they use the most uncannily accurate weapons. When men set out to avenge themselves they tend to bring out the heavy artillery, but they are also apt to over-shoot the mark drastically. Women are always bang on target. They must have an instinct for it, they know just what it takes.

You were so fond of Jennifer, right from the start. More as if she were your own daughter than your half-sister, I would say. Well, there was such a big difference in your ages, and I suppose you've always been something of a little mother, to Minna and me too. Sometimes I had the rather uncomfortable feeling that you were observing us all from the outside, with the eyes of a benevolent old aunt, thinking something like: Ah, well, as long as they're happy together, that's fine. As if you were from another world, as if you didn't think for one minute that we would understand. This could make you seem a little distant.

When I introduced you to Minna all those years ago, you immediately accepted your stepmother. You were a trusting child at that age, although still with that knowing look in your eye. To begin with I wasn't sure whether I could be completely open with you about the fact that Minna and I were a couple; I had just left your own mother after all, I refrained from kissing or any other sign of intimacy between Minna and myself. But it was as if you saw through me, you showed in your own small, considerate ways that you had nothing against me giving her a kiss when you were present, or putting my arm round her when we curled up on the sofa of an evening.

I believe this vote of confidence from you meant a lot to Minna during those first years that we were together. She had no children of her own then, you see, and felt very guilty about having entered into a relationship with a married man and father. Your trust in her, your regard for her, rendered her more, how shall I put it . . . more *human* in her own eyes. She became very attached to you.

You may never have given it any thought, but Minna and I waited as long as we could before having a child of our own. To some extent during those first years we were enough for each other, and then you were with us a lot, too. Neither of us was sure how you would take to having a half-sister. But you were thirteen when Jennifer was born, you had spent the whole of your childhood as an only child and Minna had reached the age where a woman has to decide whether she is going to have children or not.

I took you to the hospital the day after Jennifer was born, remember? You were so excited about your new half-sister and respectfully affectionate towards Minna, but it struck me that you were a little distant to begin with, as if you were not quite with us.

You were the one who decided we should call her Jennifer. It wasn't a name that either Minna or I knew, but there was never any doubt that that was what the baby would be called, it was our concession to you, I suppose I would have to say that. Since then we've both come to love the name; I've never met anyone else in Norway called Jennifer.

Both Minna and I like to be a little bit different. So does Judith, for that matter, she probably takes after her mother in that respect; neither Ebba nor Judith is a common name in these parts. When Mama and I were picking a name for you I had the horrible feeling that your grandmother had the deciding vote. When all's said and done, isn't that always the way: it's the women who call the tune.

Jennifer's birth was pretty dramatic. I was there for the first part of it, and I gave Minna all the support I could, but there's not that much a man can do in such situations, you really feel more in the way. Minna's labour was so different from how things had been for Judith when you were born that that experience was of little use here. And I hadn't been so involved on that occasion, I had managed to keep a pretty clear head. This time, though, I did my best to help Minna with the breathing exercises we had learned at childbirth classes, the same ones that had been of such help to Judith and I when you were born.

When they found that the baby had turned and was lying in the breech position things became pretty fraught for a while and I was sent out of the delivery room. Minna had surrendered to her body, she was no longer listening to me, it was as if another motor had kicked in, one that neither she nor I had known anything about. More doctors were called in; I was ushered out and left in the hands of a male student nurse while preparations were made for a tricky breech birth. He can't have been any more than twenty, and couldn't possibly have had any experience to talk about, certainly not as a father and probably not as a midwife either. None the less, what I remember best from Jennifer's birth is this young man's solicitude and quiet sympathy. He sat beside me on that clammy hospital sofa, talking softly and earnestly about all the births in his ken and making me feel confident that the doctors and the midwife in there with Minna knew what they were doing.

I saw that guy on the street about six months ago. He's a grown man now, he looks a little like Erlend. He was with a lovely woman of his own age, he had his arm around her shoulder. He didn't see me, but a surge of happiness ran through me at sight of him.

Do you remember that time when you lived with us, after Jennifer was born? After Minna and the baby came home from the hospital you came to stay for a few weeks. It was me who arranged it, as you may know. I'm so glad we were able to have you there. Minna had lost a lot of blood and needed time to get her strength back, so you were a big help to us during those first weeks, even though you were only thirteen. To be honest, I was also pretty wasted. I've seen pictures of myself from that time and I can see how thin I was, thinner than was good for me.

Your mother didn't like the idea of you staying with us, naturally. I don't know how much you discussed it, you and she, but for once I got my way. It was incredibly important to me that my two daughters should form a bond right from the start. From then on you used to wash and change Jennifer, and play with her as if she were your own daughter. Which, strictly speaking, she might almost have been – from time to time it did strike me that had there been only another three or four years between you, Jennifer could have been the daughter of a very young, skinny and rather distant teenage mum who paid us a visit once a week and every second weekend. You have always had the ability to make people think of you as being older than you actually are.

But you were still just a child, and I think it was a long time before you stopped hoping that Judith and I would get back together. I want you to know that I know this, Ebba. I've known it all along. It was only after Jennifer was born that you stopped bringing me your little drawings, the ones that were meant to remind me that you and Judith were my real family. Once when you were about eight you cut out a picture of Judith from the newspaper and put it into the pocket of my jacket out in the hall. Remember? The clipping was neatly folded and it may have been there for some days before I discovered it. It was the sort of stupid tabloid piece that Judith has a habit of agreeing, ever so reluctantly, to do, although in actual fact they satisfy her powerful craving for attention. In the picture she looks, as always, fabulous.

I didn't know what to do with that clipping. Minna would obviously have been hurt if she had found it in my jacket pocket. In the end I slipped it into your schoolbag and never said a word about it.

I know that I didn't manage to do the right thing that time Ebba. Forgive me. Grown-ups don't always know the right thing to do either.

I have a picture here in my wallet, it's of you and Jennifer. Taken around that time. I took it one day when you had fallen asleep together on the sofa. We often used to pile on to the sofa together, all four of us, when Jennifer was being fed, do you remember, I would read aloud to my three girls and once she was finished feeding Jennifer, Minna would pass her to you, to burp her and lull her to sleep, the way you do so well. Lovely moments those were.

I think maybe you were pretty run down yourself at that time, maybe a little anaemic, maybe I should have made more of an effort to find out how you and Mama managed at home, whether you were getting enough iron in your diet, for instance. Maybe I should have got in touch with the school nurse? But I had a lot on my plate just then, and you were so capable and independent and so easy-going; besides which, I was a bit of a coward; I baulked at broaching touchy subjects with your mother. Our telephone conversations were usually unpleasant, she always managed to make any such inquiries on my part sound as if I didn't think she was a good mother. And my insisting that you stay with us for those first weeks after Jennifer was born didn't exactly improve matters.

The picture's not quite sharp, see? I didn't use the flash, I didn't want the light to wake you. You're snuggled up close together on the sofa. Jennifer is lying with her face nestling into the hollow of your throat, and you must just have been dropping off to sleep too, overcome by a weariness of sorts. The peace and the beauty surrounding the two of you leaps out at me every time I open my wallet. I saw it for the first time some weeks later when I collected the pictures and opened the folder on the street just outside the photo shop. This picture took my breath away. It reminded me of another picture I must have seen at some point, it must have been a photo of Mama and you in exactly the same position, when you were a tiny baby drifting off to sleep after your feed. But behind this picture lay yet another one, an age-old picture which I couldn't dredge up from memory, it must have been a picture of the inviolable unity that exists between mother and child, possibly the Moon Queen and her daughter, I mean the real Moon Queen and the real princess, the ones in the fairy tale, suffused with a beauty so powerful that it gives hardly any pleasure at all, only pain.

Maybe it's a picture from the parchment scroll deep inside that dark cave.

I think you felt very much responsible for Judith back then, although you never spoke about her to Minna or me. As if you had to take extra good care of your own mother, now that I had consolidated my new family by having a child by the woman for whom I had left you two.

Minna never asked about your mother. I know this was out of a certain respect: for you, for Judith and for me. You understood that too, I'm sure. She respected my previous life, and she knew that there had been something special between Judith and me. She knew you were a child of love. But she preferred not to hear too much about that, not unless she absolutely had to.

As you got older you used to take the train out to see us every Thursday afternoon after school. And you insisted on collecting Jennifer from nursery on Thursdays, didn't you, I think you both looked forward to it. It also left Minna free to go shopping and buy something special for dinner. Not that she's normally much of a one for cooking, is she? To be honest she's not exactly gifted in that department. But on those Thursdays you have to agree that she really did make an effort.

Usually I was the last one home on Thursdays. It gave me the strangest feeling, to hear the sound of my three girls' voices coming from the kitchen. I often felt a little bit shy about joining all of you, as if I might be interrupting something important, as if something would come to an end the minute I walked into the room. There was that feeling again. That the shadow looming out there on the horizon will never get to me also means that all of real life takes place when I am not present, and that everything becomes different and less real the moment that I try to get involved. As if I am imposing myself on reality, as if I weaken it.

But eventually of course I did walk in. I have no reason to believe that you weren't all three glad to see me.

During dinner I always brought up the subject of Judith in exactly the same polite fashion. I would ask: 'How are things at home?' And you would answer brightly, 'Fine', and give a slightly unfocused smile, as you sometimes did when such things came up in conversation. Then you would busy yourself with a potato, or your napkin, and there seemed no good reason to pursue the matter. I didn't want to bother you.

And Minna would nod at me. Did you notice? Always the same strained, warm smile when she nodded like that, so different from her other smiles, of which there are so many.

I don't think Jennifer gave any thought to the fact that you had a mother elsewhere, in another town. She was just a little child and little children don't need to worry about things like that; they live in the moment. Jennifer's moments on those Thursday afternoons were filled with joy, she had the undivided attention of three people who loved and adored her. I'm pretty certain she knew she was loved. Don't you think so? And she knows it still.

She's so incredibly like you were at that age.

Judith's car is in the garage.

She didn't have a driving licence when I lived here; she refused to learn to drive, but she passed her driving test in record time once she was on her own. She must have started taking driving lessons the minute I walked out the door. It was you who first told me that she had passed her driving test and needed our old car, which I had taken with me, and which I badly needed for getting to work. This was during one of our Thursday dinners. I could tell by your eyes that Judith had instructed you to pass on this information. It was her who told you to do it, wasn't it?

You can't live a lie, Ebba, not in the long run. It rots away at you. You become rotten inside from living up to another person's image of yourself. You have to be your own image, only in one's image of oneself is there truth. And only in truth is there beauty.

Yes.

Only in truth is there beauty. Without truth you die a little every day.

Maybe I hadn't understood it until this moment. I thought I understood it, but maybe I didn't really understand it until this moment. Don't go.

She might not be asleep in there. Do you think she's asleep? Maybe she's standing right behind me, peering through the peephole in the front door. Sometimes she has such a piercing look in her eyes, she can make a man feel like there's a needle boring into the back of his neck.

A lie can be beautiful for a while, a lie can in fact have a lustre all its own, unlike any other, and it can last for quite a long time. But then it begins to rot from within.

Maybe I've known it for ages. Maybe that was what I perceived when I saw Minna coming over to me in the library that day. It wasn't her smiles, it was the truth in her. I did so want to be with her there in that truth.

Something was in the process of rotting away from the inside back then, the way the apples from the apple tree in your grandfather's garden when I was a little boy tended to turn brown and mealy on the inside, starting at the core and working outwards. Once that process had begun it usually wasn't long before the first brown spots appeared on the skin, and then you knew that the apple was rotten to the core.

And yet one of the things that shocked me most about the whole break-up was that I should have found it so easy to detach myself from Judith. I don't think it took any more than a few weeks. When I left I packed only the bare essentials in the way of clothing, there wasn't room for any of my things in Minna's tiny bedsit anyway. And later, when we were settled in our own flat, it was important to us that we should start afresh. New view. New furniture. New stories.

At night, after Minna had fallen asleep I would lie in the new double bed, under the new, easy-care, all-year-round, synthetic fibre duvet and be aware that the lining inside me was gone. Although this made me much more vulnerable to impressions from the outside, none the less I was relieved. Sometimes, though, I caught myself missing things from the old house: the underfloor heating in the bathroom, the spacious cellar, the view from the bedroom window. Down-filled duvets.

I changed the whole rhythm of my day after I started living with Minna, I fell into new habits. I got up earlier to have more time with her; I found that I really needed a couple of hours with her before we both had to leave for work. And it was at this time that I bought a sailboat, something I had dreamt of doing since I was a boy, as I'm sure you knew. We couldn't afford it, of course. There was never any thought of me asking Judith to buy me out of this house, I went on paying my share of the mortgage – there was obviously no way she could afford it on her own – and for me to demand that you two find a cheaper place to live would have been unthinkable. But at the same time I had to pay child maintenance for you, another big expense. So from a financial point of view I was no great catch for Minna. But I'm not going to bother you with all that. Luckily, she had a bit of capital, in the form of her share of the profit from the sale of the big flat in town that she had shared with her previous boyfriend, and she knew, without me having to say anything, that it was more important for me to have a boat than to live in an expensive flat. So we moved into that run-down little three-room flat, the one you know so well, in a tower block in a cheap part of town, and bought a sailboat with the rest of the money we didn't have. You could say it was because of that sailboat that you have to share a room with Jennifer when you stay at our place.

Minna has never much liked being out on the water, she gets seasick so easily. I was a little disappointed about that, I must admit. But you love to go sailing; during our holidays together you and I have always spent as much time as we could on the boat, ever since I taught you to swim when you were seven or eight. Do you remember when you learned to swim? Jennifer is still too small to come out with me, but in a few years' time I hope she'll get as much pleasure from it as you do.

Did.

Oh, God. Don't go.

Of course the humdrum of everyday life was bound to catch up on Minna and me too. We soon fell into a steady round of working, eating, going to the cinema or the theatre, walking in the park, doing up the boat, seeing her old friends. I would most definitely say that we were happy. It meant a lot to me, the air of tranquility that had developed between us; I felt it was a good substitute for the first mindless passion of those days when everything we did was forbidden.

And yet sometimes I would find myself looking at her with a stranger's eyes almost, as if she had nothing to do with me. At such moments I felt a chill that scared me. It came from the inside. I didn't see my own darling Minna, the woman without whom my life would have no meaning; my cool gaze saw only a blond public librarian with a round, ingenuous face, a less than sophisticated taste in clothes and rather heavy hips.

Then the image of Judith's long, slender legs would flash through my mind. The image of her sitting naked on the toilet with her huge pregnant stomach in the mornings before we went to work, telling me what she had dreamed.

And on a handful of occasions I have woken, befuddled with sleep, in the middle of the night or the grey light of dawn and reached out for the woman lying in bed beside me, only to pull it back in shame when I realised that it was not Judith lying there, but someone whose name I couldn't even recall. And I have been left with the desperate feeling that I am all alone.

But I have my books of course. I'm so glad you inherited my love of books. I have the pleasure of walking into a second-hand book-shop and stumbling over a work that I've been trying to track down for ages. I have the almost physical air of suspense when I get home, Minna and Jennifer have gone to bed, and the house is still. The moment when I can sit back in my chair with the book, a glass of whisky and a cigarette. The odour of glue and paper wafting out at me as I open the book, at the very back, always the very back first, and run my finger down the keywords in the index. The index tells me all that I can expect from the book, it reveals the author's intellectual horizon. I can think to myself: you don't fool me. And I always look forward to telling you about what I've been reading. I can tell you everything.

You may not know it, but when I met Minna she was as avid a reader as I am. Doesn't sound much like the Minna you know, does it? But since Jennifer was born she hasn't had so much time for pursuing her own classical studies; the academic side of things has really had to take a back seat as far as she's concerned. I think she's very happy with her job, with her role as a mother, you whom she is so fond of, the girls whom she has kept up with since primary school and our own little circle of friends. All of whom you know. Interests change, naturally, just as everything changes. It would be silly to insist that everything stay just as it was.

I suppose you could say that I've gone beyond her, it just turned out that way. There's a kind of loneliness in that too, although not so much for Minna, I don't think, mainly for me. That may be one reason why my talks with you have come to mean so much to me.

Your mother isn't a great book person either, although I have the decided impression that she comes from a bookish home. After I helped your grandmother to move into the terraced house out here my back ached for weeks from lugging heavy boxes full of books.

Judith has invested all of her talent in music, egged on by Granny's lofty ambitions for her, of course. I think the whole of her childhood must have been subject to a pretty strict régime of music lessons and practice. In your mother, her tremendous talent still goes hand in hand with that rather strained clever, conscientious side of her which speaks of the need to do well from an early age. It might not be so easy for you to see, but in a way this is her shame. I'm not sure if she is aware of it.

I've deliberately avoided keeping track of her career in recent years, apart from whatever you've happened to mention in passing. I have a terrible feeling it's on the wane. I think she spends more and more time teaching these days, and less on her own artistic development. Wouldn't you say so? And of course it may well be that she's a good teacher. But it seems to me that she reached her peak during the years when she and I were together. Not that this necessarily had anything to do with her meeting me, don't get me wrong, I think it had more to do with a sort of personal clock, ticking away inside us no matter what we are doing or who we are mixing with. I believe that I came into her life on that spring morning eighteen years ago simply because her clock was telling her that she was about to become queen, and the story about her required that there should be a king by her side when she came to power. If there's a vacancy in a fairy tale, then somebody has to fill it. And I, with all my complexes and my deep fascination with music and beauty, was easy prey. I felt she endowed me with all the things I lacked. To me that time was like a period of grace: after so many years of struggle, humiliation and confusion, suddenly you enter a time when everything comes to you. Music, love, everything.

When it was all over between us that period of grace, too, came to an end. I no longer had any desire to see the orchestra in concert. When we split up, most of the people from the orchestra took Judith's side. I felt I was no longer welcome there, although her colleagues were polite and pleasant enough if they happened to bump into me on the street or in a shop. Apart from Jørgen, who has always been the same cheery, amiable soul with me, none of the orchestra crowd ever asked about my new life or made any move towards meeting Minna and Jennifer. In many ways I can understand them.

Actually, though, I did take Jennifer to the opera not that long ago; after all these years I felt it was about time. Did she tell you about it? They were doing *The Magic Flute* again, a long advertised, shorter version for children. It had had good reviews, I thought it was safe, that by then it must surely be possible to go back.

The cloakroom attendant recognised me. She gave me a friendly nod as she handed me the programme.

'Well, you're no stranger to this piece anyway,' she said and winked at me. I winked back at her, disconcerted. Incredible, after all those years she actually remembered me. I located our seats and sat there watching her as she stood in the doorway, selling programmes. I found it touching that she was still there, in her little uniform.

I had your sister on my lap. She was all dressed up in a dark-blue velvet dress and black patent shoes and she held the programme in her hands with her usual concentration, like a little lady, you know the way she is sometimes. It made me feel quite shy; I buried my face in her velvet back, she turned and laughed and said don't tickle, Papa, stop it, it tickles, exactly the way you used to do at that age.

And all at once I was back at the première of *The Magic Flute*, back when I had just started seeing your mother. I was all dressed up in a suit and tie on that occasion too, for once I was sitting in one of the front rows, it was a big night for Judith and for me. In those days I felt rather proprietorial about the opera as a whole. The last rehearsal I had caught had been a disaster. The singer who was singing the part of Sarastro, one of the opera's big stars, was running late, everyone had to wait, the musicians were fed up, they wanted to call off the rehearsal. But just as they were about to put down their instruments he had taken the stage with every ounce of his persona, with that tremendous voice of his, and sung Sarastro's aria from the second act. *In diesen heil'gen Hallen*, he sang, *kennt man die Rache nicht*. That magnificent voice. It rammed me right in the solar plexus.

I had no idea what *Rache* meant, but I found the text of the aria in a music book in your mother's music room at home and learned it by heart that same evening, and some evenings later, when she was at the opening party with the other orchestra members, I sang it in the bath.

Rache means revenge. I've picked up a fair bit of German over the years.

Minna and I have had our rough patches too, I see no point in denying it. It's not her fault, and I've done my best not to burden her with my moods. Reading and studying has, I suppose, been one way in which I've taken my mind off things when my thoughts become too black.

I remember sitting in the battered old armchair in the flat that Easter when you weren't with us, reading about Mozart and the Freemasons. I was going through one of my bad spells, I was missing you, I had been thinking that over the holiday we could make a start on spring-cleaning the boat, you and I, maybe even manage some nice trips out on the water. But Judith had decided to be difficult, she had got hold of some cheap, last-minute tickets to Italy for herself and your grandmother, and she had insisted that you go with them. I couldn't face getting into a fight with her, couldn't take any more of the poisonous bitterness that laced her tirades against me, it left me drained. Bitterness is a poison.

Minna had her usual nights out with her girlfriends that Easter, she had of course been expecting you to be with us, and as I'm sure you know, it was an unwritten rule between us that she went out a lot in the evenings over those holidays, to allow you and I some time alone together after Jennifer was in bed. I assume that she and her girlfriends spent their time talking about men; isn't that usually what women talk about when they get together in a café and drink red wine, which they order by the glass, as if to say that honestly they hardly ever take a drink, when in fact they are knocking it back. But you would probably know more about that than me.

When I'd finished the book about Mozart I started reading *Thus Spake Zarathustra* again. In a way it was like discovering it afresh. I found it even more terrifying this time. It reminded me of something I thought I had forgotten, something that had to do with your mother.

I had to restore myself to normality that Easter. I did so by telling myself that what I had seen in that book, overwhelming though it certainly was, was just like being in love, and that fortunately, unlike the time when I fell in love with Minna, there was no risk involved in giving in to it, nothing of the old life that would have to be sacrificed. After all, it was only a book, a mad philosopher, a shaman. In due course this too was bound to ease off, I said to myself, the way my infatuation with Minna had eventually done, and turn into calm, clear insight, a sort of amicability, that is to be lived with.

I stuck a postcard with a picture of the extravagantly moustachioed philosopher above the mirror in the bathroom. You must remember that card, it hung there for ages. That Easter, when I was shaving in the mornings, with Jennifer hanging affectionately around my legs and Minna organising breakfast in the kitchen, I would cast a glance at Nietzsche and force myself to remember that I had a lot going for me. Normality surrounded me like a blessing. And you were a part of that, Ebba, even if you were in Italy at that point.

But maybe this obsession of mine didn't die out altogether. I went on reading just as avidly after the Easter holidays. The interest triggered by Nietszche branched out in all directions, leading me first to mythology and from there to other philosophers. It wasn't as if I were doing a course or anything, I sat on my own at home in the flat after work with my books when Jennifer was asleep and Minna was busy with bits and pieces round about me. I read slowly and intently, usually in English which was the only foreign language I felt I knew well enough. I read about initiation, about the ancient Greek rituals and the myths from which they sprang. The Eleusinian mysteries. And Plato, of course, I always came back to Plato, to his kindly, patient, enlightened clarity. I had my dictionaries to hand, I systematically wrote down the words I had to look up, to memorise later the way we used to memorise vocabulary at school: *Progression. Persecute. Inhabitant. Sanctuary.*

And basically it went on from there. My current method of study is radically different from the way I used to study at engineering college. In those days what I had to master was, for the most part, a practical skill, a skill which did involve having to read up on a fair bit of theory, but which had nothing to do with me as a person. Reading mythology and philosophy is a different matter. I don't know how to describe it, except to say that it involves an element of lust.

The sense of something shameful pervades this too. I probably shouldn't talk to you about it. To begin with I thought I was ashamed of all the things I read about of which I knew nothing; I was glad that I was studying alone and didn't have to reveal my ignorance to any teachers or fellow students. The people who had written the books and articles I read bandied about names and historic events I had never heard of; I had to invest in expensive reference books, I had to look up the most elementary things. But I can see now that what I was actually ashamed of was the lust.

The Eleusinian mysteries are based on the myth of Demeter and Persephone. Demeter is the goddess of fertility, the mother who lost her daughter, Persephone, to the underworld. A young man came and stole her daughter away, she was married to the king of the infernal regions and thus she became the queen of the dead. But Demeter mourned so bitterly for her daughter that all life came to a standstill, nothing would grow and a blight was on the earth. She shut herself away in her house and refused to come out until her daughter was returned to her. I suppose you could call it a sort of mourning strike. In the end, Zeus had to give in to her unrelenting sorrow and arrange for Persephone to be brought back up from the underworld, to be restored to her mother. As soon as she was back everything started to grow again. That reunion between mother and daughter must have been a moving sight, I'm sure the Athenians must have made much of the Eleusinian myth.

Pindar once wrote something to the effect that happy is he who is initiated at Eleusia, for he need no longer fear death. I sat in my armchair pondering this statement. What took place during the initiation rites at Eleusia? What did the Athenians see that meant they no longer had to fear death? How did this fit with Demeter grieving for her daughter? And what was it that Mozart had seen when he was initiated into the Freemasons in Vienna? Why did he write that he did not fear death?

These are the sort of questions with which I wrestled, and I began to develop a notion that the music from *The Magic Flute* might hold the answer to everything. To what Mozart had seen that led him to take the extinction of which his music speaks with such reassuring lightness; and that, since there obviously had to be a close connection between the Freemasons' initiation rites and the rituals carried out at Eleusia, there had to be a direct link between Demeter and Mozart. Through Mozart's music one could arrive at an understanding of that divine mother's relentless grieving. And if one could understand that, one would also be able to understand women and fertility. And if one could understand women, one was well on the way to having a happy life, that much I had understood. At any rate it was clear to me that the opposite was certainly the case: not to understand women can only lead to a life of misery, since that is where the power lies.

But while thoughts of this sort left me feeling elated and eager to know more, and fired me with the urge to look up lots of new English words, I always had this sense of shame at being interested in such things. It may be that this shame sprang from my feelings of lust. A lust for something ancient and secret, something which in the final analysis had to do with women. I had to keep it to myself.

None the less, as time went on I began to think that perhaps university was where I belonged. The picture of my office at the University of Chicago, with the shelves full of books and my lectures timetable pinned up on the door, was still tucked away somewhere at the back of my mind.

To get into university I had to start from scratch and do the Prelim. This was a bit of a bind, but after lengthy discussion with Minna I put my name down for an evening class run by the Free College. One evening a week I found myself, much against my will, having to take part in a study group, along with four other students. We were given the use of a dreary little seminar room; the others usually came unprepared and seemed to take it for granted that I, as the oldest, should take the place of the lecturer and tell them whatever was worth knowing. I suppose they were used to having a teacher standing over them, spoon-feeding them information. The difference in our ages bothered me; I could have been their father. Next to them I felt I cut such a ridiculous figure: a staid middle-aged man, totally out of place in a weird world of trendy fashion mags, Coke cans and the incomprehensible techno music that drifted out of their head-phones on those rare occasions when they thought it worth the trouble to remove them from their ears and leave them dangling around their necks. The way they behaved, anyone would have thought they had been press-ganged into being there – and who knows, maybe they had. They were so unlike you, somehow nothing about them seemed at all familiar to me, they seemed so unfocused, and a little aggrieved – although over what they could not have said.

But there was one who stood out from the rest. It's not easy to talk about this, Ebba. You know what I'm going to say. His name was Erlend, he was nineteen years old and he seemed to have a good head on his shoulders. He and I were the only ones who asked questions during the lectures and the only ones who came prepared for the study groups. We became friendly, possibly thanks to our joint efforts to cut through the rest of the group's solid aversion to philosophy. In a way he reminded me of myself when I was his age: the same affected air of self-assurance and, just beneath the surface, layer upon layer of inadequacy, shame, the urge to make something of oneself, not to be like everyone else.

We got talking during one of the breaks and very soon came to the conclusion that the study group was not for us, we would rather have our own meetings, just the two of us, and work on our own. We got hold of other works by Nietzsche that were not on the syllabus, and on Wednesdays, after lectures, we would sit in the Workers' Café, losing ourselves in long, earnest conversations about *Thus Spake Zarathustra*. We formed a great liking for one another.

The difference in our ages no longer seemed to matter. He told me a bit about himself: like me he was a music lover, he had a season ticket for the symphony orchestra – I was quite impressed by that, I doubt if many nineteen-year-olds could have said the same. I never mentioned my own past, with your mother and her music, but we had some great discussions about Shostakovich.

It wasn't until the exam was almost upon us that I discovered that Erlend was actually . . . your first love. At the same time as he found out who I was. I'm sure you remember that moment as well as I do. I passed the two of you outside the library one Thursday afternoon, I had come by in the car after work to pick up Minna. The arrangement with you two girls was, of course, that you would come out on the train after school as usual and collect Jennifer from nursery, and then all four of us would have dinner together.

It was Jennifer I caught sight of first, as I was walking across the car park outside the main entrance to the library. Her red snowsuit looked almost luminous and she was wearing that special bunny hat that Minna had knitted for her, the one with the ears, you know the one I mean, she looks so cute in that hat. She was holding your hand and smiling up at a young man who was bending over her and tweaking her bunny ears. And who should this young man be but Erlend. I think we were a bit taken aback, all three of us, weren't we? I've never asked you about this before, but it must have been pretty embarrassing for you, me finding out about the two of you like that; you hadn't wanted to say anything to me about your boyfriend, although I think Minna had heard something. You had told Minna, hadn't you?

Erlend blushed and stammered and suddenly seemed much younger than I remembered from our talks at the Workers' Café. Jennifer alone was all smiles, sparkling at Erlend, with all of her diminutive femininity radiating right to the tips of the bunny ears she was waggling at him; evidently this was not the first time they had met.

You pulled yourself together and introduced us; we laughed a little shamefacedly, having to admit that we already knew one another quite well. Erlend made his apologies and sidled off as Minna came out of the library's main entrance and spotted us. You and Minna smiled at one another, that wordless woman-to-woman smile that says: we can talk about this later when we're alone. I felt left out. There was something up ahead that did not want to meet me. I repelled it with my magnetic force.

Nothing more was said about Erlend, neither in the car on the way home nor during dinner. It was all very awkward. I couldn't help wondering what the two of you got up to when you were alone, how far he had got with you. You were only sixteen, for heaven's sake, little more than a child in my eyes, even though I realised that you probably seemed older. I know only too well what goes on inside the heads of young men at that age, it's not all that long since I was floundering about in a sea of hormones myself. I suddenly remembered your mother telling me how as a teenager she had been so disappointed in her first boyfriends, because all they could think of was getting their hands under her skirt. Maybe she told you about that too. I had felt slightly abashed when she told me this, as if she had divulged something that I could not talk about. I didn't want you to know about it. I wanted everything to be beautiful for you, Ebba.

All these thoughts were running through my head during dinner, while you, my three girls, chattered on about matters of your own. After dinner I retreated to the bedroom – to rest, I said. Do you remember? It wasn't like me, I know. I felt as though a glass wall had sprung up between you and me, not that you were to blame, of course, nor Erlend either for that matter, but it was a wall. I know you sensed it too.

Once you and Jennifer were in bed Minna pottered about the sitting-room on her own, as I usually do. She switched on the television, I lay in bed listening my way through the sounds of news broadcasts on several different channels before she finally came to bed. I had been looking forward to her coming to bed. I think maybe I simply needed a bit of comforting.

But she didn't get into bed straight away, as she usually did. She came and sat down next to me on my side of the bed, like a mother with her son. She asked me tenderly if it was hard for me, you having a boyfriend. I didn't answer. She stroked my brow gently and said she knew how I felt, but that I should be proud that you had found yourself such a mature and sensible young man. After all, Erlend was a lot older than you, and he seemed mature for his years. I asked how she could tell. She said that she had met him briefly a couple of times at the library; he had been in to order some books by Nietzsche. They had talked about *The Birth of Tragedy*, he had complained that there was a lot in it that he didn't get, she had recommended that he read *Classical Philology*, he had taken out a volume. They had talked a little bit about it when he came to return the journals, he'd been raving about it. He seemed very bright, she thought.

Then she got undressed and snuggled in under my duvet. I felt her warm, sweet hand running over my chest. I lay there stiff as a board and could not touch her, I turned my face to the wall. I'd had no idea that she had read *The Birth of Tragedy*, she'd never told me that.

I didn't go to lectures the next week. I decided I would do the reading for the Prelim, but not sit the exam. Say I passed and got into university, what good would that do me? I'd really only be biting off more than I could chew: I already had a full-time job and a family to think of. There was no question of taking out a study loan, I had enough calls on my finances as it was, what with child maintenance for you and Judith's mortgage to pay. I would rather spend my afternoons with Jennifer. And I could continue with my classical studies on my own, during the holidays and in the evenings once Jennifer was in bed and if you weren't staying over. If you were, then I'd obviously want to spend time with you.

Eventually I abandoned the set books for the Prelim completely. I adopted a freer approach to my studies. I went back to the Eleusinian mysteries and began to take a closer look at the process of initiation through which the high priest Sarastro guides the prince and princess in *The Magic Flute*. You see Mozart was a Freemason, as your mother's father was, and I discovered that he had had a friend, Ignaz von Born, who was an expert in ancient Hellenic rites as well as the spiritual head of the Viennese Freemasons. Now here, surely, was a vital clue! Von Born died in the summer of 1791, the summer in which Mozart composed the music for *The Magic Flute*, before he too died, two months after the opera's maiden performance. It seemed only natural to assume that the character of Sarastro had been modelled on von Born, and there can be no doubt that the latter must have told Mozart about the Eleusinian mysteries. Perhaps on the occasion of Mozart's initiation into the Freemasons? Perhaps that was when he stopped being afraid of death. That lightness of his. I thought of that.

I sat with my headphones on, listening to the music from *The Magic Flute* with a fresh ear. I unearthed more books on Mozart at the library. I felt I was following a totally unique and original line of thought – if not exactly brilliant, at least it showed that my self-imposed studies were starting to bear fruit, and that I was capable of combining several branches of learning – always a sign of a certain intellectual maturity, wouldn't you say. Had I had a course supervisor at university I would most certainly have been encouraged to pursue the idea, no doubt about it, I thought to myself.

It was hard not to become a bit distant when I had all this to think about, it got to the point where a great deal of my time at home in the evenings was taken up with making sense of it all. There was such a vast amount of material on Mozart alone, some of it only available in German, so I had to get hold of a new German dictionary too. I tried to involve myself as much I could in day-to-day life with Minna and Jennifer and you, but I suppose I always knew this was an area that was mine alone, an area that you three had neither the possibility nor the desire to visit. There were evenings at home in the flat when I felt it would be best for everyone if I were to move out, find myself a little room and kitchen somewhere, so that I could bury myself in my work without bothering anyone.

But I love my little family, Ebba. I belong with it, without it I am nothing. And it hurts to lie beside your wife in bed at night taut as a bowstring and feel so alone. It was very wrong of me to withdraw the way I did when I found out about you and Erlend. I knew very well that I was the one with the problem, and that to retreat even further was not the answer. It occurred to me that I ought, instead, to gather my family together, we ought to do something together all four, to bring back the happy times. We ought to explore a mystery together. That was it! We could travel to Eleusia together, I thought, we could make a voyage of discovery into the mystery, together we might be able to make sense of all this business surrounding the initiation rites of the ancient Athenians. We could try to find out what it was that Ignaz von Born knew about what went on during these rites, knowledge to which he then made Mozart privy. We might be able to uncover the link between the Masonic rites and the myth of Demeter. We might well have the makings, there, of an article for some journal or other.

You know the rest. One Sunday morning a few weeks later when we were having breakfast, I mentioned these plans of mine to you and Minna, just in passing, as it were. And although I doubt if Minna realised how important it was for me to make this journey, she was, as you will remember, quite open to the idea, she was probably pleased to see me showing a bit of initiative again; she knew as well as you did that I had been a bit depressed recently. And you, of course, were over the moon. These days Eleusia is, by all accounts, a drab industrial area, but remains of the excavations can still be seen, so Minna told me, as if to save me from being disappointed. As if I didn't know. She suggested that we book a package holiday to Athens in the summer. You nodded eagerly. I was a little disappointed, I would have liked to set off right there and then, as soon as it could be arranged. But I realised that insisting on such a move would mean giving away too much.

It was hard to have to wait. I decided that in the meantime I could perhaps tell you about this secret interest of mine, the way I had once told you about the invisible boy sitting next to the radio and the effect the music had on him. I knew you would understand, I could talk to you about anything without feeling embarrassed. And it would whet your appetite for the trip. You've always taken my interests seriously, that is a great source of comfort and inspiration. It's nice to be able to share things.

And I know you remember that afternoon when I told you about all of this, and played Mozart's music for you. Of course you remember. I waited until Sunday had come round again and we were alone in the flat. Minna and Jennifer had driven off to one of the innumerable birthday parties that little girls are always being invited to these days. I can't recall there being so many birthday parties when you were little. Were there? Before they left, you helped Jennifer make herself pretty and wrap the present while Minna was in the bathroom, putting on her make-up. You kept up a conversation through the bathroom door, the usual cosy girl-talk which I loved having around me, I took it as a good sign.

You asked me to take a picture of you and Jennifer just before they left. Minna was standing next to me, looking at the two of you as I clicked the shutter; I think she was every bit as proud of you both as I was, it could just as easily have been her who took the picture.

I could tell that I was a bit tense; I had set things up the night before. I had weeded out the relevant books on Mozart and the Freemasons and placed them on the table next to my reading chair along with the books on Greek mythology, and I had put the CD of *The Magic Flute* into the CD player. As soon as the door closed behind Minna and Jennifer I came over to you and said there was something I wanted to show you. I think you were a bit taken aback, you had just settled yourself on the sofa and switched on the television, and I suppose it's not really like me to be so impulsive. But if you thought I was acting strangely you didn't let on. You immediately switched the television off and followed me over to the books on the desk; at my invitation you sat down in my reading chair, while I remained standing on the other side of the table, like a lecturer. I felt eloquent and rather proud, I outlined in brief what I knew about Mozart, the Freemasons and the initiation rites at Eleusia. I recounted the myth of Demeter and Persephone, the mother who grieved so relentlessly that she succeeded in having her daughter returned to her from the underworld. You listened quietly and attentively to my words, and afterwards, when I came round to your side of the desk to show you the books, you promptly started to leaf through them. I don't think your enthusiasm was affected.

After a while I retreated to the kitchen on the excuse that I had to see to the washing-up. I handed you the headphones and put on the CD of *The Magic Flute* for you, to save you having to get up. I said that I'd been thinking of buying a pair of really good headphones for you to keep back at home with you and Mama. And I kept my word, didn't I.

From where I was standing out in the kitchen I could see that you were really listening to the music, with the same concentration that you had shown ever since you were tiny. That made me so happy. I squirted a green jet of washing-up liquid into the sink, thinking to myself that this was something different from brooding and bleak thoughts, this had meaning.

I had got to the pots when I noticed that there were tears in your eyes. It moves you as deeply as it does me, I thought when I saw that, it's almost like old times, when we used to dance around the sitting-room. You understand me.

For a mere sixteen-year-old I thought you were very mature, I simply felt it was too early for you to start going out with men, that's all.

I know. You're right. I have to get up now. I have to brush the dust off my trousers. I have to ring the bell.

It's taking her a long time to open the door. She's probably had the safety chain on.

JUDITH SAYS

There's your father's car. Still the same hideous old banger! He's not driving right up to the door, see, he's parking out on the street. He's just sitting there. What's he sitting there for, it must be like an oven in that car . . . I need the binoculars . . .

What's he fumbling about for?

He's lighting a cigarette. Is he still doing that? Hasn't she even managed to get him to stop smoking? Has she no control over him?

He's just sitting there, see? He probably can't get it lit, his lighter's run out.

No: there.

Have to get on with the tidying up – can't let myself get distracted by him sitting out there fiddling about, he's such a coward, doesn't dare to come up to the house – mustn't let myself be distracted. Oh, it's hopeless, look at all this stuff of yours . . . do you have to be so untidy . . . look at this, all over the floor, what is all this . . . Look at these shoes, you grow so fast, your feet . . . it really is quite hopeless, if only he would take you in hand a little, but then he's never here, he doesn't care.

No. I'm just going to leave the whole lot on the floor. He can help sort it out, it's the least he can do, he is your father, after all.

He's looking up the driveway, oh yes, but he can't see me. I didn't think he would come. It's so late, I thought he'd changed his mind.

He's aged. I didn't realise he had aged so much, you never said anything about that, he's an old man, for heaven's sake. If I adjust the binoculars slightly he comes closer, comes right in to my eyes.

His hair's so short. He never wore it that short before! It used to annoy him if I so much as suggested cutting his hair for him, even though he knew I was a dab hand with the scissors, he liked it long and flowing.

When he lived here, it was always me who cut your hair, and he always said he thought you looked just lovely.

'My, don't you look lovely, my little caterpillar,' he would say. And you would giggle and wriggle about on his lap.

I saw a rat. It was lying quite still on a bench in the hospital gardens, but it wasn't dead. It had dark, glittering eyes, I could see it breathing. Its tail was long and glistening and coiled up alongside its body. It stared at me. I stared back. I had my mobile in my hand.

My fingers are cold. They smell bad. I saw a rat.

There's something itching here, it smarts. Someone will have to make it go away, put some salve on it. Come. Won't you come and make it go away.

Go on sitting here by the window, hold the binoculars up to my eyes, two spears shooting out from my eyes, d'you see, I poke them between the slats in the venetian blind. Or I could pull up the blind and bang on this pane of glass with the flat of my hand.

It'll make a clatter.

Pull up the blind. Clatter, clatter. There. You see.

Yes, love. I know.

Must calm down. Mustn't let my mind start thinking for itself, it can't take it. Must think of something concrete, something that keeps still. Must think of the words, mustn't leave out any of the words. Must say *I*.

I'm thinking about a rat. I saw a rat.

I'm thinking about it now. It was hot that morning too. That was a few days ago, wasn't it. I was sitting on the bench outside the hospital, it was early, but the traffic was heavy on the roads outside the hospital grounds. I was wearing my blue linen suit, it was all creased, I'd had it on all night. And my hair was dry and flyaway, I was like a walking electrical element in summer sandals, if anyone had come near me they would have got a shock.

But no one came near me. I couldn't see how they could fail to notice me, how people couldn't see just by looking at me that I was electric. They passed by on either side of the bench, wheeling bikes, or with children in pushchairs, busy with their own affairs.

The bench was an island. I was a stranded electric seal, on a bench a little further on lay a stranded electric rat. And the people passing by me were carried off by currents in the ocean; they had no will of their own, they were just swept away, to their jobs, to their schools, their offices, all the other places. Home. They had Home written in bright letters across their faces. I shook my head back and forth, not knowing whether to call out to them and point out the rat or let it be.

I don't understand why you did it. How could you conceive of such a thing? What were you thinking of?

The rat disappeared; all of a sudden it was gone, it made no sound.

It's half-past eight, isn't it? I know how late it is, you don't have to tell me, and I can count the days too, if that's what it takes. I can count any length of time you like, there's no end to the amount of days, or the amount of numbers with which to count them.

An endless stream of days. People who let themselves be swept along, the currents in the ocean, parting around the island.

An endless succession of numbers.

The low, almost imperceptible hum of the electrical element.

If time is to be counted then you have to organise it, right? Splitting it up into days is just one way of doing it. One also has to divide it up into hours. Or minutes. Or years.

An endless stream of years.

In each year a summer.

In each summer many, many nights.

An endless ocean of nights. The currents part around the island and flow past and the people flow with them, they pass by, not knowing that I am electric.

My nights have been spent with you. I don't remember any other nights. There are no other nights. When you don't remember something, it doesn't exist.

I don't think I've eaten anything lately. And I've stopped peeing, it must be the heat, don't you think?

I saw you. You were lying in the cold room. There were blue blotches on your face. You were wearing the pale-blue blouse that Mama ironed for you the other week, it had got all creased again, that's not like you, it's all wrong, clothes hardly ever crease on you, not even linen.

I nodded my head, the sign they needed. Mama and the vicar were waiting out in the corridor, not long afterwards Mama's sisters also appeared.

My voice doesn't know this language, my mouth just babbles on, listen to it, feeling so free.

My mobile phone was in the pocket of my suit jacket. I could feel the bulge of it on the outside, but I couldn't move my hand to take it out. My hand was paralysed. I had to call your father. I had tried to do so several times during the course of the night, I sat on a sofa in the hospital reception area and stared at the luminous buttons before pressing 180, I couldn't remember his number, I had to get the lady at directory enquiries to help me. It was a different lady every time, they all sounded as if they came from the west of Norway, they all spoke with the same crisp lilt, they had no idea who I was.

I sat on that leather sofa and pretended to be waiting for someone. I didn't want to be sent home. Mama and your great-aunts were hovering about somewhere in the background, I pretended not to know them, they were talking to doctors and nurses, they looked so pale, I wanted nothing to do with them, and they left me alone, as a mark of respect, maybe, I don't know. They seemed to be so busy all the time, sorting something out, sticking their heads together, putting their arms round one another, like an ice-hockey team going into a huddle before a match. They patted each other on the back. I whispered your father's name to the luminous buttons, so that no one would hear me.

'Sorrr-ay?' said the lady at directory enquiries. 'Could you rrre-peat that?'

I didn't want to ask for his home phone number, his and Minna's number, the phone was obviously under her name. I asked for his mobile number instead.

It would have been easier if I had had his number stored in my own phone. But I've never taken the time to find out how to do that, I don't even know what I've done with the instructions for use. If your father had been living here he could have helped me to key in all the necessary numbers, I wouldn't even have had to tell him which numbers were important. There were times when he could tell what I needed help with before I knew it myself. He knew my language. It calmed me and left me with a tiny red flame of joy somewhere inside me. It's a strange thing, to feel under-stood. I don't think I can have been used to that before I met him.

In the end I stopped calling. He must have switched his mobile off, there wasn't much likelihood of his switching it on again during the night, he was sure to be asleep. Nothing would start to function again until he woke.

When your father lived here people didn't carry mobile phones around in their pockets. Mobile phones came in big bags that looked a bit like intricate, old-fashioned cassette recorders, with the receiver sitting across the top; they came with a strap for slinging over the shoulder and they cost a fortune. Your father and I didn't know anyone who had a mobile phone in those days, we didn't know anyone who had a fortune. We two had the biggest mortgage of anyone we knew; when you were born we lived on crispbread every time the payments were due. This house turned out to be much more expensive than we had expected, but all the lovely, exclusive little details that we had come up with together made us happy. We wanted you to have the best. You like beautiful things, don't you? It's no accident that you have been surrounded by beautiful things all your life.

It's not true that material things don't bring happiness. And the fact that you really can't afford them only makes it that much better; then you look at one another and laugh as you pull out the soundless sliding door separating one room from another, you catch the scent of the oil in the lovely wood and run your fingers over the little brass hollow of the handle.

I was so weak in the knees after I had been to see you in the cold room. I must have stayed at the hospital all night; Mama and the vicar and the aunts may have gone home, I don't know what happened to them. They were no longer there when I woke up on the sofa, that much I know; maybe they thought that someone had admitted me, taken care of me. Maybe they had arranged for me to be in safe hands. Maybe they thought that things will always be all right in a hospital. They had probably all gone back to their own homes; maybe they were walking up and down, wringing their hands and sighing and tut-tutting. Although the vicar must have slept at home in his own bed, next to his soft vicar's wife. Vicars are heavy sleepers, he was probably deep in a dream.

When I woke up in reception, there were a lot of people round about me. I decided that I had better get up and go. It wasn't as if I didn't have a home to go to. I could take a taxi, I know how to book a taxi and Mama or one of her sisters had slipped some money into my pocket.

I said to a nurse walking by with a trolley-load of white plastic cups containing different coloured pills that I was going to go out and sit in the park for a while before I went home. She looked at me blankly, she didn't seem to know who I was, or why I was there. I got up and followed her, thinking that she was sure to be going out of the building, but she went a completely different way, she disappeared into a room and I couldn't find the way out. It couldn't have been very far away, but I was unable to find it, I walked up and down long hospital corridors adorned with hideous curtains and information posters showing pictures of children running and parents in brightly coloured sportswear with bike helmets on their heads, until someone put a hand on my shoulder and pointed towards the exit. It must have been one of the people Mama had spoken to. Maybe it was one of her sisters.

Outside the main entrance the warm summer morning beat against my face. It was so hot and dry, there was no respite from it.

Another nurse was standing smoking a cigarette next to a big round ashtray covered by a metal grating. She came over to me when I made no move to carry on down the steps. Suddenly I was perfectly lucid, the air must have helped after all. I turned slowly towards her and told her very distinctly that I had spent the night in reception after having been to identify my daughter in the cold room the previous evening. I sounded like a speech therapist. A troubled look came into her eyes. She offered to sit with me for a while on the bench I had marked out for myself. Her slim calves

148

were encased in white knee-length socks and she was wearing white clogs with plenty of toe room and hundreds of tiny air holes. I looked down at her feet and concentrated on those tiny holes. I think maybe she knew a bit about me, maybe she had been to a concert, or read about me in the paper. She wanted me to drink something. But I said no. I had decided to fast. There was nothing more to be said, it made no difference whether she was there or not.

I walked down the steps and sat down on the bench, then I took the phone out of my pocket again and pressed 180 again. That was when I saw the rat.

I got the lady at directory enquiries to put me through. By this time your father had switched his phone on again.

I think I shouted at him. All at once I was so angry. I felt unreal. I heard him trying to get me to calm down, but that only made me more angry, I could feel the sweat breaking out. After he had hung up, I sat with my eyes shut and my head lolling back; I had no strength in my neck.

When I opened my eyes again, the sky above me was almost colourless. I thought of my flowers. I thought to myself that I had better get home and water them. It was so dry, well it hasn't rained for weeks, has it. The thought of the flowers prompted me to shut my eyes again, I've started doing that lately. I make myself blind.

I don't think I thought much more that day. Possibly just that I fancied a lozenge. Something to suck, something sharp.

It was Erlend who found you. I was only just starting to get used to the idea of him having a name. I've never met his parents, but Mama says they're good people. He cut the rope from around the branch and laid you on the ground under the tree, that's what your father told me on the phone. He knows how to put such things, your father. Erlend is the sort who carries a knife.

You were stiff. You had an ugly welt around your throat, I saw it in the cold room.

Erlend will be here tomorrow, Mama says he's going to be one of the coffin bearers. I don't even know what he looks like, I've only heard his voice coming from inside your room. It was the voice of a grown man.

Where does he live? I don't know where he lives.

If I go out on to the steps and put on your boots, they will carry my feet across the grass and over to the fence between our ground and the wood. I have more rope in the car, as you know. Everything is ready. Your boots are two sizes too small, but I think I've got smaller over the past few days, I might well be able to get into them anyway. I'm not about to give up.

You mustn't be afraid. I'll always be with you. Parents should always be with their children. When they lose a child they have to look and look until they find that child. They have to put on their boots and go out into the night, even if the boots are too small, and they have to walk and walk and call and call – they have to carry flaming brands and electric torches and call out as loud as they can – they must not stop until they find her. And once they have found her they must stay with her. They must never leave their child again.

I stood outside your door, listening. Do you remember, it was early spring; outside the days were starting to get lighter, and when I got home from the Conservatory in the late afternoon there was a strange pair of trainers in the hall. Set neatly alongside your winter boots.

I supppose you could say it was a sign that he was well brought up, his shoes being lined up like that. On one of the hooks hung a battered dark leather jacket, just like the one that Johan had when he lived here, and he had hung it on the very hook on which Johan used to hang his.

I left the bags of groceries and my violin case on the sitting-room floor and crept up the stairs. The sounds from your room were soft and muffled. I could hear you laughing quietly, he was clearly repeating the same sentence over and over again, it sounded as if he were imitating something, maybe he was a bit of a comedian. You repeated something, with a giggle in your voice, he said the same thing yet again and you laughed even harder. Then, for a long time, there was silence.

I simply couldn't see what could be so funny. I couldn't bring myself to knock on the door, I just stood there, I was a chill statue. My breath was like ice, had I been one step closer to your door I could have left a frosty flower on it, a rose.

I didn't know what else to do, so I crept back down the stairs. I flopped down on to the sofa in the sitting-room like a bundle of rags in boots and coat and pulled the blanket over me.

Evening fell slowly around me there in the sitting-room. The light turned from bright yellow to greyish, then blue, then just dark. There were no sounds from the street outside. I could see the light from the lamp in the hall, all the furniture in the sitting-room stood so still round about me, as if it were guarding something. I may have dozed off.

Eventually I heard the two of you coming down the stairs. You walked him out to the hall, you were both sniggering a little, he would have been putting on his shoes and jacket, then I heard some low murmuring sounds before the door clicked shut behind him. I think it was only once you had locked the door behind him and put on the safety chain, the way I had instilled in you, that you noticed the plastic bags full of groceries strewn about the floor. When you caught sight of me on the sofa you cried out in fright. I don't remember what it was that you cried. I felt ghastly. You came over to me and sat down beside me, you took my hand gently in yours, as if meaning to lead me away from something. I sat up and laid my head on your shoulder. I had been far too hot, lying underneath that blanket with my coat on, I felt as if I had a fever.

You helped me to take off my outdoor things, went around the room switching on all the lights, turned the radio on full blast. The news was on, you promptly switched to another channel, one playing classical music; you know I hate the news broadcasts. Then you lifted the bags of groceries off the floor and carried them into the kitchen, you switched on all the lights in there too. After a while I joined you in the kitchen, sat at the table and watched you putting things away in the fridge. I said I would make dinner, but you just shook your head and smiled at me, as if to assure me that it was all taken care of. I could tell that you were worried, but you couldn't help that, you were happy too, your worry was but a thin film over the lightness, the shimmer.

But I really had to pull myself together. I was your mother, I couldn't leave you to shoulder everything alone, I had to do my share. I began to set the table, even though all I really wanted to do was to lie down, I felt so awful.

We tried to keep up a light, jokey conversation over dinner, but we made no mention of the boy who had been here. We lit candles as we always did, but nothing was the same as before. I made an attempt to say something funny, but my joke fell flat, didn't it, I don't think I told it properly.

I couldn't bring myself to ask who he was either, the question swelled in my mouth, you must have noticed, but you weren't going to help me, and I couldn't get it out. Instead I cut up small pieces of potato and put them in. Why wouldn't you help me?

When we were getting ready for bed you suggested that we read stories in my bed, remember? The way we used to do when you were little. Your face was stern. We cleared away the remains of dinner and put the dirty dishes in the dishwasher, then we went around together switching off all the lights on the ground floor, went upstairs and got into our nighties, each in our own room. We met in the bathroom and brushed our teeth standing side by side in front of the big mirror. I looked at your reflection in the glass, as you stood there next to me. You had grown so tall, almost as tall as me; by the time you stopped growing you would probably be as tall as your father, I thought. We brushed each other's hair, gently as always. We have the same tender heads, and take the same care not to tug, don't we? We're so alike. Behind us in the mirror we could see the reflection of the wood outside the bathroom window. Then we went through to my room and got into the big bed. We left the window open to the night outside.

You had fetched the old, dog-eared collection of fairy tales from your bookcase and left it ready and waiting on the bedside table, the way you always did when you were little. I laughed and said you were way too big for this sort of thing, what was all this; I reached for my reading glasses on the bedside table, but you stayed my hand. You opened the book. It was you who did the reading. It was all wrong.

It's only words. It can't hurt that much if it's just words. They link up. I can get them to fit together, do you hear?

I was in such a deep dream that afternoon before the vicar rang the bell; it was so hot, I lay under the blanket on the sofa, sweating. I dreamt that I had gone out to the cottage to fish. It was twilight. I stood on the shore and looked out across the fjord. There wasn't a breath of wind – I saw a sailboat out there, it wasn't moving.

I hadn't caught any fish. Then suddenly I felt something really heavy on the end of my line. It was so heavy that it threatened to pull me into the water. When I finally managed to land my catch I found that it was a large seal. It was white, with big solemn eyes. I'm sure it must have been a female, a full-grown female, it was plump with blubber and had long whiskers. The fishing hook had lodged in its tongue. The seal opened its mouth to let me remove the hook, but I couldn't get it out. I grew more and more upset about this, my fingers stiffened up, I did not want such a seal on my line, it was far too big for me to kill it, and I couldn't get it back out into the water as long as it was caught on my line.

In the end I just walked away. I left the fishing rod lying next to the seal. It felt I had failed. I told myself that I was going to fetch help, but I knew that it was already too late. The seal turned its head and followed me with its great big eyes.

The vicar only rang the doorbell once. He ought to have rung it more than once. Possibly three times; a clear signal for special occasions of this sort.

Ring. Ring. Ring.

Only one ring and it could be anybody. It could be someone selling raffle tickets.

Don't ask me why I'm telling you about that dream. We always tell each other our dreams.

Someone asked me once: who would you most like to be stranded with on a desert island? This reporter called one evening, she didn't really seem to have any idea who I was; some editor had probably given her my name, maybe just someone on the desk. This was years ago – you must have been about eight or nine, we were in the middle of reading your bedtime story when the phone rang. We had slumped down against one another under the duvet in my bed, we knew that tale by heart: *And still she sat, and still she reeled and still she wished for company*.

Anyway, the phone rang. I was annoyed at being interrupted and replied that if I was ever unfortunate enough to be stranded on a desert island I would have more to think about than being sociable. I'd much rather have my violin with me, so that I could use the time to practise.

It did not look good in print. It was quite a big piece, accompanied by a picture they must have had in their files, from the time when Johan was living here; I looked radiant and inspired, but the picture didn't go very well with the text. Afterwards I regretted having been so brusque with that reporter. It's best to keep in with reporters, you never know when you're likely to run into them again.

Later I noticed that you had cut out that picture, you had obviously come upon the newspaper. You had snipped evenly along the edges, with the big kitchen scissors I assume, and folded it neatly, and kept it in your album. I didn't discover it until much later. I found it rather embarrassing that of all pictures you should have kept the one from that stupid interview, but I couldn't exactly turn round and offer you one of my good reviews instead, I realised that. I knew that you were proud of me and that you were too young to understand that I actually came over in that interview as being a bit arrogant. I guess you must just have liked the picture; maybe it reminded you of something. I could hardly take your memories from you, now could I, that would have been heartless. I've only ever wanted the best for you, I know you know that.

Ebba.

Who will look after me when I'm old if you're not there? Who will come to visit me and buy me flowers for Mother's Day? Who will come and pat my hand and put moisturiser on my parched face when I'm so weak that I can't lift my hands to do so myself? Not Johan, that's for sure. Johan will never come to visit me. It will be a relief for Johan when I am gone.

Who will look at me and smile? Who will look at me?

If you aren't there to look at me, I will disappear.

My hands are so cold. They smell bad – here, sniff them.

When Johan lived here he instinctively knew if I needed help. He helped me to comb out my hair after I had washed it.

Look. He's leaning forward in the car seat, looking up at the house. He can't see me, all I need is a little chink between the slats. My knees are stiff, I've been kneeling here on the sofa for such a long time. I'm keeping a lookout. He took his time getting here, I thought he had changed his mind. Normally he doesn't like coming to see me, as you well know – it's been hard to hide it from you, usually he'll do anything to get out of it.

The taxi brought me right to the door that morning when I came back from the hospital; all I had to do was to walk up the steps and put my key in the door. The house was full of people, far too many people. I decided to be awkward and sent them all home again. I think they had the idea that I was angry. They left after a while, but they keep coming back, Mama and her sisters and a few of the neighbours, people I normally never see anything of. It was your father who knew the neighbours. I feel like telling everyone who comes to the door just to turn right round and go away again. But it becomes more and more difficult with each visit, they are digging themselves in here, they have seen to things in the kitchen and put food away in the fridge, buns and dishes covered in cling film and no doubt stuff in the larder in the basement too, I haven't been down there.

And they have arranged flowers in vases all over the place. See? There's an enormous coffee urn on the bench in the kitchen; I couldn't help thinking of a chapel when I went in there and saw it, I sat down on the floor.

Before the last of them left some time ago they said that all the arrangements for the funeral had been made. It's set for tomorrow, it's not that long until then, only a few hours; the hours flow off with the current and part around this island on which I sit. I don't need to think about a thing, they have told me a thousand times, all your father and I have to do is agree on where we are to sit in the chapel, and on the order of the speeches. Whether one of us will say a few words.

I am going to sit at the front in the church, next to Mama. Johan and Minna and your sister will sit behind us, or across the aisle.

It's important to distribute the weight evenly between both elbows on the window-sill, so as not to put so much strain on the back. If I waggle the binoculars up and down a little the double image of his old man's head bobs up and down. I almost feel sorry for him, he looks so pathetic bobbing about in his car like that.

These are good, clear binoculars, although I don't need to tell you that, it was you who gave them to me, for my birthday some years back. Five years ago, was it? Yes, it must be five years. I don't know where the years go.

It was just the two of us for my birthday dinner. Mama was meant to be there, too, as usual, but she had called a couple of hours before we were due to sit down to dinner to say that she had received an invitation which she could hardly turn down, from one of her women friends who wasn't feeling well. Mama has a lot of friends, wouldn't you say, they have their yoga class and their gardening club and their subscription to the theatre.

When I told you she wasn't coming you were so disappointed. I could tell that you went out of your way to be the life and soul of the party, so that I wouldn't feel sad. My little girl. We made a lovely birthday dinner together, we two.

On the table was the annual bouquet of flowers from Jørgen. He always remembers my birthday, I find it just as touching every year. And you had made one of your colourful birthday cards, just as you have done ever since you were a little girl; you're so good with your hands, the colours were so pretty, pink and green wasn't it, done in pastels, with glitter sprinkled over glue; it lay on my plate. You had made everything look so nice, you're so good at that sort of thing, you have such a good eye. Your present was lying next to my wine glass, I could tell by the paper that it came from a shop near Johan's place. You fetched a pair of scissors that I could use to unwrap the parcel with care, in case I wanted to keep the lovely paper. That's something you've picked up from your grandmother, I know; I've never seen the point in hanging on to old bits of paper. It only clutters up the place, you never actually get round to wrapping other presents in the old stuff. When you buy a new present in a shop they'll always giftwrap it for you anyway if you ask. But it's a nice thought, it says something about you. Carefully I cut off the sellotape, folded the paper and stuck it under my plate before turning to admire the binoculars. I realised that you must have had help to buy them; you didn't have much money of your own in those days – you were only eleven after all.

I knew that Johan had been away from home for several weeks on business, so someone else must have helped you to buy them. It wrenched my heart. But I didn't ask you who had helped you, I merely pretended to be thrilled.

The binoculars are collapsible – they make things that are a long way off seem uncannily close. We tried them out on each other during dinner, but we were far too close to one another to begin with, sitting there on either side of the big table, we were nothing but a dancing blur at the other end of the lens. They needed to be trained on something much further away.

After dinner we went into the garden and tried them out there, that was better. You could stand here, outside the house, and study every blade of grass, every tiny insect on the other side of the lawn, remember? When we trained the binoculars on the forest we could see the pine needles on the ground in there.

Do you remember how they work? If I turn this knob here and hold them steady, I can bring the image of your father in his car sharply into focus in my field of view; there.

He is almost unrecognisable, it's so long since I saw him. His hair is still dark, but he has shaved off his beard. Do you see? You never told me that. Why did you never tell me anything about Johan, Ebba?

I can't ever remember seeing his chin so smooth before, it looks like india rubber.

Dark and shiny, his hair is. You have his hair. He planted such a dark daughter inside me. The first time I laid eyes on you I couldn't believe that you had come from my body, your eyes were all screwed up and you had hard little fists and dark woolly hair. You were red all over, with a thin layer of pale-yellow grease coating the folds of your neck. I got such a fright when I saw you, you got a fright too, you screamed like a belligerent little animal. All the time you were inside me you didn't make a sound, but now you were a siren.

The first movement I saw you make was a clenched fist lifted to your eyes. But they put you to my breast and you seemed to unfold in my warmth. My belly was a garden on the outside too, just as the inside had been a garden for you, my belly was big and soft. And you quietened down and took root in me, you were my flower, your roots were my veins, carrying the blood around my body. And one by one the petals opened, allowing your eyes to open up to the light, allowing your tiny fingers to open out one by one. The redness faded and you became pink and pure and transluscent.

After a few weeks the black hair fell off in tufts. It was left behind on your pillow, every evening we had to brush it away. And in its place grew a silky down, much lighter than his, but still darker than mine. As the years went on it turned quite, quite dark. You looked like me, but in your hair colour you favoured him, it made you even more his daughter. Neither your father nor I knew what to think about it, we never talked about it. We, who used to talk about everything. We, who were so used to letting the words flow between us, like a current, like water. We, who bathed in our own words and laughed every time we dived under.

I have read that almost every woman who picks up a child will hold it to her heart side. I kept this to myself, but I watched your father closely the first few times he lifted you, and he always held you against his left side. He would stand over by the window, his heart side turned away from me; first he would hold you in to his heart, then he would hold you up to the window to let you see. I would have done the same, if I had been able to get up on my feet. He's a woman, I thought to myself, and I don't think I liked the idea. He doesn't know it himself, but he is a woman. It's really he who should have had you, you should have come from his body. That's what I thought back then, Ebba.

Look at the way he holds his head. There's something there that he's not yet aware of. He is not broken. His neck is whole and unbowed. A bit stiff. See?

I don't know where he gets it from, his father perhaps, your grandfather; he's always been like that.

He hasn't seen you. I'm the one who has seen you. He doesn't know that there are blotches on your face and a dark weal around your neck. Only I know that.

No. He knows something too. He is not in the right and he's no longer young either, but a long corridor stretches out behind him, see, it runs on down the road. I don't want to know any more.

I have seen that corridor before.

Shall I tell you how we met? I don't suppose I've been all that good at telling you about those days.

He was sitting on a bench in the park. I walked up to him. I was wearing leather gloves – the ones I lost later on when your father and I were on a winter break to Poland, and the fur hat that Mama had bought for me the winter that I broke up with Jørgen.

He had on his brown leather jacket, it was cold for the time of year. I knew he wanted me. I pulled off my gloves and placed my hands over his ears. I bent down and blew a king into him.

I was so young then. Such short skirts and not a care for whether my shoes were sensible or not, but always a fur hat in the wintertime. Not surprisingly I was forever catching cold, but I never gave it much thought. Not like now; these days the slightest hint of a cold and I'm on my back with a blanket over me, aren't I, tucking it in at all the corners, packing it round my feet. Back then I laid myself open to everything, germs, smiles, all the words that came my way. That didn't stop me from blowing my top every now and again, though. I could change my mind so fast, as fast as the whims of fashion. And I did follow fashion, I did it by instinct. My instincts have altered since then. Wouldn't you say so?

Before I met Johan, I had a picture of a man in my mind. I thought of this as being a picture of the man of my life and I looked everywhere for him. I didn't know how he looked, but I knew what would happen inside me when I found him. It would start as a swelling, then this swelling would start to sway, as if in a kind of dance inside me. I know exactly how that dance would be, it would make me feel like . . . Judith. A wave that started in the pit of my stomach and wound its way up to my throat and my face and caused my mouth to open in a surprised . . . gasp. Yes. A gasp.

Sometimes I thought I had found him. He might come walking towards me along a street. I'd have seen him the evening before at a table in a restaurant, he'd be with some other people, but I would feel that he looked as though he needed me. And I would feel that I recognised something in him. In time this man whom I imagined was Johan would come closer and closer and

161

before I knew it we would be in bed together, our arms and legs loose and easy, and we'd be discussing who should shower first.

But I was wrong, of course, he was not Mr Right at all, he was Mr Wrong. And he was definitely not Johan. He was usually a musician. For a long spell he was Jørgen. It was all wrong. Well, Jørgen isn't your father, is he?

In the end I always had to turn my face away, it would become more and more evident just how wrong I had been. The swelling I had felt for the man who came walking towards me along the street or was standing over by the window at a party for the orchestra was not the true swelling. He had not made me feel like Judith at all. I had simply happened to give a somewhat ill-considered wave of the hand, flashed a particular glance, raised a glass. And then of course there was a terrible fuss, with me having to explain to the man who was Mr Wrong how it was all a mis-understanding. Such things are not easily explained.

This was always followed by a long phase of going over the same old ground of wooing and rejection, breaking up and making up. Long, accusatory phone calls in the middle of the night, neck muscles that tensed up and made it impossible to play, the same old stress and aggravation that I had had with other men. All the time I expended on them, you'd think I would have known better. This one wears glasses, I would think, searching for excuses and paying the price. This one wears glasses and grinds his teeth in his sleep. He doesn't check that the door is locked before he goes to bed. So he can't be the one.

Or else he was the one who left me, who let me stand alone outside his house for a whole night, watching the windows being shut one by one, the way Jørgen did it.

Well, almost a whole night. A whole hour, then I caught cold again and lost my voice. You know how little it takes for me. One by one the windows were shut while I stood alone and freezing on the street outside.

And then, on that afternoon in March, I saw Johan sitting there on a bench outside the town hall. I was probably on my way to rehearsals at the Opera, I had my violin case with me, and a letter to Mama in my pocket. This was at the time when I used to write down my dreams and send them to her; she and her friends had developed an interest in the interpretation of dreams, they had started their own dreams group. I think that interest is on the wane, didn't you get that impression too, they've taken to going to the theatre instead.

We were working on *The Magic Flute* at the time. The moment I saw him sitting there I could tell that he was someone who would enjoy *The Magic Flute*, and I wanted to be the one to present it to him. Not that he didn't already know it, of course, he was a member of the Friends of the Orchestra after all, but none the less I was proved right: it was me who presented it to him. He loved watching me in the orchestra pit, he always sat up in the gods so that he could see the whole of the pit; he attended as many rehearsals as he could, I think he skived off work. I liked to think that we were playing just for him, that somewhere way up there he was perched like a bird, watching, and knowing that we were giving him our best. He looked a bit peaky, sitting there on the bench that morning, as if the light was too bright for him. His hands were clenched into fists in his jacket pockets.

I walked right up to him and sat down beside him. I was sure that I would soon feel that swelling. Like a bud. I didn't doubt it for a minute, this time it was different. I took off my gloves, placed my hands over his ears and felt how cold they were.

I can see his ears as clear as day, I can make them as big as I like, all I have to do is adjust this setting on the top of the binoculars. They're something else, those ears, they don't really seem to be aware of one another. Like twins who have lived all their lives not knowing that the other one exists: brought up in different families, living their own separate lives on either side of his head, and yearning for one another all the time. They are tuned in different directions. What the one ear hears the other doesn't catch, you can tell by the way he shifts his gaze. You've noticed it too, haven't you? His eyes avoid looking in the direction from which the sound comes. There is something he does not want to hear.

When he lived here I could reach out a hand and trace the line of his ear with my finger; nice rounded arches. I could lean forward and whisper in his ear:

'What are you listening for?'

And I would follow the way the sound was transmitted through the narrow orifice of the ear and further into his head, along narrower and narrower passages until it struck the little hammer and the little anvil deep within and set something in motion. Something began to vibrate deep inside his head and those vibrations produced a meaning somewhere in the brain.

Now and again he would think what I wanted him to think. But usually he would think something quite different, it was the same with you. Something dark. You were so obviously his daughter, it wasn't just the hair.

He looked at me back then and he listened to what I said.

He's different now, though. Look, he's heard a sound. It wasn't me who whispered. Was it you? Both his eyes are turned towards the sound. Was it you, Ebba? Was it you?

Then it must be the birds in the wood behind the house he hears, their singing is so supernaturally loud and shrill.

No. They're quiet as can be. Not a sound from them. Not a sound, I tell you.

It was he who let go, not me. If my voice could carry that far back I would shout that to myself, from now to the day when I sat on the floor in the hall with you in my arms after he had gone, thinking that I stank of cod:

'Judith, my love, it's not your fault.'

But there's no guarantee that I would hear. Maybe I wouldn't want to hear. Maybe I wouldn't recognise my own voice, it's so different now, everything is different, it's hard to remember exactly how things were back then.

His shirt is blue and frayed. It's not the smartest of cars, is it, it's the same one that he bought just after I passed my test and needed our family car. I've seen this one parked out there once before, in exactly the same spot. That time it was Minna who was sitting in it. I haven't forgotten, if that's what you think.

He can't be that much better off after all these years. He may even be worse off. His hand rises off the steering-wheel and stops in mid-air; smoke curls from his cigarette.

In our early days together we would make love a hundred times a day. We couldn't get enough of one another, it was almost painful, we were like kittens, rolling around together and biting one another in the scruff of the neck the minute we had a room to ourselves. We laughed, and we were so solemn that we wept. We often talked while we were making love. I don't remember what we said.

Our love was all consuming. There was so much within us that we had not discovered before and suddenly there we lay, face to face, wide open, like fresh maps marked with no names except those of the best known peaks and rivers. We were forever coming up with new names.

I was playing better than ever before, several people remarked upon it, I was given lots of solos, and more compliments from colleagues and reviewers than I had had in a long time. It was as if everyone knew what was going on and were sending discreet messages of congratulation.

I became conscious of my body in a new way. It was at one and the same time lighter and stronger. I was supple as a rock climber, I didn't have to apologise for anything whatsoever. I began to consider applying for the position that was due to become vacant with the symphony orchestra.

We were so happy when we found out that I was pregnant. I had been away on tour for some weeks before that so it wasn't too hard to calculate the exact date of your conception. It must have happened here, on the sofa in the sitting-room, the house was scarcely finished, we had just moved in, I think.

I remember that morning when I came home from the hospital with you. Johan had done up the nursery so beautifully while I was away, he had finished papering the walls and fixed up a little night light, made up the little cot with the freshly ironed bedclothes that I had laid out. Mama had been over and hung new curtains sprigged with tiny pink flowers, and the window was slightly open. A gentle breeze passed through the room as I opened the door with you in my arms, it made the curtains billow out, I could tell by your eyes that you could see them. Well, your certainly not blind, I thought, and you're not deaf. I don't know why such a thought should have crossed my mind.

I laid you in the cot and spread the tiny duvet over you, closed the window. Johan was down in the kitchen preparing a special dinner, he had it all planned out, he had heard that lamb chops were the right thing for a new mother. Lamb chops and red wine. His thoughtfulness really touched me. At the hospital, the morning after you were born, he had given me a beautiful pearl ring. I was wearing it that evening; it was a bit tight, but I didn't tell him that, I thought maybe I could take it to a jeweller's and have it enlarged without him knowing. He did so want everything to be perfect.

He had brought in an old chest of drawers that I had had in my room at Mama's house in town. I expect he had stowed it away in the loft at the terraced house when she moved out here, they must have agreed between themselves that it should go into the new room for you when you were born. I remember he had a sore back for weeks after helping Mama move; I've often wondered since then whether it was because of that heavy chest of drawers, and the thought makes me happy, and a little sad.

On top of the chest of drawers someone had put two photographs in lovely silver frames – Johan and me as children. And I said to myself: that's Little Judith and Little Johan. I don't think I've ever told you about them. It's a bit complicated, I'll explain it to you some other time perhaps. See how they smile, I thought. Little Judith and Little Johan are talking to one another, now they have a little sister.

You went to sleep in your new cot straight away, I think you felt secure. I sat for a while on the floor beside you, my back against the chest of drawers. I thought to myself: now I can't ever die. I'm a mother now, and a mother must not die. That thought came as a roll of thunder from some place beyond my view, it ruined something for me, something ended when that thought struck me.

The thought that the child might die and leave the mother did not cross my mind. It did not exist. Now it exists.

Help me.

During those first days we were quite obsessed with your mouth. You had a little rosebud mouth, it puckered up, seeking, you twisted your head and your mouth knew where to go, to my breast. Your father and I immersed ourselves in your mouth, we gazed at your little hands, watched how they searched your face, almost invariably lighting on the area around your mouth and nose. Later we noted your ears, how they conducted sound into your head and prompted you to turn towards the spot from which the sound had come. My smacking lips or his clapping hands. We both agreed that you had his ears, which he, in his turn, had inherited from your grandma. 'She's not blind,' we told each other, 'and she's certainly not deaf.'

But there was something in him that turned him away from you and me right from the start. Something alien inside him, a dark core that I could not reach.

I discovered that core before he discovered it himself.

We had been one entity, one big *we*, a sum that was greater than our two parts. As individuals Johan and I were two small, separate and insignificant figures, but together we were a *we*, we were your parents, it was vast, it was like a ballroom. And I so badly needed to be a part of that grand room. It did me so much good. I needed to breathe as freely as I breathed there. I did not know what I had been missing until I found myself there.

But I could do nothing about that dark core of his. All the signs told me so.

Maybe he wasn't big and secure enough in himself to inhabit the room we had created. Maybe he was just a little boy, his mouth seeking his mother's breast, a little boy with fingers like little bitty thin strands of rope and dark woolly hair that eventually fell out in tufts.

He did not want to see that I knew about this side of him. He saw it, but he did not want to recognise what he saw. He was blind, and his ears could not hear; there were times when I couldn't stand being near him, he made me sick, with that bewildered look on his face.

I think the first time I saw that look must have been when he discovered that I had dug flower beds in the garden and put pots of nasturtiums all the way up the drive. I had inherited the shrubs from Mama's old garden, those dahlias are over forty years old, did you know that? She planted them while she was expecting me. They were superb. He didn't understand why I should have done such a thing, he didn't know what I meant by it, he was very annoyed and confused. And I couldn't explain it to him. I realised that there were some things he simply could not understand. Not ever. All at once I felt so lonely; somehow I hadn't been prepared for such loneliness, I had to go and lie down, my fingers puffed up with fluid; I had the most confusing dream. In this dream I was sliding down a banister, down and down, I never did reach the bottom. I remember that I told Mama about it, I wrote it down when I woke up.

He let go of me. First he was holding me, then all of a sudden he let go of me. It hurt so much when I fell. There was no one there to catch me. I simply slid all the way down.

When he let go of me he also let go of you, and I'll never forgive him for that. He knew what he was doing, you and I went together, he couldn't let go of me without letting go of you. You had your arms round my neck, he knew that, your skinny arms were wrapped around me, I had to talk to you in a calm, adult fashion.

You mustn't ever let go of anyone. Once you've started holding on to them you have to keep holding on to them, because if you don't they will fall and hurt themselves. Do you hear me, Ebba!

For the first few nights after he moved out, Mama slept here with us. I doubt if you remember. She was my strength, she slept in our double bed, on his side, she took up more space than he had and she lay down to sleep with her back to me. She thought she might have snored a bit she told me the first morning, but I hadn't heard a thing, I had slept heavily and dreamlessly. I'd taken the pills she had given me and when she came to wake me I didn't want to know, all I wanted to do was sleep. I wanted to slide down into the darkness and warmth.

But as time went on I did have to manage on my own, and I couldn't go on taking such strong medication, both the doctor and Mama said so. I had to stay awake in order to look after you, it seemed as if they had discussed this and were in agreement. I was a subject for discussion.

But it was so hard to be strong and alert, Ebba. My eyes were so dry and strained, there was so much they had to watch out for, and all they wanted to do was rest. One afternoon I found you out in the hall; you were right at the back of the corner where we keep the umbrellas, wrapped in your father's winter coat, I had to dig you out. I held you in my arms for a long, long time, we both sat there among the shoes and wept. And I could see that you were nursing a sorrow of your own inside that coat, but I was cold too. I propped my eyes wide open, but I couldn't share my sorrow with you. You were so young, I had to look after you; it was all so unreal, I couldn't get to grips with your sorrow, it was like mist. There was a terrible smell from my hands. I wiped them on my thighs, but it wouldn't go away.

I felt ashamed. I couldn't understand how nothingness could hurt so much and smell so bad. I was only breathing high up in my throat, my breath was thin and cold. We got up, went through to the kitchen and made cocoa, I mixed it strong and sweet. Later that evening I hung Johan's winter coat in the loft in a storage bag. When you have children you have to make an effort, you can't give up. As long as the children are awake you have to be awake too. You have to hold them close, Ebba.

I felt ashamed for a long time after he left. Of the way I smelt, as if I were disintegrating; of my strained, ugly eyes, of the fact that I couldn't make a decent meal, that there were so many things I had to ask Mama, that I didn't know how to change a fuse and was the only mother in your class who came alone to parent-teacher meetings. Johan said he would come, but he never did. Maybe he made a separate appointment to talk to your teacher.

Mama said it wasn't my fault, I shouldn't blame myself. She had seen it coming right from the start, he had never been right for me. But I didn't believe her. I could see why no one would want me, I had got so thin and I stank of fish.

Things are different now. I can see that I had got it all wrong; luckily Mama and her friends have helped me. She would ask me what I had dreamt and I would draw and describe and do the best I could. She helped me to shake off the shame and she showed me that I mustn't let him have power over me, mustn't allow him to make me think such things about myself.

It was he who had let go, not me.

It may be that I taught him something about the nature of betrayal back then, once I eventually pulled myself together a bit. I got him to look at himself. I held a big mirror up to him, I forced him to look into it; I held it and held it, with my last ounce of strength I held it. I felt I had to, for the truth's sake, for my truth's sake. For your sake.

Mirrors do not flatter; they are smooth and shiny and they show the truth. But they are so heavy when you simply have to go on holding them and cannot let go, Ebba. Your grip becomes so stiff, your fingers go to sleep.

After he left I watered my flowers as if they were thirsty children.

I think I could have put up with him having other women, if only he had told me about them himself. I had to know that I could trust him.

I know it is possible to love more than one person, as long as you don't love them in the same way. One mustn't be allowed to take anything away from the other. It's like being a mother, everyone knows that a mother can love more than just one of her children. That's not the problem. I've talked about this a lot with Mama, she understands these things.

What I could not put up with was him undermining our *we*. But the fact that he let me fall the way he did could only mean either that he could not be trusted or that he did not understand, which to my mind at that time amounted to the same thing. And still does, really. If I can't trust a man he becomes nothing to me but a passer-by, just one among all the other spineless, oversexed characters out there. I have enough men like that in my life, the sort that's looking for someone who will pet him and look up to him. That's what they are. Oversexed and spineless.

I thought Johan and I would hold on to one another. I thought he was different.

I could tell that something was going on even before he knew it himself. I wasn't sure who the other woman was, but I took it that she would be different from me. I'd known about it all winter, certainly long before I went on tour that summer when you were three and a half. All through the spring he had been getting on my nerves slightly; my symptoms began to crop up more frequently, my playing suffered and I saw how this pushed him away from me. I noticed it long before he was aware of it himself; I just didn't know what to do about it.

I knew only too well what he was thinking: it had gradually become clear to him that life with me was not what he had expected. But it had also become more and more obvious to me that he would never be able to live up to my standards where certain things were concerned. He wasn't a great one for socialising, for example, which made it difficult for me, since I had to attend so many functions to do with the orchestra. Often I had to go on my own while he stayed home to watch you, even though Mama was always offering to babysit. Other times he would make the excuse that he had some job to do around the house: there was always something that needed fixing or doing up, some alteration that had to be made; he was never satisfied and even when you were just a tot you seemed to like nothing better than to be his little helper.

And then there was the fact that he didn't much like travelling either. Apart from the woodwork side, and all the other stuff to do with the house, for which, as it turned out, he proved to have a real gift, he was not nearly as good as I had imagined when it came to practical matters or decisions that had to be made.

I remember one time when Mama had given him the job of investing some money left by your grandfather; she'd had it lying in an ordinary savings account, where it didn't earn much interest. He made such a big deal of it, went to see a financial advisor at the bank and read the financial pages in the newspapers for weeks before putting the money into shares which plummeted in value only a couple of weeks later. Mama was extremely annoyed, naturally. Your grandfather had never made a bad investment in his life, she wasn't used to that sort of thing, she was used to being taken care of, of feeling secure. I felt embarrassed for Johan too. Mama got one of Papa's old friends from the lodge to transfer what was left of the money into some unit trusts that were as safe as the bank and the matter was never mentioned between us again. But for a long time afterwards I could not help feeling that Johan had let us down. He didn't seem to have any sense for – how can I put it – our family standard, the standard that Mama and I were used to from when Papa was alive. You never met him, he was an incredibly strong, distinct character.

Because your father was so unspeakably naive he thought that the moment he felt attracted to another woman he would have to choose between her and me. If only he had known the number of men to whom I had felt attracted. A love affair is nothing but a lot of hormones running amok in your system for a while, they have names, it's only chemistry, and after a while they run out of steam and disappear. You can't make choices that affect the rest of your life on the basis of a load of chemicals in your system. Not when you have children. Not when you have a *we*, a ballroom in which to breathe, bigger than any other room.

He loved me, he would always be there for me, that's what he had whispered to me the first night we spent together. And I laid myself open to his words, I laid myself open to what he was, I lived in that, I surrendered to those words. They made me strong and distinct, to myself and to all the world.

And then he let go. It was nothing but words, he forced me to see that. He had lain in my bed and said that he had never been so real as when he was with me, but it was only some words that he'd cobbled together. When something is nothing but words, it comes undone almost immediately, there's no way you can hang on to it if it's nothing but words.

It's so simple you could scream, that's all there is to it.

You have to learn to hold on to yourself. And you have to hold on to your child. You don't have to be afraid, I won't do what he did, I will never, ever let you go. You can trust me.

After Johan left I knew I couldn't go back to Jørgen. I'd given up any thought of living with him. We'd tried it before, several times, but it was no use, we fought all the time. You know what he's like, he's a great musician, certainly, but he can be so difficult. He seemed to enjoy telling me how hopeless he thought I was, every time I did something he didn't approve of, though he never made any attempt to see things from my side. Besides which he's far too fussy, and he would make plans for the both of us without checking with me first.

The holidays we took when we were living together were generally sheer hell. People around us had grown used to our fighting, one or other of us was forever running off to mutual friends in the middle of the night, after we had had too much to drink and got ourselves embroiled in yet another argument which offered no way out except for either him or me to storm out, spend the night in a sleeping bag on somebody's sofa and come home late the next morning, hungover and remorseful. Then we would throw our arms around one another and make up as always. The sex was great, the conversation rotten.

Finally we agreed to call it a day. He moved in with his little Bodil, whom he had been cultivating on the side for some time, and I tried a few others before finding Johan. Bodil had long contented herself with the crumbs, but now suddenly she had hit the jackpot. She positively bloomed, started wearing tailored jackets and got pregnant almost at once. It can't possibly have been planned, but Jørgen didn't seem to have anything against it, he went around with a permanent, self-satisfied grin on his face, it was really quite irritating. Actually, it's quite remarkable how full of themselves men can be if they manage to make a woman pregnant; for months they have living proof of their own potency at their sides, you get the impression that they would like as many people as possible to stop and contemplate exactly how this fertilisation was effected. Jørgen strutted about with his short-winded Bodil, cracking bad jokes about procreation. 'Carrying on the line and all that, you know!' he would say with a stupid grin on his face, and pat her stomach.

I believe those two are actually pretty happy with life, despite the obligatory ups and downs. But Bodil had to hang up the tailored jackets when her weight shot up during her pregnancy and as far as I know she's never taken them out again, except on special occasions: receptions for the orchestra and that sort of thing, and then she always looks a bit over-dressed. She piles on too much jewellery. Their son was born by Caesarian, he's asthmatic and spoiled; when he was a little boy one lens of his glasses was always blanked out, which didn't make him look all that bright either. I expect he wears contact lenses now. You might remember him, Harald – you and he spent quite a lot of time together as pre-schoolers, and of course Bodil worked at the nursery you both attended, we mixed with the same crowd, celebrated Midsummer's Eve together several years in a row. Do you remember anything of those days? There was never any problem, I think Jørgen and Johan got on really well.

But then, as luck would have it, Jørgen won a position as trumpet player with the symphony orchestra, which I had just joined. Vacancies for trumpeters come along only once in a blue moon, so it was pretty much on the cards that he would apply, every trumpeter with any respect for his or herself was doing the same. But it was a bit of a blow when he got the job. At first I thought maybe he had done it just to spite me. I knew it wasn't going to be easy having him there, so close at hand, it made everything that much more complicated.

And of course we ended up seeing too much of one another. We had a tendency, when we were on tour for example, to fall back into our old ways. There could be a deal of tiptoeing back and forth between our two hotel rooms – well, we'd always been good together in bed. Our affair was soon common knowledge within the orchestra and no one took it too seriously, even if they did feel a bit bad about Bodil and Johan. Strictly speaking we wouldn't really have needed to keep it a secret, had it not been for them. Jørgen's little childminder, or nursery school teacher as he insisted on calling her, was apparently very jealous.

Every now and again I would drop in on them unannounced: quick visits to deliver something or pass on a message from someone. But mainly for the sake of the mild titillation derived from seeing what their home life was like on any ordinary day of the week, when I happened to catch them unawares. Little calls of this sort unsettled Jørgen. Maybe I did find it a little bit amusing to tease him in this way; it was so obvious to us both that in his heart of hearts he was ashamed of his nonentity of a wife and the poky rented flat full of playdough figures and checked tablecloths that Bodil had run up herself. The sewing machine was always set up on the cluttered living-room table.

When these little manifestations of mine got too much for Jørgen he was liable to pay me back by making his relationship to me obvious in one way or another at some orchestra do. Always discreetly, I grant you: allowing his hand to linger on the small of my back a moment longer than necessary as he ushered me through a door, or tenderly and a mite demonstratively lifting my hair away from my fur collar after helping me on with my coat – you know, the sort of thing that only lovers do, and only those who know the secret language can spot. In fact, though, he was perfectly harmless, and he never took any such liberties when Johan was around, I think he had a lot of respect for Johan. I liked that. If it hadn't been for that I don't think I would have had any interest in continuing our relationship. As it was, we both knew exactly what we were doing, the game we were playing could have been likened to the interminable bickering of two old friends who know each other too well to really try to make a go of it together.

And none of this had anything to do with Johan and me. Johan was someone to whom I laid myself wide open. What we had together was sacred. And if something is sacred, I know when it is threatened. I hurt inside.

But I miscalculated when it came to this love affair of his that I saw coming. I thought he just needed some fun. To begin with I wasn't really worried, I must have been suppressing the symptoms. For a while I actually toyed with the idea that it would be Bodil he fell for, they had always got on well together those two, the one was in some ways as blandly pragmatic as the other and they didn't fit in with the orchestra crowd – to be honest I don't think either of them liked the people there. As it turned out, however, it wasn't Bodil, but a librarian called Minna. I should have known. The name itself reminds me of the Disney films you liked so much when you were little, it sounds cheap.

For a while there, on that tour of England, Jørgen and I were skating on pretty thin ice. He was feeling frustrated about the situation at home: Harald was sick a lot and I suspect that Bodil was totally worn out, what with working full-time at the nursery and having the boy to see to. It didn't sound as if Jørgen was getting the attention he needed at home. We slid back into our old ways, got a little bit too drunk on a couple of evenings after a concert, and after I had made my daily call home to check how things were with you and Johan and say goodnight.

We sat in my hotel room talking far into the night. It was one of those endless, intimate moments, so familiar from the days when we were living together. I stroked his back and he said that he missed me more than he cared to admit, and that it wasn't the same with Bodil. I suppose maybe I got a little bit sentimental. Felt a little flattered. Maybe we were meant for each other after all, I thought, or at any rate maybe we had changed. Maybe we could have a harmonious, creative relationship, if we just gave it one more try. I thought: Maybe we're mature now. I think I was pretty drunk.

We made wild, energetic love, even though Jørgen was a little the worse for drink. We woke the next morning, with limbs aching and heads pounding, to the sound of one of the flautists banging on the door. It was past ten, the coach was about to set off for that day's venue, but we'd never make it down in time. We would have to let the others go on without us, we had to skip breakfast, pack in a rush and follow on in a taxi that ended up costing a fortune. I had to pay the fare, somehow Jørgen never manages to have the right currency on him when we are on tour. He really is hopelessly impractical where such things are concerned; I was very annoyed with him and I was feeling awful. You know how little patience I have with that sort of thing.

There were a lot of raised eyebrows when we finally showed up for rehearsal. We both made a bad job of that evening's concert, I had a thumping headache and my hands were trembling, for long stretches of time I couldn't seem to focus on my music and had to trust to memory.

I was so humiliated, it was all Jørgen's fault. And I felt a sudden stab of fear at the thought of how I had come so close to letting . . . I don't know. Come so close to letting my nice, secure life slip through my fingers.

I never told Johan about that last fiasco of a concert. I steered well clear of Jørgen all the way home, I saw him disappearing into Bodil's billowing embrace as soon as we exited from customs at the airport.

You and Johan were standing a little apart from the others, waiting for me in the arrivals hall. I always forgot how shy you both were. My heart stopped when I saw the two of you. You looked so small and vulnerable, you were my little angel; I couldn't imagine how I could have risked my home and family for a nobody like Jørgen. And Johan looked so warm and solid and loving, standing there with you in his arms. Almost too loving, I thought, much more so than he usually is in public.

I had no chance to give Jørgen the bottles I had smuggled through customs for him, I had to make the best of a bad job and give them to Johan instead; as usual he was the one who unpacked my bag when we got home and the only explanation I could offer for having brought back so much booze was that I had wanted to surprise him. He popped my dirty clothes into the washing machine and put the bottles of duty-free in the drinks cabinet. He seemed rather distant. When I eventually took you up to bed I fell asleep with my arms wrapped close around you and slept for almost twenty-four hours.

I have to look in the mirror. Haven't looked in the mirror for days. I've given the mirror a wide berth. Have to look at myself in the mirror, check that I'm there. Not just yet, though.

Maybe I should paint my toenails. What do you think? I've a bottle of nail polish up in the bathroom, barely touched. I'll be wearing open-toed sandals tomorrow, can't show up with my toenails looking like this. Have to file, paint. Have to go up to the bathroom. L'Oréal, best nail polish there is. You do know that, don't you. Not cheap, but it's long-lasting and it dries fast.

That summer, after our tour of England, I discovered that I was pregnant. I didn't know what to do with myself, I swung between black despair and fury. I felt used and let down by Jørgen, it had always been up to him to take care of the contraception side, or at any rate to make sure that we didn't run any risks, and I had simply assumed that this rule still applied. But he'd been too drunk, of course. Too drunk to take any precautions whatsoever, too drunk to be capable, later on, of explaining what had happened. You can never trust them when it comes to things like that, Ebba, you have to take your own precautions.

I called him from the phone box next to the petrol station a month after our return. By then I was sure, I had been sure of it for over a week. I didn't think twice about ringing his home number. It was Bodil who picked up the phone; I asked if I could speak to Jørgen, I had no desire to make it easy for him. I heard Bodil shout his name and put down the receiver, then I heard the television being switched on in the background. It was the evening news; I could just picture her, enthroned on the sofa with one eye on the television and the other on Jørgen talking on the phone. She was probably wearing one of those angora-look acrylic sweaters, you know the kind I mean, they make her look like an

Easter chick. It took a while for Jørgen to pick up the phone and say his name. I had noticed that she hadn't said who was calling when she shouted to him.

I came straight to the point, told him what he had done. There was silence at the other end of the line. I said he'd better come up with some way of sorting out this mess. He said he couldn't discuss it right now. Maybe he should have thought of that before, I hissed, when we were in that hotel room in London. He'd had plenty to say for himself then. I heard him telling me, in this artificially chummy, businesslike voice, that we'd have lots of time to discuss the allocation of rooms for group practice on Wednesday after rehearsal. I slammed down the receiver and went for a long walk on my own in the bright summer evening. When I got back, Johan was in bed. He had left a letter for me on top of the chest of drawers.

Then things really started to go downhill. I was cold all the time. My breasts felt tender and I had that familiar metallic taste in my mouth, like I'd been sucking on a dirty coin. That's one of the first signs. I was sure it was a little boy.

I had an abortion, unknown to Johan. Jørgen drove me to the hospital. He was confused and upset, he talked non-stop, a stream of alternate threats and promises. He wanted us to try again, wanted us to move in together, we would make a lovely, little, extended family, he thought, you and Harald were such good friends. We could even have joint custody, you could be brought up as step-brother and sister, you could both come and stay with us every second weekend, he just knew the two of you would love to have a little sister or brother.

But I was just worn out. Johan had written more letters to me, I had read them, but said nothing. It was too much for me, I felt as if my brain were about to burst, it couldn't absorb all of this at once – it had to concentrate on one thing at a time, and my main concern right then was that I simply could not afford to have another child. I had enough to do just looking after you. As usual, Johan seemed to be wrestling with abstract questions that were quite beyond me, and as usual, no pictures presented themselves in my mind when I read what he wrote. Your father has to think a thing through from a hundred different angles before he can get his ideas clear in his head, for him words are a means to thought, it's all words to him. I, on the other hand, must follow my heart, the heart always knows what it wants. Considering a matter a hundred times over won't make the heart any more or less happy. You're like me in that respect, aren't you. You're so certain.

What I hadn't told Jørgen was that I couldn't be sure whether the baby was his or Johan's. Although all the indications were that it was his: Johan was so much more careful and conscientious where such things were concerned, he had a lot more self-control.

So I suppose my answer to his letters was a kind of dull silence which could probably have been interpreted in lots of ways. I was so fragile, I needed him to look after me, and you of course, I didn't need his philosophising. I know it sounds as if I didn't understand what was going on. But understanding is not everything, Ebba. Understanding is only the start.

I wouldn't let Jørgen accompany me into the hospital, he had to drop me outside the main entrance and drive off home again. I didn't want to be seen there with him, it was too risky. His face was so pale when I slammed the door shut, he looked like a man who has lost everything. I simply felt cold. Just you drive on home to Bodil, I thought, I'm sure you can find solace at home, I've got enough to do consoling myself.

The abortion clinic was in the same building as the maternity unit where I had had you, but it had a separate entrance and was on another floor. There were pregnant women waddling about all over the place, slippers on their feet and weekly mags in their hands. In the corridors were tables piled with free publications on pregnancy and childbirth.

My last thought as a quietly efficient nurse pulled a pale-blue hospital shirt over my head was that if this little boy had lived, my secret name for him would have been Little Johan. Jon in real life, but Little Johan in secret.

He would have been your brother. I knew exactly how he would have spoken. A sensible little boy, a bit shy. Like me in looks. There would have been no trace of Jørgen in him, not the slightest trace.

Something is breaking here, I don't know what it is.

What is it that's breaking, Ebba?

Have to paint my nails, mustn't make a mess – there, look at that now, what a mess –

It was Johan's fault that you had to live in two worlds, you know. I never wanted it that way. I couldn't believe my ears when he demanded to have you every Thursday and every second weekend. I had to pack your little bag and stand there waving to you, while you sat with your face pressed up against the rear window of the old car that had belonged to both of us, flapping both hands at me.

When he brought you home on Sunday evening we would exchange no more than a few curt words in the hall as he handed me your bag, with you hanging round his neck and refusing to take off your jacket. It was always him who had to ease it off you, tenderly lifting your chin as only he could do and sliding down the zip, talking to you all the time in soft, warm, soothing Papa tones. It was a rotten way of stealing something inalienable from me, it was such a blatant demonstration of power, as if he were gloating, showing that only he really knew how to take care of you, only he could strike the right note.

When he left you would hover round me like a little bee. Nothing you could do was too good for me, you stroked my hair and did all the little things that you knew would please me: pinched the dead leaves off the potted plants, snuggled up close to me when I was reading the paper. Sometimes you would come home from his place with your hair done differently – Johan and Minna never could get the hang of clasps and scrunchies and all that, could they? You would stand in front of me with a consoling look in your eyes, take down your hair and ask me to redo it. I would venture a few questions as to what you had done over the weekend while I combed and plaited, but you never told me anything, you just smiled at me.

Even after your little sister came along, you never said one word about them. That really hurt me. His new family was a part of your life which I could not share, wasn't it? My own life seemed so beggarly in comparison. I hated the fact that I was always having to make comparisons, I could never relax and enjoy my life with you when I was always having to make comparisons. They had everything I didn't have. They could give you everything. They had each other.

When I read the notice of your sister's birth in the newspaper something fell apart.

Johan called the next day and bullied me into letting you stay with them when the baby came home; the summer holidays had just begun; he was probably going to use you as child labour, changing nappies and sterilising bottles. You were far too young to be doing such things, you needed to rest, you seemed awfully list-less around that time. It made me ill just to think about it, but I had no energy left for arguing with him, he had been waging a devious campaign of attrition designed to end in this victory over me, although I didn't realise this until later. Mama had to get the doctor to write me a sick note. She took me to the cottage for a break, do you remember, somebody had to stand in for me with the orchestra, I had no will of my own, she had to see to everything.

Mama and I went round and round one another at the cottage, with the rain pelting down outside. I went out fishing in the fjord in the rowboat, but we had to throw most of the fish away, I had no appetite and Mama was on a diet as usual. She did crosswords and talked about the weather; I said not a word, she had to switch on the radio for the sake of hearing someone talk; it got to the point where the radio was on for most of the day and half the night. I suppose she did try to cheer me up, but I wasn't capable of talking, I kept picturing how you were all getting on in the city that I could see from the shore, how you snuggled up together in the double bed, all four of you, how you put your arms round one another, whispered little words to one another, burst out laughing, watched over the new baby.

When my sick note ran out and we had to go home, you came back. But I felt as if I had to shut myself off from you too, to save you from being smitten by my grief. I felt almost as if you had betrayed me, by going off like that and taking Johan's side. Did you notice, Ebba? I never meant for you to notice.

You couldn't get through to me, I know that; I had to spare you, and the only way I could do so was to sit still and say nothing. Which made for long, oppressive afternoons, the hours threading bleakly into chains – you spent a lot of time in your room, reading, didn't you? Luckily you had Mama.

Later on, Johan – being his usual devious self – always made a point of having your sister in his arms when he called you. And he called often, didn't he? It was usually me who answered the phone. We would exchange stiff, polite banalities or discuss practical arrangements to do with clothes or driving you to music lessons or a birthday party; I could hear your sister gurgling at the other end, he must have had the receiver shoved right up against her mouth. Then I would put down the phone and call you. You were always hovering about close to the phone when I was talking to Johan, you always knew intuitively when it was your father who was calling. I think you must get that from me, your intuition for such things.

But you stood with your back to me when you were talking to him. And when you spoke to your little sister you would wedge yourself into a corner of the room with your face to the wall and make little cooing sounds into the phone; you shut out the rest of the world. For a long time after you'd had your chat and hung up you would avoid my eye. You found it hard to wipe off the soft, secretive, little smile that played around your lips. And when you eventually did glance at me you looked guilty. I said nothing.

Yes, love, I know you kept quiet because you didn't want to hurt me, that was your way of caring for me, just as my silence was my way of showing that I cared for you. But it meant that the house was so quiet, do you remember how quiet it was, that quietness made me feel so hopeless. I had this terrible urge to scream and shout and wave my arms in the air.

I thought to myself: Johan, what are we doing to her, what sort of a life are we giving our daughter? Is it really supposed to hurt all the time, when will it end, won't it be over soon?

But there was no answer to these questions. Johan had no say in my house, and if he had said anything I wouldn't have listened, you do see that, don't you, I would have been liable to strike out, had he tried; strike the cold flat of my hand against the glass.

And yet I could so clearly see the imprint of myself in you. I saw it in all the little things: the neat way in which you laid your knife on top of your napkin after buttering your bread, so as not to stain the tablecloth. I knew that you saw the tablecloth with my eyes. This filled me with gratitude. I buried my face in your hair as we lay side by side in our matching nighties in the big double bed that your father had deserted. You turned towards me in your sleep. You turned towards me. You turned to me. I caught the sweet whiff of toothpaste from your mouth. I took such good care of your teeth, you didn't have a single cavity until fourth grade, remember? I was so proud of you.

Now and again I would look in on you when you were asleep in your own room. At such times I felt like my own mother, she used to tiptoe into my room at night too and stand there watching me. Sometimes I wasn't asleep. I kept my eyes shut and sensed Mama's presence in the room, she seemed like a stranger to me then. Like someone who had come to inspect her property. And now here I was, watching you.

Sometimes, when I stood watching you like that, it was as if I were seeing you dead. As if you had stopped breathing, as if something had run out of you, as if all the life had drained out while you slept, while you were somewhere else. And I had to lay my hand on you to bring you back. You were not dead, you pulsated under my hand. My heart beat hard and fast.

It was evening, a year before your sister was born. I was on my way home from a concert. You were a big girl, past needing a babysitter; you were in bed at home, waiting for me.

It was so dark. I had parked the car further up the road, I wanted to walk the last bit of the way up to the house. I do that occasionally. It makes me feel like a guest in my own home, as if I'm coming to it as a stranger. I can see who lives in this house much better that way. I get so deeply entangled in my own life sometimes, I need to see it from the outside.

A little further down the road there was a strange car, it was parked right outside our driveway. I drew closer to it. The headlights were off, I could see a woman sitting inside. I came up on it from behind, I doubted if she could see me, unless she were keeping an eye on the mirror. Suddenly it dawned on me that it was Johan's car. A hideous old thing.

Just as I was about to turn in to our driveway the car door opened. I stopped short. She still hadn't seen me. She got out and stood with the door open, looking up at our house. All of a sudden I felt so afraid. I recognised her from pictures you've brought home from your holidays with Johan and Minna.

It was her. Minna. I stayed rooted to the spot a little way up the street. She stood still, looking up at the house that I would shortly be entering. It looked as though she also needed to see it from outside, like me. Then she turned abruptly, got back into the car and drove off.

The car headlights lit up a broad sweep of the wet tarmac ahead of her as the car disappeared down the road.

And I felt as if I were seeing it with her eyes. I saw the illuminated strip of tarmac ahead of the car, I felt the accelerator under my foot. I was her. I felt as though it was me who had climbed into Johan's car and driven off, out of my own story. It was raining. I longed to be where she was going.

I didn't sleep well after that evening and I starting putting on the safety chain on the outer door once you were in bed. I had such a strong feeling that something was going to happen. I had already been given a forewarning, it was something ordained by him, something I couldn't bear to think about. I became convinced that he had sent Minna to spy on me, that they were going to demand custody of you, that they had dug up some unsavoury tit-bit about me. Possibly concerning a rather unfortunate incident with a babysitter whom I had offered a drink one night when I got back from a concert, but who, as it turned out, could not hold his liquor. It was all a long time ago, and we got it all sorted out. He kicked up such a row when I refused to go to bed with him, drunk as he was. But suddenly I got it into my head that Johan and Minna had found out about what had happened that night, and because of this they had decided to take me to court, to prove that I was an unfit mother.

I made my few small, secret preparations for running away with you. I packed a little suitcase which I kept in the cellar, in the workroom. You didn't notice anything, did you? It was important that you shouldn't notice anything, I didn't want you to worry, to get upset. I cleared the bottles out of the drinks cabinet, carried them out to the garage and tucked them behind the winter tyres, just in case they had also taken it into their heads that I was an alcoholic – that would have been disastrous for me.

It was a bad time altogether. Jørgen had started sniffing around one of his new pupils, a tasty little trumpeter with a tightly belted waist and soulful eyes. Things weren't the same between us, he seemed to have lost interest a little. I did consider giving Bodil a hint as to what he was up to, but I pretty much came to the conclusion that no good could come of such a move. I really didn't mean Bodil any harm, you know, she was just so pathetic, her and her fulsome admiration for her notoriously unfaithful husband. It annoyed me.

My finances were in an awful mess, too, something else I had to keep from you. I'd had this horrendous bill for tax arrears: I had forgotten to send in my tax return for the year before, so the tax people had come up with an estimate based on the figures they already had. I'm hopeless when it comes to keeping my accounts, as you well know; when Johan lived here he saw to all of that side of things, and before that I had Papa to take care of it for me, he filled in the forms for my student loan and all that sort of stuff.

The minute I received the letter from the tax office I called Johan at work: an instinctive reaction from the old days. But that only resulted in yet another bitter exchange: there was no way he could help me out, he was barely able to keep himself and his family. Or so he said, although I knew very well how much he earned. So I had to take out a loan, and in order to meet the payments on that I had to take on a lot more new pupils, it became a real juggling act: coordinating babysitters and school for you, as well as my own rehearsals and concerts with the orchestra; many a time I had no choice but to take you with me to the Conservatory and let you do your homework while I took a class. Do you remember how you used to sit there with your books, at the little table out in the foyer? So quiet and intent. You've always had such focus, Ebba.

Then one evening a year later, the doorbell rang; this was just after you had got back from staying at Johan's when your sister was born. I was sitting on the sofa here with a glass of wine and a pile of newspapers: I was up to my eyes in work at the time and only got round to reading the papers a couple of evenings a week. I had known for some time that it was bound to happen soon, but even so, when I heard the doorbell I jumped as if I had had an electric shock. I scurried about the sitting-room, looking for my shoes, my lipstick, folding the blanket I had had over my knees. When I finally made it into the hall to open the door Minna was already on her way back down the drive, she was walking quickly, she had a short leather jacket slung around her shoulders and all at once I was so afraid that she would go away and leave me. I shouted her name.

It was a shrill shout, unnecessarily loud; she stopped and stayed where she was for a moment before turning to face me. I stood on the doorstep feeling like something the cat had dragged in.

Only when she turned round did I see that she was carrying a bundle in her arms: it had to be your new baby sister. That threw me. I could not believe that she would have the nerve to bring that child to my house.

She looked so serious, and much shorter than in the photos. And you've never described her to me, of course. She didn't appear to have particularly good taste, unless she was following some fashion that I hadn't come across yet. But she had nice hair, I noticed that right away, and a round and somehow gentle face. She walked up the steps towards me, shifted the sleeping baby over to her other arm and put out her hand. She introduced herself, giving both her Christian name and her surname. She doesn't have the same surname as your father you know, in some way that made her more of a person in her own right than I had imagined. I didn't take Johan's name either when we got married. The thought never crossed my mind.

I didn't give my name, but I stepped to one side and asked her in. She didn't hang up her jacket in the hall, I didn't offer to hold the baby for her; she kept the jacket around her shoulders. I could tell that she recognised your outdoor things and your shoes in the hall, it made me almost mad with worry. I got it into my head that she had come to get you, that she and Johan had been granted custody of you without my knowledge. I put the safety chain on the door behind her.

We stood face to face in the sitting-room. It struck me that I had actually met her long before at various social gatherings, along with some of the orchestra crowd, she had been seeing one of the second violinists at the time, I think; he got a job abroad and moved away some years back. But she had seemed taller then.

On one wrist she wore some fine silver bracelets, and her hair seemed to rise in a froth. I have exactly the same bracelets myself, did you know that, in the jewellery box upstairs in my bedroom. I thought to myself that I was glad I wasn't wearing them that evening. Something had stopped me in the morning, as I was about to slip them on to my wrist. I had put them back in the box, the one I inherited from your Granny.

Your sister was wearing a pale yellow suit. She was fast asleep. I noted that Minna was still left with a distinct pot-belly after the birth, she probably wasn't the type to go to all the effort of doing sit-ups to flatten her stomach, the way I did after I had you. Maybe she knew that she was loved the way she was, with her plump, cushiony stomach, podgy white overarms and a little double-chin wobbling above her polo-neck sweater. You know how soft she looks.

I invited her to sit down on the sofa. I sat on the edge of a chair, not knowing what to say. Minna's coming was like an ambush for which I could not possibly have prepared. She laid the baby down on the blanket under which I had just been sitting and began to extract it from the suit. It was sleeping soundly; the tiny, infant arms barely stirred. I could see that she looked like you, the way you were for the first few weeks, she had the same dark, woolly hair. Johan had succeeded in setting his bloody genetic stamp on both his daughters, I thought, like a mark of triumph. I told myself that very soon that hair would be falling off. I told myself that I would have to be strong.

I looked expectantly from the baby to Minna. I tried to look confident.

She began to talk in a soft, deep voice. It was a long time before I said anything myself. She said she knew this was difficult and unpleasant for me, but she had been thinking a lot about it since the baby was born, and she could no longer live with the fact that we had not spoken to one another. She felt that in some way we were now on an equal footing as regards Johan: we each had one child by him. She didn't think she would have any more children. She wanted us to get to know one another a bit – for your sake. Our daughters were half-sisters after all, they were going to have a lot to do with one another. You were already becoming attached to one another. She said she thought it bothered you that you felt you could never say anything about your life here with me, when you were with them.

She made quite a little speech. I didn't say all that much, but it was as if the anger and anxiety inside me withered away and I sank into a sort of trance. After a while the baby woke up and began to howl, she lifted it, pulled up her sweater, undid the little flap on her nursing bra and put the child to the breast. Now I had a clear view of her flabby white stomach. She had no moles, as far as I could see, she looked smooth and warm.

A few minutes passed. I stared at them apathetically. She was struggling to get the baby to latch on to the breast, it waved its head from side to side and didn't seem able to focus its hunger on the right point. I saw the milk beginning to stream from both her nipples, forming large dark circles on her bra, it was so frustrating to watch; I felt that same sensation again in my own breast – that overwhelming feeling that you are about to burst – from the time when I was struggling to breastfeed you, and your father and Granny were hovering around me, giving good advice that was of no help.

For some time I went on sitting rigid in my chair, observing all of this. Minna was becoming more and more frantic, she was breathing heavily. It was impossible not to feel sorry for her, she seemed so helpless sitting there. I got up from my chair, went over and sat down next to them on the sofa. Then I placed my hand gently on the back of the baby's head and guided its face towards the nipple. I put one of the sofa cushions under Minna's elbow for support, the way I remembered the children's nurse at the maternity unit doing when I had you.

At last your sister settled down and begun to suck, the little face and the closed eyelids working intently. The whole of the cotton-clad form relaxed. Minna smiled gratefully at me. She thought everything was all right now.

That's all there was to it. We didn't say much. She sat on my sofa, she fed your sister, and in this way, warmly and gently, she claimed a place in my life. Afterwards I walked down to the car with them and helped her fasten the baby into its car seat. It was a totally different type from the one your father and I had when you were that age, this one looked as if it were specially designed for newborn babies, it was padded and sat at exactly the right angle. She had it in the front, fixed to the passenger seat; Johan and I had always put you in the back seat. I didn't mention this to her. I went on standing and waving for some time after the car had disappeared around the corner.

Back in the sitting-room I kept going round and round, from window to window, howling. I would stop and bend over as if I were about to throw up, but what came out was sound, not vomit: a stifled scream, very faint, because I didn't want you to hear me. I switched the radio off and on several times, hauled saucepans clattering out of the pots cupboard, opened and closed cupboard doors. In the end I gave in to it, slipped on my boots in the hall, ran out to the garage and retrieved two of the bottles I had hidden there. I settled myself on the sofa again, pulled the blanket over my head and made a little tent, then I sat in there and drank. There were no windows in the tent.

I didn't sleep at all that night. The next morning I felt like death warmed up, I must have looked terrible. You had to make your own way to school that day, do you remember, I barely heard the door closing behind you when you left.

I felt so confused. I couldn't get Minna and your sister out of my head. She thrust herself on me, it was brutal, it was as if she had taken a picture of herself and stuck it up in front of my eyes.

I knew Minna worked at the library. One day I got in the car and drove down there. I don't know why I did it, I just got in and drove. I called the Conservatory that morning after you had gone to school and said I was sick, then I just drove to the town where they live, it's not all that far away.

I parked in the square and wandered round and round the town centre. I'd been there lots of times before; it's not the most desirable of areas, it's kind of dirty-looking.

I saw the shop where you and Minna must have bought my binoculars. I stopped at a café in a garish shopping centre and sat there for nearly an hour sipping at a cup of tepid tea. Then I went to the library.

It had never crossed my mind that she might not be there. She was on maternity leave of course, I'd forgotten. I'd been sitting by the periodical racks for some time, flicking through all sorts of magazines and journals, before it dawned on me. I didn't know what to do. It was almost as if I were missing her. I trailed out of the library. Then I sat on a bench outside for a while, just in case she might happen to come by with the pram.

And all at once I seemed to see her. It was that picture that she had stuck up in front of my eyes, it wouldn't go away. I stared and stared at it. It was uncanny, it was real as could be. In my mind's eye I saw her and your father walking with the pram along the street that ran past the library. Your father was pushing the pram with one hand, his other arm wrapped firmly around her shoulder, they were chatting and laughing together, she had something important to tell him, I could see. He came to a halt while she was talking, regarding her earnestly. They stood there in the middle of the road, cars swerving around them. She told him how she had paid me a visit, told him what I had done, what I had said. What she had felt. His face, as she spoke, was full of sympathy. When she was finished he put the brake on the pram with his foot, threw both arms round her and hugged her, long and hard.

And I couldn't seem to stop. I pictured how they would be once they were home again and had eaten dinner and put the little one down for the night. They're tired now, I thought. They switch off all the lights in the flat, go through to their cosy, warm bedroom, fitted up by her with furniture from Ikea. Close beside one another they get undressed. Everything is so nice and tidy in here, no clothes lying about. The baby is sleeping peacefully in the next room, he pads through naked to check on it one last time, he leaves the little night-light burning and the door slightly ajar.

By the time he comes back to the bedroom she is in bed. She lies there, smiling at him, that warm, gentle smile of hers. She lifts the duvet with one hand. He switches off the light and snuggles down beside her. She is warm and smooth and soft, she has no stretchmarks or spots. She laughs quietly, she has all the time in the world, she wants to hear what he has to say. If he needs comforting, she will comfort him. And if it is she who is restless, he will run his hands over her stomach.

I ran back to the car and drove home. I drove far too fast. I couldn't face driving all the way up to the house, I parked down on the street. I was back before you got home from school.

Our Sunday breakfasts were one of the nicest things we had together, you and I, wouldn't you say so? They were sacred, they were my greatest solace. Every second Sunday we would be bright and gay and rested – we both liked a long lie-in, didn't we? As soon as you woke up you would creep through to my bed and slide under the duvet, and then we would lie there like that, dozing and talking about little things and listening to the radio until our stomachs said it was time for breakfast. You would go down to the kitchen ahead of me and start to boil eggs and make tea while I went to the bathroom and applied a face mask, plucked my eyebrows, had a shower, washed my hair and shaved my legs: the weekly ritual, you know. The sort of thing that, deep down, I so enjoyed. If you were ready before me you would come into the bathroom and sit on the edge of the bath and watch while I finished off. Then you might let me wash your hair with the hand shower and untangle it slowly and carefully with the soft hairbrush.

We would sit in the bright kitchen in the big bathrobes that Mama made for us, wouldn't we, eating our long, leisurely breakfast, reading the papers and chatting. And afterwards we would get dressed, stroll down to Mama's and ask her to come for a walk with us.

It made me happy to see you and Mama together, in sturdy shoes and windcheaters, on those Sunday walks. I often took photographs of the two of you, didn't I, you were my little family, you know. It reminded me of how she and I used to do the same, walking and talking about this and that, when I lived at home. Mama has taught me almost everything I know, I think. I don't know what I would have done without her.

You might not remember this, but when you were younger, too small to go for proper Sunday walks, Mama and I often used to take you into town on Sundays. We would go to a café, or a museum; you had the sweetest little red coat that Mama had made for you, and a little bonnet in the same material, all lined with silk, it was a lovely piece of workmanship. You had that coat for years, I think there's a picture of you in it in your album. I just let the sleeves out and let down the hem as you grew.

You walked along between us holding our hands, so nice and well-behaved, you were never any trouble. When we saw other children lying down and screaming and kicking, or charging about, arms flailing, we both used to shudder.

I remember one time when we were at the Historical Museum. Mama had met some people she knew and we left her chatting to them while we carried on into the exhibition rooms. The place was packed, it was a busy family Sunday.

I got stuck in front of one glass case, studying some old coins, it was so beautifully lit, I became totally engrossed in it, the way I sometimes do, and suddenly you were gone. I wasn't too worried to begin with, you were four years old and pretty independent, and you couldn't have got very far in such a short time anyway. I started looking around for you, I went through room after room, I couldn't see you anywhere; there were people all over the place, they blocked my view, I had to zig-zag through the throng; I started to call out your name softly, I broke out in a sweat, I couldn't think where you could have got to in such a short time. I asked one of the attendants, but he hadn't seen any four-year-old in a red coat wandering about on her own. I ran back down the stairs to the foyer to ask Mama to help me look for you, but she was still standing talking to this middle-aged couple, I couldn't bring myself to go over to them. I ran up the stairs again and back into the large exhibition rooms, which were positively heaving with people, all gazing at objects behind glass.

At long last I caught sight of you. You were standing at the far end of one of the rooms, next to some old, cordoned-off pieces of furniture; you were gazing round about you, but you didn't look frightened, you had just . . . how can I put it? Turned away. You had turned away from the world. You had your hand round the cord that marked how close to the furniture on exhibit the public could come, as if you were clutching a lifeline. I ran over to you and picked you up, pressed my face against the breast of your coat and asked you where you had been, but you just looked at me, calmly and remotely. I asked you if you had been frightened, but you shook your head. When I told you that you ought always to tell me where you were going you just looked at me. Well, it wasn't you who had lost me, it was me who had lost you.

Neither of us said a word to Mama about this, did we, somehow we just never got round to it.

It had no nose, and no mouth. It just stared at me, Ebba. You've always had it in you, haven't you. I don't know where you get it from.

And towards the end, when Johan was living here: I scared away the neighbours' kids when they came to ask if you would come and play in the wood, didn't I? I was a horrible bird that stood on the steps and flapped its wings, exactly the way I did that evening when Minna had been to see me. A witch. They ran away. I went back inside and smoothed the duvet over you. Johan was nowhere to be seen, he was always doing something else.

He's getting out of the car. He's not locking the door. I don't know why he can't drive right up to the house, there's plenty of parking space up here – well, he ought to know, he built it himself.

He's walking slowly, look, he's all hunched up. He follows my pots of flowers up the drive – I'll have to put down the binoculars, I'll duck down so that he can't see me from the window. What's he doing now? Has he sat down on the steps?

I put my hands over my ears, I don't want to hear the doorbell . . . but no sound comes, he must have sat down on the steps, yes, that's it. Maybe he needs to rest, like me.

200

I'm so tired, I have so much to do. He's far too late getting here, why can't he let me know when he's going to be late.

There's just no dealing with people who are so unreliable, look at all this mess, and look at my toes, no, I can't tidy up right now, I have to look at him, have to look through the peephole in the door –

Oh, look. So slight. An old man.

I can only see his back and the nape of his neck. The peephole isn't all that big.

I saw things that Johan didn't see, back then. In him too. I couldn't share this with him, he would never have understood. You had the same darkness inside you both, you and he, but in you it lay deeper. I didn't know what it was, it made me feel tired and afraid.

That night when I got back from the English tour I was woken by an awareness that he wasn't in bed beside us. It was a light summer night, like tonight, not dark at all. He had gone downstairs to read or play music as he sometimes did when he couldn't get to sleep. You were sound asleep beside me; I didn't switch on the lamp, I didn't want to wake you and it wasn't necessary anyway, it was quite bright in the bedroom; I just tiptoed down the stairs and into the sitting-room.

I stopped short in the doorway. He was sitting in his chair with his headphones plugged in to the hi-fi and a book on his lap as usual, a whisky glass on the table next to him. But I could tell that he wasn't himself, he was a dark figure with a cloudy, introverted look in his eyes. He was gone from me, he seemed to be in another world and behind him I saw that long corridor that I had seen before, it ran off into the luminous night. That corridor was full of other figures like him. They didn't see me, they were busy with their own affairs.

I said nothing. He didn't see me, he had the headphones over his ears. I ran back up the stairs and hid under the duvet. I pushed it away. I fell asleep again and dreamed it away, I piled layer upon layer of dreams on top of it, like almost transparent brushstrokes, until it was almost invisible. And the next morning he was lying there beside me as usual, he was Johan, not a dark shadow; there was no corridor behind him and there was no way I could have explained to him what I had seen.

Seeing too much doesn't make you any wiser. It just makes you scared, Ebba. You don't know what to make of what you have seen.

I loved him so much, we were one. I told myself: if it doesn't exist for him, then it doesn't exist for me either, of course it doesn't. I pushed it away. And when I saw it in you I couldn't even bear to think about it.

But he didn't want me any more. And he forced me to accept his conditions. He had already found himself a lawyer.

The night before he and I were due to go and see the lawyer you and I slept at Mama's house. I was in such a state. I don't know what I would have done without Mama that night. She let me curl up in her bed and held me like a little child, I cried and cried. She whispered into my hair that everything was going to be okay, that we would manage just fine, we three, she would help me, it would be all right. It would never have worked out with Johan in the long run anyway.

In the end I must have nodded off. You were asleep in your own room, in the bed that had been both Mama's and mine when we were little. I don't think you woke up, I tried not to talk too loud.

We were up early next morning. Mama chatted away to you and put some slices of cucumber on the liver pâté sandwiches for your lunchbox and some on my swollen eyelids, she left me sitting like that in an armchair in her dressing-gown, with my head tilted back, while she took you to nursery. I did my breathing exercises, the way she had shown me. When she got back she helped me to wash my hair, put on my make-up and practise what I was going to say. She painted my nails, neatly and with a steady hand. She lent me a pair of her own tights, mine had a ladder in them. Then she drove me into town. We had agreed on exactly what I had to say, it was important that I came over as being cool and clear and firm, since these were the conditions on which my new life would rest. She repeated this several times, and I knew myself that it was true.

But when I saw your father I almost broke down again. Mama had dropped me off and driven away, she was going to park the car and wait for me in a nearby café. I was standing outside the main door of this large office building, about to go in. He came striding down the street towards me at a great rate of knots, not looking where he was going; I could see that he hadn't slept either, I could tell at a glance. He looked as if he'd been dragged through a hedge backwards. I wanted to call out to him to mind the road, there were cars coming from all directions, charging straight for him. But I didn't call out, I was no longer the sort of person who would call out like that.

And during our meeting with the lawyer I could tell that he was lying. He didn't know he was doing it. He said things he didn't mean. His thoughts were dark, a dark skein of rope coiled around his mind. As it did in mine. I felt mean, and I had every reason to be.

Sometimes, when people are talking to me, I can tell whether they are lying or telling the truth. I think the same goes for you, doesn't it? We've never talked about it. It's not so much that you can see it with your eyes, you just have the feeling that they are lying, isn't that right? Then you pull back a bit, you don't even know what it is they are lying about. Johan was lying in that office, he was lying to himself and to me. And Mama was right, it was there that the conditions for my new life were laid down.

I don't know whether it's dangerous, this ability that you and I have, it's more like a kind of music that some people can hear, while others only hear a lot of noise, or nothing at all. But it's complicated to explain. I tried to explain it to your father on a number of occasions, but I always regretted it. He had stuck a postcard on the notice board over the kitchen table, on it were the words *I think, therefore I am* in Latin. I can't remember how it goes in Latin, but I think he found those words comforting. I've taken down all of his bits and pieces now, I did it despite your protests.

'But supposing I don't think, what am I then?' I asked him one morning when we were having breakfast and I was feeling empty and fragile. He asked me to pass the salt. With that he dismissed it, he didn't think I took him seriously; with a wave of the hand he reduced me to a person with whom he couldn't have a sensible discussion.

He was the reader of the family. I think he felt I ought to read more, too, it's as if he was never really content with me as I was. He stuck to his books the way I stuck to my music. I don't know whether he has done much reading since he moved in with Minna, but when he lived here with us his nose was never out of a book. I'm not sure whether you know, but those boxes of books in the cellar belong to him; he's never come to collect them so they can't matter that much to him, he's never even asked about them. He doesn't know the first thing about music, he never has done, but words are supposedly his forte. When he was living here he tried to sort out the world by sorting out words. As if it were the same thing. It was an idea he had come up with. But it's not the same thing at all, not when you can see things that you can't explain, for which there are no words, and which aren't there for other people to see.

And you can't wipe out what you have seen by not talking about it, that much at least I have learned. It only becomes more dangerous, it takes on new forms and starts to coil round and round, it finds voices that begin to talk to themselves, they get out of control, they feel free to say anything at all.

On Wednesday morning, when I realised that you weren't home, I went and lay down on the sofa. I felt unreal, and cold, I itched all over. I knew something terrible had happened. I could tell, I was itching. I knew it the minute I walked into the kitchen and saw that the dishwasher had finished its cycle. When I opened the door the hot steam billowed out at me, it was a really bad sign. I looked out of the window, at the croquet mallets lying in a heap over by the birch trees. Nothing was as it should be.

I let the whole day go by before contacting anyone. I didn't even call Johan to ask if you were with them, I was numb. All morning I could hear his voice in my head, that soothing, rather weary tone he adopted when he didn't like the way I was behaving.

'You're over-reacting, pet,' he told me, time and again. I got so used to hearing him say that. I even started saying it to myself.

And what could I have said to explain my unease? That you had gone out on a summer's morning, and switched on the dishwasher before you left? That was nothing to get in a flap about, I couldn't point to anything unusual in it, I mean, you're a big girl now, almost grown, you've often done things recently that you haven't told me about until afterwards. It was the summer holidays, and you had just got yourself a new boyfriend, you were spending a lot of time together, early in the morning, too, I'm sure.

But that thought didn't help at all. I got it into my head that the worst had happened, that you and Erlend had run away together, that he had lured you on to a plane and out of the country. I raced over to the bureau to check if your passport was there, but it only made me more uneasy when I found it in its usual place.

I don't know what I did for the rest of that morning. It was early afternoon before I phoned Mama. I knew that she would take over from there, she's so efficient, far more so than me, and I had this terrible, terrible tiredness inside me. It was the end of everything, the big wide world had taken you, I knew in my heart that Mama wouldn't be able to do anything about this. I went and lay down on the sofa again and pulled the blanket over me.

From somewhere just below the surface I heard Mama letting herself in. I heard her organising things and talking on the telephone, her voice seemed to come to me from the end of a long corridor. She was obviously working her way through all the numbers, for your friends and mine, listed in the index that lay open on the top of the bureau. I may have shouted something to her from where I lay. I don't remember what, it just slipped out.

I don't think she called Erlend until the very last. She called him on his mobile, he answered straight away. It was him who found you: he knew where to look, he knew more than I did. You must have told him a lot of things, Ebba.

He called an ambulance; it arrived without the siren on, that must be why I didn't hear anything, lying there under the blanket on the sofa. Then they took you to the hospital. I don't see why they couldn't just bring you here, this is where you live, after all, and I *am* your mother, why couldn't they just bring you home?

The vicar rang the doorbell. I jumped, I fell out of the dream about the seal – I had just put down my fishing rod and gone for help, even though I knew really that there was no help to be had for such a big seal with a fishing hook lodged in its tongue. The nearest habitation was far too far away, and there was far too little time. The seal watched me go, it had great dark eyes.

The air in the room was hot and dry. I had slept as if I were drugged. A ribbon of saliva had run across my cheek from the corner of my mouth and my limbs were heavy and stiff. Mama must have gone home to rest or to carry on ringing round from there, she was no longer in the house at any rate. In the telephone conversations I had heard through my dream she hadn't sounded particularly concerned, just officious.

I have an idea she also thought that I was overreacting. I suppose she was used to me lying on the sofa like that and she didn't like it, she took it as a sign that I was going into one of my bad spells.

The vicar was an old man, he couldn't have been much short of retirement age. I remembered him from the church when you were confirmed. I was so annoyed when I saw him standing there on the steps gawping at me. It was obvious that he didn't know what to say. How dare he come to see me like that, I yelled at him, intruding on me in the privacy of my own home and gawping like a fool. I was still dazed from the dream about the seal, and he made me so mad, him and his helpless pity. I simply could not understand what he was saying. Nothing had happened to you, it couldn't have, you had just gone for a walk by yourself! You'd be back any time! You were a big girl now, almost grown, and you knew how I worried when you went off like that, no doubt you had a good reason for not being home, one of your chums having boyfriend trouble maybe; girls of your age have so much going on in their lives and most of it, of course, to do with boys. Well, I'd prepared you for that, hadn't I? Men – spineless and oversexed, the lot of them.

I could have hit him. My hands were covered in hard, jagged spikes, they were full of poison. But he gripped my wrists, he was very strong and steadfast for such an old man. He steered me backwards into the hall and from there into the sitting-room.

He had just got me down on to the sofa when Mama came in. She took one look at us and then she started wailing. She sank to the floor. I saw her sink, it was pathetic, like something out of a second-rate movie, she really annoyed me, her slip was showing, now who's overreacting, I thought. She could have done with losing a few pounds too.

I didn't understand one word of what she or the vicar said. I excused myself and went up to the bathroom. I locked the door and stood in front of the mirror. I couldn't see myself.

The vicar stayed a long time. For the most part, he and Mama talked between themselves. I stayed in the bathroom for ages, they didn't try to persuade me out of there. I unlocked the door and came out all on my own. I had sprayed myself with perfume and unearthed the brightest lipstick I had; I had gone into the bedroom and put on my new linen suit. I felt unreal, but I could now hear what they were talking about and I must have seemed quite composed – it's amazing what some bright lipstick can do, an elegantly cut jacket. I noticed in the mirror that the woman who came striding out of the bathroom had such a taut neck, there were little white nodules under the skin, like peas.

The vicar said that it was Erlend who had found you. An ambulance had come and taken you to the hospital, they needed me to come down there and identify you. Erlend was at the police station: just a routine interview. The vicar asked Mama where your father lived, he wondered whether it would be a good idea for him to call the local vicar and let him know what had happened, so that this colleague of his, who we gathered was also a good friend, could go over to Johan and Minna's place and break the news to them. He droned on and on, and I broke in and told him that your father hated all churchmen, that he would never allow a man of the cloth to set foot inside his flat. The vicar asked if I would contact him myself; I said I could call him on my mobile. But first I was going to the hospital.

He drove Mama and me to the hospital in his own car. We took the main road into town and drove right across to the other side. We glided through every intersection on a wave of green lights. The vicar was a good driver. He had a nearly new Volvo, it seemed solid. I remember everything about that car journey, every detail. He had an old copy of the Norwegian Automobile Association road atlas on the back seat – it seemed out of place in such a new car – and several cassettes of classical music, but he didn't play any music for us, he kept quiet. He left us in peace. I sat in the back seat, Mama sat in the front. I felt I could have been their child.

He and Mama arranged things with the undertaker, the hospital had procedures for such things, numbers to call, forms to sign. There are telephone numbers and forms for everything, all you have to do is call. In due course her sisters also arrived, I don't know where they came from, they just appeared.

They had wrapped you in a sheet and laid you in cold storage. It was cold in the ante-room, too. White coats hung on pegs in a little cloakroom. I shivered. The vicar and Mama were waiting outside.

I don't know whether I nodded or what. I suppose I must have nodded. A little nod of the head can be enough, then you've said what you have to say. They had hung a label on you, with all your details; maybe they were afraid you might get mixed up with someone else.

I would have done better to shake my head. Shake it hard from side to side. But if I had shaken my head they would only have called Johan, and then he would have nodded instead of me. I wanted it to be my nod, my say-so. I was your mother, only a mother can say whether her child is alive or dead.

The next day you were to be taken to the Institute of Pathology. A post-mortem has to be carried out on all suicides, you know that, don't you, they have to be sure that the person concerned has hung herself from that tree by her own hand, that she hasn't been hung by anyone else.

But now he's getting up from the step, Heavens above, would you look at this place, must get it tidied up, look at this mess, and look at my toes . . .

. . . it really is hopeless, the mess you make . . .

Now he's ringing the doorbell, what's he ringing the bell for, why can't he just walk straight in?

must have put on the safety chain. Have to open the door, have to open the door for him. Have to say I.

THE STORY

It is evening. In the houses of the neighbourhood everything has changed. It is as if people had suddenly woken up, as if someone had grabbed hold of them and shaken them and screamed something into their ears while they were asleep. They are still dazed and bewildered. They would rather not know, they'd like to run and hide. The word has spread from house to house, as if conveyed by a distant transmitter known to none, but feared by all. They don't know what to do, they pace restlessly to and fro, move things about, reach for their children.

As soon as they heard the news they passed it on, ran over to a neighbour or picked up the phone and called a number, as if they wished to be free of what they had heard, not wanting it to stop at them. The residents' association has organised a wreath, and several members are planning to attend the funeral tomorrow.

The death notice had been in the paper. In a way that made it all a little easier to take in, since then it actually seemed to concern more people: in principle everybody who read the newspaper, you might say. And there were so many death notices on the day it was published, there seemed to be no end to them.

In the notice of Ebba's death Judith's and Johan's names appeared side by side, under them came Minna and Jennifer's names, and under them again her grandmother's.

Those who are going to the funeral have ironed shirts and blouses and hung them ready on hangers. Several have thought to themselves that they would also have washed the car in which they'll be driving to church tomorrow, had it not been for the water rationing. It doesn't look good, going to church in a dirty car. But there's not enough water left for such things, the dry spell has gone on for so long, there are heavy fines for anyone daring to use a garden hose.

No one can believe that she actually did it. This death just does not fit.

No one has seen anything of Judith, she's probably keeping to the house. But there's been a steady stream of people in and out of her door these past few days, Judith's mother and what the neighbours take to be other relatives, people they've never seen before. They carried plates and dishes of food out of the cars, up the steps and through the door, and a while later they came back out and drove away. Then the traffic tailed off.

At first, when Johan drives up and parks down on the street that evening, it is only the old couple across the road, Runa and Isak, who notice him. They stand at the window, each behind their curtain, observing how he goes on sitting and sitting in the car. He looks as if he has turned to stone. After a while they give up watching to see what happens, their old legs get so tired. They drop the curtains. Runa takes to pottering about in the kitchen, Isak sits down on the sofa in the sitting-room. A fair bit of time passes and then they are drawn back to the window, only to find that Johan has got out of the car. But he has not gone into his old home, he has sat himself down on the front steps. He looks as if he is frozen to the spot.

The two old folk remember him from the days when he used to live here. They feel they know him better than they know Judith, although it's years since they spoke to him. Judith can seem a bit standoffish, hard to make out, but when Johan lived here everyone in the neighbourhood knew him to be a helpful, easy-going man, always ready to lend a hand when there was a job needing done, and always happy to lend out his tools. It seems almost unreal, that he should be back here now, and that he doesn't go in. That must mean something.

They remark to one another on what they observe, softly, as if afraid that Johan will hear them. Then they see him pull himself to his feet on the steps, brush the dust of his trouser-legs, turn and ring the doorbell of Judith's house. And all at once the tiredness seems to wash over them, it is like a warm weight on their faces, they can hardly keep their eyes open. They sigh and mutter something about it being just about time, then they wander through to the bathroom to get ready for bed. They brush their teeth, get undressed, clean their nails with a nail file, break off a suitable length of dental floss and wind it around an index finger. All unknown to each other, every neighbour goes through precisely the same motions.

All of the houses lining this road are built to the same standard design, furnished in the same style, from the same era, the bathrooms are more or less identical, the distance from the bathroom to the main bedroom is exactly the same length, even though some people take long strides and others short, faltering steps. And all the double beds in all the bedrooms are positioned in exactly the same way, with the headboard underneath the bedroom window and just enough space on either side for a bedside table.

Within an hour of climbing between the sheets, in most cases with no duvet because of the heat, the majority of the neighbours are asleep. But not Runa and Isak; they lie awake and stare at the ceiling.

Erlend too is awake. He is lying in bed in his room at his parents' house, only a few blocks away. On the floor sits a tray with sandwiches and a glass of milk, next to the milk glass lies a sleeping tablet. It seems to him that every time his mother has spotted him slipping upstairs and into his room these past few days, she has been up after him only minutes later, with this tray. She must be dashing into the kitchen the second she sees me, he thinks, slinging open the fridge door and hauling out butter and salami, cheese or jam. Every time she comes up she has put something different in the sandwiches. As if trying to tempt him, she's trying to tempt him to eat and sleep, she brings him food and medicine. Emergency aid, that's all she knows.

But he doesn't eat, and he never sleeps. It's too hot. He has tucked the sleeping pills under his pillow. There's quite a little pile there now.

On the cupboard door, next to the desk, hangs the dark outline of a figure with no head and limp arms and legs. It's the suit he will wear to the funeral tomorrow. Ebba will be lying in the coffin that he has promised to help carry. He knows exactly how much she weighs, he has lifted her lots of times when she was alive, he liked lifting her. That was only a few days ago, less than a week; how can such an awful change come about so suddenly, it's just not possible, it can't be right. Every time he thinks of how much she weighs he feels the weight of her in his arms, and he imagines the burden of that weight in the coffin tomorrow morning. The hollowing out of the cave behind his face is steadily progressing, whenever he thinks like that he can feel it. Is she fixed to the coffin or will her body slide about in there when they lift it up? Will she slide? Is she stiff or limp? Will they have to be careful to keep the coffin perfectly level? What if he trips?

The hollow space behind his face is quite big now, it must be windy in there. It won't be long now before those who are busy digging in there have worked their way right through. He doesn't know what they can have been digging through. Right through his head, maybe; soon they'll have dug right out through the back of his head, leaving behind them a yawning tunnel. His face is nothing but a thin grimace covering this tunnel.

He can't bear to think any more. He can't bear to think about the last day he and Ebba were together either. But he does it anyway, something inside him says he has to force himself. Thoughts can't just settle down, like the wind. Or trail off to their den, like a weary dog and drift off to sleep. No, they can't. Thoughts have to stay on the alert, chase each other, make the wind blow, send it whirling up.

He remembers the day before she did it. In the bathroom that morning, as on so many others, he had told himself that soon he would have to tell her what was on his mind. It was Midsummer already; school was out, she and her father would shortly be going out sailing, and he and some of his mates were going to a rock festival – there might be a few girls coming along too, although that wasn't quite decided yet. He had come to the conclusion that it would be best to tell her just before she went on holiday, so that she would have time to get over it while she was away. He knew she was looking forward to it, she and her father were planning a long trip on the sailboat.

Ordinarily, she didn't tell him much about her father and his family, not since that day last spring when he had run into them outside the library. Things had been more difficult since then. Prior to that meeting she had spoken of them quite a lot, she seemed almost relieved to be able to talk about them. But she seldom mentioned her mother. He got the impression that she was protecting her from something: that there was something he wasn't supposed to know about Judith.

They both had jobs for the summer, he in a brewery, she in a psychiatric hospital. Usually, if their shifts allowed, they would meet after work. They would go for a walk, or sit in a café and drink coffee – it was all they could afford, they were both saving up for their holidays. Once or twice she had mentioned that she and her mother had a cottage down by the fjord, that they could perhaps ask if they could borrow it for a few days in the summer, get away from it all, just the two of them. It wouldn't cost them anything, it would do no harm to ask, she had said, looking at him with eyes that shone, but each time he had managed to talk his way out of it. He wasn't sure when he was going to have to work, he had to take all the hours he could get at the brewery, he said, the pay was good, and the money would be a big help in the autumn when he left home and had to manage on his grant. She understood, of course. She hadn't gone on at him, she wasn't that sort of person.

But he just couldn't tell her that he wanted to break it off. He tried to, he truly did; from the time he got up in the morning and all day at work he would be firmly resolved that this was the day when he would tell her. But when he saw her walking across the square towards him in the afternoon it was as if she became too real for him, somehow her presence gained the upper hand, rendering him weak and indecisive. She was always so happy when she caught sight of him, she had no way of hiding it. There was something about her that was too open, such an open person is bound to get hurt, he had thought.

But he can't remember there being anything unusual about her that last day. They had gone for a coffee after work, she had actually seemed more relaxed than usual, she had talked about her little sister, about all the funny things she had been saying on the phone lately. The two sisters evidently spent a long time talking on the phone in the evening before Jennifer went to bed, it was a little ritual they had established this summer, he gathered. He had noticed that she was speaking of her family again, she hadn't done that in a long time. She had told him how, the evening before, Jennifer had asked her what was inside the earth, they had talked about earth and rock and mountains and red-hot lava. Her sister had asked again and again about this red-hot lava. How could you get all the way in there? To the centre of the earth, to the very core. She was so sweet, Ebba said, she had become really fascinated with lava recently, she talked about it all the time. And he had nodded, agreeing; Jennifer was a lovely kid – he'd met her quite a few times, of course. Not for a while, though.

Ebba meant to spend the evening with her mother. They were going to try out a new dish they had seen some celebrity chef make on this television programme that they always watched, and Ebba was going to do the shopping on the way home. And he had arranged to meet a couple of mates at a bar near the town centre. They would have a couple of beers, he'd made no secret of the fact, why should he? She didn't seem unhappy that he didn't spend all his time with her. In fact she didn't seem unhappy at all, he thinks, if anything she had been more relaxed than usual, clearer, somehow. Did she seem older perhaps? He's not sure. In any case, all of this is just what he's reading into it after the event, no such thoughts were going through his mind at the time.

He had paid for both their coffees, pecked her on the cheek that she turned to him, before unlocking his bike, clipping the weighty bike-lock around his waist and pedalling off along the pavement. She was going to walk up to the station and take the suburban line home.

'So long!' he had said, lifting his hand in a wave. She had merely smiled, a quiet, intent smile. It occurred to him that he hadn't got round to telling her that day either. It'd have to wait till next time.

He rolls over in bed. This is as far as he ever manages to get, before having to start all over again. She hadn't replied to his 'So long,' she had merely smiled at him. That was the last thing that passed between them. There was no way he could have known what was going to happen. No way. There were no signs. Not beforehand and not afterwards. It was impossible to interpret anything that had passed between them as a sign.

He turns his head and looks over at the dark suit hanging on the cupboard door. He bends his knees and stretches them again. The sheet is creased and drenched in sweat, it sticks to the soles of his feet and slips up and down the mattress. It's far too bright outside. How can a person sleep when it's so bright and warm.

The suit is a shadow. It hurts so much. It hurts so much. Yet again he goes over in his mind the last time he saw her alive. What she said. How she looked. What lies at the earth's core?

Lava. 'So long,' he had said. She hadn't replied. His chest constricts, it's hard to breathe. What lies at the earth's core? Lava.

He could easily disappear in that bed; all that would be left would be the sweat-soaked sheets; he could become a shadow, slipping away. His gaze flickers across the walls of the room, over the bookshelves, the posters tacked to the wall. The bright evening around him is too close, everything feels cold and utterly meaningless, suddenly he is filled with a deep loathing for it all. What is the point in lying here, tossing and turning, unable to sleep; what, come to that, is the point of enduring all of this pain, it would be easier if one could just let go, see it all smoothed out into a soft white light, and after that – nothing. He wonders how many sleeping pills it would take to sleep like that. He's quite sure he doesn't have enough, he thinks, possibly not even enough to fall into a doze.

He can no longer live with himself. This thought leaves him panic-stricken; he can't hold himself together any longer, his thoughts break away from him, take physical form: a wrathful child which aims a violent kick at his chest.

And at the very moment when he is overwhelmed by this kick to his chest, everything inside him seems to loosen up. His thoughts slacken their grip. All at once everything goes still. Within a fraction of a second a weight seems to have lifted off him. Lifted off his chest, as if the wrathful child had simply evaporated. He is sucked into what feels like a whirlpool, it drags him into the void, and he realises that this void he sees is the cave that has come into being behind his face. Maybe in a moment he will lose consciousness. He lets himself fall.

He doesn't know how long he has been out. The pills are still there under his pillow when he comes to himself again, but it is as if he has become someone else. He notices it first with his hearing, it has intensified. His body is limp and numb. His attention is drawn to the sounds outside in the garden, and inside the house. All sounds are amplified, become clearer; he hears a car starting up and driving off, a dog utters three short, sharp barks then falls silent again. The steady flow of traffic on the main road hums in the background. He hears the sound of his own breathing.

And he hears the silence within all of this. The pauses between the dog's barks. The space between inhaling and exhaling. And within this space he is caught by a fresh surge, he is swept towards the suit hanging on the door. It envelopes him. He feels the dark cotton fibres against his face. He feels calm and light. It's not so hard, it's just empty and bright, a wide-open space. He is aware of his breathing. He is nothing but this breath. He breathes into the suit.

He hears his mother's footsteps on the stairs. She passes his door and goes into her own room, just like the neighbours in the other houses round about them, who are also going to bed now. It is almost as if he can see them.

He hears the silence between his mother's footsteps. The same silence that hangs between the footsteps of the others. Everyone who is walking. They are all exactly alike, they have no faces.

Johan also hears the silence. His breath is also strained, it catches in his throat, he holds one hand against his breast like a shield.

And Judith too must become part of the soundlessness, she has opened the door now, she stands before him in the doorway. She is still almost as tall as him, and her hair is just as he remembers; he realises that it must be her. But her face is strange to him, it's so old. There must be some mistake, he thinks. He doesn't belong here any more. He wants to get away.

He doesn't live here any more. Ah, yes, this is what it was like. He pulls himself together and tries to get things clear in his mind. Something happened, and he could no longer live in this house, it became too cramped for him; he made himself hard and clear as crystal and drove off in the old car. Something between them had been shattered. Now he remembers.

Judith is staring at him with those stranger's eyes. He knows that she is going to claim him back. This house is a trap.

But Judith, too, is bewildered. To her, *he*'s the one who has grown old. She can't get it to add up, surely it's not that long since he left? Ebba was three and a half at the time, she thinks, working it out, it was early autumn, it took a while for her to realise that Papa wasn't coming back, but when it finally dawned on her she tore up and down the gravel driveway, screaming blue murder, she fell and hurt herself on purpose, she acted up something awful. Judith had to get her a plaster and a glass of blackcurrant squash, she remembers it well, they cuddled up together here on the step and Judith told stories. She told the story of the pancake that rolled and rolled away down the road, away from Goody Poody, the husband and the seven squalling children, she told the story of the cock and the hen in the nut forest, she plaited Ebba's hair and rubbed her back and promised that she could sleep in Papa's bed. They went to bed early.

After he left them, she was the one who had to be big and strong. You mustn't ever let go of your child, she thought, you have to lie there beside her in the double bed until she is breathing peacefully and you can tell that she is asleep. You feel yourself slowly withering away, growing weak, but you must not let go. You have to be on guard, be strong. Make things right again.

Neither of them moves. And as Johan stares at her, Judith's stranger's face begins to change. Her features slip into place, growing familiar to him, uncannily familiar, more so than he cares to admit. So many times he has run his fingers over these lines. It seems he had forgotten that he can tell from her eyes what she is thinking.

Between them time has solidified. In the warmth of the evening it has turned into an almost transparent sheet through which they can barely make one another out. And he wants to shout at her: All the things you're thinking about me, that was all a long time ago, Judith! Everything's different now, look at me, I'm a different person. There's Minna, and Jennifer, they're lying in bed, back at the hotel, waiting for me. They're relying on me. I'm not going to let them down, not going to let you get the better of me. You're so strong.

But he stands there, paralysed, her eyes shining on him, the sun shining on him; it is a long, light summer night, the sun is not about to give in, the look in her eyes is not about to give in, it hasn't rained in such a long time. It's now four and a half days since Ebba went off into the forest.

He climbs the last step towards her. She stays where she is. From the hall behind her the heat hits him: a wall of fug. The sun has been beating down on the windows for days, the flowers inside emit warm gusts of scent and noxious vapour. He has to brace himself, to save reeling backwards.

Her eyes are wide open. He half expects her to flap her arms at him and shoo him away, she is a witch. But she stays quite still.

He knows it's a dangerous sign when Judith does not move.

Then things start to move again, complete with sound. Judith steps back a pace into the hall, he is drawn in after her; neither of them says anything. She stands aside, locks the door behind him with an audible click, fumbles the safety chain into place with stiff fingers, he hears the chink of metal on metal. He stands with his back to her, unmoving, while she locks up; the poison from the flowers is already starting to work, it seeps into his pores. It wouldn't take very long for them both to suffocate in here, he thinks.

But he can't stop now. He moves further in towards the sitting-room, his feet know the way, they want to take him with them, he automatically lays his car keys and mobile phone on the chest of drawers as he passes it. Someone has spread a white crochet cloth over the chest of drawers, and there is a big bouquet of white flowers sitting on top of it: white roses, lilies, gypsophila. A white condolence card.

There was never a cloth on the chest of drawers when he lived here, he didn't know she owned a white crochet cloth. And there have never been so many flowers in the house before. He can tell that Judith must have a lot of friends, but he no longer knows who they are.

She follows him from the hall into the sitting-room. Her feet are bare, he glances down at her toes and notices that she has painted her toenails, she has smeared nail polish all over the toes themselves, it looks pathetic. She appears to have made some attempt to smarten herself up, her dress is white but creased.

In the middle of the sitting-room floor is a heap of clothes and stuff. At first he can't think what it can be, but then he recognises Ebba's things: her hairbrush, her swimsuit, pairs of dressy shoes and trainers. The sight of this heap makes him feel like being sick.

But his throat has knotted up. He has to open a window, create a draught, he has to get some air.

'It's awfully stuffy in here,' he says, taking a step towards the window. This is the first thing he has said to her, the sound is back now, so there must also be words, but he can hear that what he says is wrong. Wrong sound. None the less he continues:

'We need to open some windows. We need to get some air in here, these flowers . . .'

But she just stands there staring at him with those same stony eyes. Then a sound escapes her, a kind of howl. He pulls up short and lowers his arm.

'*We!*' she hisses between clenched teeth, he shudders when he hears how toneless her voice is. 'Why do you say *we*?'

'But we . . .' he starts, but checks himself. She steps right up close to him, eyeing him with menace, he has never seen her like this before.

'There is no *we*! You may *not* open the windows!' she shouts, full in his face. 'They're my windows! And I want them shut! I'm not having any air in here! Get away from that window!'

He jumps back in alarm.

'May I sit down?' he asks, nodding towards the sofa.

'No! You'll stand!' she yells. Then she starts marching rapidly around the room, circling him.

It's really weird, as if this house were already beginning to absorb him. Helplessly he submits to being sucked in. She may be play-acting, this may all be an act or she may be genuine, he can't tell, and it makes no difference now anyway, he is powerless to resist.

'I saw a rat,' she says eventually, still circling him. 'It was sitting on the bench outside the hospital, staring at me.'

'A rat?'

'It was sitting on the bench outside the hospital, staring at me. I called directory enquiries to get your number. All the ladies at directory enquiries sang their words, Mama and the aunts wanted me to drink blackcurrant squash, and you were in bed asleep, your

228

mobile was switched off . You never hear me when you're asleep, you never have your mobile switched on.'

He doesn't know how to reply to this. He endeavours to understand this language she is talking.

Judith reaches down stiffly and starts picking up clothes from the heap on the floor and folding them, her movements brisk and impatient. Her voice sounds as if it is babbling on all by itself, feverishly, it mutters that she is sick of tidying up after Ebba, that it's about time that young lady started tidying up after herself . . . this cannot go on . . . just can't keep anything tidy . . . look at this . . . dirt and filth everywhere . . . her hands smell so bad . . . it hasn't rained for ages . . . it's ridiculous having to carry all that water from the kitchen . . . that heavy garden sprinkler . . . her hands are all blistered, just look . . . it's ridiculous . . . she needs to put on some salve . . . why does he never have any salve with him . . .

He has to interrupt this torrent.

'Hey. Look at me,' he says, softly and insistently. 'We need to . . .'

But she will not look at him.

'Sorrr-ay?' she says. 'Could you rrre-peat that?'

He tries to get her to meet his eye.

'And what sort of a time is this to come at?' she adds, her gaze riveted on the wall behind him. 'You might have called! Why didn't you call me? Ebba's been asking for you! She always gets so excited when she knows you're coming, you know that, when will you learn to call and say when you're going to be late? I'm not being unreasonable, I would just like to know, so that I can tell her when Papa will be here. Now you can see what I've got to put up with. Look at this mess, it's actually quite hard work having a teenage daughter in the house, she's sixteen now, or hadn't you noticed? She's reached puberty, in case you didn't know? Did you know that!? It's a difficult age! Just you try getting her to eat some decent food for a change! And to clear up the mess she makes! Look at all this! The place is like a tip! Just you try clearing up, and see how easy it is. It's all so slippery, things just keep sliding away from one another, they just . . .'

He stands there with his hands hanging by his sides like heavy weights, it's all he can do not to laugh. He covers his mouth apologetically with one hand, the other dangles limply.

After a while her words degenerate into heaving gasps and she sinks down on to the heap of clothes, a trickle of white spittle running from the corner of her mouth. She gropes about, rummaging in the heap, he doesn't recognise her when she is like this. He wades through the heap to get to her and tries to put his arms around her, but she pushes him away.

'You didn't want to be here any more, you just drove away!' she hisses. 'This is not your house, it's mine! You left it! You just dropped everything and drove off!' Then she seems to fall back into herself.

'I saw a rat,' she whispers again, fainter now. 'It was outside the hospital, it was staring at me, then all of a sudden it was gone, I don't know where it went, it just disappeared. You weren't there. You're never there.'

But he is still not sure whether she is play-acting or whether she really is unbalanced. He knows of old how she can put on an act in order to get what she wants.

'Hey,' he says. 'Stop it. I'm here now. I did get here on time, but I've been sitting in the car for a while, I needed time to think. I don't know what to say. We have to talk about Ebba.'

'The princess!' she cries.

'Yes. We have to talk about the princess. The princess is dead.'

The sitting-room is smaller than he recalls, more compressed, there is less space between the furniture than he recalls. But that can't be right, surely it's only those rooms that you haven't seen since childhood that seem smaller when seen again in adulthood? He looks at the curtains, the folded blanket on the sofa. It all seems very nice and tidy, except for the heap of Ebba's clothes and stuff on the floor.

He turns to Judith. She lifts her face and gazes deep into his eyes. He makes to say something about the heap on the floor, but she breaks him off and starts speaking to him in an exaggeratedly bright, storyteller-lady voice, as if recounting something to a dull-witted child.

'Once upon a time . . . there was a goodwife who had seven hungry children,' she says, keeping her eyes fixed on him. 'One day she made pancakes for them. She made them with new milk, and the first one lay in the pan sizzling and bubbling until it was lovely and thick.'

Johan stares at her in bewilderment, trying to grasp what she is saying. He feels her fastening her grip on him with that voice, he remembers it from the time when he lived in this house and she used to read to Ebba. He had always wondered why she had to sound so coquettish when she read aloud, it was as if she wanted to show everyone who saw her that she was also an excellent actress. I suppose this is what she thinks of as 'spellbinding her audience', we're talking tip-top acting here, he tells himself. There would soon be no way of getting out of this house again.

Judith goes on with her tale, growing more and more frenzied, her voice getting louder and louder. She darts about the room; he makes a grab for her, but she dodges him, she's quicker than him, she is a squirrel.

'But the pancake flipped over on to its other side,' she cries, 'and when it had cooked for a little on that side, too, and felt a bit firmer, it sprang out on to the floor and rolled off like a wheel, through the door and down the road.'

At this point she brushes against him, he reaches out and catches hold of her. He checks her flight so roughly that she simply flops like a rag-doll. He grips her tightly.

'Judith. Look at me,' he says, as she struggles to pull away. 'We have to talk about Ebba. She's dead. Do you understand?'

But Judith manages to wriggle free. She flits about the room, playing the pancake, she wants him to follow her. She rolls off as fast as she can, away from the goodwife, the husband and the seven squalling children.

'It had been rolling for some time when it met a man,' she cried, in a thin, fierce, little-girl voice now. '"Good-day, pancake," said the man. "Greetings to you, Manny-Panny," said the pancake. "Dear pancake," said the man, "don't roll so fast, but stay a while and let me eat you!" But the pancake said: "I have run away from Goody-Poody and the husband and seven squalling children, and I can run away from you, too, Manny-Panny," and it rolled and rolled until it met a hen.'

This is ridiculous. She has come to a halt by the kitchen door, she is gasping for breath. He stands still too, on the other side of the heap of clothes.

'Stop it!' he says quietly. 'Stop all this. I know you're only play-acting. I'm not going to play along with you, Judith. You can't make me.'

She looks straight at him. Her eyes are suddenly perfectly clear. Somehow it's even more disturbing when she looks at him like that, he senses that she is, in a way, stronger than him, but this does not stop him from holding her gaze.

'We have to talk about it,' he says. 'We were her parents. Are. We are her parents. We're having the funeral tomorrow, we need to discuss how we're going to arrange things. *We*. We have to talk.'

He can tell that she understands what he is saying. But she's not going to allow him to take charge, she walks up to him and does something with her eyes again, she glares at him with child-like sternness. He decides that he had better try to play along, it doesn't look as if he has much choice.

'Don't talk to me like that!' she says, seizing his wrists, pulling them towards her and shaking them. 'Say: "Dear pancake, don't roll so fast, but stay a while and let me eat you."'

'Dear pancake, don't roll so fast, but stay a while and let me eat you,' he repeats obediently. She stares at him in amazement. He is aware that he is losing a battle, the whys and the wherefores of which are lost on him. He has to pull himself together, gather his thoughts.

'Oh, no, no. I have run away from Goody-Poody, the husband and the seven squalling children, and I can run away from you, too, Manny-Panny!' she murmurs tentatively, and makes to run on, pulling him along with her. But he wrenches his hands back and restrains her.

'Judith. Stop it,' he says. 'It's not funny. I don't want to play.'

'You never want to play,' she answers sulkily.

I've managed to shake her out of it, he thinks with relief.

'No, you're probably right,' he responds, hoping that he can keep her here, in the real world. 'You're probably right, I'm no good at playing. But now we have to talk about Ebba. She's dead. Do you understand? She didn't want to go on living. Why didn't she want to go on living, Judith? You must know, you were her mother.'

She just stares at him.

'She's dead,' he says again. 'You do understand that, don't you? Why didn't she want to go on living?'

In his bed at his parents' house a few blocks away, Erlend has at long last fallen asleep. The unreal experience with the suit has passed, he has sunk back into himself, then drifted off; he is not dreaming. From somewhere in his sleep a wave of weeping is rolling in, like a wall of pressure. But as yet he is not aware of it, in his sleep there is nothing but darkness and warmth and heaviness.

But in the sitting-room in the house at the top of the drive Judith slumps, dark and motionless, in the heap of Ebba's clothes. Her bizarre pantomime appears to be over now. Yet she is breathing so strangely. Her name is an anchor attached to a slender line, but it may not be heavy enough to hold her fast, she feels as if she is being pushed away. The line grows longer and thinner, she seems to be floating, she feels light-headed.

Johan treads softly around the room. It has suddenly become so quiet. He feels sick. He moves from one bouquet of flowers to the next, reading the condolence cards. The flowers don't really seem to have anything to do with him. Nor do they, he thinks, these flowers were sent to her. But he reads the cards anyway. He notices that a number of people who used to be his and Judith's mutual friends have sent two bouquets: one to him and Minna and one to her. He feels a stab of pain at the realisation that people don't even believe they can share the flowers for Ebba's funeral. But they're right of course. They can't even share the flowers.

After several bouts on the phone with Judith's mother over the past couple of days he has agreed to let the undertakers arrange for a wreath bearing the legend 'Thanks for everything. Mama and Papa.' But he hasn't dared to tell Judith this, and he knows that this is not the moment to tell her. She is probably correct in saying that he has abdicated the right to be a *we* with her, and 'Mama and Papa' is most clearly and heartbreakingly a *we*. He hopes her mother has told her about the wreath, but it would not surprise him if she has left it for him to say. She has never made any secret of the fact that she thinks he needs to be schooled, as if his character weren't actually fully formed.

He pauses behind Judith and tries to place his hands on her shoulders. She wrests herself loose with a convulsive twist of her body. He jumps back as if burned.

Judith is starting to sink now, the thin line has become slacker, something weighty has begun to open up inside her, something other than this airy transparency that makes her so light-headed. She wants to be with Ebba. Far too late, she knows. She wants to be heavy. She goes on sinking.

She is breathing so rapidly, he turns to look at her and sees that she is close to hyper-ventilating, her gasps transporting her into a state that cannot be good for her. She may have been putting on an act for him when she was haring around playing Goody-Poody, but this is something else – hyperventilating can be dangerous, he remembers them saying that at the childbirth classes they attended when Ebba was on the way.

Amid the panting he can hear that she has started mumbling something, a song of some sort, a murmur, her body is the resonance chamber for a murmuring that is trying to get out, but her voice is turned inwards and her breath is like a bellows. He tells himself that he'll have to speak to her, say something, anything.

'What's that you're singing?' he says. She mumbles louder, as if meaning to show him something, but her breathing is so heavy that it's hard to hear.

'Hey. What's that you're singing?'

She won't look at him, but he steps closer and now he can hear:

All the little billy-goats came over the hill
to ask if Ebba was home, home, home
Yes, said Ebba's mama, yes, she said
and all the little billy-goats were glad, glad, glad.

He remembers that song. It's one of the old nursery rhymes. It belongs here in this house. It is so old. He is so old.

'Ow!' she cries suddenly, like a child that has hurt itself. 'Ow! It hurts!'

'What hurts?' he asks in alarm.

'It hurts!' she cries again.

'What hurts? Where? Where does it hurt?'

'Here!' she cries, clutching at her breast. 'Here! Oh, the pain. Ow!'

The last thing he needs now is for Judith to have a heart attack. He wades into the mound of clothes to get to her, wraps his arms around her and sits down on the floor, holding her to him. She permits him to do this now, her hands are clenched across her chest and she looks genuinely frightened. He places both his hands over hers and searches frantically through his memory for something he can do, he doesn't remember any first-aid apart from mouth-to-mouth resuscitation and that's not what she needs, he can see that. The only other thing he can think of is the breathing exercises they learned at those childbirth classes.

He tries to tune in to his own breathing, he doesn't know whether he has any breath left, he can't feel it anywhere, but it must be there, he thinks, it's bound to be there. He thinks back to the childbirth classes, trying to remember what they had been taught; the teacher had been a big, strapping Finnish midwife, a nice woman, although they had had difficulty understanding what she said.

But he's been here before. Judith is in pain, just as she was that time when he was by her side in the delivery room, with his mother-in-law waiting outside in the corridor. Now, as then, something is trying to get out of her, her body contracts and wants to push, although this time whatever it is appears to be in her chest, not in the huge pregnant belly she had back then.

It was so long ago. But surely he can remember the breathing, he thinks. Everything is stored away in the brain.

And then it all comes back to him. He bends his head down to her and begins to whisper to her, telling her how to breathe. Inhale slowly. Exhale slowly. Inhale slowly. Exhale slowly. He breathes with her, holds her hands, as if trying to quieten this heart to which she is clinging. And in the end he gets her to calm down, the breaths flow between them like a gentle breeze; he talks softly, confidentially to her between each inhalation and exhalation, as if she were still his woman giving birth, as if some living being were still working its way out of her, as if he were an earnest and hopeful father-to-be, awaiting the arrival of something that looks like him, something that cannot be anything but good. He feels her body relaxing, she lets go. Something slides out of her. He can't see what it is, it slides off and is lost among the heap of clothes.

And at last he can tell himself that now she will return to this house. He has done it. Her song sinks down inside her again, until it is almost gone. He starts to murmur, singing along with her:

All the little billy-goats came over the hill
to ask if Ebba was home, home, home
No, sighed Ebba's mama, no, she sighed
and all the little billy-goats they cried, cried, cried.

When they reach the last line he is able to take his hands from under her arms and let his head drop on to her back. For a long time they sit like this in the heap of girl's clothes on the floor.

When, wearily, he attempts to get up, she pulls him back down on to the floor beside her. She twists her head towards his and tries to kiss him, but he turns his face away.

Then she seizes hold of his face, wrenches it round and says: 'Say my name!'

He is looking her straight in the face. Her hands are a vice.

'Judith,' he says. 'You are Judith.'

She releases him.

The sitting-room is such a mess, they can't have it looking such a mess. They have people coming tomorrow, they have to get Ebba's things back up into her cupboards. Or into boxes. Into boxes and out into the garden? Or down into the basement – it might start to rain, her things mustn't get wet, they can't be left to stand out in the garden, everything could start to fall apart.

No, he thinks. It's not going to rain, it hasn't rained for weeks. Someone will have to come with a trailer and collect the whole lot. He has no idea who would normally come and collect this sort of stuff, maybe there's somebody one can call. Maybe they're in the phone book. Yellow Pages, he thinks.

He bends down, his bones creaking, and starts folding bits of clothing. Judith sits and watches him, then proceeds to copy his actions. She folds the clothes hesitantly, quite unlike her movements a little earlier, as if she has never done anything like this, as if he were having to teach her everything afresh, like a father. They work like this for a while, each on their own side of the heap of clothes, and facing in different directions. She looks at him, he looks away. Blouses and sweaters and tights, they put them into piles, set matching shoes neatly side by side. A sort of peace settles over them.

'Hey,' he says softly after a while, still with his face turned away from her. 'We have to talk about it. She didn't want to go on living, Judith. We were her parents. Are. We are her parents. We're having the funeral tomorrow, we have to talk about how to arrange things. We have to talk about why she did it.'

'Where's Minna?' she asks airily, holding up a blouse.

'Minna and Jennifer are waiting at a hotel in town. I have to be getting back soon. We've a lot to discuss. We have to decide where we're going to sit in church, whether we're going to be in the same pew. Minna and Jennifer would like to sit with us. They're grieving for her too, you know. These are things you have to think about. I don't want to keep them waiting too long. We've all got a long day ahead of us tomorrow. We need to get some sleep.'

But then, yet again, a change seems to occur. It happens so suddenly, he doesn't know what to make of it, she is so unpredictable, he must have said something wrong, he thought she was calmer now. Her glance slides away from him.

'Yes, that's right,' she says, throwing down the blouse. 'We're going to lie down and go to sleep! You're not going back to town! You're staying here with me! *I'm* the mother! You're sleeping here with me. You used to sleep with me, you used to like sleeping with me. You liked holding me.'

'I'm here now,' he says.

'Hold me,' she says, coming up to him.

'Judith. Grow up. Don't make it more difficult than . . .' He tries to stay calm.

'We've got to lie down!' She grabs hold of his hand and tugs at it like a little child.

'All right,' he says reluctantly. 'We'll lie down on the sofa. I'll hold you. Come here and . . .'

'We have to lie down here!'

Her arms are strong, she drags him down on to the floor, into the heap of Ebba's clothes. Then she rakes the clothes together around her to make a bed. He has fallen on to his knees beside her. She settles down with her back to him, takes his arm and pulls it towards her, compelling him to lie down too. She places his hand on her breast. He lets it rest there.

They lie quite still.

'Tell me about us,' she whispers after a while. 'Tell me that we were a couple. That we had a child together. Tell me about it.'

'We were a couple,' he repeats. All at once he is so tired. He feels drained of energy, the poison has started to work. He can hardly keep his eyes open, the thought of just giving in is so tempting. His voice talks on all by itself.

'We had a child,' he says dully. 'Now she is dead. She didn't want to go on living. Tomorrow we are going to bury her. We have to talk. We have to decide where we're going to sit in church.'

Even the thought is too much for him, he doesn't know how he's going to manage to stay awake for this conversation, or what chance they have of agreeing on anything before tomorrow comes and it is too late. He wishes sleep would come and help him. He wants to drift away, into the warmth.

'No, don't say it like that!' she protests. 'Tell it beautifully.'

'I don't know if I can tell it beautifully. You'll have to show me how to do it.' He yawns.

'You're no good at playing let's pretend. You never were any good at playing let's pretend. You have to pretend to be telling me a story. You've done it before. Don't you remember?'

'Yes.'

'You used to be able to improvise!'

'I'm not like that any more.'

'I want you to be the way you were! We have to play let's pretend!'

'I'm not sure I follow this game, Judith.' he says. 'Can't we just have a normal conversation? Can't we just work it out. I'm so tired.'

She lies quietly for a few minutes, as if she is thinking. He drifts further into sleep then wakes with a start when she removes his hand from her breast, gets up and goes out into the hall. She is away for some time; when she comes back he sees that she has brought her old fur hat from the hat-rack.

She tosses it down beside him in the heap on the floor. Then she lies down again, burrows down beside him, tucks the hat under his head like a pillow, lays her head on his arm. He is fighting to keep sleep at bay, he is almost overcome by it again, it has him, it is too strong, he lies there like that. He holds his eyes wide open, feeling the muscles of his face twitch.

She turns, stares straight at him for a few seconds, then places her hand on his chest and proceeds to rub, round and round. Round and round. For a long time they lie like this. He lets himself go, lets his eyes fall shut, dozes off. He hears her whispering in his ear:

'Johan. Johan, dear. Now we're going to play. You have to tell me a story. And this is how you have to begin: Once upon a time . . . in a land far, far away . . . there lived a king and a queen. They were a couple. They had a beautiful daughter.'

And he succumbs. Maybe he is asleep.

'Once upon a time, in a land far, far away, there lived a king and a queen,' he mumbles, faintly. 'They lived in a house on the outskirts of a town. The king had built the house with his own hands. They had a beautiful daughter. No. This isn't right, Judith.'

'Hadn't he built the house with his own hands?' she asks ingenuously.

'I can't do it. I'm exhausted. I can't tell . . .'

'Couldn't the king build the house?'

'I can't tell stories. You've got to let me rest.'

'But wasn't he good at building things?'

'Oh, yes, he was good at building things,' he says, fighting to get the words out. 'He enjoyed it. But it turned out that he wasn't a king. He had married the queen, but it wasn't long before he discovered that marrying her did not make him a king, only a prince consort.'

'I don't understand. What's a prince consort?'

'A prince consort is the person who is married to the queen. He makes a good match, but he doesn't get to rule.' Johan can scarcely get the words out, he is all but paralysed now.

'When did he discover this? That he was only a prince consort?' she asks.

'He discovered it on the very first morning after the wedding, when he woke up early and turned over in the bed in the bedroom in the house that he had built with his own hands, and looked at his new wife.'

Johan turns his head with difficulty and looks at Judith lying there. She snaps shut her eyes and pretends to be sleeping. She is playing herself.

He can't go on lying beside her like this, everything inside him cries out against it. He has to get up. Finish the story. Get up on to his feet.

'It was the first morning of their marriage, he was so tired, he didn't know whether he was asleep or awake,' he says. 'He had to force himself to wake up. And she slept on; he could see that she still had traces of make-up from the previous evening's celebrations under her eyes, and nail polish on her toes, a crumpled dress; she slept with her arms folded under her breasts, but it was not hard to see that she was of royal birth. She would always be a queen, no matter what life did to her. He saw it in the way she stretched out in bed in the seconds before she awoke. She stretched like a queen, like a cat.'

'Like a cat?' Judith asks, with closed eyes.

'Yes. Like a cat,' he replies.

'Then I don't see the problem.'

'The problem was that he realised, in the moments before she woke up and smiled at him with those shining eyes, that he would only ever be a man who had married into that family.'

He senses that he is starting to wake up now. He has talked himself out of it.

'That's right, Johan,' she says slowly. 'That's how it was. He was just a prince consort, and she was a queen.'

'A cat-queen.'

'But he was good at building things!' she smiles, opening her eyes.

'Yes indeed. He was good at building things. He built their house almost single-handedly, he only hired people to lay the foundations and put in the wiring and the plumbing. He put his heart into that house in a way he'd never done with anything before. He felt so close to it all, to the materials, the ground, the wind gusting around the trees as autumn came and went and winter drew on. Once the roof was on he held a topping-out ceremony all by himself with a beer and a cigarette. They moved in in May.'

'You sound as if you're reading from a book,' she says.

'But that's how it was. They moved in in May.'

'Yes. That's how it was. They moved in in May. And he was a happy man. It was a fine house he had built.'

'He was indeed a happy man,' he continues, trying to figure out where to go from here. 'And they had her mother, the Moon Queen, living in a terraced house not far away. Some evenings she would pay them a visit. She would sit and watch television while she knitted and talked with a decided look on her face about goings-on in the kingdom. But most of the time she was busy with her own concerns in her own residence. She had lots of sisters, and lots of women friends.'

'The Moon Queen, was that what she was called?' asks Judith in surprise.

'Yes,' he replies.

'I didn't know that.'

'I have told you before, you must have forgotten.'

'Was it him who came up with that name?'

'Yes.'

'He didn't say anything about that.'

'Oh yes he did.'

'But the Moon Queen didn't come to visit them all that often.'

'No, sometimes the queen went to visit her, it's true. And when she did she was usually gone all evening.'

'She felt secure with her mother.'

'I'm sure she did,' he says. 'And she was always happy to take advice from her mother on how things in the kingdom should be run. Her advice was sound and well-meant and based on long experience, it was always better than the prince consort's advice – whenever, that is, he brought himself to offer any. When the mother wasn't visiting the daughter or the daughter visiting the mother they could talk on the telephone for hours, discussing internal affairs. On those occasions the queen would take the telephone into the bedroom, he would see the cable vanishing under the door.'

'I don't think he was too happy about that,' Judith remarks mildly. 'I think he felt neglected.'

'Sometimes, perhaps,' he replies. 'He may have felt a little uneasy when he heard them talking like that, he may have begun to wonder whether he was fit to be a prince consort at all, he, who had no experience of this life.'

'But generally he thought it was just fine that the mother and the daughter got on so well together,' she says.

'Yes, generally he thought it was fine. Actually he was quite happy about it, after all they were the ones who knew what it was like to be royal. He was only an ordinary man of the people, a computer engineer who had been drawn into this fairy-tale without really understanding how it happened.'

'He didn't understand it?'

'He didn't really understand it, no.'

'But what was there to understand? I thought they loved one another. I thought what they had was special.'

A trace of doubt has crept into her voice. He realises that it is beginning to dawn on her that he has the upper hand, that he has woken up and is about to break out of the fairy-tale.

'There was a lot to understand,' he says. 'Too much for him, perhaps.'

They stare at one another.

'I thought it was enough that they loved one another,' she says. 'The queen didn't think there was anything to understand, she thought it was enough that they loved one another. They were so happy.'

She has reverted to that sulky little voice that he knows so well. It's never a good sign when she puts on that voice, but at this moment it's also reassuringly familiar, he knows that voice inside out. It seems he had forgotten how she used to punish him by talking like this.

'Well, they may have differed slightly on that point,' he says guardedly. 'The prince consort had always felt it was important to understand whatever happened to him.'

'Yes, because if he didn't understand he felt trapped, and that made him uneasy,' she says coldly. She is visibly annoyed now. 'Oh yes, I know. And when he was uneasy, he felt sick.'

'Yes,' he says.

'Like now.'

'Yes. Like now.'

'Don't stop,' she says, though looking away. 'Keep talking to me. Don't let it go all quiet in here.'

He drags himself to his feet. He can't give up now, not when he's come so far, this is too important for them both to let it slip away, he has to try to get her to understand. He will have to keep talking her language, trust that he'll be able to figure out what he's saying as he goes along. That's improvisation for you, he thinks. He used to be able to improvise, back when he lay in bed with her. Everything is stored away in the brain.

'They were possibly more different than they thought,' he says.

'She was certainly a queen, but he wasn't even a prince consort. He was just an ordinary man, all but invisible until he met her. He needed to understand, she had other needs.'

'How do you know that she didn't need to understand? I'm sure she needed to understand just as much as he did!' she snaps.

'But he had a feeling that she needed to understand rather different things from him. Maybe.' He's on thin ice now.

'But they loved one another,' she says.

'Oh yes. And she filled him with joy, she let her royal light shine on him, she made him visible. That was a great gift.'

'Yes,' she says.

'And he really tried to understand her,' he goes on. 'Because she meant all the world to him. He felt that it was her who lent him light, and if he could just understand her, he would also understand himself, and then perhaps he could be his own light.'

'What was there to understand?' she asks. 'Why do you keep going on about understanding?'

Now he has to think. Think. Remember how it was. Everything is stored away in the brain. But he has never spoken to her like this before, and it's so hard to explain. He doesn't really understand it himself, so how is he supposed to explain it to her? He'll have to tread very warily.

'Everything about her,' he says. 'He wanted to understand everything about her. The way her mind worked, how she saw the world. What was going on inside her head when she went all quiet and didn't talk to him. Why she could sometimes seem so afraid. What she was seeing when she just stood and stared.'

Yes. That was it. He remembers now, he's there now.

For a moment there is silence.

'She was frightened because she had seen something that she didn't understand,' says Judith simply, as if what he has been struggling to put into words was the most obvious thing said so far this evening.

'She had seen something she didn't understand?'

'Yes, something she didn't understand and he didn't want to hear about.'

'Why didn't he want to hear about it?'

'I'd have thought you'd know that better than me!'

Now she's lost him.

'Well, but couldn't you explain it to me,' he pleads. 'What was it she had seen in him that he didn't want to hear about? What was it, Judith?'

'There was no point in trying to explain it to him. He wouldn't have understood anyway. As far as he was concerned it didn't exist, even though it was in him she saw it. There's no point in explaining it to you now, either, you haven't changed.'

'How do you know?'

'You've no sense for that sort of thing.'

'What sort of thing? What was it you saw in me? Stop talking in riddles!'

'I saw something that doesn't bear thinking of, something I just had to take in, then carry on and try to forget.'

'I have no idea what you're talking about.'

'No, exactly. See what I mean.'

'But try to explain it to me. Don't you realise it's me you're talking about! Us!'

Now it's Judith's turn to think. Her face is working overtime, her parched lips move, but no sound comes out, he stares at them. She knows that what she has seen gives her power over him, he can tell.

'Do you remember the postcard you had stuck up in the kitchen?' she asks at length. 'That one with the Latin saying on it. I've taken it down now. I took all that stuff down after you moved out. I've got it all packed away down in the basement, it's just a matter of going down and rooting it out.'

'*Cogito ergo sum*,' he says. 'It's not a saying, it's Descartes. I think, therefore I am.'

'Yes, that's it. But what if I don't think, what am I then?'

'You can't go turning it around like that.'

'There, you see!' she cries in exasperation. 'That is exactly why there is no point in telling you about things like this!'

'I don't know what you mean.'

'No, exactly. That's just what I'm saying!'

He gives up. She's so stubborn, so irrational, he has never been able to get through to her, it's like banging your head on a brick wall. She talks in riddles. She hasn't changed.

Judith is thinking the same thing: it's like banging your head on a brick wall.

He goes over to her bookcase and scans the titles on the shelves.

She doesn't have that many books. Most of them are from different book clubs. Neither he nor Minna has ever been a member of a bookclub, he thinks. He gets most of his reading matter from second-hand bookshops, and Minna borrows from the library.

'Did he think she had changed?' Judith asks eventually, addressing his back from the heap of clothes. 'Was that why he left?' He turns to face her with a book in his hand.

'I don't think he left just because of that. But that was part of it. She changed, and he changed too. There was no way to stop them from changing. Just as there's no way you can stop a body from growing.'

'So he grew, while she merely changed?'

'That's not what I said. Stop twisting everything I say.'

'But it was she who started it?'

'I don't know,' he responds reluctantly. 'But something had certainly changed between them. It made him uneasy. Nothing was the same any more.'

'How had she changed?'

'Maybe it was the way she would change her mind, without any warning. The way things he thought they were agreed on suddenly no longer stood. The way the patterns shifted. The way he thought he had been allowed into the inner circle, only to find himself out in the cold again.'

'What inner circle? I don't know what you're talking about.'

Johan places the book back on the shelf and crosses to her, he pulls an armchair over with him and sits down in it. It feels more appropriate to sit in a chair; it's no good sitting on the floor, he can't think when he's sprawling about like that, so low down.

'Oh, I think you do,' he says. 'Take, for instance, that time just after the house was finished. They'd agreed to leave the ground untouched, hadn't they? They wanted a wild garden. They had talked about it a lot, and they felt the same about it, or at least he was under the impression that they were agreed on this. It made him feel good to be so in tune with another human being. It made an end of the loneliness. And then out of the blue one day, without saying anything about it, she had gone into town and bought a whole pile of pots which she then planted with nasturtiums and set down either side of the driveway. Those flowers grew like mad, they spread like a carpet over the gravel, it wasn't natural. Then she got hold of a spade and started digging flower beds round the sides of the house and planting begonias. Right from the start they made the house look so bourgeois, it wasn't at all the way he had pictured it, it could hardly be called a wild garden now. That's the sort of changes I'm talking about.'

'Dahlias. Not begonias, dahlias. They were from Mama's garden.'

'Dahlias, then. At any rate, this wasn't what they had agreed on, this garden sent out quite different signals from those he thought they had agreed that they wanted to send, it made him feel confused, he didn't know what to make of her doing things like that. Why did she want to be so bourgeois all of a sudden?'

'What do you mean: "doing things like that"? Didn't she have a right to plant flowers around her own house? Was he supposed to make all the decisions?'

'No, it was *them* who were supposed to make all the decisions, *together*! That was how they had always done it! He thought he knew her!'

'No,' she mutters crossly, not listening to what he's saying. 'He didn't want any flower beds, not him.' That old, familiar, reassuring sulkiness of hers, he finds it hard not to smile.

'He had absolutely no sense for things like that,' she continues. 'He didn't like people planting things. He thought the

252

only things that could grow were things that had sown themselves. Everything had to be so natural.'

'But he didn't understand her!' he yells, suddenly consumed with vexation, as if the feeling from that time has unexpectedly welled up in him again. 'Those flowers confused him! Until then it had never been necessary for him to say that he wanted something different from her! They had always wanted the same things! He knew that she thought exactly as he did! They thought alike – they took pleasure in the same things – all impressions were like a wave that reached them both at one and the same time, because they were standing side by side on an endless beach – and all impressions came rolling in on a warm wave that hit them both together – that was their strength, that was why nothing could touch them.'

'There you go again,' she says tartly. 'I know just what's coming when you start talking like that.'

'Like what?'

'"Standing side by side on an endless beach." When you start talking like that it's because you're trying to worm your way out of something.'

'Judith,' he says, lowering his voice with some effort. 'I'm only trying to come up with a metaphor for the way in which nothing could touch us. We used to smile at the same time back then, at the same things.'

'You're always trying to come up with metaphors. You never talk about what's real.'

'I do the best I can.'

But she turns a deaf ear.

'Is it true that nothing could touch us?' she asks.

'Yes,' he says. 'It's true.'

'And I ruined this? By planting dahlias from Mama's garden around this house? You grew, I merely changed and ruined everything? It's hard to take you seriously when you talk like that, Johan.'

'The thing about the flowers was just an example, for Christ's sake,' he says. 'But that's how I saw it. I was sure that we'd been in agreement right from the start. I had no idea that we weren't in agreement. I thought we were one! You didn't tell me you had other ideas. How was I supposed to know, if you didn't say anything?'

'Not everything can be put into words. Not everything can be thought out either. Some things you just know. Not everything is cogito cargo sum.'

'Ergo. Cogito ergo sum.'

'Ergo! Ergo!' she screams. 'I'm trying to tell you that there are some things you just do, even though you can't explain why. There's a little voice somewhere inside you, whispering that *this* you have to do, and so you do it. And it's the right thing, even though you can't explain it.'

'I know,' he says, controlling himself with difficulty. 'That's how I see it too. There was a little voice, and it was telling me something. Maybe that was why I had to move out. I couldn't have said why, but my life depended upon it. Something had changed, we couldn't go on as we were, our life had got on to the wrong track, a little voice inside me told me so.'

'That would be Little Johan, I suppose,' she sneers. 'He's still alive and kicking, is he? Still the little boy who wants his Mummy? He said so many things back then.'

Johan glares at her.

'Don't start dragging all that up again,' he says. 'Don't spoil it.'

'If you didn't know what made you move out, apart from a little boy talking inside your head, then I think you ought to have stayed,' she breaks in. 'It's just too banal, Johan.'

'Yes, I know you think that.'

'You didn't know what you were doing.'

'No, maybe not.'

'You don't know the harm you've . . .'

'Don't try to sidetrack me,' he interrupts. 'I want to get back to whatever it was that changed between us. To the point where it went off the rails. We have to try to understand it, otherwise we're never going to be able to move on.'

'Well we can't bloody well go on talking about dahlias!' Judith has taken a step backwards, as if to gather momentum, she hurls the words at him.

'Yes, we can,' he says bitterly, he is a stone now. 'I think that was where it started. We need to know how it began. We have to try to understand what happened. It had such far-reaching consequences, Judith. Something fell apart when we went off the rails. Ebba is dead.'

'You're unbelievable!' she cries.

'No. We have to get to the bottom of this. Why was it so important to you to prove that I didn't understand you?'

'You're unbelievable, Johan!'

'Try to explain it to me, anyway.' He is hard as stone, right down to the tips of his toes, he can feel it.

She stares at him, open-mouthed.

For a moment there is silence.

'Why are you making such a big deal out of this,' she says, more softly, sadly even. 'I don't know what I think. There was something – ancient about those dahlias.'

'Something ancient. Oh well!' he retorts cheerfully. 'That changes everything! Christ Almighty, Judith!'

'Why are you so angry?' she says. 'What's happened to you? You never let on back then that you were angry.'

'I didn't know I was angry.'

'Well you're angry now.'

'No! I am not angry!' he shouts. 'I'm simply trying to explain to you how I felt back then. You're not listening.'

'Oh, I'm listening all right, *do* go on,' she sighs, with what sounds like feigned forbearance.

He needs a break. A cigarette.

'Is it all right if I have a cigarette?' he asks.

'No.'

'You can't deny me a cigarette.'

'Oh, can't I? This is my house.'

He lets it go.

'I was confused,' he says. 'I had received the first sign that maybe we weren't one after all. Those flowers that you planted changed everything. Not because they were flowers, the flowers were just a symptom. But because the ground rules had altered. I had to change my way of thinking.'

'And that made you feel confused,' she says, still feigning concern and forbearance. 'But now you're angry. You hate the thought of something being beautiful and ancient and mysterious if you can't understand it. Not dahlias, and not anything else either. It has to be understandable, otherwise you can't cope with it. If you can't understand something then you'd rather it didn't exist.'

'No, Judith, that's enough now,' he says wearily. 'That's not what all this is about.'

'Yes, that is exactly what it's about,' she insists. 'Whenever you see something that you don't understand you become blind and mad as hell. Just like now. Look at yourself. You're angry with me because I know something you don't know. Something ancient and beautiful and mysterious. And because I had seen something in you that you didn't know was there, you felt trapped with me. That's why you left Ebba and me, I realise that. Ebba and I knew that there was something that made you feel trapped, we had something that was beautiful. You were just a clumsy clod. And you were afraid of me. Go on, admit it! You were afraid of me because this thing that I knew and that you didn't understand made me too powerful, you were afraid that I would use it against you. You're still afraid of me, I can see that. It made you even more inferior. You hate being inferior. You couldn't simply admit that to yourself, you had to invent some other excuse for leaving. Minna was just an excuse.'

Judith's voice has worked itself up into a screech again. And Johan has had enough. He is staring at her lips again, as if he can't really believe that they can just keep going on and on. Then he slumps forward in the chair, he crouches over his knees, wraps his arms around them, hunches his shoulders up around his ears. He can't stand to hear what she's saying, can't stand that shrill voice of hers, and he can't stand listening to what lies behind her words either. What lies there is the betrayal, he knows that. But it's too much to both know and listen, the one reinforces the other, he has to shut off, bend double and cover his ears. He must remember that he left this house because he had to save himself. He must remember that if you try to stop growing, you die.

No. They're not going to get anywhere with this. It has no bottom. He is falling.

'You die!' he murmurs under his breath.

Then suddenly the telephone rings out in the hall. They both start. Johan jumps up to answer it, but Judith holds him back, clinging on to him with both hands. She is still very worked up; he's not to answer that phone, she screams, this is her home, he has no business answering her phone. She hangs over the instrument for what seems like an age, letting it ring and ring, before snatching up the receiver and shouting 'Hello.' Johan is standing right behind her, on tenterhooks, like a man about to be saved from drowning.

It's Minna. He knew it had to be her. Judith yells down the phone at her that she has Johan here, he's not coming back to the hotel, he's going to stay the night here with her, and not just this night, but probably many more besides, this is where he most wants to be, he wants to touch her, that's what he most wants to do, he's happiest with what he's used to.

Minna tries to say something, but Judith snaps her off short and slams down the phone. She tugs open the top drawer of the chest, pulls out a pair of scissors and cuts through the telephone cable at the socket down near the floor. She tosses the scissors back into the drawer and rams it shut. Then she picks up the mobile phone that he had left lying next to the bouquet of white flowers and goes over to the window. Slowly she raises the venetian blind, as if hoisting a flag, and pushes the window wide open.

'There,' she says. 'That's better. Let's let some air in here.'

Then she throws his mobile out of the window as hard as she can. She has always had a powerful throwing arm. She shuts the window again before any air has had a chance to penetrate into the room.

'What the hell do you think you're doing!' he yells. She eyes him with mute triumph.

'What the hell do you think you're doing!' he repeats. 'Have you gone completely mad!' She doesn't reply.

'I'm leaving!' he yells again. 'I'm not staying here if that's how you're going to behave! I'm going back to the hotel! You can do your own tidying up!'

She just looks at him. He is about to yell something else at her, but thinks better of it, opens the window again, leans out and scans the lawn. He can't see his mobile anywhere. He's getting desperate now.

When he pulls his upper half back into the room, Judith is gone.

She must have been out of there like a shot. He leaves the window open, hurries through to the kitchen, but she's not there. Then he runs up the stairs to the first floor, flings open the door of every room, calling her name again and again, but she is nowhere to be seen. He stumbles back down the stairs; she must have gone outside.

He finds her sitting on the front steps. Ebba's boots are there, she's struggling to pull them on. Her breath is coming in quick, short gasps like before. His heart sinks. The boots are too small for her, but she squeezes her feet into them, and when she hears him coming she gets up and teeters down the steps. He runs after her and grabs her by the shoulder.

'Where are you going?' he says. She doesn't answer.

'Judith! Where are you going? You can't just walk off!'

'You have to take care of your child,' she mutters under her heaving breath, breaking away from him and heading off across the lawn in the too-small boots. 'You mustn't ever let go of your child. If that child gets lost you have to go out and look for her. You have to take flaming brands and electric torches.'

Johan follows her, catches hold of her again.

'What are you talking about? Why are you wearing her boots?!' he shouts, shaking her.

'There's no point in trying to explain it to you,' she mutters. 'You'd never understand anyway. We'll never understand one another, we two.'

'Don't say that! We used to understand one another before, for years we understood one another. We can be like that again. We have to try. For Ebba's sake, Judith. You have to pull yourself together.'

'No, it'll never work. And there's no point, anyway, she won't be coming back. I know, I've seen her. Someone has taken her from me.'

'How can you say such a thing!'

'I know it, I've seen her.'

Johan blocks out what she is saying. He doesn't want to know.

'Why are you wearing her boots?' he asks. 'Where do you think you're going? Answer me!'

'I'm going to her,' Judith replies. 'I can't get to her without her boots. She left them on the steps for me, she left everything ready.'

'No, Judith!' he cries. 'This is madness! Ebba wants you to stay here!'

'How would you know? You've spoken to her, have you?'

'I . . .'

'Have you spoken to her, I asked.'

'No.'

'There you are then. You never talk to her, not properly. Parents have to be with their children. They have to talk to them, and listen to them.'

'Oh, cut it out, Judith! You know very well that I always talked to Ebba! No one talked to her the way I did.'

'When parents lose a child they have to look and look until they find her,' Judith chants on, she doesn't seem to have heard him. 'They have to put on their boots and go out into the night – and walk and walk and call and call – they have to carry flaming brands and electric torches and call out as loud as they can – they must not stop until they find her. And once they have found her

260

they must stay with her. They must never leave her again. They have to be strong, they must never let go.'

Johan gazes at her in disbelief. This is it, now they're getting to the heart of it. And that heart is absurd. He has to make sense of this.

And then it comes to him: someone has stolen away Judith's princess and carried her off to the underworld. And she has grieved so hard that the land has grown barren and dry, nothing will grow. The neighbourhood is bereft of life, devoid of sound, everything is so dry and parched. The queen is wrathful Demeter and now she is preparing to go after her daughter and bring her back. Such is her power, there is nothing she cannot do. She is living the story.

'Did someone steal her away from you?' he asks gently.

'Yes!' Judith answers. 'He came and took her!'

'Who?'

'Him!'

'And now you are going to fetch her?'

'Yes! And you can't stop me!'

'But how will you get to where she is?' he asks. 'How do you expect to be able to find her? Answer me, Judith!'

'I'll find her when I go out to the wood with the rope,' she says. 'She's waiting out there. It's so quiet there. Everything is ready.'

'No! You mustn't do that!' he cries in desperation.

'Why not?'

'You have to stay here!'

'Why?'

'Because . . . because you're her mother! You have to stay here with me. We are her parents. We have to see to it that things go on! We have to organise the funeral.'

'But things don't go on.'

'Of course they go on.'

'Oh? Where?'

'Here. In this house. For you and me. For all the people we love. Things go on. We have to stay here with them. They need us.'

'Not me.'

'Yes, you too. You have to stay here.'

'Who needs me?' says Judith. 'Ebba's not here any more. Somebody stole her away, she knew what was going to happen, she knows things like that, she takes after me. She left everything ready for me, the boots were there, she's waiting for me. Everything's ready.'

'But you have to stay here, Judith,' he repeats. 'Lots of people need you. Your mother! You have to think about your mother. And all your friends, all those people who sent flowers . . .'

'They're not my friends. They're just people from work, and the residents' association, and old pupils and lovers. Nobody needs me. My child's the only one who needs me.'

'No, Judith, you're wrong. There is someone . . .'

'Speak up then, so people can understand what you're saying!' she screams, tearing herself loose. 'Who needs me? Tell me!'

'I do.'

'You're lying.'

He does not answer.

In the house across the street Isak and Runa have been woken by the sound of voices from the driveway of Judith's house. They tumble out of bed and totter back to the window. Startled, they stand there, concealed by the curtains. One might almost think that the two out there sense that they are being watched; amid all the commotion they instinctively lower their voices, as parents do when they are arguing at night, so as not to wake the children.

Johan takes hold of Judith's hand and leads her back to the front steps, as though she were a little girl. She is surprisingly compliant. He sits down on exactly the same spot where he had sat some hours earlier, before he stood up and rang the doorbell, and he pulls her down beside him.

In the thick of this thing that is unravelling around them it comes as a relief to Johan to be outside once more. The night is still warm, but he feels his brain starting to function normally again now that he has escaped from that poisoned house and got a breath of air. He could really do with a smoke now. He doesn't ask permission, and she doesn't seem to notice him dipping into his shirt pocket and pulling out a pack of cigarettes and a flat box of matches from some restaurant.

They sit like this in silence. Judith stares dully at the boots on her feet. After a few long drags on his cigarette he turns to look at her and says:

'You're the grieving mother, aren't you?'

She doesn't answer.

'And you're mad at me,' he continues. 'You think I took her away from you.'

'I never said that!'

'No, but it's true. And now you want to be with Ebba.'

'Yes,' she says.

'You don't want to stay here with me. With the rest of us.'

'No.'

'We're not enough for you.'

'No.'

'Only Ebba will do.'

'Yes.'

'Only she can fill you.'

'Yes.'

Judith turns to him and meets his eye, she looks surprised to find that he suddenly seems to understand. He takes another drag on his cigarette.

'But how do you know you'll find her?' he asks, slowly exhaling the smoke. She immediately looks suspicious.

'What do you mean?'

'How do you know what will happen after you – jump, out there in the forest?'

'I don't understand what you mean. She has gone on before me, she'll be there. She knows everything. Everything is ready.'

'Are you sure she'll be there?'

'Of course she'll be there!' Judith cries indignantly. 'She's waiting for me! She needs me!'

'But what if you don't find her. What if she's not there. What if there is nothing after this?'

'I don't know what you mean!'

'What if everything just comes to an end when you jump. What if you just disappear. What if everything simply unravels and turns to nothing?'

'What do you mean – nothing! Don't talk like that! How dare you talk like that!'

He ignores her, takes another deep drag on his cigarette.

'What if it all just unravels. Imagine if that's how it was for Ebba, too. Imagine if everything just unravelled and disappeared when she jumped.'

'You don't know anything about this! Don't talk about things you don't know anything about!'

Judith has started hitting him now. Isak and Runa gape at them in horror from the window across the street. She pounds and pounds on his chest and shoulders and thighs, while he just sits there with his cigarette between his fingers. He holds it up to save her from burning herself. She is utterly distraught, he is amazingly calm; that cigarette has done him good, he has knocked her off her perch.

He is still a stone. As if from very, very far away he sees the weeping break over her in waves. He, on the other hand, feels nothing. Eventually, all that is left of the cigarette is the butt, and by that time she has quietened down. She collapses into a sobbing heap, he stubs his cigarette out on the step and lays a tentative hand on the back of her neck. There they sit. The two old folk across the street shuffle back to bed.

After a long while, Johan pulls the too-small boots off Judith's feet and leads her back inside the house. She lets him, she has no fight left, she feels that he has stripped her of her last shreds of resistance. She will never forgive him for that.

Back in the hall, he locks the door behind them and puts on the safety chain. Then he leads her into the sitting-room and over to the sofa. She lies down on it, exhausted from weeping, tears still streaming down her cheeks, her upper-lip damp and glistening with snot. He places the boots on top of the heap of Ebba's clothes, next to the fur hat.

While all this is going on, the wall of pressure that began to build up in Erlend's breast as he was sleeping in the house a few blocks away reaches the surface. He is woken by the sound of his own crying. His tears might be Judith's tears, the sobs are the same, the same crumpled heap. His body is racked by sobs; snot and tears pour from all of his facial orifices too. It comes as a relief. Both he and Judith continue to weep like this for some time, he in the bed in his old room at home, she on the sofa in the house that Johan built.

Johan sits in the armchair amid the heap of Ebba's clothes on the floor. The spaces between the sobs from Judith, over on the sofa, gradually lengthen. The storm passes, and eventually only the odd shudder still runs through her. Then there is silence. Johan fetches some paper towel from the kitchen. He hands it to her with a paternal look on his face.

Judith takes the towel and blows her nose hard. She drops the used paper on to the carpet. Then she starts talking again, so abruptly that Johan jumps.

'So the prince consort didn't want a bourgeois life,' she continues, in a voice so clear that nothing might ever have happened. There is no trace of all that weeping, it's as if she had blown it all out of her nose. She appears to be back inside the fairy tale from which he thought he had extricated them.

She gets up from the sofa and goes over to the window. She is suddenly and inexplicably bursting with new and wayward energy; she means to pay him back for what he said about Ebba not being there. She pretends to feel a fresh breeze on the back of her neck from the window he left open. She lets it waft over her, inclines towards it with a smile on her face.

'He didn't want dahlias, no, not him. He didn't want linen tablecloths and silver cutlery,' she says.

'No, he most certainly did not,' Johan responds, astounded. How can she simply pick up the conversation again as if nothing had happened? What happened to the snivelling bundle he held in his arms only a moment ago? What happened to Demeter, all set to take herself off to the underworld? But he really shouldn't be so surprised, she's always been the same, he thinks, she has always carried on as if nothing had happened. This is her way of manoeuvring, her folly. She may be Demeter in flashes, but for the most part it's merely play-acting, before you know it she's her old self again, shallow and unpredictable. She knows what she's doing.

'Well maybe it wasn't so smart to marry an aristocrat,' she goes on, in the same blithe tone.

'You could be right,' he replies, afraid that she is about to have hysterics again. A white coat and a syringe would come in handy right now, he thinks. But he says:

'He didn't know what he was doing. He was blind and in love.'

'Don't be so hard, Johan,' she says sweetly.

He gives himself a shake. He realises that she is punishing him for what he said out there on the steps. Women are so accurate in their punishments.

'The prince consort began to feel uneasy about the fact that he had married an aristocrat,' she continues, in a voice that is as warm and modulated as that of an actor. 'It wasn't easy living with a queen if you didn't want linen tablecloths or dahlias or silver cutlery. He messed things up for himself, he started thinking too much. He would sit up at night and listen to the radio. He stopped coming to her concerts, on the excuse that he had to look after the princess, or fix something. There was always something needing fixing. As if they didn't have her mother, as if she wouldn't have been only too happy to babysit. As if there were no such thing as tradesmen.

'And then suddenly, one summer, he took it into his head that he was in love with another woman. It was an effective way of fooling himself and it had the most terrible consequences. In just a few days he threw away everything they had had together. He left the queen and their daughter. It was as if they no longer existed. As if there had never been any story about them. He rubbed it out completely, as if he had a big eraser for rubbing things out. His whole head was one big eraser, smooth and white.'

Her voice has altered, but he realises that she is trying to wear him down. The words come so easily to her, one might almost

267

think she had copied it all down from a book and learned it by heart.

He breathes a couple of heavy sighs, but makes no move.

'No, Judith,' he says at last. 'It wasn't like that at all.'

She jerks warily to the side like a boxer in the ring.

'Wasn't it?' she asks from her new position. 'Have I misunderstood it?'

'Yes, I think you misunderstood.'

It's a feeble punch and it doesn't hit anything but empty air, it can't even be called a punch, he's just swinging wildly.

'Okay, you tell it then. Read the book yourself.'

'I don't think I've read the same book as you.'

Another feeble swing.

'Well, read your own book then!'

She is more agile than him, her footwork is better.

'I don't want to talk about *them*. I want to talk about *us*,' he says. He tries to shift himself, get into a better position.

'By all means. Say whatever you like. No one's stopping you.'

She dodges out of the way, causing him to lurch forwards.

He recovers, then he too essays a couple of sidesteps across the canvas. It's tough to have to keep changing tactics like this.

'In my book it says that we lived in this house for over four years,' he says. 'I thought I was as one with you, I loved and adored you and Ebba, I saw how much she resembled both you and me. Her dark hair and her long slender hands. But sometimes I had the feeling that it wasn't healthy for us to be so wrapped up in one another. I saw how it made me try to be something I couldn't be. I tried to be an image, the image you wanted, and as a result I stiffened up, I died a little every day.'

'You died?'

'Yes, I died a little every day. There was a little voice inside me that gradually grew fainter and fainter. I missed it.'

'Little Johan?'

'I don't know. But eventually it became so faint. And one summer when you were on tour and Ebba and I were on our own here, I found that I could hardly hear it at all. I would sit up long into the night after Ebba had gone to bed. I listened to the radio. I thought about my life. I thought about all that I knew and all that I didn't know. I missed all the things I didn't know. I missed myself. I thought that something was stiffening up inside me. I thought about music.'

'Music?'

'Yes. It was as if you owned the music, I thought. You owned it because you thought you were the queen, there had never been any question about that. Who had the talent, the power – the secrets in this house? Who could permit herself to talk in riddles?'

'I don't follow.'

'I had learned that as far as you and your mother were concerned talent and power were one and the same thing. And I thought about the music that Ebba and I shared, the music that you knew nothing about, because in this house the rule was that you were in charge of the music and the secrets. And I told myself that I couldn't go on living without this other music. It was the music that was alive.'

'I don't understand one bit of this!'

'No. I know,' he says.

'Tell me about this other music.'

'You would never understand.'

'*I* wouldn't understand? You're the one who doesn't understand. I understand more than you think. That's part of the problem with you, you don't know me. You don't want to see me. You're blind and mad as hell.'

'It seems to me that I've spent years of my life trying to see you, Judith.'

'Tell me about this other music, then, if it's so important! Show it to me!' she says.

'You can't force it out of me.'

'Well, maybe I'll have to coax it out of you then. Shall I . . .'

She moves in on him in the ring, tries to get close enough to stroke his chest, but then she starts to flail her arms, sticks out her elbows, clenches her fists, as if she is about to punch him again, pummel him. He checks her, grasping both her wrists and pinning her arms behind her back, as if he were putting her under arrest.

'Stop it!' he breathes. Don't touch me. I'll tell the story. But don't touch me.'

He walks her over to the sofa, as if she were his prisoner, and pushes her down on to it.

This cannot go on. Judith is back on the sofa, looking small and defiant, her hands are still pinned behind her back even though he has long since let go of them. She is sitting in the same awkward, lopsided position in which she landed when he pushed her down on to it. Her whole being is a protest.

He needs to find other words, needs to pull her out of this, get her on his side. He has to explain what was so beautiful. It is his last hope. Judith has a sense for beauty as he well knows. He knows her. She eyes him expectantly. He wavers.

'I don't know whether I can explain it,' he says. 'It was the . . . music in everything. A music that made me feel so light and open, music that, to me, felt almost like a breeze, the way it flowed out of the radio. It was the music inherent in everything I wished for, but could not have, a music that could only be heard when I put my ear to things and kept it there for a long, long time. A music that was like doors.'

'Like doors?' she says. She has been listening attentively.

'Yes.'

'Doors to what?'

'I don't know. To what was there in my work when I had been working long and intently and didn't have a thought in my head. The *presence* of it. The music. A music so simple that it was almost beyond comprehension, music that I would never be able to speak about to anyone. A music that – that was – sheer presence.'

'I don't understand a word you're saying,' she snaps. 'Talk in a way that I can understand. When I was away, you lay in our bed with Minna. I've known it all along. You and Minna in our bed, rolling about, all legs and arms – that was your music, that was the secret, there was nothing so strange about that.'

'I don't know what you're talking about,' he says, she has put him off. This is not beautiful.

'No, I'll bet you don't,' she says. Why don't you tell me something you know about, damn it! Tell me about the summer when you lay with Minna in our bed! It can't be that hard to describe if it was so important to you! I'll tell you what, Johan: I think all this stuff you're spouting is just words. There's nothing behind it. You've always been the same. "The music in everything." I listen to you and I try to understand what you are saying, but then I see that it's just a lot of words. I can't take any more of it. There's nothing behind it, no doors, just pasteboard, just dry pasteboard.'

He has to stop her.

'We put the pillows at the foot of the bed,' he says.

'Who?'

'Minna and I. The one time she spent the night here.'

'At the foot of the bed? Why did you do that?'

'I don't know. We just did. Anything else would have been out of the question.'

'Go on.'

'Listen to me. I want to tell you something that's – important. The thing with Minna is not important.'

'Not important! You're living with her! She had your child! Isn't your child important! Is that the sort of person you are?!'

'Of course it's important,' he says. 'But that's another story. We mustn't mix up the stories, Judith. We have to try to keep them separate.'

'They can't be kept separate!' she screams. 'You're the one who mixed them up! It's your fault that everything got into such a mess! I didn't want them to get mixed up!'

'You have to listen to me,' he says, desperate now. He brings his hands down heavily on her shoulders, as if meaning to press her right through the sofa.

'I'm trying to tell you something. I danced with Ebba. There was a tune playing on the radio. You were in the kitchen with the extractor fan on, you didn't hear us. It was The Mammas & The

Papas. They were singing 'Dream a Little Dream of Me'. I whirled Ebba round and round, and I heard her singing, she had learned all the English lyrics by heart, although she didn't understand a single word, she sang them in her clear, piping voice, her pronunciation odd, yet perfect. The words she sang were hers alone, it was a language all her own, and it was so obvious that she was keeping her voice down so that you wouldn't hear. *Seem to wispa ay buv yoo –'*

'I love you, you mean.'

'No. Ay buv yoo. And that's how it felt back then, how it feels now. As if I had done something wrong. As if I had caught a glimpse of something that must never be mentioned, a perception for which, were it ever to come to light, I would be brought to book. The music came to an end, we heard you switch off the fan over the cooker in the kitchen and call to say that dinner was ready. We acted as if nothing had happened.'

He lets go of her shoulders.

She has sat quietly listening to him, has unclasped her hands, brought them from behind her back and laid them in her lap.

'When we were together,' she says at length in a small voice. 'I just wanted to show you something beautiful. I just wanted to make you happy and strong. I saw the light within you, I wanted you to feel it shine. I saw Little Johan, I just wanted to see him come alive.

'Sometimes you could tell what I needed help with before I knew it myself. You knew my language. That made me calm and full of joy.'

With these words she turns everything around yet again. He loses his grip. He sees that she has stepped out of the boxing ring, she sits on the big sofa like a little girl and doesn't know what to do with herself, he hears that she is talking with Little Judith's voice. His strength fails him, he lets her talk. She withdraws into herself.

'I remember New Year's Eve, the year I was four,' she says. 'Mama and Papa were holding a big New Year's party, this was in the house in town. There were lots of children there and lots of adults, I was so excited, I had got a new dress for Christmas, burgundy silk, and Mama had plaited my hair the night before while it was still wet. When she combed it out in the morning my hair was all curly, I had never seen myself with curly hair before. Papa had invited several men from the lodge with their families to the party. The atmosphere in the house was always a bit fraught when any of the Freemasons came to visit. Mama had help in the kitchen; all day they were busy making the food and making the house look nice, no one had any time for me. I hung around the yard on my own, I had taken off my woolly hat and put it in my pocket, I didn't want my curls to go all flat. I wandered about by myself over by the garage, with my hands over my ears to make sure that I didn't get earache.

'And at long last evening came. I was washed and dressed up and allowed to join the party and sit at the children's table set up in one of the rooms. I didn't know the other children who were there, they were all older than me, they played rowdy games and ran around, arms flailing. I joined in their games, but the evening felt awfully long to me. I was determined to stay up till midnight and see the fireworks.

'I grew so tired, though. I tried to stay awake, but in the end I must have fallen asleep on a sofa. I was woken by Papa trying to pull my hat over my ears – he was going to take me outside. I must have had some sort of tantrum, I started screaming and lashing out, I didn't want to go outside. I didn't want my hat on, I didn't want to spoil my curls, and I . . . I hit Papa.

'He was so angry, he slapped me. Then he went out to the others. I was left sitting on the sofa, howling.

'I kind of went to pieces. I was crying for Mama. I didn't know where she was, I thought she was gone. I could hear the rockets outside, the banging was so loud, I thought there was a war going on.

'At last I heard the front door open and someone come in. It was Mama, in a fur coat and wearing a hat and leather gloves. She picked me up, shushed softly in my ear and carried me over to the window; we two could watch the New Year fireworks from here, she whispered, in fact we would have a much better view.

'I remember how my body relaxed. I laid my face against the cool fur of her coat, the snow melted on my cheek. Rockets tore across the sky outside.

'Then she got me undressed and carried me to bed. And I didn't have to brush my teeth.'

The bathroom is large and white. There is a mirror on the wall opposite the window that looks on to the wood. The mirror reflects the image of the wood back into the darkness.

The taps on the wash-basin can be switched to both cold and hot water; the water gushes down on to the white porcelain when the taps are turned.

Judith and Johan moved into this house together seventeen years ago, it was Johan who built it for them. A warm thrill ran through him when he bent down to his toolbox to find the right tool. He didn't have a lot of experience with this sort of work in those days, but he seemed to have a feel for it all the same, like some sort of unmerited legacy from a distant ancestor.

One forenoon at the end of May he painted the frame of the big window in the bathroom with a thin, round brush; then he stood looking out at the wood while he rubbed spatters of paint off his hands with a rag dipped in white spirit: threadbare cotton, one of Judith's old tops. He had fitted the bath that same day. And before that he had worked long and intently at the job of putting up the tiles, he was so precise, the grout lines ran straight and true over the white glazed walls. Like a grid, beams across ice. She had come in and watched him work.

They were two bodies in one back then. Their shared intimacy lent a drowsy look to their features, it was a badge they wore without even knowing it. They weren't conscious of their own faces then. They could not see themselves from the outside.

In the morning, after sleeping entwined in the big broad bed, they would stagger out to the bathroom together while they slowly extricated themselves from sleep. Judith would sit peeing thoughtfully and describing what she had dreamt while she watched Johan showering behind the transparent shower curtain, drying himself with his back to her, hanging the towel on the rail next to hers without folding it first, taking the deodorant out of the cabinet, rolling it over his own armpits and leaving it on the side of the wash-basin for her. They shared their deodorant, just as they shared the bread in the bread bin and the newspaper in the mailbox. It was a neutral, unperfumed deodorant from the chemist's.

But seventeen years have passed since then. They sit in the sitting-room. They are tired now. There's not much more to be said.

Judith looks like a stranger. She is still the little girl who fell asleep on the sofa on New Year's Eve. He is the father who tried to pull her hat down over her curls. She hit him. He is scared of her.

He understands what she has been telling him, and he understands that he has to stay the night here. He can't leave her now, she will go to pieces if he does. She hears the rockets outside, she thinks maybe there's a war going on. She wants to lay her cheek against his cool fur and feel the snow melt. She needs her Mama. He has to be the Moon Queen for her.

He knows that Minna will be beside herself with worry, but he can't bear to think about that.

'Judith,' he says. 'Judith, love. There's something I have to tell you.'

She doesn't answer, she sits on the sofa staring into space. He has to get her to become grown-up again.

'I have something to tell you, too,' he says. 'I want to tell you something I remember that is true.'

She turns to look at him, still without saying anything.

'I know what it's been like for you,' he continues. 'I know what it's like to feel that Ebba needs you. I know all about how it feels to miss her. Because that's how it's been for me all these years. I couldn't stand not having her with me. Even years after I moved out of this house. I think I must have suppressed a lot of things from that time. But one incident in particular sticks in my mind, it must have been the last day before the summer holidays. This was just before Jennifer was born. Ebba and the rest of her class were going to be singing at the school closing day, in front of the whole school. It had been quite a while since we had spoken to one another: some weeks earlier I had promised to take her sailing and then forgotten all about it, she was still feeling hurt. I felt very bad about it. But I had noted the date of the school closing day in my diary and I had done everything I could to make sure that I would be there.

'I had planned to leave early in the morning to be certain of getting there in good time, but something came up at home. Minna found a leak in the kitchen. She was heavily pregnant at the time, of course – the baby was due any time – and I couldn't leave her to take care of it alone, we couldn't get hold of a plumber at such short notice . . . When I finally got out of the flat, the car wouldn't start, and there was no way I could make it in time if I took the train, so I ended up taking a taxi all the way to the school. By the time the taxi turned in to the playground the sweat was running off me.

'When I walked into the big gym hall with the simple stage at one end they had already begun. I tried to slip past some of the other parents, but met only with irritated requests to be quiet, so I stood where I was, near the back of the hall.

'She was standing in the middle of the group of children, a head taller than the rest, she seemed so much older than them. You were sitting down at the front with the other mothers, looking as attractive and well turned-out as always. You were thinner. You didn't see me. Ebba didn't see me either. I noticed the way she ran her eyes over the hall, looking for me; there was something resigned about the look in those eyes. I didn't dare to wave, I didn't want to attract any more attention than I already had.

'They sang some songs I had never heard before. They weren't like the songs we sang when I was at school.

'Then she spotted me. Our eyes met at a point somewhere in mid-air. I saw a kind of a flutter run over her face. She didn't wave, she was far too well-behaved for that, and shy, like me.

'I didn't wave either. But we held each other's eyes. They formed a cord running through space, a note that spanned the room. I could have climbed up on to that cord and walked along it to her.

'But the song just went on and on, there were a lot of verses.

'I vibrated.'

It is hard to tell whether she has taken in this story. She seems so apathetic. He can't figure out whether the Judith sitting there is a child or an adult.

'I remember that time in the gym hall too,' she says. 'That's when you took her from me.'

She stands up and comes over to him, growing enormous in the time it takes to walk a couple of steps.

'You climbed up on to that cord and took her away with you,' she says. 'I had to go home alone.

'She wasn't there when I woke up the next morning either. And after that I couldn't see any point in getting up. A grey fog drifted in over me.

'I couldn't stop myself from picturing how she was when she was with you and Minna. My mind conjured up pictures of her, laughing and happy in your flat, the flat that I've never visited. And it only got worse after Minna had been to see me.'

'Minna came to see you!' he says.

'Yes, didn't she tell you?'

'I don't believe you!' He stares at her in shock.

'Didn't she tell you about that?' Judith says, she seems a bit brighter now. 'Does she have secrets from you?'

'Minna and I have no secrets from one another,' he says. 'We're always totally open with each other.

'But she came here to see me. Just after Jennifer was born.'

'Jennifer has been here, too!'

'She was just a tiny baby. I helped her to take the breast. She didn't want to take it, she kept waving her head from side to side, but I helped her.'

Johan is lost for words.

'From then on I had a picture of Minna stuck up in front of my eyes,' Judith goes on. 'Whether I wanted to or not, in my mind's eye I would see her in your kitchen at home, frying eggs for you and Ebba. Or see that she had an interesting and difficult book lying open on her bedside table.'

'Minna doesn't read much any more,' he says.

'But she had everything that had once been mine.'

'Minna didn't take anything away from you, Judith. I left of my own free will, because I had to. I didn't leave because of Minna. I've tried to explain that to you.'

'Would you listen to what I'm saying,' Judith answers wearily, though still looming menacingly over him. 'For once would you just listen to me. Hear me out, if you can.

'I felt old and dirty and used up. On those Sundays when she wasn't here, I stayed in bed, couldn't bring myself to get up. I just lay there thinking, I couldn't stop thinking. The mind doesn't stop turning, it just keeps on working away. What was I doing here – what point was there in getting up – was one supposed to get up merely to shower and clean and shave the body, to make it look better, so that some man would be attracted to it and desire it – shovel food into it so that it wouldn't become weak – take it for walks so that it wouldn't stiffen up. Was that how it was supposed to be? Was one supposed to use Sunday to prepare for a new working week, so that one could earn the money to heat the house, so that the body wouldn't get cold, and to buy food to shovel into it, so it wouldn't weaken and die? Was that the way of it?'

'I had no idea you felt like that,' says Johan.

'Weaken and die,' she continues, ignoring him. She turns her back on him and crosses to the window.

'It wasn't hard to imagine what I would leave behind me if I were to die there, in bed, at that moment. I wouldn't be found until Monday afternoon when Ebba came home from school. The orchestra would arrange a memorial service with some fine musical contributions, and then they would find some gifted replacement for me, maybe someone better than me, maybe that much talked-about girl from the conservatory. You would be horrified, but in truth it would be a weight off your mind. Minna would obviously be relieved, and she would know just how to console you when you were feeling low. She would be patient and tell you, in her warm voice, that you did your best, that the fault lay with me.'

'I've never said that.'

'Mama would mourn me and blame herself, but after a while she would be fine, she has always managed just fine, she's so strong. It would be just like when Papa died. She and her sisters and women friends would go through my clothes and give them away to slim women of their acquaintance, they would be too small for them to wear themselves. The things that no one wanted they would throw out or donate to a jumble sale. My clothes would be spread on a table-tennis table in the school gym hall at the autumn jumble sale, strangers would pick them up and sniff them before dropping them again.

'And my flowers. The neighbours might take them, maybe Runa and Isak across the street, they would dig up the dahlias, carry the heavy pots of nasturtiums over to their place and go on watering them, every bit as well as I could if not better. The house would be sold, other people would move in and paint the walls of the bedrooms different colours, hang wallpaper with a decorative border running all the way round the top. There would be nothing left of me but a faint grey hush.

'Apart from Ebba. Ebba would be heart-broken. Ebba wouldn't be able to bear it. Ebba was my reason for living. A mother can never die and leave her child.'

All the time that Judith has been talking, Johan's eyes have been fixed on her grubby feet and painted nails. He doesn't want to hear any more.

'I think you could do with a bath,' he says.

'Now?'

'Yes, now. And then you ought to go to bed. We've got the funeral tomorrow. You need to be clean and rested.'

'I'm not up to it. I just want to sleep. I can sleep down here on the sofa.'

'I'll run a bath for you,' he insists. 'I'll help you with everything.'

'My dress is all creased.' She runs her hands over the white fabric.

'I'll iron it for you,' he says. 'First thing in the morning. But first I'm going to give you a bath.'

'I want you to stay here tonight,' she says in a little-girl voice.

'I know,' he replies. 'And I will stay here tonight. But you'll have to let me call Minna first. I'm sure she's anxious, Judith. She must think something has happened to me. You have to let me talk to her. You have to let me run over to Runa and Isak's house and use their phone. I'll come straight back, I promise.'

'You can use my mobile,' Judith says. 'It's in the top drawer of the chest of drawers.'

He gets to his feet, takes her hand and leads her out of the sitting-room and up the stairs to the first floor. In the bathroom he turns on the taps, pours in bubble bath from a bottle in the cabinet; he still knows where everything is kept here in the house, nothing has changed. He asks her to get undressed while he goes downstairs to call Minna. She shouts the PIN code for her mobile down the stairs after him.

The call to Minna doesn't last long. She snatches up the receiver at the other end almost before the phone has had a chance to ring. He knows she has been anxious, they are both equally relieved to hear the other's voice. He explains the situation in a few short sentences; she says she understands, that he mustn't worry about her. Jennifer is fast asleep, she says, she didn't even stir when the phone rang, she is lying right beside her in bed. He is not to worry, she repeats. She reminds him that his clothes for the funeral are at the hotel with her. She asks him how they are going to work things in the morning. He says he doesn't know. But that it will all sort itself out.

'Okay, but call me,' she says in a small voice. 'Call me, if you should need anything.' He nods at the receiver. Then he wishes her goodnight and blows her a silent kiss, the way he did that night when he was out on the sailboat.

When he comes back upstairs to the bathroom, Judith has taken off her clothes and got into the bath. She has left her dress and underwear in a heap on the floor. She says nothing; he picks up the clothes and carries them into the bedroom. He lays them on her chair. Then he hesitates for a second before slipping his hand under the big double duvet on the double bed and locating her nightie. It is lying exactly where it always used to lie when he lived here: on her side of the bed, a little more than halfway down. He sits for a moment on the edge of the bed; his knees are so weak, he has hardly any strength left. Beyond the bedroom window all is quiet. The wood is out there, he thinks.

He returns to Judith in the bathroom, sits down on the toilet seat. She still says nothing. He considers her white body; he remembers how, only a few hours ago, he stood watching Minna and Jennifer take a bath at the hotel. He thinks of Minna's body, the way she avoided his eye.

Then he feels something building up in his throat. Tears. They work their way up, like a wall of pressure welling up towards his chest and throat, his face. He can't hold them back. He bends over

284

and hides his face in his hands. They flood out of him, in a wave.

'Oh, Johan love,' he hears Judith say from the bath, her voice soft. 'Johan, love. Are you crying?' He doesn't answer. She lets him cry. She soaps herself, slowly and steadily.

'Yes. I think I'm crying now,' he whispers at last.

'Are you crying because you called Minna?'

'I'm crying because Ebba is dead, Judith.'

'Yes, she's dead.'

'She's dead! You don't understand what I'm saying,' he sobs.

'Oh, but I do. I do understand what you're saying,' she replies, still steadily soaping herself.

'Tell me you understand what I'm saying!' he breathes.

'I understand what you're saying.'

'You don't understand! You don't understand! Tell me you understand!'

'I've been there. I understand what you're saying.'

'No! You haven't been there! Tell me you haven't been there!'

'I've been there,' she murmurs. 'I understand what you're saying. Ebba is dead. Her body is covered in blotches. There's a dark welt around her neck. She is stone cold.'

Slowly Judith stands up in the bath. He stands up too, reaches out to her; he staggers, bends forward and grabs a bath towel, holds it out for her, wraps it around her and helps her out of the water as if she were a child. But once she is out of the bath it is he who leans on her, an old man leaning on a child; he cannot stand unaided. He stays like this, swaying from side to side, while she waits patiently for him to regain his balance.

He takes a deep breath, then proceeds to pat her dry all over; he hangs the towel to dry, finds her nightie and pulls it over her head. He takes her hairbrush from the cabinet and brushes her hair very gently; he knows how tender-headed she is. Then they both walk through to the bedroom.

The window overlooking the wood is open. Johan has opened it; there is not a sound out there. He stands looking through the window while she pulls the bedspread off the double bed with one brisk sweep and moves the four pillows down to the foot. He doesn't see what she has done until he turns to face her once more. He says nothing. She looks very, very tired now, clean and pale, her contours almost obliterated. She crawls under the duvet on her side of the bed.

He takes off his trousers and shirt and socks and places them on the chair, on top of her clothes, but keeps on his T-shirt and underpants. She lies there, gazing at him, but he cannot bring himself to get into bed. He walks back out into the hall, checks that the bathroom light is switched off, the towel hung up neatly. Like a caretaker. He pauses for a moment on the landing, in two minds. Then he enters Ebba's room.

It's in an awful mess, garments scattered all over the floor. Judith must have dropped a lot of things when she was hauling Ebba's clothes out of the wardrobe and down the stairs to the sitting-room earlier in the day. No one has made the bed. Ebba's nightie is lying in a ball near the bottom. He sits down on the bed and gently picks it up. He folds it neatly and slips it under her pillow, smooths the pillow the way he used to do when she was little and he would make her bed before running her to nursery. He gives the duvet a shake, settles it into place, tucks in the edges.

As he is leaving the room he switches on the little night-light that has been here ever since Ebba was born. He fixed it up himself, on the day that he collected her and Judith from the maternity unit. She never really outgrew that night-light, he thinks, she always had to have it on.

Then he closes the door quietly behind him and goes back to Judith.

He is not used to seeing her like this, at the foot of the bed. She looks at him with tired eyes, lifts the double duvet with one hand to allow him to climb in beside her on his side. He lies there on his back, rigid, listening to the last of the water in the bath draining away.

They don't make love. How could they, they have no strength. But the thought crosses both their minds, the movements are there in their bodies, just under the weary skin, they know how it feels to curl a leg over, turn one's face towards, pull oneself on top, slide underneath. They know one another so well. They have lain entwined in this bed on so many nights, nights without number, like one interlocked night unfolding before them.

It's hard to say how much time passes. He sees the luminous digital numerals on her clock radio, but he can make no sense of them, time seems in some way to have unravelled. He lies with his eyes open, thinking that she's asleep; her breathing speaks of sleep. But all of a sudden she throws back the duvet, swings her legs over the edge of the bed, gets up and walks across to the chest of drawers under the window. She opens a drawer and starts to rummage about in it. He asks what she is looking for.

'The letter,' she says.

'What letter?'

'Jennifer's letter.'

'Jennifer's?'

'Yes. The letter Ebba wrote to Jennifer.'

'What are you talking about?! You have a letter from Ebba!' he says, appalled.

'Of course. Or didn't you know about that? I must have forgotten to tell you.'

He stares at her in stunned disbelief.

'Where did you find it?' he asks.

'In her room, when I was clearing up her things. She'd stuck it inside her photo album, it wasn't hard to find. It was tucked in among some loose photos and newspaper cuttings about you and me. I was meant to find it, you do realise that, don't you.'

'How long has it been lying there, do you think?'

'How would I know? I don't go poking around among her things.'

Judith produces a white envelope from Ebba's underwear drawer. She crosses over to the bed again, hands the envelope to him. He feels hot and flustered; he seizes the letter, holds it up in one taut hand while she calmly gets back into bed and closes her eyes. He recognises Ebba's neat, swirling copperplate on the envelope, he knows which pen she has used, a calligraphy pen which Minna gave him for Christmas one year; he usually has it lying on his desk at home, and keeps it for special purposes, such as writing Christmas cards, or gift tags. 'For Jennifer on her 16th birthday,' it says on the envelope. The letter is sealed and there is no sign that Judith has attempted to open it.

'We have to keep it safe,' Judith says, still with her eyes closed. 'It's for Jennifer.'

'Yes, of course,' he replies. 'But what do you think is in it?'

'That's not for us to know,' she says. 'She wrote it to her sister, not to us.'

'But there might be something important in it! Something we need to know.'

'Like what? Is there any more *to* know?'

'But we have to . . . There might be . . . It's not like her not to want to explain things to us. She's always been so – thoughtful, always so good about letting us know where she'll be, and – we need to know. What we have done.'

'She's stone cold now,' says Judith. 'There's nothing else to explain. We know where she is.'

Johan heaves himself on to his elbows and props the letter up against the display of the clock radio on Judith's side of the bed, blocking the luminous red numerals from his view.

'I'll keep it safe,' he says. 'I'll put it in the safety-deposit box at the bank and leave it there until Jennifer turns sixteen.'

Judith makes no reply. Her eyes are still closed.

A glassy film has settled over the neighbourhood, transparent and yet impenetrable. The funeral is only hours away now. There is not a stirring of air. In almost every house someone is asleep. Isak and Runa sleep facing one another, like brother and sister. Erlend is asleep in the house down the road, his fists so tightly clenched they might be locked like that.

Hardly any cars pass on the main road. The petrol station is closed, but well lit up, the hatch at Eddy's Snack Stop is shuttered and barred, the stall itself in darkness, except for the glimmering letters of the sign.

Judith and Johan lie beside one another in the big broad bed, rigid, on their backs. The letter from Ebba gleams whitely on the bedside table in front of the clock radio. Something has come to a stop, but there's no way of telling what, it is impenetrable. It seems as if nothing now can ever be said. It is all too late.

None the less, after a while Judith starts talking again. She doesn't turn to face him, she addresses her words to the ceiling immediately above her head. The words are uttered with great effort.

'She didn't want us to read it,' she says. He jumps. She gropes for his hand, still without turning her head.

'What did you say?' he asks, a little too loudly, and turns his head to look at her, reaches out his hand to her. She grips it and turns to him, she holds it tightly, a little too tightly, but he doesn't pull it away.

'She didn't want us to read it,' she repeats.

'No,' he says.

'She didn't trust us.'

'Didn't she?'

'She didn't trust us. She didn't want us to read it.'

'No, maybe not.'

'That's what it says in the letter. That she didn't trust us.'

'But why didn't she trust us?'

'I know what's in that letter. So do you, if only you would allow yourself to see it.'

'You said you hadn't read it.'

'I haven't.'

'Then how can you know what's in it?'

'I'm not just talking about what's in the letter. I'm talking about all of this. About her. What we're going through now. There are some things you just know, Johan. I've tried to explain it to you so many times. I know her. She had it in her.'

'What did she have in her, Judith? Answer me!'

'This.'

'Are you trying to tell me you know something about Ebba that I don't know? Do you know why she didn't want to go on living? Talk to me!'

'Try to listen to what I'm saying, Johan. Try just being here for once.'

'I'm listening. I *am* here.'

Judith lets go of his hand and edges a little further away from him in the big bed. She starts to recite, in the low chanting voice that has always alarmed him before. But he is too tired now to be alarmed, he lies still and listens. He does his best not to let his mind wander while she is talking. He recognises that she does know something.

'She always had it in her,' she says, still with her eyes closed. 'There was nothing I could do about it. She had it from you. It was the same darkness that I sometimes saw in you when you lived here. When you got out of bed again at night and listened to music. I crept down after you.'

'Were you spying on me?'

She ignores him.

'And maybe I had it in me, too,' she says. 'I saw it in her and she saw it in me. In you and in her it lay behind you, like a kind

291

of shadow that never managed to close in on you completely. You weren't aware of it yourselves. In me it was something heavy and black that lay deep down in the earth.'

'Down in the earth? I don't know what you're talking about Judith,' he says, trying to keep his voice light. 'You'll have to try to explain it to me.'

'In me,' she repeats, 'it lies deep down in the earth. It is dark and heavy and I don't think it has any sound, it seems to block all sound coming anywhere near it. That's how heavy it is. And sometimes it led me to let go of her.'

'You let go of her?! You mustn't ever let go of your child!' he says, aware even as he utters them, that these are her words he is mouthing. 'Why did you let go of her, Judith?!'

But she doesn't appear to hear him.

'I have to find it,' she says. 'That's what shut me out from her, that's what drew me away, drew me down.'

'Judith, why did you let her go?!'

'I have to dig in the earth,' she carries on. 'I have to dig and dig until I get to it. I have to look at it. Have to look at it now.'

He doesn't know what to say. He doesn't understand what is happening, but everything around him is telling him that a change is occurring. Sounds are now coming from the wood outside.

'What is it you have to see?' he asks.

'It takes all my strength,' she says. 'I'm digging, there's dirt under my fingernails, it hurts: look, it takes such a long time to clean up afterwards, you have to scrub and file . . .'

He makes no answer, he wants her to go on, but gives her no encouragement. She doesn't need any encouragement, though, she is running on automatic now.

'But I know that I have to dig,' she continues. 'I have to find this thing down there that is so heavy, whatever it was that drew me away from her, even though I know it's no use.'

'What makes you think it's no use?' he asks. He feels thirsty. He has a powerful urge to get out of bed, to interrupt this thread she is pursuing, wash it away with a glass of water from the bathroom tap. My toothbrush glass might still be in the cabinet, he thinks, but he stays where he is.

'Because I keep being stopped by things lying in the way,' she says. 'I can't get any further. There's something blocking the way and it's stopping me from getting down to where I'm going, to see.'

'I don't understand,' he says. 'What's stopping you? Why can't you get to where you're going?'

'It's lying right here in front of me.' She gropes at the air in front of her and blindly pats his side of the bed with both hands.

'Here? In the bed?'

'Yes. And down in the earth. In the bed and in the earth.'

Johan realises that this is no time to dwell on whatever he doesn't understand. There seems to be some peculiar logic to what she is saying, he has to try to follow it. His mouth is totally parched now. He presses his tongue against the roof of his mouth, to see if he can produce more saliva that way. A glass of water, he thinks.

'But how do you know where you're going?' he asks. 'How do you know where to dig?'

'Don't ask such questions!' she snaps. 'Don't spoil it!'

'I'm sorry,' he says. She doesn't answer. The thought of mineral water comes into his mind. He is consumed by lethargy. Thirst, that's a form of torture too, he thinks.

'What is it that's blocking your way, Judith?' he ventures again after a while.

It is a long time before she answers. He wonders if she has snapped out of it. Maybe he could slip out to the bathroom now.

'It's you,' she says. 'And Minna. It's always you two. You're always lying side by side. Now you're both here in this bed. You're covered with earth. You're blocking my way. I can barely distinguish the two of you from the earth I'm digging through, I have to run my hands over you. Only after I've been feeling your faces for some time do I realise that it is you and her.'

'Then what do you do?' he whispers. He is starting to get hooked, there is something hypnotic about what she is saying.

'Then I put down my spade and sit down beside the two of you and cry,' she says.

'You cry over Minna and me?'

'Yes.'

'Why do you cry?'

'Because you're in the way. I can't get past you. You merge with the ground. And it's so hard to tell the difference between you and the earth I have to dig through to get to where I'm going. I brush the dirt away from your faces and only by your clear, pensive eyes can I tell that it is you and her. That you are not earth.'

'Are we looking at you?' he asks. He is totally caught up in it now, he sees what she sees, he is no longer thinking about mineral water.

'Yes,' she says. 'Minna and you are looking at me. You both have such clear, pensive eyes.'

'But you feel that you have to shovel us out of the way,' he says and blinks, runs a hand over his eyes.

'Yes, I have to shovel you out of the way so that I can dig down deeper, I shovel earth over you, earth and bedclothes.' Judith scrabbles at the bed. It looks weird.

But now Johan has to have something to drink. He pushes off with his hand, rolls over on to his side and out of bed. He is not in full control of his movements, when he tries to get up he bumps his head hard against the wooden foot of the bed. He feels dazed and defenceless, as if someone has come along and hit him over the head with a blunt instrument. Judith doesn't turn a hair.

'But can't you get past us?' he asks at length. He is sitting doubled up on the bed, clutching his head with both hands. 'Can't you get any further? Does it have to be such a problem for you that we're lying there?'

'No, I can't get any further,' she says. 'I'm trying, but it does no good. I don't know how I can possibly shift you. You're in the way. All I can see is the two of you.'

'Yes, I see,' he says.

'That's why I have to give up. I'll never learn what's underneath you at this rate. You are the guards. I have to leave you lying there, half uncovered. I have to make sure that your mouths and eyes are cleared of earth, so that you can see and breathe, and then I have to pick up my spade and leave. I'm never going to learn what lies underneath you. What it was that shut me out from her.'

'So you can never learn what lies underneath us, because we're blocking the way,' Johan says. It is intended as a sort of summing-up, but he can hear how dry and schoolmasterish it sounds. Well, I guess that's me, he thinks. Dry and schoolmasterish. Thirsty. Head aching.

'No,' she says wearily. 'I just have to come home again, home to this big, empty house, where you didn't want to live any more. I have to lie in this bed. You're not here.'

He remains sitting on the bed with his head in his hands, saying nothing. He studies her face to see if he can find any clue there, that might lead him in the right direction, he knows that it is up to him now. But Judith turns away and will not help him. She is deep inside herself. Unlike earlier in the evening, when she was racing around the room being the pancake, he has the impression that she is not playacting. It feels as if something has been shaken loose inside his head when he bumped it against the bedstead, and all the pieces have fallen into a new pattern. Now I'm going to get up and go to the bathroom and find my glass, he thinks.

He pulls himself to his feet and stumbles out to the bathroom. He finds the glass in the cabinet, fills it with water from the tap, drains it in a couple of great gulps, fills it again. Not until he puts it down on the side of the wash-basin does he realise that he has been drinking from Ebba's glass. His own has been cleared out of there years ago.

He studies himself in the mirror. The bright light lends a greenish cast to his skin, it looks eerie. He goes back to bed.

'What do you think you would have found if Minna and I weren't blocking the way, and you could dig deeper?' he says, as he climbs back into bed. His head is no longer aching. He can hear the cold water burbling down into his stomach, like a little brook, running very, very slowly.

'It's not possible,' she says desolately. Her eyes are open, but she doesn't looks as if she has even registered his absence.

'But if it were possible, Judith?'

'You don't know what is possible and what is not possible for me. You don't know me any more.'

'But if I asked you. If I *begged* you to dig deeper.'

'Are you begging me now?'

'Yes.'

'You don't look like someone who is begging.'

'I don't know how a person who is begging is supposed to look.'

'No, exactly – that's just what I'm saying.'

'How do you want me to look then?'

'Like someone who is begging me,' she says. 'Like someone who is in deadly earnest and understands what is going on. Someone who knows me.'

Johan breathes a heavy sigh. He has no idea how to answer her. He can still feel that little burbling brook trickling down through him. Soon it will be the intestines' turn, he thinks. To welcome it in. It is pitch dark in there. It is all very clear. I am a schoolmaster. Judith shuts her eyes and feigns sleep again.

But then Johan starts to sing. He sits up in bed, his head is light and spacious, he sits upright and sings the high priest Sarastro's aria from the second act of *The Magic Flute*. *In diesen heil'gen Hallen*, he sings, *kennt man die Rache nicht*. Judith's eyes fly open in surprise, then she lies with her head resting on her hand and listens.

He doesn't sing loudly, he sings softly. He is no longer himself, he is a voice singing softly, he is the schoolmaster, the high priest who is in deadly earnest and knows what is going on, who knows her. He is playacting, and not playacting. He sings with his eyes shut. Now he is begging her, he does not know any other way of begging her, he has never begged anyone for anything in this manner before.

When he opens his eyes again she has closed hers. He sits and looks at her.

'You have a nice voice,' she murmurs.

In the house across the street, Runa is cuddled right up against Isak now; she has curled her fingers round his pyjama jacket. Both old people breathe with their mouths open. They sleep.

In Judith's house the tap in the bathroom has started to drip. Johan can't have turned it off properly when he was in there a moment ago. It makes a rhythmic sound, like a slow, stylised roll from a drum-machine. He hears it. He tries to think what it reminds him of. Hypnosis, he thinks. He still has the song inside him, like a priest.

'Judith, love,' he says after a while, cutting through the steady tap, tap from the bathroom. 'Would you please dig deeper into the ground underneath Minna and me. You have to find out what is down there. It's important to you. It's important to me, too.'

'And to Minna,' she says.

'Yes, to Minna, too.'

'And to Jennifer.'

'Yes. To Jennifer.'

The tap drips.

'And to Ebba.'

'Yes.'

'To Ebba most of all.'

'Yes.'

'Oh, well. If you put it like that.'

'Yes. Please,' he says with relief.

'Okay, now I'm going to dig.' She raises her empty hand to him. 'Here's the spade.'

'Yes,' he says. 'The spade. I see it.'

'I'm digging with it,' she says, although she is lying perfectly still with her eyes closed. 'I'm digging now. I dig on beyond you and her. I cover you with earth. Soon I won't be able to see you at all. You are covered with earth.'

He places a hand over his eyes, as if to shield himself.

'What lies underneath us?' he asks.

'Wait a moment,' she answers, struggling to get the words out, although still lying perfectly still on the bed with her eyes closed. 'It's awfully hard work, I'm so tired. Stop pestering me. I think I'm coming to a cave. There's a big, hollow space. I don't think I need to dig any further, it's a cave. I'm so tired, stop pestering me . . .'

'What sort of a cave is it?'

'I think I've been here before, long ago.'

'When you were a little girl?'

'Yes, I think so.'

'What can you see in the cave?'

'I can't tell you,' she says, turning her face away. 'You wouldn't understand.'

'Yes, I would. I would understand, Judith. Tell me,' he says.

'I can't trust you.'

'Yes, you can. You can tell me. You can trust me.'

She turns to face him again, opens her eyes and gazes blankly at him for some moments; her vision seems somehow to be trained in the wrong direction. Then she says:

'I think it's Little Judith. She sitting in there. She's so alone.'

There is silence between them. Johan turns his attention to the dripping tap. He tells himself that he cannot possibly go out there and turn it off now. He has to stay here. He is never going to get away from here. He has been hypnotised.

'It's so windy in the cavern,' Judith says at last. 'She's cold.'

She seems exhausted. Maybe now she will sleep. Maybe she will talk in her sleep. She lies quite still. He tucks the duvet in around her.

'Judith, love,' he says. 'Don't sleep now. I know you're not sleeping. Listen to me. Do you remember when you were playing with the orchestra – that time when you were rehearsing *The Magic Flute* and I came to rehearsals – I know you remember – I sat at the very back of the theatre, watching you – remember the overture? Remember? Yes. I know you do. We had just met, I was so in love with you – I sat at the very back of the theatre, up in the gods, and I had the idea of screwing up my eyes, to distance myself from you, not to let you get too close to me – I should have had a pair of binoculars to hold the wrong way round, I hadn't thought of that. So I just screwed up my eyes, I wouldn't allow my gaze to caress you too much, Judith, you loomed too large in my field of vision, I was so much in love.'

Johan looks down at her through half-shut eyes. He is sitting up now. She lies quite still with her eyes closed; he doesn't know if she is listening, but he goes on talking all the same.

'I sat there watching you, I listened to the overture, I let it wash over me – and I thought: this is what thinking is like. This is how it begins, with one strong chord.

'Judith. Don't sleep, I know you remember it, after all it was you who was playing it, I know you can hear me, it's a chord that is played by the entire orchestra at once . . . then that chord is split in two, remember, then it sounds for a third time, transformed by then from an assertion to a question, one to which you musicians are not really sure you want to know the answer. Isn't that so? Then your section, the strings, comes in: insect-like, vibrant, as if you have already released the question, sent it soaring into the air. And the rest of the orchestra follow your lead, you catch and let go of the question, each section in turn, you flip it from one to another and almost imperceptibly you start to offer your own suggestions for a response: the flutes notably to the fore here, followed by the other wind instruments; you egg each other on, the tension builds up . . .'

He lays a hand on her shoulder, shakes her gently.

'. . . and it gets to a point where the whole thing reaches such a pitch that there is no longer any way back . . .

'I lose sight of you, you become one with the others, you become one great, vibrant mass which is the orchestra . . . and then come the three blasts from the wind section:

'*Ta-tam ta. Ta-tam ta.*'

He is shaking her harder now.

'*Ta-tam ta.*'

And Judith opens her eyes. He stares at her, as if hardly able to believe it.

They gaze into one another's eyes, each from their own side of the bed. They are both wide awake. She is lying down, he is sitting up. And these two, the only ones awake in this neighbourhood, do not know what is happening. They are there beside one another in the double bed, and they hear sounds coming from the wood. The tap has stopped dripping, they are left open and exhausted; it is as if something has split apart: a duvet or a cloud, and something blows away. It is not glass.

'We have to go into her room,' she says. He nods.

'There must be a sign from her,' he says. 'Something or other. Surely she wouldn't go off and leave us like that without giving us some sign.'

'No,' she says. 'I'll show you where I found the letter. There has to be something else there, something I've missed.'

They get up and walk through to Ebba's room. The little night-light is burning. Judith notices that Johan has made the bed. This throws her for a second, but she does not remark on it. She goes over to the bookcase and lifts down the big photograph album full of pictures of Ebba; they sit down on the bed and open it so that it lies across both their laps. They are like two children looking at the pictures in a storybook.

Judith insists that they start at the very first page. On this are pictures that they stuck in together when they were both living in this house: first of Judith's enormous tummy, Judith walking in the forest in a voluminous raincoat. Then the first photos taken at the hospital: Johan and Grandma drinking a toast over the baby's head – that must have been taken with the self-timer, the picture is a little squint. And then Ebba with Granny, wrapped in blankets, and Ebba with Judith, with Johan, always swathed in blankets.

Then comes the photograph that Judith's mother took of all three of them when they came home from the hospital; she couldn't get the flash to work, the image is dark, it looks as though the house were in twilight. Then come all the photos of Ebba as a baby at different stages of growth. And then the first birthday: Ebba with her bright little face covered in whipped cream and sticky fingers splayed wide – they both remember how she started screaming the second after that picture was taken.

It's easy to see who has taken which pictures: Johan always takes close-ups, homing in on the face of his subject, while Judith likes to include more of the surroundings and has less of an eye for the structure of the photograph – she, who normally has such a thing about composition. Johan produces striking portraits, but on inspection, so many years later, Judith's snaps prove to have captured more of the flavour of the times: the clothes, furniture, angles, all the indefinable elements that say something more; that make it possible for us to tell at a glance that a certain photograph was taken many years ago, and that those days are long gone now.

When they reach the photographs from the time after Johan moved out, Judith wants to flick past them, as if this she would rather keep to herself. But he stays her arm: he wants to know everything. Ebba has her own big photograph album at home with him and Minna. The pictures in that album start from when she was three, the year when he moved out. He has often looked through it with her. It contains pictures of her surrounded by his family: with Minna, then Jennifer, with Minna's parents and siblings. But he has never seen these photographs, the ones that Judith took around that same time. Wordlessly he studies the Ebba he did not know, that part of her life which he could not share, the part from which he shut himself out: children's parties, outings with the girl guides, Ebba with various musical instruments, with chums he doesn't know. Judith offers no comment on them, she sits quietly by his side. Eventually they reach photos from the last couple of years: a tall, skinny Ebba on a bike trip with the girls; at the beach; Ebba sitting on the sofa downstairs in the living room, engrossed in a book, the look of surprise in her eyes when she realises that her mother is taking a picture of her.

'This is where she had put the letter,' Judith says, leafing forward to the last page in the album. In here they find a bundle of loose photographs which have not been stuck into the album, together with some newspaper cuttings, neatly folded. Johan takes out the cuttings; he leaves Judith holding the album. The first one he unfolds is the cutting that Ebba once slipped into his jacket pocket in the hall of the flat. It shows Judith about ten years ago; she looks radiant and charismatic, a very different person from the hunched-up child sitting next to him here on the bed. The next cutting shows himself and some colleagues when they won an award for a product they had developed. He had been in charge of the project. That was five years ago.

While he is studying the newspaper cutting, Judith picks up the bundle of loose photographs and proceeds to lay them out on the bed.

At first he can't make out what these pictures represent, then it dawns on him: it is a series of small tableaux from the grove of trees behind the house. The remains of the tumbledown hut in the middle. Birds in a tree. The fence between the wood and their own garden. The stumps that Johan helped to saw up and trundle over there in the wheelbarrow the summer that he moved out. All seen from a long way off, taken from a quite different perspective than either he or Judith would use. Ebba must have taken these herself. Her approach to composing pictures is quite different from that of either of her parents.

And so they sit, looking and looking at these pictures. They don't know what to say.

'I don't understand,' says Johan.

'No,' says Judith, and lays her head on his shoulder.

THE LETTER

Dearest Jennifer.

You're sleeping now. I've just been in to check on you, your nightie is rucked up under your arms and you've kicked off your duvet as usual, but your hair is still damp with sweat from all the rolling about we did before you fell asleep. I'll leave you like that for a while yet to let you cool down. I'll take care that you don't get too cold.

Papa and Minna are asleep too. The whole flat is in darkness, except for this light here on Papa's desk. There's no risk of either of them waking up, they both seem so tired. I bet they're curled up close together in bed as always. It's a cold winter's night outside, this flat is a bit draughty.

You're too young to have noticed, but Papa has been a bit distant and not quite himself lately, I don't think he's feeling all that great. I've taken some paper and an envelope from his desk drawer and I'm using his pen to write with. I know he doesn't mind me borrowing his things. Papa would happily share every-thing with me. And with you, that's something you'll discover when you're a bit older. You're going to have to take good care of Papa, he's not as tough as you might think, though he doesn't know it himself, not really.

I'm going to put this letter in the envelope and write on the front that it's to be opened by you on your sixteenth birthday. I'll write it as nicely as I can, I have a special calligraphy pen here that I can use. I want this to be a beautiful letter, one that you can treasure. Maybe someone will find it and put it in the safety-deposit box at the bank. It is twelve and a half years until your sixteenth birthday. That's a long time.

We've had such a good time today, you and I – playing and fooling about! You're so sweet when you sing for me. I helped you get dressed up for the birthday party that Minna was taking you to. You looked so nice, and when the two of you got back from the party you ran straight to me, showed me the goodie bag you'd been given and let me have a sweet. You wanted me to give you your bath and put you to bed. I read to you and let you jump and roll about on the bed as much as you wanted. I hope you'll remember all of that when you read this. Your little body is so strong and happy. I hope you'll still have a strong, happy body when you are sixteen years old. I'm so afraid of ruining anything for you.

Sometimes I feel as if I'm standing outside a glass bubble, looking in on everyone else. All the people inside the bubble go about their business as if nothing was wrong. They seem to be doing just fine, for the most part. They go to birthday parties, talk to one another, laugh and eat, they don't worry too much. They do think, but mainly about the same things over and over again. Sometimes I feel as if they'll never let me in.

But you let me in. When you sing me that song about all the little billy-goats, and hop off the headboard into my lap with a squeal the way you did tonight, it's like you lay yourself wide open to me. I don't know what I would have done without you. Jennifer, I salute you! It was me who thought of your name. I wanted you to have a name that would be like a flag flapping in the breeze.

When you read this you will be the same age as I am now. I wonder how you will look then. Do you look like me? Will you think like me? You might well do: Papa has shown me pictures of myself at your age, he stuck them into my photo album, I looked almost exactly the way you do now, only a bit thinner maybe, and with slightly darker hair. And I'm sure I thought the way you do now.

I was your age when Papa met Minna. I've often thought that that was the beginning of you, too, even though you weren't actually born until years later. If Papa hadn't met Minna, I wouldn't have had you for a little sister. If Papa and Mama had stayed together and had another baby, I doubt if she would have been like you. Or maybe they would have had a little boy. We always carry inside us a part of the people who made us. You have yours from Minna and I have mine from Mama, but we both have something of Papa in us too, of course. That's why we're so alike.

I hope it won't hurt you to read this. It's so hard when you hurt inside all the time. I hope you'll have someone to share it with, and that you don't have the same feeling of standing outside a glass bubble. I would so like to be there when you read this letter, be the one with whom you could share it. Just as I'm going to look in on you very shortly, and stroke your hair and check whether you are still hot.

I'm writing this letter to let you know that this is how I thought when I was alive. Maybe you can think of me as someone who is still there for you. I hope so. Or maybe you have a boyfriend – a sweetheart. That, too, I hope. Everyone should have a sweetheart. I wish Mama had one.

I'm so afraid that you'll forget me, lambkin. I've made sure that Papa has taken lots of pictures of us together. He took one this afternoon, just before you and Minna left for the birthday party. When you read this, maybe you'll know the one I mean, maybe someone has stuck it into your photo album. There are lots of pictures of me in there already, I've seen to that. In the one that Papa took this afternoon you are wearing a dark-blue velvet dress and lovely black patent shoes, I'm wearing a striped polo-neck sweater. I hope you can find it. Now I'm in my nightie and slippers and I've borrowed one of Minna's cardigans, it's a bit chilly in here.

I've tried to find out how old children must be before memories of things they have experienced will stay with them, even after *they are grown up. I've asked lots of people about their earliest memories, whether they can remember things that happened when they were three and a half.*

Early this morning, before you three were awake, I stood for a long time looking at myself in the bathroom mirror. I tried to imagine that I was you on your sixteenth birthday, the day on which you will read this. I stood there staring at myself and wondering whether you will stand in front of the mirror on that day and try to understand what it was like to be me when I wrote this. What it's like to be me. Now. In this nightie and cardigan, in these slippers. Sitting at this desk. It takes so long to write this.

I've left the little bedside lamp burning in our room, you're happiest when it's not completely dark. I got out of bed again once I could tell from the sounds in Minna's and Papa's room that they were asleep. I've been listening to music with the headphones on so as not to wake all of you. It's the most beautiful music. Papa introduced me to it, it's called The Magic Flute. *By the time you read this I'm sure you'll know what I mean. I hope Papa will show you beautiful things too. He loves you so much. There's nothing to be afraid of.*

When I was standing in front of the mirror this morning, waiting for you three to wake up, I thought to myself that I would have to remember not to make this letter sound too childish. By the time you read it you'll know as much as I do now. Maybe more. I hope you know more. On your sixteenth birthday it will be summer, and the nights will be lovely and light, it won't be dark all day and snowy as it is now. Sometimes, if you concentrate long and hard enough you can almost know what it's like to be someone else. Not entirely, though.

I've seen a picture from the time when Papa was living with Mama and me. Maybe you can find that picture too. I'm wearing a red towelling jump suit that Granny had made for me, and in those days Mama used to plait my hair the way that I plaited yours this afternoon, before I helped you on with your pretty velvet dress and tied the bow at the back.

It's much easier once you've made up your mind. I see everything differently now: Mama and Papa, Minna, you. Things will go on without me, it will be better that way. It will hurt at first, but it will get easier, the hurt will kind of melt away and eventually it will pass, then everything will be very white and still.

Mama will take it hard of course, I'm all she has. I hope Papa and Minna will look after her. Maybe she could come and stay with you for a while, so she won't have to live in this big house all alone. She could have my bed in your room, couldn't she? She's going to love you so much, how could anyone not love you. And as time goes on she will cope better, she'll start to play the violin again, she always feels better when she's playing, and she'll find that it is possible to go on living without me. Papa and Minna will help her. And Granny.

Sometimes I have the feeling that I'm going to be lost without you all. And the thought of that loss scares me. But where I'm going there is no loss or longing. I have to trust in that, otherwise it's no use.

I've been thinking that Mama and Papa and Minna and Granny are going to ask themselves over and over again why I did it. None of them will be able to get that thought out of their heads. Maybe you could try to show them how to stop thinking. Maybe you'll be the sort of person who knows things like that.

There's too much pain, poppet. It's so hard to be surrounded by so much pain. There are too many people to look after, too many inside the bubble, they understand so little of what is going on, they just carry on as they've always done.

In that way I think things will be easier for you than they are for me. Even though Papa might not be living with Minna when you read this, I'm sure they'll both have managed fine on their own. It will be easier for them than for Mama. By the time you read this you might even have had another brother or sister, as I did. Maybe you'll have a little sister of three and a half who lets you bath her and shares her sweets with you. If so, then you are lucky, just as I was. Minna will probably be too old by then to have any more children, but Papa can certainly have more and there's a good chance it would be a girl. Papa loves children, you know.

That's about it, though, I think. It's almost morning again. I've been writing so slowly, my writing arm is tired. I'm going to fold these sheets and put them into the envelope and address it to you in my very nicest handwriting. Then I'll put it in my rucksack. I'm going to hide this letter somewhere in my room at my and Mama's house when I get home from school tomorrow. I think I know where to put it. Now I'll go in and cover you with the duvet; we can't have you catching cold, my little honey bee.

Your Ebba.

THE WHITE ROOM (largo)

It is early morning. The light has entered the bedroom in Judith's house.

They have lain beside one another in the double bed all night. Johan wakes up first. The belt of darkness which in the past he has always been able to stave off with his magnetic force, that darkness that has been hovering out there, watching him from some point in the future, has now closed in on him. It has crept over him during the night. Somehow his magnetic charge must have altered while he was asleep. He can feel it in his bones as he lies there in the bright morning light with his head at the foot of the bed, on top of the duvet, in his T-shirt and underpants. For some reason the sick feeling is gone.

When he awoke a moment ago he could not remember who he was, or where he was. He was a stranger. He thought: Ebba is dead. That thought came to him before the knowledge of his own identity.

And at that same moment he recognised his own body, with an intensity he had not felt since he was a little boy. As if even back then he knew. In those days he was always the first one in the family to wake in the mornings; often he would lie on in bed for hours before sounds began to reach him from around the house – the rush of water through the pipes, someone on the stairs.

He lies with his head turned so that he is looking straight at the bedroom window. The light filters through the green leaves on the trees outside, it flickers over his face, both peaceful and restless. From outside comes the dense rustle of twittering birds. It is comforting to discover that he knows the names of several of these birds. So there are, in fact, things which have names, even though on waking he had for a moment forgotten his own, and still cannot remember that of the woman sleeping next to him.

He remembers a dream.

Ebba is dead.

He gets out of bed and goes to the bathroom. He takes a quick shower, dries himself with the red towel with which he dried the woman in the bed the evening before. It is dry almost before he hangs it up again. He looks in the mirror. He doesn't seem so grey now. But his head still aches where he banged it against the foot of the bed.

On his way down the stairs he remembers the name of the woman in the bed.

He goes into the kitchen and turns on one of the hotplates on the cooker. The light in the kitchen is white, even brighter down here than in the bedroom upstairs. Judith has got herself one of those new cookers with a ceramic glass hob, they didn't have a cooker like that when he lived here. After a moment or two the red circle denoting the hotplate starts to glow red, like a wound. He has the impression, when he stares at the glass surface, that he can see right inside the cooker, it's as if it were a volcano on the verge of erupting. Lava, he thinks. At the earth's core there is lava. This is something that Jennifer is forever asking him about.

And with this thought Minna and Jennifer also come flooding back to him, with such force that it is physically painful; it leaves him weak. Are they awake now, he wonders. Are they anxious. Are they thinking about me. He looks down at the glowing hotplate and thinks to himself that Minna and he will never own a cooker like this, it looks expensive. So what, he thinks. We're fine the way we are. I have to go to them.

He finds a swish-looking designer kettle on the bench, upside down with the lid lying next to it as though it has recently been washed. He remembers Judith's habit of washing the kettle and leaving it to dry like that, he has never seen the sense in it: washing in soap suds something that has never been used for anything but boiling water. But this was just one of those things which there had been little point in discussing with her when he lived here. A designer kettle is just up her street, he can see that. It fits right in. He fills the kettle with water and sets it over the fiery wound on the hob; the water immediately starts to hiss.

Ebba is dead. On the kitchen bench sit piles of clean coffee cups and saucers with an institutional look about them. Judith's mother is evidently well-organised for the reception to be held here after the funeral.

He stands there in the middle of the kitchen, gathering his thoughts while he listens to the water in the kettle hissing: what has happened today? Woke up. Ebba. Thought: Ebba is dead; those words. Couldn't remember his name. Thought of the time when he was little and woke up early. That he knew even back then. The dream. Remembered Judith's name. The kettle, recalled the idiotic washing of it. Minna and Jennifer. Yes. That was it. Ebba is dead. The hurt. It hurts.

His brain is working slowly, but when he feels that he has things clear in his mind he goes back up the stairs and into the bedroom. Judith is still in bed asleep, her feet stick out from under the duvet. They are pale and clean now, her toenails are a flaming scarlet.

He stands for a moment, considering her. She's not moving; he is suddenly seized by a fear that she too has gone from him, that she won't remember him when she wakes up. He says her name softly. She doesn't wake up. He hunkers down beside the bed and says it a little louder. This time she stirs, she slides further down the mattress and squeezes her eyes tighter shut. He breathes a long sigh. He pulls back the duvet, eases himself down beside her, on his back with his hands folded on his chest, and waits for her to wake up. After a while he can tell by her breathing that she is awake, but that she doesn't want to open her eyes.

Then Judith lays one hand slowly over his, still with her eyes closed. They are silent.

'It's morning,' he says quietly. She nods.

'I had such a strange dream,' he says. 'I dreamed that I died.'

He is interrupted by the sound of the kettle in the kitchen starting to whistle. They both jump, as if they have been caught doing something illegal. Johan goes downstairs, switches off the hotplate and removes the kettle, the red wound on the hob promptly turns black. The volcano has died down, he thinks.

When he walks into the sitting-room, he finds Judith standing before him in the middle of the room, looking confused. She is still in her nightie, but she has brought the dress she was wearing yesterday downstairs and dropped it on the floor at her feet. She gazes at him in bewilderment.

'You died?' she asks. 'Last night?'

'I only dreamed that I died,' he says.

'Tell me about it.'

'It's hard to explain,' he says. 'Let's make some coffee. The water's boiled.'

'Tell me about your dream,' she says.

She remains where she is in the sitting-room, while he goes into the kitchen and positions himself awkwardly, bolt upright, next to the cooker. With one hand resting on the handle of the kettle he tells her about his dream. He doesn't know which leg to put his weight on, he can't make up his mind.

'I dreamed that I was in a big vehicle, some sort of tank, I think,' he says. 'I don't know who else was with me, but I wasn't alone. The tank was rolling along, not fast but with tremendous power. It had no steering-wheel, no controls of any sort: those of us who were inside it had to try to steer it by moving from side to side, rocking our bodies, a bit like you do when you're riding on a toboggan – you know.' He shifts his weight from one leg to the other and sways his hips to show her what he means. She nods.

'I was aware that we were heading into the enemy's camp. The tank had no windscreen, only small round windows on each side, like the portholes on a boat. Through these small windows I could see tall dark buildings rearing up on either side of us. I realised

that the tank was about to propel us into one of these buildings. I
and the others fought desperately to steer it, to save crashing into
anything, but it was hopeless, of course, because we couldn't see
where we were going. Then there was an almighty jolt. We were
thrown backwards. We knew that we had driven straight into a
building. The noise and the shaking were unbearable. I thought:
I'm dying. Then everything went quiet.'

'Were you frightened?' Judith asks, stepping over her crumpled
dress and coming over to him in the kitchen. She seems dazzled
by the bright light in there, everything is so white. But she doesn't
appear surprised by his dream. Maybe she was there, too, in the
dream last night, he thinks. In the old days, the one's dreams
often used to rub off on the other's.

'I don't know,' he says. 'Yes. I was frightened.'

'What was it like – the place where you went when you were
dead?' she asks, peering at him through slitted eyes. He thinks:
you need sunglasses in this kitchen.

'It was all white,' he says.

'Was Ebba there?'

'What do you mean?'

'You said you were dead. So you must have gone to Ebba. Was
she there?'

'I don't know,' he says. 'I couldn't see anything. It was only a
dream, you know. Everything was white.'

'But didn't the whiteness disperse?'

'No.'

'Say that you saw her.'

'But I didn't, Judith. It was only a dream.'

'But you must have seen something, even if it was only a
dream? I mean, you've just been telling me about all the things
you saw.'

'Yes, but not in the real world. We're in the real world here,
Judith.'

'I just want to know whether you saw her.'

'I didn't see her. It was only a dream.'

For some moments there is silence. Judith gets the coffee out of the cupboard, he takes down cups and saucers. Everything is kept exactly where it used to be when he lived here.

'But does death have no end?' she asks out of the blue, in a normal, everyday voice, as she measures out the coffee with the measuring spoon.

'No,' he says, as if he has long been expecting this question. 'Death has no end.' He has no idea where this comes from.

'I think you're wrong there,' she says calmly. 'Everything has an end. Even death has an end.'

'But Judith. What do you think comes after the end of death?' He walks across to the fridge and opens it.

'How should I know!' she retorts. 'I haven't been there, have I? No one has been there. How are we supposed to know?'

'I don't know,' he says, taking out cheese and butter. He sees that she still eats mature French cheese, and that as usual the pat of butter is hardly touched. She's probably worried about putting on weight, now as then. The butter looks as if it has been there for ages. He knows her.

'No, exactly,' she continues. 'You don't know, so you can't very well say that you do. How can you say that death has no end when you don't even know if there is such a thing as death?'

'I don't know.'

'You don't know if there is such a thing as death, and you don't know whether death, too, has an end.'

'No. I know there is such a thing as death.' Johan puts the cheese and the butter on the table.

'No! You don't know!' she hisses. 'You don't know! I'm the one who knows. It's so bright in here. Why is it so bright?'

In Erlend's house everyone is awake. His mother has woken both of his sisters and is now bending over his bed, shaking him gently. He pretends to be asleep. She can see that he has been crying. She takes the tray from the previous evening with her when she leaves the room.

Judith stands in her own kitchen in her bare feet, gazing out of the window while she pours hot water over the coffee filter. Johan has sat down at the table.

'There aren't any birds out there,' she says. 'What's happened to all the birds?'

'They were there a little while ago,' he says. 'I heard them clear as day. I knew their names when I woke up.'

'What are their names?'

'I must have forgotten them again.'

'Johan,' she says, pouring and pouring until the water overflows. Black coffee grounds swill over the kitchen bench, but she doesn't notice. 'Is there no rest to be found here? Won't it be over soon?'

'No,' he says. He crosses one leg over the other and presses his spine against the back of the chair. 'It's never going to be over. It will go on and on. We have to be strong.'

'All day? Do we have to be strong all day?'

'Yes. All day. We've got the funeral today.'

'And tomorrow? Do we have to be strong tomorrow too?'

'I don't know,' he says. 'I think so. Tomorrow I'll be going home with Minna and Jennifer.'

Even as he says it, he realises that this is out of the question; he can't leave Judith alone in this house after the funeral, it would be too risky, she is far too unstable. He will have to try to come to some arrangement whereby her mother can move in with her, he thinks.

'Then it's never going to be over,' she says. 'Then we'll have to be strong for ever.'

'Yes. I think so.'

'But what if we aren't strong? What if we should weaken again? Is there no rest to be found then either, if we weaken?'

'I don't know, Judith. Come and eat now,' he says, leaning forward and pulling out her chair for her.

In the hotel room in the town centre, Jennifer has woken before her mother. She sits up in bed and looks down into Minna's face. She runs her finger gently over her mother's eyebrows. Minna opens her eyes. They don't smile at one another. Jennifer nestles close to her and curls up into a ball, she's pretending she is a little baby. Her mother holds her close and strokes her back. They say not a word.

Judith is not eating. She stares out of the kitchen window, both hands clasping her coffee cup, but she's not drinking either. Her eyes are wide open now, she has grown accustomed to the light, her pupils are big and dark. Johan doesn't understand how they can be so open when the room is so bright. Eyes that are open that wide are bound to hurt, he thinks. Everything becomes too clear-cut.

'Tell me what it's like where she is now,' she croaks.

'I don't know what it's like,' he replies. 'I don't know.'

'Tell me,' she persists. 'You're her father. You must know.'

'But I don't know, Judith,' he says. 'Eat up now.' He pushes the plate of food he has prepared for her over to her side of the table.

'Just *know*.'

'I'll try.'

'Don't try! Just do it. Just tell me. You're the one with the words. Tell it beautifully.'

Johan gets up, walks through to the sitting-room and fetches the binoculars. He stands at the kitchen window and trains them on his car down on the street. He zooms closer.

'Where Ebba is now,' he says tonelessly, 'there is no time.'

'No. No time,' she responds. He feels her wide eyes boring into his back from her seat at the kitchen table.

'And there is nothing to see.'

'No. Nothing to see. Is that because it's dark there?'

'No, it's not dark. It's light,' he answers.

'I don't understand. Is it light there? Doesn't it get dark? Is it exactly like here? Is it Midsummer?'

'Yes, it's Midsummer,' he says.

He can see his car clearly now. It is empty. He sees the seats and the dashboard. The empty lighter lying on the passenger seat.

'It's not far away, is it?' Judith says. 'It's close by! Isn't it?'

'No. It's not far away. Just beyond Runa's and Isak's house.' He turns the binoculars on their house. He can't see anyone at the windows, they're probably not up yet, he thinks.

'Almost close enough for us to reach out and touch it?' Judith asks anxiously.

'Yes.'

'Almost close enough for us to see it with the naked eye?'

'Yes. Almost with the naked eye. Just over there.'

'And certainly with binoculars!'

'Yes.'

'Give me the binoculars!' she says. He hands her the binoculars, she places herself next to him and she too points them at Isak's and Runa's house.

'And there is a cord running from where we are to where she is!' she says. 'We can climb up on to it and walk along it to her. It's just over there, isn't it?'

He takes the binoculars from her and lays them on the window-sill. Then slowly he turns to face her. He is a schoolmaster.

'No, Judith,' he says heavily. 'There is no cord running from this room to her room.'

'But you said there was!'

'But there is no cord running to the room where she is now. She's in another room. A totally different one. Things aren't the same there as they are with us.'

'Aren't things the same? Is it a totally different room?'

'Yes. It's silent there.'

'Doesn't anyone talk there?'

'No.'

'Is it that silent?'

'As silent as – ice.'

'As ice?'

'Yes.'

'Oh, but she'll be chilled to the bone!' Judith says faintly. 'Tell me she's not chilled to the bone! She looked so cold. They hadn't wrapped her up well enough. Why hadn't they wrapped her up well enough?'

'They . . . oh God, Judith.' He covers his face with his hands, as if to break the trance into which he has put himself.

'You haven't seen her,' Judith goes on, 'how can you say that she's dead? You don't know anything about this, you haven't seen her! I'm the one who saw her! She was so cold. She was lying in the cold room. She had a dark welt around her throat. There were blotches on her face. Tell me it's not cold where she is!'

'It's not cold there.'

'Why do you say that? You don't know what you're talking about!'

'No, I don't know what I'm talking about.'

'Because you haven't seen her!'

'No. I haven't seen her.'

'I'm the one who has seen her!'

'Yes.'

'I nodded my head at them, that meant that she was mine, that I recognised her, that I understood what had happened. Say that I nodded my head.'

'You nodded your head,' he says.

'That meant that I recognised her. That she was mine. That I understood what had happened. Right?'

'Yes.'

'She was so cold, Johan! They hadn't wrapped her up well enough.'

'No.'

'Say that she's not alone where she is now! Say that there are lots of others there. Say that they wrap her up well! There are lots of others there, aren't there?'

'Yes, of course there are,' he says. 'There are lots of others there. Her best friends. Her nearest and dearest. They wrap her up well.'

'But *we're* her best friends! You and I are her nearest and dearest, Johan. You know we are! So how can you say that she isn't lonely?'

'She isn't lonely because she – has so much else.'

'So much else?'

'Yes. She is so – full, there is no room for anything else where she is now.'

'Is there no room for anything else?' Judith says. 'Is there no room for us?'

'No.'

'But we're her parents!'

'Yes. But there is no room for us there.'

'What are you talking about? Is there no room there? But she always has room for us!'

Johan sinks down on to the floor under the kitchen window and rests his head against the wall. She stands facing him, looking down at him. There is something insistent about her vulnerability that makes her strong, stronger than him, he can see that.

'What are you talking about?' she hisses again. 'What is she so full of, that there is no room for us?'

'I don't know,' he says spiritlessly, with closed eyes. 'I don't know what I'm talking about.'

'Yes, you do, you *do* know! Say that you know!'

'I don't know, Judith.'

'Well try anyway! Try to know!'

'She is full of light,' he says. 'Full of herself, her own light. If we had seen her, we would have thought: There you are now, Ebba.

You're weightless as air, your light is so bright. You are full of your light, Ebba. You are a cord running through space.'

'A cord running through space!' says Judith.

'Yes.'

'Like that time when we heard her singing in the gym hall at school closing day!'

'Yes.'

'But we can't see her.'

'No.'

'And we can't bring her back along a cord running through space, as if she were a tightrope walker.'

'No.'

'Because she's not a tightrope walker, she is the cord.'

'Yes. If you say so.'

Judith can tell that he still does not understand. He is talking in riddles. Only she understands, she thinks. She sits down on the floor beside him and leans her head back against the wall, like him.

Johan sits hugging his knees. Judith is still in her nightie. After a while she rises stiffly, walks through to the sitting-room and picks up her dress.

'My dress is all creased,' she says. 'I can't wear a creased dress today. I have to look nice.'

'I'll iron it for you,' he says. 'Didn't I promise I would?'

'You're no good at ironing clothes. You never were. You make promises you can't keep.'

'Well, maybe you could iron it yourself.'

'I'm no good at ironing clothes either,' she says. 'You know that. Mama has always ironed the clothes. She used to iron your shirts too, and Ebba's blouses, don't you remember?'

'Then I don't know what we're to do.'

'What are you going to wear?'

'My suit is back at the hotel with Minna and Jennifer.'

'You'll need to wear a tie. Did you bring a tie?'

'Yes, I brought a tie.'

'A dark tie. Have you a dark tie?'

'Yes, I have a dark tie.'

'Is that back at the hotel too?'

'Yes.'

'With Minna and Jennifer?'

'Yes.'

'You'd better call them. They're worried about you. Jennifer has just woken up, she's asking for you. She doesn't know where you are.'

'How do you know that?'

'I just do. She's scared. She's asking for her Papa. Maybe Minna could iron my dress.'

'Minna? I didn't think you wanted to know about her.'

'But can she iron?'

'Yes. She can iron. She's good at ironing.'

'Do you think she would iron my dress for me?'

'I don't know what you mean.'

'Do you think she would iron my dress for me?'

'I don't know. You would have to ask her that.'

'Could we ask her together?'

'I think you should ask her yourself.'

'Do you think Jennifer would come here? To see me? If her mother came with her?'

'You could ask her.'

'Maybe Jennifer could iron the hankies? They're not very big.'

'You could ask her.'

'I saw her once, just after she was born.'

'Yes, you told me.'

'She came here.'

'Yes.'

'Minna was with her, of course. She never told you that.'

'No.'

'We can use my mobile. We can call them now.'

'Will you speak to them?'

'Yes. But you'll have to key in the number for me. I don't know the number. I don't have your numbers stored in my phone. You'll have to help me store your numbers.'

Judith goes out to the hall, takes her mobile phone from the top drawer of the chest. She hands it to him, he takes it, keys in the PIN code, then the number of the hotel: he knows both by heart, that is how his brain functions, he never has any trouble remembering numbers. When Minna answers the phone he hands the mobile to Judith. Then he goes into the sitting-room. He stands there, listening to the conversation.

Judith speaks into the phone. She clenches her free hand tightly. Her voice is faint, he has to strain to hear what she is saying. After some moments she asks to speak to Jennifer.

Afterwards she joins him in the sitting-room.

'They'll be here in an hour,' she says. 'They just have to have breakfast and smarten themselves up. They're going to help me iron my dress. I told them to take a taxi, there are no trains or buses running at this hour.'

He gapes at her, dumbfounded.

'Tell me about Jennifer,' she continues. 'She must be a big girl now. It's years since I saw her. She sounds so sensible on the phone. So old-fashioned. Just like Ebba.'

'She's getting so big,' he replies. 'She'll be four soon.'

'The same age as Ebba was when you left us.'

'I know.'

'But you won't leave her.'

'No.'

'I don't think she should iron the hankies,' she says. 'She's too small. Only four? No, she's too small for that. She might burn herself. We'll have to watch that she doesn't burn herself on the iron.'

There is silence between them. Until Judith asks in a small voice:

'Tomorrow evening when you three go home, can I come with you?'

And now more people are stirring in the houses. The town is bathed in light because it is morning: a different light, and yet the same. Also today it streams from a young, strong sun. It won't rain this day either. Sunlight on the cars driving by and the houses lining the roads, sunlight slicing across the glass pane as someone opens a window.

Everyone is awake, the summer morning is gossamer-light and dry; full of low, murmuring voices, the sound of water rushing through pipes, someone pulling a duvet over their head, wanting to sleep a little longer. Erlend's mother stands outside his door, wondering if she should look in yet again. She hasn't the heart to go on at him today.

In the kitchen across the street Isak and Runa are sitting at the table. They are waiting for the water to boil. In just a few hours' time they will be going to a funeral, they have put on the clothes that Runa ironed and hung on hangers yesterday evening. They have spread a cloth over the table, it is white and smooth.

Judith and Johan are also seated across from one another at the kitchen table. In their kitchen all is quiet. They drink the coffee that Judith made and wait for the taxi bringing Minna and Jennifer. The coffee is almost cold now. Neither of them eats anything. They look out of the window.

'I want us to pretend that we're in another country,' Judith says. She is not using the storyteller voice now.

'Which country?' he asks.

'Anywhere. A foreign country. Some place where it's windy and it's just been raining.'

'Yes,' he says. He is not a schoolmaster. 'Some place where it is windy. On a beach.'

'In the morning!'

'Yes, in the morning.'

'Early, early in the morning!'

'Yes. Early, early in the morning. Before anyone is up.'

'Before the sun is up! The air is so fresh!'

'Yes. Before the sun is up. Early, early in the morning. And it's windy.'

'And the clouds are scudding across the sky.'

'Yes.'

'We had something that was beautiful,' she says.

'Yes.'

'There is something that opens the heart, and something that closes it, Johan.'

'Yes.'

'We had the something that opens it.'

'Yes.'

'Why don't we have it any more?'

'I don't know.'

'Where is she now?'

'I don't know. I've tried to explain that to you. No one knows.'

'But tell me anyway. Where is she now?'

'I don't know what to say. She's gone.'

'Is she gone? But isn't she here? Tell me where she is. You knew a while ago! Is it white there? You said it was white there. Say it again.'

'I don't know what to say.'

'Say it anyway.'

'She's in these things.'

'In these things? Is she in these things? In the things she touched?'

'Yes. In the things she touched and the rooms she moved around.'

'But I can't see her.'

'No. I can't see her either.'

'I can't see her, Johan! Talk to me!'

332

'You can't see her,' he says. 'But you see these things. You are sitting at the table in this room.'

'Keep talking to me!'

'I don't know what else to say.'

'Say: You see these things. You sit at this table in this room.'

'You see these things. You sit at this table in this room.'

'Yes,' she says, as if rehearsing something she has to learn by heart. 'I see these things. I sit at this table in this room.'

'Is it light where she is?' she resumes after a pause. 'Say it again. Say that it's light there.'

'Yes. It's all white.'

'Does it never get dark? Say that it never gets dark.'

'No. Where Ebba is, it never gets dark.'

'But how can it be light all the time? Doesn't the light get too bright for her. Doesn't it hurt her eyes?'

'No.'

'It's bright here too.'

'Yes. That's because she's not far away. She's right over there – just across the street, over by Isak's and Runa's house.'

'Can she see us?'

'Yes, she sees us all the time.'

'But it's so dry here.'

'Yes.'

'What is she thinking about us?'

'I don't know. I think she's watching over us.'

'Is she watching over us?'

'Yes. I think so.'

'Will she comfort us?'

'Yes, if that's what you want. She'll do whatever you want her to.'

'I feel it's so bright in here,' Judith says. 'It's too bright.'

'But does she understand that she's dead?' she asks. 'Are you sure she understands that?'

'Yes,' he says. 'She understands. She understands that she's dead.'

'And she's not going to change her mind?'

'No. She's not going to change her mind.'

'But she's been gone such a long time now. I think it's about time she came home.'

'She won't be coming home.'

'Never?'

'No.'

'But won't she get homesick? You know how she is – only a couple of days away and she's pining for home.'

'No. This time she won't get homesick.'

'Has she turned into such a big girl? In this short time?'

'Yes, she's a big girl now.'

'Doesn't she need us any more?'

'No. She doesn't need us any more. It's us who need her now.'

'I don't understand how she could get to be so big in such a short time,' she says. 'It's only been a few days. And there aren't that many hours in a day. A mere handful. I don't understand how she could get to be so big in such a short time.'

'Where she is, time is different from it is here,' he says.

'Time is different there from it is here? So how is the time in that place?'

'In that place there are – oceans of time.'

'Oceans of time?'

'Yes.'

'What does that look like – oceans of time?'

'It's just – I don't know,' he says. 'It's just bright.'

'Bright? And still?

'Yes. Very bright and very still.'

'Like a big, white room?'

'Yes. Like a big, white room.'

'Like our bathroom that time when you were putting up the tiles,' she says. 'You went on working in there for so long, you were so precise, the lamp you were working by was so bright, you had it pointing towards the door, it blinded me when I walked in. I couldn't see you, all I could see were white tiles and straight, even lines running between them, and a blinding light; I couldn't see you.'

'Even lines, like beams across ice,' he says. 'Like mathematics.' He doesn't know what makes him say that.

'Yes,' she says. 'Like beams across ice. The way we were back then. Don't say any more. Yes, do. Say that it's beautiful there.'

'It's beautiful there,' he says. 'White and still and beautiful. It is so beautiful that it hurts. Like mathematics.'

'I know there is something so beautiful that it hurts,' she says.

'Yes,' he says. 'I know you know.'

'Tell me more,' she says. But Johan cannot take any more. She is too much for him, the light in here grows too bright when they talk like this, there is too much of it; he does not know where they get these words from. It scares him. Too many things have changed. He shuts his eyes.

'I can't see anything any more,' he says. 'I'm too tired to see. You are the seer. I am blind. I'm an old, old man.'

'No, you're not blind,' she says, not looking at all worried. It is as if she has known it all along, that this is how he really is: blind, a poor old man. 'Tell me what you see,' she says.

Johan feels dazed and light-headed, the way he used to do as a little boy when he had cried for longer than he had thought he could stand to cry, then fallen asleep, exhausted.

'I see – Erlend,' he says, his voice low and tentative. He has no idea why he says this. His head is spinning, he must have hit it harder than he thought last night. But she is not surprised.

'Erlend? What is he doing?' she asks.

'He's lying in bed.'

'What is he thinking?'

Johan can tell by her voice that she knows this is important. He would so like to trust her.

'He's not thinking,' he says. 'Erlend is afraid to think. He doesn't want to get up. Someone is digging a cave behind hs eyes. He's been crying, for longer than he thought he could stand to cry. He doesn't want to wake up, his head is light and dry, he is in a daze, someone is digging a cave behind his eyes. His mother can't help him. She stands outside his door and doesn't dare to go in.'

'Who is digging inside Erlend's head?' Judith asks.

'I don't know.'

'What sort of a cave is it?'

'I don't know. I feel so dizzy.'

'Describe the cave to me, Johan.'

'I don't want to be inside Erlend's head.'

'Describe the cave to me,' she repeats.

'It's like a tunnel,' he falters.

'Can you see it?'

'Yes. It's dry. I think there is something lying over against one of the walls.'

'What is it?'

'I don't know,' he says, squeezing his eyes even tighter shut; they are nothing but narrow streaks in the middle of his face now. 'I can't see. My head feels so light. I'm blind. It's so dark, Judith.'

'No, Johan, you're not blind. You just have to accustom yourself to the darkness.'

'But I don't know if I can.'

'Just be there. It can't hurt you. Tell me what you see,' she says. 'Tell me what you see down there in the cave inside Erlend's head. You are in there now, aren't you?'

'Nothing but rock,' he says. 'Earth and rock. Someone has been digging here. It's cold. I think there's something wrong with my head. We'll have to call a doctor. I feel so dizzy.'

But she is not listening.

'Tell me more about Erlend,' she says. 'What is he doing? Is he still there inside the cave?'

'Yes, he's just over there.'

'I think I know the cave you mean,' Judith says. 'It is the one that lies under you and Minna.'

'Maybe so,' he mutters faintly. His head is buzzing. He needs a doctor.

'Then I know the way,' she says. 'Walk straight ahead. Look at Erlend. Is he bending over something?'

'Yes, I think he is,' he says. 'He's bending over something.'

'Is he picking something up?'

'Yes,' he says. 'It looks as if he's picking something up.'

'Is he holding it in his hands now?'

'Yes, I think so.'

'What is he holding?'

'I don't know,' he says. 'It's hard to see, it's so dark. I'm standing over by the far wall. I feel so dizzy. Can't move.'

'You have to move closer,' she insists.

'I daren't,' he says. 'It's such a long way off. I can't move. I'm an old, old man. I'm blind.'

'I'll help you,' she says. 'Come. Look, here's my hand.' She reaches across the kitchen table and gives him her hand; he gropes for it with his eyes closed, grips its hard when he finally locates it.

But still: 'Where are you,' he asks forlornly. 'I can't see you.'

'I'm right here beside you,' she says. 'Don't you know me? I'm holding a flaming brand in my other hand, can't you see it? Or is it an electric torch? Can you see the torch?'

'Ah, yes,' he says, still with his eyes closed. 'Now I can see you. I feel so dizzy.'

'Now you can move in closer to Erlend,' she says. 'I'll wait right here for you.'

'You said you would hold my hand,' he says tremulously. 'Couldn't you call the doctor?'

'I'm right here,' she says, her voice calm. 'It's best that you go alone, I think. I'll wait right here for you and hold the torch.'

'The flaming brand,' he says.

'Yes. The flaming brand.'

'But don't leave me,' he says.

'No,' she says. 'I won't leave you.'

'Promise me.'

'I promise I won't leave you,' she says, letting go of his hand. 'Look at Erlend. What is he holding in his hands?'

'It looks like a rolled-up piece of skin. I think it's a scroll.'

'A scroll?'

'Yes. A parchment scroll. He's reading.'

'What is he reading?'

'It's not writing. It's just a lot of pictures and strange characters.'

'Pictures and strange characters?'

'Yes.'

'What do they show?'

'It's hard to make out, it's so unclear. I think there is a king there, and a queen. But most of it is indecipherable. He's rolling up the scroll now and turning to leave.'

'Are you going to follow him?' she asks.

'Yes,' he says, more confidently now, as if he senses the end is in sight. 'Erlend is making for the way out.'

'Is he going out?'

'Yes, now he's going out. Don't leave me. I need a doctor.'

'We're nearly there now,' she says. 'I'm with you. I'm right behind you, look, I have the flaming brand here. Follow him. Is he almost out now?'

'Yes,' Johan says. 'Now he has reached the way out. It's so bright here! All white. Don't leave me.'

'Where is he?' Judith asks.

'I think he is in – his bathroom,' Johan says. 'He is standing at the washbasin. It's so bright here, a mass of white tiles. He's shaving. He's wearing a suit. He feels so dizzy. The light hurts his eyes.'

'Why is he wearing a suit?' she asks.

'I think he's going to a funeral,' Johan says, and slowly opens his eyes.

The taxi bringing Minna and Jennifer does not park down on the street, it comes all the way up the drive, running over the carpet of nasturtiums. Minna pays the driver and helps her daughter out of the car. Jennifer has on the dark-blue velvet dress and the black patent shoes she wore the time that Johan took her to the opera. They walk up the front steps hand in hand. Minna has Johan's white shirt and dark suit draped over her arm on their hangers; she too is wearing a dark dress and dark shoes, but mother and daughter bear little resemblance to one another. Minna rings the doorbell.

In the kitchen, Judith and Johan start at the shrill note of the bell. For a long time they have sat there saying nothing. They both go to open the door, bumping into one another. Anyone would think they lived together in this house. Johan unhooks the safety chain, Judith slips a hand under his and turns the latch.

And there they stand, facing one another, all four. Neither Minna nor Jennifer dares to lay a hand on Johan, he seems such a stranger, as if he came from another world. He blinks and is almost sent flying backwards by the force of these two. They have come to get me, he thinks. It will soon be over.

Judith crouches down and looks at Jennifer. Jennifer looks back, she does not smile.

'Hi,' says Judith.

'Hi,' says Jennifer.

'You look like your sister.'

'Yes,' says Jennifer. 'But she's dead. We're going to the funeral. You have to come too.'

'Yes, I'm coming,' Judith says. 'I just have to get my dress ironed first, your Mama is going to help me, and your Papa has to put on his suit.'

They file inside. Minna releases Jennifer's hand and lets the child walk ahead of her. The stupefying, flower-scented fug in the sitting-room hits her head-on. She makes straight for the veranda doors and opens them wide, then she opens two of the windows in the room. Judith makes no objection.

Jennifer hangs back on the threshold of the sitting-room for some time. Eventually she walks over to the heap of Ebba's clothes. She stands on the fringes of the heap, nudging the garments with her toe as the grown-ups pass through to the kitchen. Then she hunkers down and proceeds to hold up one piece of clothing after another. She recognises these clothes, she sniffs at them. She separates them into smaller piles, carrying on where Johan and Judith left off.

In the bright kitchen, Minna hands Johan his shirt and suit on their hangers and asks him to go and get changed. She does not look him in the eye and he avoids hers too. Dutifully he makes his way up the stairs to the bedroom with his suit held high in front of him, like a banner. Once he is out of sight, Minna turns to Judith. The two women eye one another, shyly, fearfully almost.

'We'll have to hurry,' Minna says quietly and firmly. 'Do you have an ironing board and an iron? We've the church to go to. And we have to get this place tidied up, people will be coming back here afterwards. We don't have that much time.'

'No,' Judith replies, she too a dutiful child now. She goes off to find the things Minna has asked for.

'Now let's get your dress ironed,' Minna says, picking it off the floor as Judith comes back with the iron and the ironing board. She has already cleared away the food that was lying on the kitchen table. 'Do you have shoes to match?'

'Yes.'

'We have to be there before everyone else. We have to be sitting in the church when the others arrive.'

'Yes.'

'Have you and Johan discussed the seating arrangements?'

'No,' Judith says hesitantly. 'We didn't get that far.'

'Didn't get that far?' Minna glances sharply at her. 'But you've had since yesterday evening. What have you been talking about all this time?'

'We've been talking about – I don't know what. I don't remember,' Judith says.

Minna sighs under her breath, turns her back on Judith and plugs in the iron. Judith hands her the crumpled dress, sits down on a kitchen chair and regards her. Then she stares down at her scarlet toenails. Minna irons with sure, steady strokes; the iron emits short puffs of steam. After a minute or two she turns to Judith again, as if she knows that the other woman is about to say something.

'Can I come home with you three after the funeral?' says Judith.

Shortly afterwards, Johan comes down the stairs wearing his dark suit. He steps quickly past the kitchen door. He can see the two women in there, although he can't quite see what they are up to; they seem to be talking. He is afraid to butt in, and relieved to find that they are not fighting or arguing. Maybe Minna is helping Judith into her dress, he thinks. Maybe she is zipping her up. He cannot bring himself to examine too closely exactly what kind of feeling this thought arouses in him: he does not feel anything but numb and dazed.

He goes through to the sitting-room, to Jennifer. He stands next to the bookcase and considers her, sitting there among her sister's clothes. He notices that she has arranged them in piles; she doesn't really know how to fold clothes, but she has devised her own method. As so often happens, his heart is touched by her, and it swells with pride. There is a grace in everything she does, it strikes him every time he sees her.

He treads softly past her, skirting around the clothes and over to the old hi-fi. He crouches down in front of it and begins to flick through the collection of albums. It doesn't look like Judith has played a vinyl record in years, possibly not since he lived here. She has a rack full of CDs now, almost exclusively classical music, not arranged in any order as far as he can see.

He retrieves his secret record of The Mammas & The Papas from its hiding place behind the other albums, exactly where he left it all those years ago. Gently he slides it out of the sleeve on to the flat of his hand, puts it on the turntable, presses the appropriate buttons on the hi-fi. Then he moves the pick-up arm across and lowers the needle. He finds the right track straight away, his stiff hand knows just what to do; it knows this action, it is full of precision, it has done this so many times before.

Then he walks over and lifts Jennifer out of the heap of clothes. She wraps her spindly arms around his neck and lays her cheek against his. She is crying. He runs a hand over her velvet back as he begins to move in time to the music. And as they dance he sings to her.

Stars shining bright above you
Night breezes seem to whisper 'I love you'
Birds singing in the sycamore tree
Dream a little dream of me

Say nighty-night and kiss me
Just hold me tight and tell me you miss me
While I'm alone and blue as can be
Dream a little dream of me

Stars fading but I linger on dear
Still craving your kiss
I'm longing to linger till dawn, dear
Just saying this

Sweet dreams till sunbeams find you
Sweet dreams that leave all worries behind you
But in your dreams whatever they be
Dream a little dream of me

RUNNING HOT
Dreda Say Mitchell

Elijah 'Schoolboy' Campbell is heading out of London's underworld, a world where bling, ringtones and petty deaths are accessories of life. He's taking a great offer to leave it all behind and start a new life, but the problem is he's got no spare cash. The possibility of lining his pockets becomes real when he stumbles across a mobile. But the phone is marked property, and the Street won't care that he found it by accident. The Street won't care that the phone's his last chance to change his life. And he can't give it back because the door to redemption is only open for 7 days ... Schoolboy knows that when you're running hot, all it takes is one phone call, one voicemail, one text message to disconnect you from this life – permanently.

'Lock, stock and a twenty-year-old mobile phone, at last I know my way round the North London gun belt!'—Nigel Planer, actor, writer & comedian

Dreda Say Mitchell was born into London's Grenadian community and works as an education advisor in East London. This is her first novel.

£8.99 ISBN 1 904559 09 3

ESSENTIAL KIT
Linda Leatherbarrow

In these varied and exquisite short stories, Linda Leatherbarrow brings together for the first time her prize-winning short prose with new and previously unpublished work. A wide-ranging, rich and surprising gallery of characters includes a nineteen-year-old girl leaving home, a talking gorilla in the swinging sixties, a shoe fetishist and a long-distance walker. The prose is lyrical, witty and uplifting, funny and moving, always pertinent – proving that the short story is the perfect literary form for contemporary urban life. Essential reading for short-story lovers everywhere.

'full of acute observation, surprising imagery and even shocks . . . joyously surreal . . . gnomically funny, and touching'—Shena Mackay

Linda Leatherbarrow, born in Dumfries, is one of the UK's leading short-story writers and has won many awards. Several of her stories have been broadcast on BBC Radio.

£8.99 ISBN 1 904559 10 7

GOOD CLEAN FUN Michael Arditti

'witheringly funny,
painfully acute ...
deserve a wide
audience, and will
create a wiser one'
—Amanda Craig,
Literary Review
£8.99
ISBN 1 904559 08 5

This dazzling first collection of short stories from an award-winning author employs a host of remarkable characters and a range of original voices to take an uncompromising look at love and loss in the twenty-first century. These twelve stories of contentment and confusion, defiance and desire, are marked by wit, compassion and insight. Michael Arditti was born in Cheshire and lives in London. He is the author of three highly acclaimed novels, *The Celibate*, *Pagan and her Parents* and *Easter*.

A BLADE OF GRASS Lewis DeSoto

'What fiction should
be: instructive,
moving, enthralling'
—Margaret Forster
'A masterful debut
... Clear and strong
and beautiful'—
Ottawa Citizen
£8.99
ISBN 1 904559 07 7

Märit Laurens, recently orphaned and newly wed, farms with her husband near the border of South Africa. When guerrilla violence and tragedy visit their lives, Märit finds herself in a tug of war between the local Afrikaaners and the black farmworkers. Lyrical and profound, this exciting novel offers a unique perspective on what it means to be black and white in a country where both live and feel entitlement. Lewis DeSoto was born in South Africa and emigrated to Canada in the 1960s. This is his first novel. **International Book of the Month in the USA**

PEPSI AND MARIA Adam Zameenzad

'If you can imagine
a hybrid of *City of
God* and *The Wizard
of Oz*, then *Pepsi
and Maria* comes
close'—Boyd Tonkin,
Independent
£8.99
ISBN 1 904559 06 9

Pepsi is a smart street kid in an unnamed South American country. His mother is dead and his father, a famous politician, has disowned him. He rescues the kidnapped Maria, but they must both escape the sadistic policeman Caddy whose obsession is to kill them – as personal vendetta and also as part of his crusade to rid the city of the 'filth' of street children. In this penetrating insight into the lives of the dispossessed, the author conveys the children's exhilarating zest for life and beauty, which triumphs over the appalling reality of their lives. Adam Zameenzad was born in Pakistan and lives in London. His previous novels have been published to great acclaim in many languages. This is his sixth novel.

UNCUT DIAMONDS
edited by Maggie Hamand

'The ability to pin down a moment or a mindset breathes from these stories … They're all stunning, full of wonderful characters'—
The Big Issue
£7.99
ISBN 1 904559 03 4

Vibrant, original stories showcasing the huge diversity of new writing talent in contemporary London. They include an incident in a women's prison; a spiritual experience in a motorway service station; a memory of growing up in sixties Britain and a lyrical West Indian love story. Unusual and sometimes challenging, this collection gives voice to previously unpublished writers from a wide diversity of backgrounds whose experiences – critical to an understanding of contemporary life in the UK – often remain hidden from view.

ANOTHER COUNTRY Hélène du Coudray

'the descriptions of the refugee Russians are agonisingly lifelike' —review of 1st edition, *Times Literary Supplement*
£7.99
ISBN 1 904559 04 2

Ship's officer Charles Wilson arrives in Malta in the early 1920s, leaving his wife and children behind in London. He falls for a Russian émigrée governess, the beautiful Maria Ivanovna, and the passionate intensity of his feelings propels him into a course of action that promises to end in disaster. This prize-winning novel, first published in 1928, was written by an Oxford undergraduate, Hélène Héroys, who was born in Kiev in 1906. She went on to write a biography of Metternich, and three further novels.

THE THOUSAND-PETALLED DAISY
Norman Thomas

'This novel, both rhapsody and lament, is superb'—
Independent on Sunday
£7.99
ISBN 1 904559 05 0

Injured in a riot while travelling in India, 17-year-old Michael Flower is given shelter in a white house on an island. There, accompanied by his alter ego (his glove-puppet Mickey-Mack), he meets Om Prakash and his family, a tribe of holy monkeys, the beautiful Lila and a mysterious holy woman. Jealousy and violence, a death and a funeral, the delights of first love and the beauty of the landscape are woven into a narrative infused with a distinctive, offbeat humour. Norman Thomas was born in Wales in 1926. His first novel was published in 1963. He lives in Auroville, South India.

ON BECOMING A FAIRY GODMOTHER
Sara Maitland

'Funny, surreal tales
. . . magic and
mystery'—*Guardian*
'These tales
insistently fill the
vison'—*Times
Literary Supplement*
£7.99
ISBN 1 904559 00 X

Fifteen 'fairy stories' breathe new life into old legends and bring the magic of myth back into modern women's lives. What became of Helen of Troy, of Guinevere and Maid Marion? And what happens to today's mature woman when her children have fled the nest? Here is an encounter with a mermaid, an erotic adventure with a mysterious stranger, the story of a woman who learns to fly and another who transforms herself into a fairy godmother.

IN DENIAL Anne Redmon

'This is intelligent
writing worthy of
a large audience'—
The Times
'Intricate, thoughtful'
—*Times Literary
Supplement*
£7.99
ISBN 1 904559 01 8

In a London prison a serial offender, Gerry Hythe, is gloating over the death of his one-time prison visitor Harriet Washington. He thinks he is in prison once again because of her. Anne Redmon weaves evidence from the past and present of Gerry's life into a chilling mystery. A novel of great intelligence and subtlety, *In Denial* explores themes which are usually written about in black and white, but here are dealt with in all their true complexity.

LEAVING IMPRINTS Henrietta Seredy

'Beautifully written
. . . an unusual and
memorable novel'—
Charles Palliser,
author of
The Quincunx
£7.99
ISBN 1 904559 02 6

'At night when I can't sleep I imagine myself on the island.' But Jessica is alone in a flat by a park. She doesn't want to be there – she doesn't have anywhere else to go. As the story moves between present and past, gradually Jessica reveals the truth behind the compelling relationship that has dominated her life. 'With restrained lyricism, *Leaving Imprints* explores a destructive, passionate relationship between two damaged people. Its quiet intensity does indeed leave imprints. I shall not forget this novel'—Sue Gee, author of *The Hours of the Night*